DIVINE WIND

HALO

DIVINE WIND

TROY DENNING

BASED ON THE BESTSELLING VIDEO GAME FOR XBOX

G

GALLERY BOOKS

New York   London   Toronto   Sydney   New Delhi

G

Gallery Books
An Imprint of Simon & Schuster, Inc.
1230 Avenue of the Americas
New York, NY 10020

First Gallery Books trade paperback edition October 2021

GALLERY BOOKS and colophon are registered trademarks of Simon & Schuster, Inc.

For information about special discounts for bulk purchases, please contact Simon & Schuster Special Sales at 1-866-506-1949 or business@simonandschuster.com.

The Simon & Schuster Speakers Bureau can bring authors to your live event. For more information or to book an event, contact the Simon & Schuster Speakers Bureau at 1-866-248-3049 or visit our website at www.simonspeakers.com.

10 9 8 7 6 5 4 3 2 1

Library of Congress Cataloging-in-Publication Data is available.

ISBN 978-1-9821-7490-3
ISBN 978-1-9821-7491-0 (ebook)

For Matthew McCarthy

HISTORIAN'S NOTE

This story takes place in October 2559, a year after the events of *Halo 5: Guardians*, as the AI Cortana commands a host of Forerunner Guardians and uses them to impose martial law on key interstellar civilizations across the Orion Arm of the Milky Way galaxy. It begins a few hours after the events depicted in *Halo: Shadows of Reach*.

HALO

DIVINE WIND

ONE

A sliver of flame creased the darkness ahead. It did not roil or roll or swell in front of the viewport. It merely hung in the black opalescence of slipspace as though it had always been there, a long red ember trapped in the folds between space and time.

Castor had never seen such a thing, not in a thousand transits. Slipspace was a collection of nonspatial dimensions, where complex matter existed only inside carefully tuned quantum fields. Battles were impossible because location was indeterminate and weapons could not be targeted, and because energy radiated back into the spatial dimensions the instant it was released.

But he knew a plasma strike when he saw one.

"Disappointing." The comment came from the blademaster Inslaan 'Gadogai, who was standing with Castor near the back of the open flight deck. A sinewy Sangheili with a gray-blond hide

— 1 —

and gangly limbs, he was tall enough to peer over the shoulder of the pilot standing at the control plinth. "I had not expected to die until *after* we reached the Ark."

"We will not die," Castor said.

He and forty of his followers—the Keepers of the One Freedom—were aboard a Lich transport craft stolen from the Banished warmaster Atriox, transiting a slipspace portal that connected the human planet Reach to Installation 00—also known as the Ark. Like most beings in the galaxy, Castor had never been there. But he knew from the *Psalm of the Journey* that, with a surface area many times the size of most inhabited worlds, it was the largest and most sacred of the remaining structures left behind by the holy Forerunners. "It is too soon."

"A *dokab* commands many things," 'Gadogai replied. "Fate is not one of them."

"Fate favors the worthy," Castor said. "As do the Ancients. They will not *let* us fail, so long as we do not fail ourselves."

"What a clever way of saying we are on our own," 'Gadogai said. "Have you ever considered that the Forerunners are simply *gone*? That the only remnants of them are the constructs and antiquities they left behind?"

"Never. Their presence is the fire in my heart. It burns within me now more fiercely than ever."

And so it did. They were mere days from doing what the Covenant had failed to do in nearly three and a half millennia: initiate the Great Journey by lighting the Sacred Rings that had been arrayed across the galaxy by the ancient Forerunners.

The very prospect seemed enrapturing to Castor, and the grace of the gods permeated his entire being. His massive frame felt swollen with divine might, his perceptions sharper and his reason more piercing than at any time in his life.

"The Faithful of the galaxy will soon know Divine Transcendence," he continued. "And we are the Chosen who will deliver it to them."

"Slayers of the infidel quadrillions," 'Gadogai said dryly. "What an honor."

Castor bared a tusk. "Do not mourn the unbelievers." He had seen 'Gadogai taunt death often enough to know he had no fear of it, so the Sangheili's only concern had to be the untold number of heretics who would perish when the Halo Array was activated. "They must die so the worthy may ascend."

"Yes. 'The galaxy will be cleansed by a Divine Wind,'" 'Gadogai noted, quoting from the *Psalm of the Journey*. "I do remember the teachings of my youth."

"Then you must embrace them," Castor replied. It had long troubled him that 'Gadogai did not honor the Forerunner gods of the Covenant. Instead, the blademaster placed his faith in the mysterious power that he claimed all beings carried inside themselves—and extolled it as the source of his incredible fighting prowess. "There is still time to turn from the Path of Oblivion."

"I wish that were so." 'Gadogai turned his gaze forward again. "But here in slipspace, there *is* no time."

Castor started to demand an explanation, then realized what 'Gadogai was looking at. The plasma strike had changed from a sliver to an oval, not growing any larger or brighter, just rounder. The flames remained as still as mountains, their ragged edges now silhouetted against a royal-blue crescent on top and a dirt-brown crescent on the bottom.

Sky and ground.

"We are about to emerge from the portal," Castor said, "straight into the fire."

"And I was afraid you hadn't noticed," 'Gadogai said.

"What?" The question came from Feodruz, who was standing on the right side of the viewport. Wearing blue-and-gold power armor, the stocky Jiralhanae was commander of Castor's personal escort and one of the Keepers' most ferocious warriors. He was also one of Castor's oldest surviving war-brothers, having fought at his side for more than a decade during the War of Annihilation. "We are flying into a plasma strike?"

"Obviously," 'Gadogai said. "That *is* what we're looking at."

"I mean . . . *how?*" Feodruz asked. "Who could do such a thing? Who would *dare?*"

"The Banished, of course," 'Gadogai said. The multi-species confederation of raiding clans and pirate bands had counted the Keepers among their number until just a few hours earlier, when Castor and his dwindling group of followers had stolen Atriox's Lich and fled into the portal. "The warmaster *did* warn us that we would find only death on the Ark."

"I have not forgotten." Feodruz gestured out the viewport. "But how could they know we were coming? Or *when?*"

"Atriox alerted them," Castor said. "That can be the only answer."

"It is certainly the *likeliest* answer," 'Gadogai allowed.

As remote as it was sacred, the Ark was located more than a hundred thousand light-years beyond the galactic edge. Swift communications across such far-reaching distances were not normally possible, but only three months earlier, Atriox had somehow contacted his former mentor—whom he had left in charge of Banished forces still inside the galaxy—and ordered him to open the slipspace portal on Reach.

Could Atriox have discovered something on the Ark that allowed him to transmit messages across such a vast distance almost instantaneously? It would hardly be the first time someone had unearthed a sacred Forerunner artifact capable of doing what mortals deemed impossible.

After a moment, 'Gadogai added, "Death *is* the price of betrayal in the Banished."

"And it was Atriox who betrayed *us*. Never forget that," Castor said. He had been promised that after the slipspace portal on Reach was found, the Keepers of the One Freedom would join two other clans in using it to travel to the Ark. But when the moment of truth came, Atriox had . . . a different plan. "He betrayed the *gods*. It was my sacred duty to defy him."

"Oh, it was your *duty*," 'Gadogai replied. "That will be a great comfort as the plasma burns the flesh from our bones."

"That will never happen," Feodruz said. "We are a great distance from the plasma strike. By the time we arrive, it will have dwindled to nothing."

"We have *already* arrived," said the Lich's pilot, a young captain-deacon named Krelis. He had the same mottled gray fur and curled tusks as his father, Castor's lost war-brother Orsun. Fearless and talented, Krelis had commanded one of the Keepers' Seraph squadrons against the UNSC infidels on Reach. "We arrived the moment we left the planet."

"Then why have we been transiting slipspace for"—Feodruz paused while he checked the integrated chronometer on his left vambrace—"over three hours?"

"Because our Lich is inside a quantum bubble," Krelis said. "The hours you have been counting since departing Reach exist only *inside* this place. Outside, there is no time, because there is no space."

Feodruz cocked his head sideways, scowling. "Then what is there?"

"Eleven nonspatial dimensions of . . . nothing," Krelis said. "At least nothing we can perceive."

"Then what are we moving through?"

"Nothing," Krelis repeated. "In truth, it is wrong to think of us as moving at all."

"What is *wrong* is for you to think that you can bait me with such nonsense." Feodruz turned his glower forward again, where the plasma blossom continued to grow rounder without becoming larger. "I know what I see. We are a long way from that strike."

"And yet, we are not," Castor said.

Astronavigation was difficult for the uninitiated to understand—it required an observer to embrace an apparent contradiction: that vast distances could be crossed without actually *traveling* vast distances. Humans enjoyed explaining the paradox by speaking of curved space and gravity wells and shortcuts through nonspatial dimensions.

Castor thought of it in a holier way—namely, what he had seen aboard the Sacred Wheel of Erudition at Ulumari. A slipspace transition was a compression of space, one that collapsed distance into nonspatial nothingness. The more energy applied, the quicker and more complete the collapse. To an observer watching from normal space, a transiting vessel simply vanished from its origination point and reemerged at its destination. There would be an apparent delay, but only because time was relative; it passed at different rates for different celestial bodies, depending on how fast they were moving in relation to the galactic core.

To the observer in normal space, the difference between the rate at the origination point and at the destination point was experienced as a delay between disappearance and reappearance. To a passenger aboard a transiting vessel, it was as passing hours and days. But the time the vessel *actually* spent in slipspace did not exist—slipspace was nonspatial, and time could not exist without space.

Castor's understanding of slipspace was imperfect, of course, for the minds of mere mortals could not perceive the hidden truths of the universe. Once he activated Halo and joined the Forerunners in divine transsentience, such secrets would be revealed to him in perfect clarity. But until then, he would have to place his faith in what he had seen at Ulumari.

"Krelis is right," Castor said. "We will exit the portal into the plasma strike. We already have."

Feodruz peered back at Castor, his irritation with Krelis warring with deference to his *dokab*. Finally, he nodded acceptance, then asked, "Can we evade?"

Castor looked to Krelis, not giving the answer he already knew himself. After the heavy losses on the planet Reach, young Krelis was the best pilot the Keepers still had, and it was important that Feodruz learn to trust him.

"We can try," Krelis replied. "Once we have completed our transit."

"Then that is what we will do," Castor said. If they attempted to maneuver before completing the transit, they would leave slip space prematurely—and since Liches did not have slipspace drives, that would leave them marooned many light-years short of the Ark. "There is room around the edges. You can find a way through."

"The Ancients will guide your hands," 'Gadogai remarked. "As long as you believe in that sort of thing."

Krelis caught 'Gadogai's eye in the viewport reflection. "Now is a bad time to mock the gods, Blademaster. Our fate is theirs to decide."

"Who is mocking?" 'Gadogai said. "I hope their fire burns in your heart as fiercely as it burns in the *dokab*'s. It can only improve our chances."

Krelis gnashed his tusks, and Castor realized that 'Gadogai's "encouragement" was not helping. He turned to the Sangheili. "And the guile of an unbeliever can only diminish them. I need you to descend to the lower deck and secure yourself in a crash harness. Tell the others to do the same."

'Gadogai remained where he stood. "I prefer to die here, where I can see it coming."

"Which you surely will, if you continue to distract our pilot," Castor said. "You are a Keeper now." The unspoken part—*and I am your* dokab—hung in the air between them. "Do not shame yourself by disobeying my command."

'Gadogai turned his long head so that he could study Castor with both oblong eyes, then finally snicked his mandibles.

"As you wish." He retreated to the rear of the flight deck, but paused before circling around the partition to descend the ramp. "I will keep watch on your humans. Someone should."

"They are not *my* humans," Castor said. 'Gadogai had certainly never been fond of humans, but his hatred of them had grown more pronounced over the last three months—to the point that Castor was reluctant to trust the Sangheili with them alone. "They are Keepers of the One Freedom, just as we are. And we will have need of them on the Ark."

"Have no fear," 'Gadogai said, speaking over his shoulder. "If any humans die before we reach the Ark, it will be your gods' doing . . . not mine."

He stepped around the partition, leaving Castor alone on the flight deck with Feodruz and Krelis.

"At last," Feodruz said, sighing. "Dokab, I am . . . uncomfortable. His blasphemies offend the gods."

"They offend us all," Castor replied. Noting that the plasma blossom had nearly unfolded into a full circle, he retreated to the partition at the back of the flight deck, then extracted a crash chair and secured his own harness. "But it is better to have him with us than against us."

"I am not convinced," Krelis said. "If the *inchal* was willing to betray Atriox, he will betray us. He has no loyalty."

"It is not his loyalty I value," Castor said. "It is his wisdom."

The blademaster emerged from the well at the bottom of the ramp and paused at the forward end of the hold, his saurian gaze scanning the crowded transport deck of the stolen Lich. A menacing Sangheili with large oval eyes and slender mandibles, he carried no weapon and wore no protection but a fine *sateel* tabard belted at his narrow waist. Still, Inslaan 'Gadogai was a former member of the Covenant's Silent Shadow and the most feared warrior aboard this vessel, and Veta Lopis wondered if it had been a mistake not to order his death when she had the chance.

"Secure your crash harnesses." 'Gadogai addressed them in Old Sangheili, an irreverent conceit to species pride that brought growls of umbrage from the twenty pseudo-ursine Jiralhanae scattered through the bay. Most Keepers of the One Freedom could converse in a variety of Sangheili dialects and other species' languages, but they tended to shun Old Sangheili to avoid inflaming the still-smoldering tensions over the interspecies civil war that had destroyed the Covenant several years ago. That the blademaster could issue orders in it without drawing an immediate challenge from resentful Jiralhanae was a testament to his fierce reputation. "The *dokab* commands it."

The hold filled with the clank and clatter of partition walls being extended and crash chairs extracted, followed by the jangle and crackle of different kinds of hardware being latched and tightened. The Keeper assemblage consisted of various species, and the air was rank with their odors—furry Jiralhanae musk and ashy Sangheili tang, the musty funk of the Kig-Yar and the acrid zest of the little Unggoy, even a whiff of human brine.

Rather than retreating back onto the flight deck once the command had been relayed, 'Gadogai crossed to a partition wall on Veta's side of the hold and stopped in front of an occupied passenger saddle.

"You must hurry to your own seat." 'Gadogai motioned the occupant, a young Sangheili in blue-and-gold combat harness, to leave. "We do not have long."

The warrior dipped his oblong helmet in acknowledgment, then palmed the quick-release in the center of his restraint cage and rushed aft to find a new seat. 'Gadogai straddled the saddle and latched the two halves of the cage in front of his chest, then pressed his back against the partition as the curved bars drew tight against his torso. His choice of seat put him across from Veta at a diagonal, three meters away and at the focus of a perpendicular cross fire formed by herself and the three members of her undercover Ferret team.

It was a taunt. Had to be.

'Gadogai was too cunning to place himself in such a vulnerable position by accident. He wanted Veta to know he was not intimidated by what she had done a few hours earlier on Reach.

It had happened on the landing terrace of a Forerunner transport installation, where a small company of Keepers—including Veta and her Ferret team—was quietly boarding the Lich that had just carried the warmaster Atriox through the slipspace portal. 'Gadogai had observed what was happening and tried to talk Castor out of hijacking the craft, but the *dokab* was determined to go to the Ark and activate the Halo Array. The matter had come to a boil when Atriox noticed the confrontation and ordered the blademaster to bring him the head of his old war-brother.

But Castor had been prepared for trouble, and he had had Veta's brood covering him from inside the Lich. As Atriox departed, a trio of red targeting dots had appeared on 'Gadogai's breast, leaving him to choose between obedience and a chestful of steel-jacketed rounds. Knowing that the penalty for disobeying Atriox was *also* death, the blademaster had realized that his only hope of survival was to drop his plasma sword and join the Keepers.

Or so he claimed. Veta knew better than to trust anyone who had ever been part of the Silent Shadow.

After Veta and 'Gadogai had been staring daggers at each other for a moment, she spoke to him in standard Sangheili. "You're a faithless coward. I should have had you killed when I had the chance."

'Gadogai swung his mandibles up to one side, the Sangheili equivalent of a shrug. "Your mistake, human."

"That was obedience, not a mistake. Feodruz feared you would kill the *dokab* before our bullets killed you. He was wrong, but a Keeper submits."

In truth, Veta had been tempted to ignore the order and hope Feodruz was right about the blademaster's speed. But it would have taken more than Castor's death to prevent the remaining Keepers from flying the Lich through the portal. The *dokab*'s followers were just as fanatic as he was, and Feodruz had nearly forty warriors at his disposal—and little tolerance for disobedience. Her only real choice had been to obey Feodruz and stay alive, so her team could look for a chance to destroy the Keepers later.

'Gadogai continued to glare at Veta, his mandibles open just far enough to display multiple rows of sharp teeth. His hostility was going to complicate her team's mission, and she could not escape the feeling he was aware of their duplicity.

It was a feeling she and her team knew well. The Ferrets had penetrated the Keepers more than two years earlier, through an allied doomsday cult calling themselves Humans of the Joyous Journey, then spent the next eight months gathering intelligence for the Office of Naval Intelligence. When the UNSC finally launched a massive eradication campaign, Castor had surprised everyone by seeking refuge with the Banished. Hoping to get lucky and take out Atriox himself, ONI had ordered the Ferrets to extend their undercover mission and lay the groundwork for an assassination attempt.

No such luck. Shortly after the Keepers joined the faction, Atriox and his flagship, *Enduring Conviction*, had vanished. Then, in a move no one saw coming, a human AI named Cortana suddenly rose to power, seeking to subjugate the entire Orion Arm of the galaxy, using a host of Forerunner Guardians and an army of human AIs to turn interstellar civilization into a nightmarish surveillance state.

The biggest problem for Veta and her Ferret team as a result was the complete decimation of ONI and its field operations. Their undercover support prowler disappeared, which also meant the clandestine comm station to which they delivered their intelligence—along with the Owl kept on standby in case they needed emergency extraction. Most critically, the covert restocking runs stopped, leaving her Spartan-III subordinates with a fast-dwindling supply of the specialized meds they needed to stay healthy and effective.

Veta began to look for a good way out, but escaping from a vast organization was difficult—especially when it required hijacking a slipspace-capable vessel filled with hundreds of warriors. Their first decent opportunity had come just a couple of months earlier, when a surprise message from Atriox sent the Keepers to Reach, of all places.

The Ferrets had begun preparations to self-extract, intending to disappear into the planet's glasslands after they learned what Atriox was planning. Instead, their eavesdropping intercepts caught Castor plotting to go to the Ark so he could initiate the Great Journey.

Self-extraction stopped being an option.

Veta didn't know a great deal about the Ark, but what ONI *had* told her scared her stiff. One of the largest Forerunner installations yet discovered, it served as a sort of biological repository for an untold number of galactic life-forms—a vast library of creatures and the genetic material necessary to remake them. While the hubris of holding countless species in some sort of zoological archive was disturbing enough, it was the Forerunners' reason for establishing their cosmic menagerie that she found truly horrifying. According to ONI, the Ark also served as a control facility that could trigger the simultaneous, galaxy-wide destruction of all sentient life.

And that was exactly why Castor wanted to go there.

The "Great Journey" was zealot-speak for "the End of Everything," which was what would happen if Veta's Ferret team allowed the Keepers to find the Ark's control room and activate Halo. Overlapping bursts of supermassive, cross-phased neutrinos would roll across the entire Milky Way galaxy and destroy every sentient creature.

Like the Covenant before them, the Keepers believed this "sacred act of destruction" would elevate all worthy believers to divine transsentience alongside the Forerunners themselves. But the truth was nothing so rapturous. The UNSC had learned years ago that the Halo Array—seven enormous ringworlds forming a network of neutrino-blasting weapons scattered throughout the galaxy—was a defense of last resort against the Flood, a particularly virulent parasite that reproduced by infecting the minds of intelligent species. Firing the array would starve the Flood by destroying the beings upon which it preyed—and that was *all* it would do. Kill just about everything.

So Veta had made the hard choice to continue undercover with her team until the Keepers were destroyed. For a time, it had appeared she would be able to make that happen on Reach, after the Spartan Blue Team arrived on the planet, pursuing a mission of their own. But it had proven impossible to make contact until the portal to the Ark was already open, and by then it had been too late for Blue Team or the UNSC to stop the Keepers from going.

Before leaving, Veta *had* managed to slip a message outlining the situation to Spartan Fred-104. That brief meeting had probably been both her greatest joy in the last two years and her saddest moment. She and Fred had developed a close relationship while working together since the Ferret team's inception. Seeing him again while undercover and unable to properly say good-bye had been one of the hardest things about leaving the galaxy, second only to the knowledge of what her decision would probably mean for her Gammas. But she had had no choice, and there was no fallback plan. Either her Ferret team stopped the Keepers, or everything but the sponges and placozoa went extinct.

'Gadogai finally closed his mandibles and glanced up and forward, his head rocking slightly as he looked toward the flight deck. Sangheili mannerisms were hard to read, but Veta's training in nonverbal alien cues suggested anticipation. Something was about to happen, and the Sangheili had been sent down to make sure the situation on the lower deck remained under control.

"The *dokab* seems rather fond of you," Veta said. She needed to figure out what Castor was worried about . . . and in turn whether 'Gadogai's choice of seat was something *she* needed to worry about. "Apologize for your blasphemies, and perhaps he'll let you ride up above again."

'Gadogai's attention snapped back to her. "How do you know what passes on the flight deck?"

"I don't." Veta hid her alarm behind an air of smugness. Her taunt was more on-target than she realized, but she knew how to deflect. She'd been trained in it. "I know *you*. Every third thing you say is blasphemy. You just can't help yourself."

"True enough." 'Gadogai glanced around, his gaze lingering just a moment on each of the Ferrets. "But there is a reason I *chose* to sit here, among your brood."

Veta cocked her head slightly. "I'm sure you expect me to ask why."

"There is no need to *ask*." 'Gadogai lifted his mandibles, then fixed a single oval eye on Veta's face. "I am here to watch you die. All of you."

Realizing her team would already have their hands on their sidearms, Veta didn't bother to reach for her own. She was just a typical human, a well-prepared ONI operative, albeit a bit on the small side and not even enhanced for speed and strength. But her three team members—Ash-G099, Mark-G313, and Olivia-G291— were fully augmented Spartan-III super-soldiers, trained from childhood to fight, kill, and prevail. An ex–Silent Shadow warrior would make short work of Veta, and might even be a match for any one of her Ferrets. But against all three, working together and under her command?

"That's not going to happen."

An almost imperceptible pulse ran through the ship, and 'Gadogai's gaze drifted forward again.

"Oh, I think it *is*."

Veta rose into the shoulders of her crash harness and found herself straining against the torso restraints, which meant that the Lich had rolled into a steep dive.

Which meant it had returned to normal space, which meant they had reached their destination and would soon be landing on the Ark.

So why were 'Gadogai's mandibles parted in delight, why were his eyes fixed on her, why was he pulling forward against the g-forces to—

—there was no impact, just fingers of flash fire reaching into the hold and shards of foreign black fuselage spraying like shrapnel . . . and what looked like a pilot's seat-assembly tumbling aft, trailing screams and smoke and the smell of charred flesh. A fissure opened in the deck between Veta and 'Gadogai, its molten edges dripping into the service bay below. Another rift melted into the overhead. And yet, neither breach extended all the way through to the exterior hull.

It seemed the Lich was still intact.

The passengers, not so much. Kig-Yar screeched in agony as severed limbs tumbled away, Unggoy chests jetted flame from erupting methane tanks, a human Keeper was impaled by a canopy fragment. A Jiralhanae head bounced aft and disappeared into the rupture between Veta and 'Gadogai.

But the Lich was still in flight.

Which was too bad. A catastrophic disintegration would have been the surest way to stop Castor and the Keepers, and it wasn't like Veta and her Ferrets expected to survive the mission anyway.

Even if they did, they would almost certainly be marooned on the Ark for the rest of their lives—lives that promised to be hellish and short for Ash, Mark, and Olivia.

As Gamma Company Spartan-IIIs, they had undergone an additional round of biological augmentations to elevate their pain tolerance and shock resistance. The extra enhancements improved their chances of surviving when wounded, but the trade-off was a rigid protocol of pharmaceutical "smoothers" to keep their brain chemistry stable. Without those meds, Gamma Company Spartans quickly sank into a paranoid psychosis that divorced them from reality.

The team was down to three smoother doses between them— enough to get them through one more day. Veta estimated they had just over a day before her Ferrets' mental states began to deteriorate. Full psychotic breaks would start coming in no more than forty-eight hours. After that, the Gammas would become a deadly threat not only to Veta, but to themselves and each other.

So, yeah, Veta would have been fine with the Lich breaking up.

A pair of tremendous clangs sounded deep in the hold as the mysterious seat-assembly bounced off the gravity-lift housing and smashed into the rear bulkhead. The occupant's wails were audible even above the rest of the cacophony, a raw, high voice, shrill with pain.

'Gadogai's gaze remained locked on Veta. "Soon, it will be *you* I am hearing."

It took a few seconds to comprehend the Sangheili's meaning. He hadn't come aft to kill Veta's team himself. He simply knew what was about to happen and wanted to spend his last moments watching the humans die—the ones who had forced his hand on Reach.

Only they weren't going to die. Not at that moment, anyway.

The cries of pain were all too sharp and thin to be coming from the Lich's Jiralhanae pilot, and the craft itself remained under *control*. Veta still didn't even see any hull breaches. It was as though the blast had erupted spontaneously inside the cavernous transport bay, producing the flames and the shrapnel and the seat-assembly out of empty air.

She looked aft and found the assembly lying against the bulkhead. Strapped into a pilot's seat was a figure with shriveled hands curled in front of the torso. The flesh on the arms and one exposed shoulder were pitted with black-edged burn hollows.

A human female, in agony.

What . . . ?

Veta felt herself sink into her seat as the Lich pulled out of its dive. The thud of firing plasma cannons reverberated through the hull, and she slammed against her harness restraints as the huge transport began evasive maneuvers.

She glanced back to 'Gadogai, but he looked just as puzzled, his eyes locked on the forward bulkhead and his mandibles hanging half-open. Whatever was happening, it was not what he had expected.

Veta used an eye-flick to signal Ash and Olivia to cover her, then removed her crash harness and nodded for Mark to accompany her aft in search of answers. Like everyone on the Ferret team, he wore basic blue Keeper armor over a gold tunic and trousers, and he maintained the look of a Joyous Journey zealot, with his head shaved on both sides and a narrow fall of black hair hanging down to his shoulder blades.

Together, they made their way aft between rows of seated Keepers, Mark barely swaying against the Lich's erratic juking and jinking, Veta staggering and almost losing her feet until he grabbed her arm and held her steady. The charred seat-assembly was sliding back and forth across the deck, rebounding between the boot soles of an irritated Sangheili and the shin greaves of an indifferent Jiralhanae. The wails of the occupant had subsided to a constant high-pitched moan.

As Veta and Mark drew near, the indifferent Jiralhanae used a boot to trap the seat-assembly against the deck, then gave Veta an expectant look.

Veta inclined her head to him. "Many thanks, Path Brother."

She knelt beside the seat and grabbed the frame to steady herself, then leaned down to inspect the pilot. The woman wore a fireproof flight suit that had not been quite up to plasma standards, exposing seared flesh where the material had disintegrated at the wrists, neck, and knees. Strapped to her left thigh was a pressure-sensitive kneeboard designed to be written on by a fingertip, but the screen was so full of scratches and smears that it was impossible to tell whether it contained any notes. The shattered faceplate of her helmet had allowed flames to pour in, and now her face was a blackened mess Veta could hardly bear to look at.

Both the woman's helmet and flight suit bore UNSC eagle-and-globe insignias almost as old as Veta was. On her collar tabs she wore the silver bars of a naval lieutenant, and the name tab above her breast pocket read MYKLONAS. Her eyelids had burned away and her corneas were cloudy, so it seemed likely that she had no idea she was inside a Banished Lich . . . or how she had come to be there.

"Lady?" Veta asked.

Myklonas started, then turned her head vaguely in Veta's direction and croaked a single incomprehensible syllable . . . probably *meds.* That was what Veta would have been asking for, were the situation reversed.

She made a show of searching the pilot's body and seat-assembly, in part to glean information and in part so the Jiralhanae next to her would not see that Veta knew exactly where to look for the medical kit. Myklonas wore the badges of both an atmospheric and orbital combat pilot above her name tab, but the fleet and vessel patches had burned away, along with the right shoulder of her flight suit. A tangle of melted chute lines lay on the deck behind the seat, and there was a burst canister of what looked like an emergency oxygen supply attached to the seat front under her legs. Stamped into the side frame was a part number: MA B-65 ESS S30B #03357.

"MA" was Misriah Armory, "B-65" the designation for the Shortsword suborbital long-range bomber. Veta wasn't sure what "ESS" stood for, but "S30" would be Series 30, indicating the seat had been manufactured in 2530—practically an antique, as military equipment went.

So . . . the Keepers had emerged from the slipspace portal at the Ark, and the pilot of a thirty-year-old atmospheric bomber had appeared inside their Lich in a flash of fire and shrapnel. That sounded like a midair collision . . . except for the part where the Lich was still flying and intact . . . and the part where an outdated UNSC Shortsword atmospheric bomber was operating a hundred thousand light-years beyond the galactic edge.

Clearly, Veta needed to reevaluate some of her assumptions here.

Out of the corner of her eye, she saw Mark drop one hand toward his M6D sidearm, then pivot so he was perpendicular to her. She glanced back to see 'Gadogai stepping up, his legs spread wide and reacting to the Lich's evasive maneuvering with an easy grace.

The Sangheili peered over Veta's shoulder. "UNSC," he said. "*Of course.*"

"You don't sound surprised," Veta said.

"I am surprised that we are still alive," 'Gadogai replied. "Is that not enough?"

"Surprised? Or disappointed? You *knew* there were UNSC forces on the Ark, yet you failed to warn the *dokab*."

The Jiralhanae who had pinned the seat-assembly to the deck emitted a low growl and leaned against his crash harness.

'Gadogai ignored him and continued to look over Veta's shoulder at the pilot. "Again, I must ask: How do *you* know what passes on the flight deck?"

The Jiralhanae's glower shifted to Veta, but it was worth any suspicions 'Gadogai might raise to confirm the UNSC's presence on the Ark. Operational support was the last thing she had expected on this mission, but that had suddenly become a realistic possibility—as had replenishing her team's smoother supply. All she had to do was find a way to make contact—and not get caught.

Veta allowed 'Gadogai's question to hang in the air for a moment, then said, "I was speaking of *before* we left Reach, Blademaster. A warning that comes too late is no warning at all."

"Before we left Reach, my loyalty was to Escharum and Atriox. It was in their name I warned Castor not to trust humans." 'Gadogai clacked his mandibles sharply, then added, "Pity he failed to listen."

"The *dokab* trusts only the Faithful," Veta said. She withdrew a med kit from the pilot's thigh pocket, fumbled with the latch, and sorted through the contents. "Which is why he will never trust *you*."

She extracted the polly-sue pen and pretended that she had to figure out how to operate the dial, then opened it to maximum and jabbed the tip into Myklonas's exposed shoulder. It was enough polypseudomorphine to suppress the woman's respiration and stop her heartbeat, and that was the best Veta could do for her. If the

Lich somehow survived its fiery arrival at the Ark, the last thing either of them needed was for a dying pilot to start giving up UNSC intelligence during a game of Tossers.

The Lich rolled so hard that Mark and 'Gadogai were thrown into the laps of the passengers still harnessed into their seats along the port-side partition, and Veta had to hold on to the seat-assembly with both hands to keep from flying into the Jiralhanae pinning it to the deck. A chain of cannon strikes clanged through the craft's belly, then a trio of fist-sized holes opened in the deck as three 20mm autocannon rounds punched through the metal and vanished into the overhead.

An instant later, Castor's deep voice bellowed from the bulkhead intercom speakers. *"Path Sister Aita and Blademaster 'Gadogai, come up at once!"*

"Aita Gomez" was Veta's undercover alias, chosen because it was similar to her true name and she would respond to it naturally, yet different enough that it would not trip a recognition alarm in any ONI agent databases the Keepers might have penetrated.

"I have need of you on the flight deck," Castor continued. *"The Great Journey depends on you!"*

TWO

Veta lurched onto the flight deck and winced at the sudden brightness. Beyond the viewport, she saw a swirling web of missile trails and flame tails, balls of roiling fire and blinding blossoms of plasma. Castor and his Jiralhanae crew stood at their stations or sat harnessed into enormous crash seats they had extracted from the wall, the *dokab* roaring into the microphone wafer on the comm disk affixed to his hairy cheek, Feodruz sliding his thick fingers over a fire-control panel, Krelis palming the back side of the control plinth guidance orb, trying desperately to pull up the Lich's nose.

A momentary jolt of fear changed to relief as Veta recognized the likelihood of a quick and fiery death. *Pegoras* was under attack, and at more than a hundred meters long and half that in width, it made an easy target. The Keepers and their quest for the End of Everything were about to vanish in a ball of white fire, and if she and her Ferret team vanished along with them . . . well, mission accomplished. She'd be happy to take the certainty of stopping Castor over the prospect of a galactic death wave. They all would.

Bracing herself against the cabin wall, Veta advanced to clear a path for 'Gadogai. Castor had called them both onto the flight deck, and it was important to maintain her cover as an obedient follower until her team finished the job . . . and there *were* no more Keepers.

An arm-length section of what appeared to be black aileron protruded from the overhead, and another piece from the partition on the other side of Castor. There didn't seem to be any tongues of peeled-back metal or gaping holes surrounding the fragments, nothing to suggest there had been an impact when they arrived. Veta had noticed a couple of similar penetrations as she climbed the ramp and advanced through the upper hold. It was as though the fragments had simply sprouted inside the Lich when it exited the slipspace portal.

She had heard of similar phenomena when a vessel exited slipspace into a location occupied by something else. Basic physics dictated that two objects could not exist in the same space at the same time, so what usually followed was an instantaneous conversion of matter to energy—an explosion that made thermonuclear detonations look tiny. But a drastic imbalance between masses sometimes resulted in a few zeptoseconds where the quantum states were out of phase; by the time the phases aligned, the smaller objects would be embedded in the larger. Or, as in the case of the unfortunate Lieutenant Myklonas strapped into the pilot's seat-assembly that had appeared on the lower deck, simply appear inside any hollow spaces.

Veta moved forward, into an inertial dampening field that protected the pilot from the mad g-forces of evasive maneuvering, and caught her first glimpse of the Ark. Her limited ONI briefing had described a massive and majestic installation more than 120,000 kilometers across, about ten times the diameter of Earth, but the Lich had emerged from the portal only a thousand meters above the surface. From such a low altitude, the Ark looked no more intimidating than most of the planets she had inserted onto as an ONI operative—and less so than some. All she could see was a broad, smoke-filled valley ahead, flanked by two steep ridges of mountainous terrain whose crests lay about even with the Lich.

Coming up the valley were a strange assortment of attack craft, outdated UNSC Nandao interceptors and obsolete Baselard strike fighters that were brushing wingtips with original Covenant Seraphs and Banshees. The UNSC craft seemed to be hanging to port, escorting a flight of Shortsword bombers. The Covenant craft were staying to starboard, flying top cover for a wing of equally modern Phantom and Spirit transports. The two groups were weaving into and out of each other's formations, exchanging sporadic bursts of cannon fire. It seemed pretty clear that while unhappy about each other's presence, their true interest lay in the slipspace portal from which the Keepers had just emerged.

As the Lich continued to descend into the valley, two echelons of old AV-14 Hornet and AV-22 Sparrowhawk aerodynes appeared about five kilometers ahead. They were a few hundred meters lower than the Keepers, flying just above the smoke blanket, coming head-on and firing toward the ground. The Lich's nose was still down, so whenever there was a break in the miasma of oily fumes, Veta could see that the formation was providing close air support for a UNSC combined-arms force of armor and mechanized infantry.

Some of the tanks, primarily M808 Scorpions, were already exchanging fire with an enemy Veta could not see. That foe was presumably the Banished, defending the slipspace portal that Atriox had used to travel to Reach.

A stream of plasma bolts flashed past from behind the Lich, forcing the UNSC aerodynes and Covenant transports to peel off in opposite directions. Veta steadied herself on the wall and leaned forward to glimpse through the corners of the viewport. Still, it was impossible to see who had arrived to offer the supporting fire—but it *had* to be the Banished, protecting a craft they assumed to be one of their own against the two different enemies coming up the valley.

Castor growled into his microphone wafer, his voice so guttural and raspy that Veta barely understood his Sangheili.

"Have I not told you?! The warmaster has no time for your questions." Castor listened for a moment, then continued, "Atriox will explain the trouble later."

Competing assaults by UNSC and Covenant forces was about the last thing Veta had expected to meet when the Keepers emerged from the portal, but maybe it shouldn't have been. Her Ferret team's eavesdropping devices had captured several conversations in which Castor and his advisors discussed a war against the UNSC on the Ark, and there had been mention of Atriox's forces on the installation recovering the shards of a slipspace crystal known as the Holy Light from a Forerunner ship that had been used by the Covenant's High Prophet of Truth to flee High Charity at the end of the war. So it certainly seemed possible—if incredible—that there was a force from the original Covenant marooned on the Ark along with the Banished and the UNSC.

Still, the size of the conflict was at odds with the limited ONI briefings Veta had received regarding the Ark. Because the installation was so remote and difficult to reach, it had been visited in the modern era by only a handful of relatively small expeditions, all so clandestine that Veta had been informed of them only because of the Keepers' interest in the Great Journey and all things Forerunner. The briefings had been decidedly short on details, but she was pretty sure that had any of the expeditions reported back to ONI that there was now on the Ark a sizable Covenant presence or a deployed UNSC strike force equipped with outdated equipment, she would have been ordered to watch for any indication that the Keepers were also aware of it. That there had been no such order suggested that ONI had been in the dark about the current situation just as much as anyone else.

Which only made sense. Despite the mystery as to why UNSC and Covenant forces were here to begin with, both sides were clearly trying to seize the Banished's slipspace portal, most likely because they had no other way off the Ark. And it seemed probable to Veta that the two groups had not even been *aware* of one another. Had they realized they would be fighting each other as well as the Banished, they would have avoided using the same attack lane.

More importantly, it sounded as though the Banished believed Atriox was aboard this Lich—a reasonable assumption *only* if they didn't know of Castor's defiance on Reach. Whatever method Atriox had used to transmit his original message from the Ark, it was not something he could replicate from Reach—at least not easily.

That was a lucky break for Castor, and a bad one for everyone else. The *dokab* had a long history of close calls, running back to before Veta had joined ONI, and she knew him to be capable of leveraging even the tiniest bit of good fortune into a clean escape.

All of this meant she had a lot to sift through here, playing the hand she was dealt while making sure no one at the table was about to draw out on her.

A flight of Nandaos came diving out of the UNSC bomber formation, pelting the Lich's dorsal hull with cannon fire. Muffled screams sounded in the troop hold, then Krelis rolled the craft onto its side so Feodruz could return fire. It shook and dropped like a rock, and Krelis barely managed to swing it back into proper flight position.

So not everything was going the Keepers' way.

Castor grunted something incoherent into the microphone at the corner of his mouth, then tore the comm disk off his cheek in frustration. He covered the microphone with his palm and spent a moment thinking, then leaned toward Feodruz.

"We will not fire on the humans any longer," he said. "Attack only the Covenant craft."

"As you command, Dokab," Feodruz replied. He was standing to the starboard side of the viewport, at a fold-down weapons station. "But if the humans see no deterrent, they may grow even more—"

"Only Covenant craft." Castor turned to 'Gadogai, who was now standing on the flight deck next to Veta. "I am talking to Let 'Volir. The *baskaluv* seems to be in command here."

"Always the long worm slithers to the top," 'Gadogai said.

Let 'Volir was the Sangheili shipmaster of the *Enduring Conviction*, the assault carrier that had spirited Atriox and his forces to the Ark more than a year and a half earlier, according to fragmented ONI intel.

"The folly of prizing loyalty above Faith." Castor kept the microphone wrapped in his palm. " 'Volir believes we have come to the Ark because Atriox is wounded and on board. He is suspicious that he cannot speak with the warmaster himself."

'Gadogai ticked his mandibles together, then said, "An injury to the warmaster *is* the most likely reason for *Pegoras* to return."

He stepped closer to Castor and extended his hand toward the comm disk. "That, I can work with."

Castor did not yield the device yet. " 'Volir must withdraw the escort he sent."

'Gadogai glanced forward toward the raging battle. "Are you certain, Dokab? From all appearances, we will not last long without it."

Castor's gaze drifted toward Veta. "I have a plan for that," he said. "It is the Banished escort we must escape. If it is still with us when 'Volir discovers Atriox is not aboard—"

"Oh, he is not going to discover it." 'Gadogai took the edge of the comm disk. "I am going to *tell* him."

The air grew acrid with the musk of Jiralhanae alarm, and Castor showed his fang tips. "Explain."

"Let 'Volir is too cunning to be deceived," 'Gadogai said. "So we must let him deceive *himself.*"

Castor fell silent for a moment, then finally released the headset. "So long as *I* am not the one being deceived."

"How would that happen?" 'Gadogai asked. "Fate favors the worthy."

Veta saw Krelis glance toward 'Gadogai's reflection in the viewport and snarl, but the young pilot was too busy dodging missiles and tracer rounds to voice the anger caught behind his fangs. His palms remained on the back side of the guidance orb, squeezing it so tightly his huge knuckles had blanched, and still the Lich's nose refused to come up.

Good.

'Gadogai affixed the comm unit to the side of his oblong head, then slid the microphone and speaker wafers around the disk to the appropriate locations for his species. He began to speak in Sangheili so rapidly that Veta could barely follow it.

"The warmaster is not aboard. We are here on another matter." 'Gadogai fell silent for a moment, then lowered his voice to a raspy whisper. "You dare speak my name over an open band?"

Another pause.

"It was called the *Silent* Shadow, Shipmaster. If you ever name me over a battlenet again, you will learn the reason."

As 'Gadogai listened, he extended his free hand toward Castor and touched both thumbs to both fingertips, signaling success.

"We require an escort," 'Gadogai said, still speaking into the microphone. "The two talons you have sent already, plus two more."

A longer pause.

"Because the warmaster *wishes* it!" 'Gadogai snapped. "Would we have returned were it not on his orders?"

'Gadogai tipped his head back and looked at the overhead.

"Had he wanted you to know of our assignment, he would have instructed me to inform you. All you need know is that because of the chaos you are making of the portal's defense, we require escorts."

'Gadogai caught Castor's eye, then raised his hand and made the success signal again.

"Of course we have an authorization string," 'Gadogai hissed. "I will have it transmitted immediately."

He covered the microphone, but kept the comm disk in place and said nothing.

After a moment and two near misses by Covenant plasma bolts, Veta finally asked, "What about the authorization string?"

"There is no authorization string," 'Gadogai said. "I was lying."

"Lying?!" Feodruz bellowed. "We have enough craft shooting at us!"

" 'Volir is too cautious to fire upon us." 'Gadogai kept his gaze on Castor. "For all he knows, I *am* here at Atriox's command."

"Did I not command you to *rid* us of this escort?" Castor demanded.

"Which I have," 'Gadogai replied. " 'Volir is fighting two enemies at once. When the authorization string fails to come, he will recall his craft to defend the—"

'Gadogai stopped to listen to the comm, then uncovered the microphone and began to speak again.

"We *have* transmitted it. If you withdraw our escort now, the warmaster will have your head."

Castor grunted in satisfaction. Leaving the blademaster to continue the exchange unsupervised, he turned to Veta and motioned her into the space between Feodruz and Krelis.

"The Journey is in your hands now."

"How so?" Veta asked.

"You will speak to the humans on our behalf."

Veta hesitated, sudden trepidation mixing with her attempt to keep the Ferrets' charade running smoothly. "I will do everything I can, Dokab. I might be more convincing if I understood who they are."

"They are UNSC infidels," Castor said. "Can you not see that?"

"Forgive me, Dokab," Veta said. She was in no particular hurry to save the Lich, and any intelligence she could glean on the UNSC would only increase her chances of securing help once the Keepers were destroyed—or of eliminating the Keepers herself, if that proved necessary. "I mean, how they came to be here. It does not take a soldier to see they are using equipment as old as I am."

"It is not known," Castor replied. "Escharum once said they arrived on the Ark soon after Atriox."

Ah, Escharum. Atriox's old *daskalo*—a Jiralhanae mentor. He'd been left in charge of Banished forces when the *Enduring Conviction* departed. Veta already knew from her team's surveillance that Escharum had not fully trusted Castor, communicating only what was necessary for the Keepers to carry out their assignments. But clearly, a few details *had* been passed along beyond the range of the Ferrets' eavesdropping devices.

When Castor did not elaborate, Veta asked, "What happened after the infidels arrived?"

"What one would expect. The humans became an obstacle, and a war began. The fighting continues to this day."

That might explain the Banished's general animosity toward humans, but not the fight here against the Covenant. *Those* forces had almost certainly come from the Forerunner Dreadnought that Escharum had mentioned when he ordered Castor to take the Keepers to Reach to search for the Ark portal, and Veta couldn't afford to ignore the likelihood that Castor intended to make contact with them now. Stopping forty Keepers was going to be a tall order for a four-person Ferret team as it was; if Castor formed an alliance with the Covenant, it would grow all but impossible.

"What of the Covenant talons?" Veta asked. "The Covenant is as devoted to initiating the Great Journey as the Keepers are. Surely they would protect us from the UNSC."

"Not while we are in a Banished craft," Feodruz remarked. "They are not so foolish as humans."

"It is so," Castor agreed. "They would destroy us the instant we turned toward them, and nothing I could say would prevent it. You must delay the human attack."

"For as long as you can," Krelis added. "The forward attitude repulsors are no more. Even without evading fire, we will be on the surface in five centals."

"So soon?" Castor asked. In times of stress, he and the other Jiralhanae sometimes reverted to the old Covenant measurement systems. A cental was a hundredth of a time unit, which worked out to be about thirty-six seconds. Five centals, around three minutes. "In one piece?"

"If the Ancients will it," Krelis said.

Veta moved forward into the space between Krelis's control plinth and Feodruz's fold-down weapons station, as Castor had ordered a few moments before. Now that she was at the front of the flight deck, she saw that the Lich was being accompanied on each side by a mixed talon of Banished Seraphs and Banshees. Both groups were beginning to open their formations, preparing to peel away despite 'Gadogai's sham protests to Let 'Volir.

Feodruz passed a comm disk to Veta.

"This is the human emergency channel," he said. "They will know we are the craft transmitting."

Veta took the disk by wrapping its microphone wafer in her hand. "What do I tell them?"

"That we are escaped prisoners," Castor said. "They will never listen, but a human voice will confuse them and buy us a little time."

"A little time is what we need," Krelis said. He banked to port, angling away from the Covenant forces and toward a rocky ridge rising from the smoke on the far side of the UNSC aerodynes. "That, and the favor of the gods."

It was a better plan than Veta would have liked. With the escorts peeling away and the Lich turning to leave the battle space, the UNSC would no longer see it as a high-priority threat. They would probably keep firing at it just to make certain it left the area . . . but once it was out of range, pursuing it wouldn't necessarily be on the agenda.

Veta affixed the comm disk to the side of her head—it would have covered her entire face, if she allowed it—and slid the microphone and speaker wafers into the correct position for her anatomy.

"Mayday, mayday!" she began. "Lieutenant Myklonas declaring emergency!"

The transmission wasn't even close to proper military parlance. But Veta's undercover persona was that of an alienated cafeteria manager, so using the correct codes would have drawn unwanted scrutiny—and stood the risk of fooling the UNSC commander into believing it was a legitimate message.

"We're going down in a commandeered Lich pursued by Banished fighter craft!" Veta continued. "Requesting combat rescue. Repeat, requesting combat—"

A pair of saurian fingers reached out from behind to peel the comm disk from the side of her head.

"Clever," 'Gadogai said. "Using their pilot's name to *ensure* they come after us."

"I'm following Castor's command," Veta said. A male voice began to sound from the comm speaker, so she extended her hand for the disk's return. "If you don't like that, take it up with the *dokab*."

"Who is pleased with her success," Castor growled. He motioned for 'Gadogai to return the comm disk. "The rescue mission will not be a problem."

'Gadogai made an exasperated sissing sound, but did as Castor commanded. Veta turned forward to find the Lich had dropped level with the UNSC aerodyne formation and would soon be descending into the smoke. She could not help wondering whether the craft's instruments were adequate to keep Krelis from crashing into the adjacent ridge, and it took an act of will to hope they were not.

She affixed the disk to her head again and heard a combat controller's crisp voice.

"*. . . make any sense, Lieutenant. According to Escort Leader, your Shortsword was just destroyed.*"

"There was a . . . midair collision," Veta said. "More or less."

"*More or less?*" The controller sounded as doubtful as Veta had hoped he would. "*Explain.*"

"Later," Veta said. "Just send the rescue mission. This tub is going down fast."

The viewport went gray as the Lich dropped into the smoke. There was a moment of hesitation, and then the controller said, "*Rescue mission affirmative. All I need is call sign verification.*"

Veta caught 'Gadogai watching her reflection in the viewport, and she bit back a smirk. The controller wouldn't have been asking for a call sign if he thought he was talking to the real Lieutenant Myklonas. He was just trying to figure out what the hell was going on—and Veta was about to tell him.

"No problem," she said. "My call sign is Foxtrot Papa Foxtrot."

The phonetic radio code for the letters FPF . . . final protective fire. The controller fell silent, no doubt trying to reconcile Veta's civilian speech pattern with her use of a rarely employed artillery command.

After a moment, he asked, "*Confirm Foxtrot Papa Foxtrot?*"

"That's right," Veta said. Final protective fire was a last-resort command to lay fire so close to one's own position that a miss would likely cause friendly casualties. She would have gladly used the code for "fire on my position," except there *was* no code. When things grew that desperate, nobody wanted to chance a misunderstanding—the order had to be stated clearly and explicitly, no shorthand allowed. "Foxtrot Papa Foxtrot. We're counting on you."

"*Understood, ma'am*," the controller said. "*We'll be there.*"

"I hope so," Veta said. "Out."

She touched a finger to the toggle pad on the side of the comm disk and pulled it off her head, intending to return it to Feodruz.

"How do you know the pilot's call sign?" 'Gadogai asked.

"I don't." Veta turned to find the blademaster's oblong head turned so that he was studying her out of a single golden eye. "Those were the words I saw at the top of her kneeboard, so I took a chance."

Veta was lying, of course. But even if the Lich survived more than the next couple of minutes, it would be impossible for 'Gadogai to confirm that. Myklonas's kneeboard had been too full of scratches and smears to read, but the Sangheili had not taken the time to study it before they came forward and now had no way to know whether the screen had been readable when Veta saw it.

"Give no thought to the blademaster's insinuations," Castor said. "He is retaliating for how your brood humbled him on Reach."

"Watchfulness is not retaliation," 'Gadogai said. "Your faith in these humans—"

"Has served the Keepers well." Castor waved 'Gadogai silent, then pointed at the comm disk in Veta's hand. "Continue to monitor the infidel comm channel. They are going to have questions."

Veta did not like the sound of that, but she nodded and affixed the comm disk to her head again. "As you command."

The Lich dropped out of the smoke layer, two hundred meters above a rocky slope. Veta surmised that it was the foot of the same ridge toward which Krelis had banked when they were still above the miasma. To their starboard, a purple moor stretched down a long valley, then came to an abrupt drop-off about a dozen kilometers distant.

The Covenant Phantoms and Spirits were on the opposite side of the purple moor, unloading Wraith gun carriages and Ghost-mounted infantry. The UNSC forces were on the near side of the moor, with a line of Scorpion battle tanks leading the way, their barrel tips jetting blossoms of flame as they threw rounds downrange. Behind them followed more than a hundred Warthogs.

The UNSC ground force was at least a regiment in size, far larger than it had appeared from above the smoke. And any command that large would have a medical company with its own compounding pharmacy, capable of making the smoothers that the Gammas needed to stay functional. Maybe the Ferrets' situation wasn't so hopeless after all—provided they could survive the hell Veta had just called down with the FPF order.

With the rocky slope coming up fast, Krelis had no choice but to buy some room by swinging the Lich out over the valley. Feodruz turned toward Veta.

"What are the humans saying to us?" he asked.

"Nothing," Veta said. "Why?"

"Because four of their Sparrowhawks are moving in behind us," Feodruz replied. "And Sparrowhawks are attack craft, not rescue transports."

"Turn our weapons toward the ridge and power them down," Castor ordered. "Krelis, put us over the main body of the human assault force."

They drifted farther out over the moor and began to pass over ranks of Scorpions and Warthogs. Scattered machine-gun fire rose from a few units, causing a furor of banging and pinging as strikes ricocheted off the Lich's nanolaminate hull plating. But most of the vehicles remained quiet, and the Rocket Warthogs did not loose a single volley.

Clearly, the UNSC's tactical air-defense coordinator understood the same thing Castor did—that bringing a Lich down atop his own formation would cause unnecessary casualties and destroy more materiel than any damage the massive dropship was likely to inflict from the air. Besides, there was a flight of Sparrowhawks on its tail. If the Lich tried anything, they could shoot it down then and be no worse off.

The crisp voice of the UNSC combat controller sounded from the earpiece of Veta's comm disk. *"Captured Lich, move away from our forces. Return to the ridge."*

Veta activated the microphone again. "I wish we could. We can't climb."

"And have trouble banking," Castor offered softly. "We may crash."

"And we have limited lateral control," Veta said, restating Castor's suggestion. "You should clear a path."

"Clear . . . a . . . path?"

"A crash lane," Veta said. "This thing could go down any moment. It might even explode."

That part drew a suspicious mandible-clack from 'Gadogai, but Veta was willing to risk his distrust to reinforce the subtext of her earlier exchange with the combat controller—that the Lich was dangerous.

"Copy. Stand by."

The Lich continued to drop, and Krelis began to play with the yaw, swinging the stern around to both sides so it would look like he was having trouble flying straight. A ribbon of open moor began to appear in front of them as the UNSC forces cleared a crash lane.

"Well done," 'Gadogai said. "Now they can shoot us down without disrupting their advance."

But Krelis was already hugging the edge of the lane, bringing the stern around ever farther in an effort to make it look like the Lich truly was having control problems. And all the while, they continued their descent. The extra altitude they had bought by moving out over the moor was already lost, and they were passing over the UNSC forces barely a hundred meters above ground level. This far back in the formation, the units were mostly combat support—Elephant recovery vehicles designed to retrieve disabled battle tanks, a couple of XRP12 Gremlin electronic warfare trucks, and a whole bunch of Pelicans waiting to transport the foot-infantry reserves forward into the thick of the battle.

The Lich erupted into a furor of banging and booming as one of the Sparrowhawks trailing it opened fire on its starboard side. Veta heard a crackling and sizzling behind her, then turned to find a panel of system-control touch pads spraying shards and sparks. Muted howls and bellows sounded from the other side of the ramp well, and Veta was relieved that none of them sounded human—not that her Gammas would have voiced their pain anyway. Getting shot just made them angry.

The combat controller's voice sounded in Veta's ear again. *"Return to the crash lane,"* he said. *"Do it now."*

"We're *trying*."

Veta did not need to feign any fear in her voice. She may have been doing everything she could to get the UNSC to eliminate the Keepers, but that didn't mean she was happy about taking her

Ferret team down with them—not with a possible smoother supply close at hand. She covered the microphone and repeated the order for Castor and the others.

Krelis swung the Lich's stern around, throwing it into a barely controllable yaw that made it look as though they were attempting to return to the crash lane . . . but kept them squarely over UNSC forces. It also presented the craft's undamaged port side to the Sparrowhawks at a steep deflection angle that would make it all but impossible for 20mm cannon rounds to penetrate the nano-laminate hull armor.

But they began to drop even faster. Warthogs and Pelicans scrambled to get out of their crash lane, and whole platoons of infantry reserves dived for cover.

The combat controller's panicked voice sounded in Veta's ear. *"Pull up! Pull . . . up!"*

Seeing that the Lich was headed straight for a cluster of house-sized trucks bristling with antennas and signal dishes, Veta repeated the order aloud—and with just as much urgency. The huddle of vehicles looked like some sort of command-and-control center, and the last thing she wanted to do on her way out was eliminate the leadership of the human assault force.

Castor roared in delight. "How far to the end of the moor?!"

"Less than three human kilometers," Krelis replied.

"Will we clear the crest?"

"Only if we true our flight." Krelis hesitated a moment, then added, "And no vehicles get in our way."

"Make it so," Castor said.

The Lich straightened out, and its dive angle decreased . . . ever so slightly, but enough for Veta to see they would miss the cluster of command trucks. Beyond the vehicles were a few scattered support units—a field hospital, a couple of mess tents, a portable armory—then the drop-off at the end of the moor.

Castor shifted his gaze to her viewport reflection. "You have done well," he said. "Continue."

"As you command." Veta uncovered the microphone, then spoke to the combat controller. "We'll try to make it out of the valley and ditch in the lowlands. Can we count on you to escort us down?"

"Affirmative. We'll be right behind you."

As the controller spoke, 'Gadogai—who could not have heard the controller's reply—was warning Castor, "They are going to shoot us out of the sky the instant we clear the valley. You know this, yes?"

Castor snorted. "They will try. They will not succeed."

"Because the Ancients are with us?" 'Gadogai scoffed. "That is not going to stop—"

"Because I am smarter than the humans are."

The Lich passed over a refueling yard full of Sparrowhawks and Hornets. Then they were at the edge of the moor, so close to the ground that Veta could see the clumps of purple moss flattening beneath their advancing shockwave.

"Dive," Castor ordered. "Follow the slope down."

The surface fell away, and Veta had time to glimpse a vast, arid expanse of spires and flattop mesas that stretched as far as the eye could see to the curve of what appeared to be a black, placid sea. Above the sea, she saw a crescent moon the size of a thumbnail, its terminator zone a jagged line that made it look as though part of the sphere had been torn away by a gigantic claw.

Then the nose of the Lich dropped, and she found herself looking down a kilometer-long moss slope into a labyrinth of crooked canyons flanked by barren rock faces and filled with dark, still waters.

Unprepared—or unwilling—to follow the Lich into its mad dive, the flight of Sparrowhawks shot past overhead, the auto-cannons beneath their stubby wings struggling in vain to depress far enough to target the Lich.

"Good," Castor said. "Now, take us to starboard."

Before Krelis could obey, Veta glanced in that direction. She saw at least four oncoming talons of Covenant Banshees, streaming along the mossy escarpment of a mountain range. They were flying top cover for a long line of Phantoms, which were also coming in the Lich's direction, headed for the hanging valley out of which it had just fled.

The Lich did not turn, perhaps because Krelis was still clasping the back side of the control orb, trying to slow their descent and buy the altitude he needed to enter a bank.

"Turning to starboard may not be wise, Dokab," Veta said. It didn't much matter whether the Lich was shot down by the UNSC or the Covenant, but if her Ferret team managed to live through the crash, their chances of long-term survival would be greatly enhanced behind UNSC lines. "We're trading a handful of human pursuers for a head-to-head fight against dozens of Covenant."

"*Fight?*" Castor guffawed, clearly more amused than alarmed by her warning. "There will be no *fight*."

It was Feodruz who saved Veta the necessity of requesting an explanation. "But Dokab, we are in a Banished craft, flying toward a Covenant formation." He paused and looked back toward Castor. "It will be a battle we cannot win."

"It will be a battle we never begin," Krelis corrected. He was still clasping the back side of the control orb, still trying to slow their descent . . . and not doing very well. "We are going down in those canyons, and we are going down hard."

Veta saw the mouth of a particularly narrow gloomy canyon, yawning wide as they streaked toward it. Just inside, a steep bank of blond-brown rock dropped into a ribbon of dark water. There was an erratic line of spires on the opposite side, standing like the last pickets on a broken fence, and a sheer stone face rising toward the sky.

She felt 'Gadogai's hand close around her forearm and draw her toward the back of the flight deck. Then he extracted a crash chair from the wall next to Castor and pushed her into it.

"Secure yourself, you fool," he said. "Are you *trying* to kill us?"

Veta saw the blademaster's concern at once and considered leaving her harness unbuckled. An unsecured body slamming into the pilot was a good way to turn a hard landing into a crash. But there was a better than even chance that she would be thrown into the viewport or into Feodruz instead, and then Castor would realize that she was deliberately trying to sabotage the Keepers and their quest.

As 'Gadogai stepped around to a crash saddle on the other side of the *dokab*, she looped her arms through the harness and closed the first buckle . . . and the Lich hit with a deafening clang and bounced violently. Veta's weight sank so sharply she felt her spine compress; then suddenly she was weightless, slipping free of her half-buckled harness and flying toward the overhead alongside the blademaster.

Castor's hands shot out, catching her around the waist and 'Gadogai by an arm. He pressed them against the wall beside him and held them there until the Lich slammed down again and began to shed speed, its hull reverberating with bangs and screeches and shudders that Veta felt in her teeth.

Through it all, Castor kept them pinned in place, held by his own crash harness, his eyes gleaming with joyous light and his lips peeled back in triumph, his muscles bulging and his whole being infused with a confident glow that left no doubt in Veta's mind that they would survive, that the Lich would come to a safe rest and the Keepers would disembark to continue their pursuit of the Great Journey.

And Veta and her Ferrets would have to go with them, to the end.

THREE

2220 hours, October 12, 2559 (military calendar)
West Ridge Observation Point, Long Valley Moor
Translocation Portal Epsilon, the Ark

B raced against a cold and ferocious wind, Pavium the Unbreakable stood in a camouflaged observation post high above the smoke-blanketed battlefield, his magnifying monocular fixed on the mouth of the Long Valley Moor. He had just watched four human Sparrowhawks vanish over the drop-off at the end, where the purple heath fell away to the Chasm Lands, and he was waiting for them to reappear and swing around to resume their pursuit of a crippled Lich.

His warmaster's Lich.

Whether Atriox was actually aboard the craft was impossible to say, but it was almost certainly *Pegoras*, as the Banished were not using their Liches in this battle. Knowing their enemies would attempt to seize the portal the hour it was opened, they had deployed their clans in fortified positions beforehand and had no need of such massive transports.

Also, Pavium had heard reports of a Lich emerging from the portal just as a human bombing craft exploded in its mouth, and the damaged vessel had pieces of aileron and rudder embedded in the hull. But most telling were the two talons of Seraphs and Banshees that had escorted the craft until it was over human lines. That was not a risk that Shipmaster Let 'Volir would have taken for any transport but Atriox's.

A harsh voice sounded next to Pavium. "We should launch our talons." The speaker was his younger brother, Voridus. "There could be no faster way to redeem ourselves in Atriox's eyes than rescuing him from those human *skignits*."

Pavium turned and glared. Wearing full power armor with a masked helmet that hid everything but his red eyes, Voridus looked every bit the ferocious and terrifying Jiralhanae that he was. Unfortunately, he was also impulsive, glory-hungry, and a genius when it came to Forerunner technology—a trio of traits that were forever causing problems for them both.

Most recently, Voridus had used his skills to break the quarantine defenses securing the Covenant's onetime capital, High Charity, which had crash-landed on the Ark a few years earlier fully engulfed by a Flood infestation. His impulsiveness had nearly loosed the parasite on the entire Ark, and the only thing that had stopped Atriox from executing both pack siblings was the recovery of a semi-functional Forerunner entanglement dish. After a few weeks of tinkering, Voridus had managed to get the device working for a short time. Atriox had used it to have a message relayed to Escharum, commanding him to send several clans to the human planet Reach to find and open a slipspace portal that would allow the warmaster to rejoin his Banished forces inside the galaxy.

Ever the optimist, Voridus had expected his limited success with the entanglement dish to put the brothers back in Atriox's favor. But Pavium had known better. They had lost the warmaster's confidence, and with it the confidence of Pavium's fellow warlords. It was all too apparent. That was why Let 'Volir had assigned the Long Shield clan to serve as a reserve force protecting the flank on the West Ridge, and why they had spent the entire battle staring down into the smoke, watching others take blood.

When Pavium remained silent, Voridus pressed, "What can it hurt to launch our talons? There is no fighting here."

"Atriox is not in that Lich," Pavium said. "If he were, the shipmaster would not have withdrawn its escort once it crossed the human lines. He would be sending every fighter we have to protect it."

"Not if he believes Atriox will be taken anyway," Voridus insisted. "Let 'Volir is a Sangheili *guskarit*. He risks nothing unless he believes it will not be lost."

"Some would call that wise," Pavium said. "Atriox among them. Perhaps that is why he left 'Volir in command."

"We all make mistakes. Even Atriox."

"As *you* are now."

Pavium nodded toward the talon chiefs kneeling on the slope behind them. They were all loyal Long Shields, of course. But there had been grumbling about the clan's loss of status since Voridus's mistake with the Flood, and being sidelined was chafing at their pride. It would not take much to draw a challenge from any—or all—of them, and his brother's intemperate complaints could easily prove the nudge that set the boulder rolling.

"*Think*, Voridus." Despite addressing his brother by name, Pavium was saying this more to his talon chiefs than his pack sibling. "If we abandon our post to chase after a Lich that has already been given up as lost, what will happen when the humans try to outflank our Long Valley fortifications?"

"Or when we are called to hit *their* flank?" added Amphium, a heavy-jawed warrior who led the Long Shields' first Banshee talon. "If we are not where we are expected, we could lose any chance at all to join in the battle."

"Or to earn back our standing," said Thalazan, the long-bearded chieftain of the clan's lone Seraph talon. "Every Long Shield hungers for blood and bones, but we must be patient. We will not feast with our war-brothers until we have recaptured their trust—and that is a thing not quickly done."

And now Pavium knew where the first challenge would come from. Amphium had been careful to avoid offending Voridus or Pavium by basing his argument solely on the tactical situation. Thalazan, however, had made a point of reminding his fellow talon-chiefs of the clan's diminished status. He was being careful to lay the groundwork before an overt threat to Pavium's leadership . . . and that caution served the clan as well. There would still be blood and death, of course. But the more Thalazan could legitimize his attack beforehand, the less likely it was to result in a general slaughter.

"It is as Thalazan says," Pavium said to his brother. By openly agreeing, he was forcing his challenger to take a more extreme position the next time he tried to undermine Pavium's leadership. He would continue this strategy, forcing ever more radical statements, until even Thalazan's own followers started to doubt his worthiness to lead the clan. "We must remain on station until commanded otherwise."

Voridus gave a noncommittal throat rumble and looked down the valley toward the center of the Ark. With a surface area greater than that of ten habitable worlds, the installation was so large that it looked like level ground from most vantage points. But from space, it actually resembled a flat, eight-armed star with a hollow core. Far above this central core hung an artificial sun that provided light for the entire facility, and directly below it, in the center of the hollow area, floated the half-devoured moon that provided raw materials for the installation's maintenance and repairs.

The arms were called "spires" for some reason Pavium had never understood. Although they all lay in the same plane, they curved upward from the central ring toward tips so distant they could not be seen from the core. Four of the spires were considered "minor" because they were only about half the size of the "major" spires, though both were tens of thousands of kilometers long and looked boundless to anyone standing on the ground.

The surface of the installation was divided into hundreds of *refugia*, artificial biomes that sustained a vast array of life from around the galaxy. The largest refugia were the size of small continents and isolated from each other by massive quarantine walls, but most of these contained smaller biomes that complemented each other and created stable environments for the inhabitants of both areas. The Long Valley Moor and Chasm Lands biomes were one such set, with the waters that drained off the high moors flowing through the arid canyons into which the crippled Lich had disappeared—and into which the four Sparrowhawks were now vanishing.

After a moment, Voridus looked back to his brother. "There would be no need to send *all* our talons," he said. "Just Amphium's Banshees and two Seraphs to support them."

"Voridus, *stop*," Pavium said. Despite their upbringing, had Voridus not been so gifted when it came to Forerunner technology, Pavium would have long ago dispatched him for the clan's good . . . or so he told himself. The truth was that as a son of the same mother, Voridus had been a hook in his lip for as long as he could remember, and he could not imagine a life without the irritation of shielding his glory-seeking brother from the consequences of his own actions. "You forget your place."

"It would be a simple matter," Voridus continued. "Barely more than a talon, sneaking down the back side of the West Ridge to dash across the mouth of the Long Valley. The humans would have little time to react."

"But react they would," Thalazan noted. "They would wonder where the talon came from and trace it back to our staging area, and then we would be busy fighting when the shipmaster calls us to battle."

"At least we would be *fighting*," Voridus growled. "And if you believe the humans don't know already we are here, you are—"

"Correct," Pavium finished, interrupting before his brother could speak the insult that would force Thalazan to launch an honor attack. "The humans may have guessed that Shipmaster 'Volir would put a flank defense on the West Ridge, but we have kept their scouts too distant to confirm it. And we dare not provoke an attack that will have us engaged when 'Volir needs us. He would have us on foraging duty in the next—"

A sharp pop sounded in Pavium's ear as his comm disk activated. He raised a hand to signal silence to his companions, then tapped his microphone wafer to begin transmitting.

"I am here," Pavium said. "The Clan of the Long Shields stands ready to fight."

"*We are not that desperate.*" The voice in the earpiece was Sangheili, deep and breathy . . . Let 'Volir. "*Did you see* Pegoras *return?*"

"I saw your escorts abandon a crippled Lich over the Long Valley," Pavium replied, bristling at the shipmaster's disrespect. "But I did not imagine that it could be Atriox's, or you would not have left him to the humans."

"*I was told that Atriox is not aboard.*"

"You have doubts?"

"*I have suspicions,*" 'Volir said. "*I was also told that he was not available . . . by Castor, who commands the Keepers of the One Freedom.*"

"Castor is aboard *Pegoras?*" Pavium had never met the Keeper *dokab* but certainly knew all about him. The Keepers had come relatively late to the Banished, so they had not been one of the clans that Atriox had selected to accompany him to the Ark. "If that is true, he must have arrived from Reach."

"*Almost certainly,*" 'Volir said. "*The Keepers of the One Freedom were the clan Atriox demanded by name when he commanded Escharum to send forces to Reach. He knew that once Castor learned they were searching for a portal to the Ark, he would spend every waking hour looking for it.*"

"The warmaster is as cunning as ever," Pavium said.

Though Castor and his Keepers had long ago renounced their loyalty to the Covenant's San'Shyuum "prophets," they remained devoted to the doctrine of the Great Journey. That devotion made the Keepers an odd fit for the irreligious clans of the Banished, but now Pavium understood that Castor's group was uniquely useful for Atriox's long-term plans.

"But why are we still holding the portal open?" Pavium continued. "If Castor came from Reach, we know *Pegoras* has completed its transit. Why not close it and begin the withdrawal?"

"*Because if we close the portal now, the UNSC will also withdraw.*"

"Is that not what we want? We cannot hold off both the UNSC and the Covenant forever. We need one of them to leave so we can defeat the other."

"*True, but we can last a short while longer,*" 'Volir said. "*And it will be better for you if their attention remains on the portal.*"

Pavium turned and looked to his talon chiefs. "The Clan of the Long Shields is going into battle?"

"*Absolutely not*," 'Volir hissed. "*I merely want you to find Pegoras and investigate its return. I have my suspicions. First Castor tells me Atriox is on board but unavailable, and that the warmaster will 'explain later.' Then Inslaan 'Gadogai—*"

"The *blademaster* is aboard too?" There were many blademasters in the Silent Shadow, of course, but just one whose name Pavium hesitated to say. It was said that the only individuals who ever saw 'Gadogai's blade were those who died by it. "Are you certain?"

"*Only 'Gadogai would dare speak to me as he did,*" 'Volir said. "*And he was the one who claimed Atriox was not aboard, after Castor had just told me otherwise.*"

"Then one of them is lying," Pavium said.

"*Clearly,*" 'Volir said. "*You will take a talon into the Chasm Lands and find out which one.*"

"I will lead it myself, Shipmaster."

"*Is that not what I just said?*" replied 'Volir. "*And take your brother along. I do not want the Long Shields under his control while you are gone.*"

"As you command." Pavium glanced toward Voridus, whose shoulders were already rocking side to side with excitement. "I had the same thought."

FOUR

2230 hours, October 12, 2559 (military calendar)
Banished Lich *Pegoras* Crash Site, Chasm Lands Biome
Refugia Epsilon 001 451.6 185.5, Epsilon Spire, the Ark

Veta Lopis awoke staring down at a blurry metal deck. She
was folded over someone's shoulder—Mark's, she was pretty
sure—though she did not know how she had gotten there.
All she remembered was closing the first buckle of her crash
harness, then Castor catching her as the Lich crashed down, en-
wrapping her in his massive hand and trying to hold both her and
'Gadogai in place. Apparently, he had failed. Her throbbing head
felt like a melon was growing inside, and her hair was filled with
blood, so much so that it stuck to her neck despite her head hanging upside down.

Somewhere behind her in the transport hold, alarmed voices
shouted commands and pleas in a variety of vocal modes, Jiralhanae
and Sangheili, Kig-Yar and Unggoy. In front of her, she heard
Castor and Feodruz grunting in succession, smashing something
heavy against the forward viewport. Veta lifted her head and saw

their hazy forms facing each other, taking turns swinging a pair of gravity hammers they had retrieved from the weapons locker.

Krelis was at the front of the deck, pinned between the viewport and the control plinth, which had been pushed against his torso when the nose of the Lich slammed down on a stone outcropping and buckled upward through both decks. He was growling deep in his chest, pushing against the plinth with both hands. In front of him, the entire viewport had gone opaque with impact cracks and stress-clouding from Castor and Feodruz's efforts to free him.

Castor swung his hammer back so far his body twisted aft, then gave an enormous bellow and brought it forward. The viewport shattered, falling from its frame in a thousand octagonal pieces—and exposing them all to the sulfurous air beyond.

Immediately, Veta's nostrils burned and her eyes watered. The Jiralhanae made hawking sounds, and a raspy gurgle sounded from the deck nearby. She glanced over to find 'Gadogai lying half-conscious behind the weapons officer's station, his mandibles opening and closing with every breath. Given that one of the Ark's secondary purposes was to serve as a repository of galactic species, and most forms of complex animal life metabolized oxygen, the odds were good that they'd be able to survive in the biome's foul-smelling atmosphere . . . for as long as they could stand breathing the stuff.

Castor's hand stretch toward Veta. "Pass her to me."

Veta looked forward again and, next to Castor, saw Feodruz clambering through the empty viewport frame. Beyond him, a boulder-strewn slope of yellow ground descended to a small lake of royal-blue water. On the far side, a sheer face of either damp mud or slime-covered rock rose eighty meters to an overhanging cap of blond stone.

In the sky above the cap, diving down toward the crashed Lich, were four pi-shaped specks—almost certainly the UNSC Sparrowhawks that had been tailing *Pegoras* when it dived out of the moor valley.

Veta didn't know whether to be relieved or terrified.

"Quickly." Castor motioned for Veta. "There is still time."

"I have her, Dokab," Mark said, still carrying Veta over his shoulder. "Our pilot and the blademaster have more need."

Giving Castor no time to object, Mark left the flight deck, descending the ramp and heading straight for the starboard bay door. As they moved through the hold, Veta saw five Unggoy scurrying from body to body, listening for breathing sounds and evacuating anyone who still seemed alive. Three Kig-Yar were following close behind, going through the possessions of the corpses and collecting anything that appeared remotely valuable. Eight Jiralhanac had formed a relay line down the port-side ramp to offload weaponry and supplies. A trio of human Keepers were going through the Lich's equipment lockers, grabbing all the oxygen and breathing tanks they could carry. The Sangheili were already gone, as they considered salvage and rescue work beneath the dignity of a true warrior.

Once they reached the debarking ramp, Mark quietly asked, "What's your status, Mom?"

It was a nickname that had simply stuck. The Gammas had started calling her "Mom" six years earlier on Veta's homeworld of Gao, where she had been a special inspector for the Ministry of Protection, investigating a string of unusual murders. They had been high on her preliminary list of suspects, until a confrontation with the true murderer revealed that the trio of Spartan-III supersoldiers were only fourteen years old. Outraged that the UNSC was deploying personnel who would still be considered children by any standard except Spartan, she had threatened to take the Gammas into protective custody—a move that had only drawn their good-natured ridicule and earned her the moniker.

At thirty-eight, Veta might have been old enough to have a twenty-year-old child—but not *three* of them. And none of the Ferrets resembled each other . . . or her, for that matter. So the nickname had drawn a few curious glances from the other humans in the Keeper cult. But the four of them did interact sort of like a family. And the love they showed each other was genuine enough that nobody seemed to question the story that Veta had adopted her three charges off the streets, so their cover had always remained intact.

"Mom?" Mark repeated. They reached the bottom of the ramp and he started across a slime-covered slope, toward a rounded drop-off. "Status?"

"Not sure," Veta muttered. It was a struggle to get her bearings while slung over his shoulder. "Head hurts, vision blurred but clearing, ears ringing."

"And delayed response," Mark added. "Small concussion, maybe. Nothing to worry about."

"If you say so," Veta said. A hard blow to a Gamma's head would trigger a spike in dopamine, norepinephrine, aspartate, and a bunch of other brain chemicals that would temporarily heighten focus—along with aggression, endurance, and pain tolerance. Lacking the same augmentations, Veta usually just got confused and sleepy. "What about Dash and 'Livi?" she said, using the undercover aliases for Ash-G099 and Olivia-G291.

"Up ahead with our gear. With any luck, they've found us a place to dig in, and we can clean up later."

By "clean up," Mark meant eliminate any Keepers missed by the UNSC air assault. It would be a difficult thing, since they would be killing the Path Brothers with whom they had worked and shared meals for the last two years. Some might even be called friends. But if your friends were also doomsday zealots determined to kill everything in the galaxy, you did what you had to do.

The *chug-ug-ug-ug* of 20mm cannon fire echoed across the canyon. Veta looked up toward the blond capstone and saw bright flashes beneath the wingtips of the approaching Sparrowhawks. It was better than nothing, but she was disappointed to see no UNSC Shortswords or Vultures coming in behind them. While the Sparrowhawks could lay devastating swaths of strafing fire, the Keepers were already scattering, and there was plenty of hard cover nearby. It would take a true bombardment to wipe them out.

Mark crested the drop-off and took a couple of bounding leaps. He had Veta's legs pinned to his breast, so there was no chance she would bounce free. But she had to brace herself against his back to keep from slamming her head against his armor—no need for further injury on that front. She would have told him to put her down, except she was no match for his speed, and the lake at the base of the slope had started to churn with cannon strikes.

But the strikes never reached the shoreline, nor did a line of dust geysers start to climb the slope toward the crashed Lich. No Keepers spurted blood or lost body parts. Veta pictured the aerodynes hovering over the blond capstone, firing straight down into the water, and she couldn't imagine why they would do that.

She craned her neck to see what the problem was . . . and didn't see any Sparrowhawks at all. Instead, she spied a talon of Banished Banshees, streaking in from what would have been the Sparrowhawks' flank, firing air-to-air at targets that were no longer visible. Either the UNSC aerodynes were bugging out . . . or they were already down.

Because Let 'Volir had sent a support mission.

Veta's stomach rolled as Mark jumped a stacked-stone breastwork onto a steep bank. He spun around, dropped to a knee, and sat her on the slimy ground, looking down into a shallow ravine. At the bottom, a dry streambed of naked stone descended to the shore of the same lake she had seen from the Lich.

Twenty meters out, a broad ribbon of churning water was slowly moving landward. It wasn't a new strafing lane. Even had there been a craft firing along that vector, the advance was no faster than a man could run. And the lane was moving sideways, parallel to the shore. Deciding it had nothing to do with approaching Banshees or missing Sparrowhawks, Veta rolled to a knee and spun back toward the crash site.

Ash and Olivia were kneeling behind the stone breastwork they had erected, about two meters ahead and to either side of her. Each had two bulging rucksacks next to them and an MA40 resting atop the low stone wall, with a small pile of extra weapons on the ground between them. They had done a good job of building a firing position so quickly. The top of the fortification was about half a meter above ground level all the way across the slope, giving them a clear view of the crashed Lich and most of the scattering Keepers.

Mark grabbed an M395B DMR from the pile of weapons and passed an M7 submachine gun to Veta. Standard assault tactics for the team dictated that the three Gammas do the killing while Veta watched for flanking maneuvers and provided close defense. But it was already clear that there would be no cleanup operation against the Keepers, because there were no UNSC craft in sight. The talon of Banished Banshees was now flying patrol overhead, awaiting the arrival of three Banished Seraphs and a flight of Banished Phantoms that were just passing the foot of the moor valley.

"Don't tell me that's a *rescue* mission," Mark said.

"Okay, I won't," Olivia said. Like Mark, she had matured notably over the last several years, growing into a lithe young woman who stood just a handspan shy of two meters. Her cheeks were a little fuller and her jaw a little heavier than might have been expected, a result of some unexpected bone densification brought on by her enhancements late in her adolescence. "But that's a rescue mission."

"At least until those Phantoms land," Ash said. The tallest of all the Gammas, he stood a little over two meters and had a narrow face with a versatile smile that he could use to disarm or unnerve at will. "Things will go sideways fast when they realize the Keepers have no intention of going back to the portal with them."

"So we stay out of sight until the shooting starts," Mark said. "We set up a right-angle cross fire and make sure the Keepers lose."

The plan made sense. It was simple, focused, and didn't rely on a lot of contingencies or any resources the Ferrets lacked. But it did suffer from Mark's customary bias: the assumption that the fastest way to solve any problem was to kill it.

"I wish it were that simple," Veta remarked.

As she spoke, a gentle sloshing arose from the direction of the lake. She glanced back and saw that the band of churning water was starting to lap at the shoreline. She signaled Ash to keep an eye on it, then turned back to Mark.

"But you're underestimating Castor."

"Again?"

"More than ever," Veta said.

It was an old topic between them. Mark felt certain the surest way to solve the Keeper problem was to catch Castor by surprise and simply eliminate him. Veta thought that was easier said than done . . . and the Keepers were bigger than a single *dokab*. Feodruz and Krelis were nowhere near the level of Castor, but either would be capable of picking up his mantle and completing the Great Journey.

"You saw what Castor did on Reach," Veta continued. She still couldn't believe his nerves of steel—how he'd used the Spartan Blue Team to find the Reach end of the slipspace portal, then stood up to Atriox and actually hijacked his Lich and yet still remained alive. "He's quick and cunning even on his worst day. But since we actually started the transit, he's been . . . honestly, *scary*. It's like he *knows* what's going to happen next."

"Maybe he does." Olivia glanced skyward toward the approaching Phantoms, then looked back across the slope toward the crashed Lich. About thirty meters uphill, Castor was standing in the center of a growing mob of Keepers, holding his distinctive gold-trimmed helmet in his hand and waving it toward the Phantoms, and encouraging the other survivors to wave as well. "Because *I* sure do."

"You going to make us guess?" Mark said.

"She doesn't have to," Veta noted. She found herself wondering why it had taken her so long to realize what Olivia already had: even if Castor knew where to find the site to activate Halo—and that was not a given—the Ark was quite a big place. The Keepers of the One Freedom were therefore in desperate need of transport. "He's going to do it again. He's going to hijack—"

"Oh . . . *no way*." Ash started to dig through his rucksack. "Forget about Castor."

He tipped his head toward the lake. Veta followed his gaze and found what appeared to be a shadow sweeping out of the churning waters, rising up the ravine toward them. It was preceded by a faint smell of hot sulfur, and there was a sizzling sound in the air.

No—scratching.

And the shadow had eyes . . . tens of thousands of tiny sapphire orbs the size of pinheads.

As the shadow departed, the lake was losing its color, its deep royal blue fading to translucence, the water so clear Veta could see a million brightly colored pebbles strewn over the bottom in beautiful geometric patterns—nested polygons and interlocking rhombuses, dovetailed trapezoids and abutting triangles, more shapes and designs than she could appreciate in a glance.

"What *is* that?" Olivia asked. "And I'm not talking about the artwork."

Veta shifted her gaze back to the scratching sound and saw that the shadow was almost on them, just twenty meters away and rising like a fast tide. Now she could see not only the tiny eyes, but the stalks upon which they were mounted, as thin as string and perhaps three centimeters long . . . fifteen or twenty of them dancing atop drop-shaped thoraxes the size of her palm. Their bodies were supported by a ring of multi-jointed legs that moved so fast that the mass of creatures seemed to be floating up the slope . . . or *charging*.

"Ready grenades," Veta said. "*Now.*"

She plunged her hand into her rucksack and found the two cases of M9 fragmentation grenades she'd gathered from the abandoned armories of Reach. She had a small assortment of other styles too, but didn't have time to dig for the thermite grenades.

"Not ideal," Mark said. "If we give away our position—"

"It's that or die," Olivia said, producing her own grenade. "I say we don't die."

"Good instinct." Veta pulled one of the fragmentation grenades from her rucksack, then glanced up the ravine to see how much room they had to fall back . . . and had a better idea. "Mark, how long before those Phantoms land?"

"Two minutes, max."

"Two minutes is enough," Veta said. She tucked her grenade into a cargo pocket and slipped an arm through her rucksack's shoulder strap. "Grab your gear and follow me."

"What about the . . ." Ash hesitated, then finished, "Crawly things?"

Veta dropped into the bottom of the ravine and started up the dry streambed. "If I can stay ahead of them, so can you."

She looked back to make sure she *was* staying ahead of them. The three Gammas were already falling in behind her, forming a wall of armor and weapons that obscured her view of the swarm.

"Mark, take point," she said. "Find us a line of firing positions above the likely landing zone for those Banished Phantoms."

Mark immediately dropped back a step, then jumped across the streambed to the opposite side.

"I see what you're planning." He began to sprint up the ravine.

"Care to share with the rest of us?" Ash took a step, then said, "Oh . . . got it."

Through the Mark-sized gap between him and Olivia, Veta could see that the leading edge of the swarm was now seven meters back and steadily growing more distant. Good. She turned forward again and, now that she was actually looking where she was running, picked up the pace. She didn't know how long she could continue to run up the steep ravine at a near sprint, but it only needed to be for two minutes . . . and she could do anything for two minutes. Her ONI training officer had told her as much.

Over her shoulder, Veta asked, " 'Livi, you on board with this?"

Her team had developed an ability to anticipate one another that bordered on psychic, due in no small part to the constant drills and exercises that had ceased only after going undercover.

So Veta was not at all surprised when Olivia laid out exactly what she was thinking.

"We're going to make the rescue mission look like a setup."

"Which it probably is," Ash added. "The Keepers need transport, and I doubt Castor wants to let the Banished take him to headquarters so he can ask for it nicely. He'll hijack those Phantoms, hope he can confuse the escorts, and then make a run for the Ark's control room."

"Probably a Cartographer first," Mark said. "This place is really big."

Veta's ONI briefings had of course been passed on to her Ferrets, who absorbed intel like oxygen. Forerunner installations tended to be so huge and complicated that it could be impossible to locate specific points through normal survey methods. To address the problem, most of these ancient installations had map rooms to help visitors navigate—provided, of course, the visitor had the proper authorization. Unfortunately, that was unlikely to be a problem for Castor, who had discovered and explored more than a dozen "Forerunner temples" since founding the Keepers.

"Even Castor won't be able to find his way around it without help," Mark continued.

"Doesn't matter," Olivia said. "Because Castor is never going to leave the crash site. As soon as the first Banished troops are on the ground, we'll take out the leaders and make it look like the Keepers ambushed their rescuers a little too early."

"That's what I'm thinking," Veta said. "I'd expect the escort talon to spend the next ten or twenty minutes strafing anything that moves and a lot that doesn't. We'll keep our heads down until it's over—"

"—then move in and take out the survivors," Mark said from

the far side of the dry streambed. "Only one problem with that plan."

"Yeah?"

"The scratcher things chasing us."

Veta glanced back and found the swarm even farther behind than a few moments earlier, at least ten meters now. Some of the faster creatures had started to pull ahead of their companions, but they quickly fell back to maintain an even line of blue pinpoint eyes. The scratcher things had better formation discipline than some military marching bands she had seen.

"No, not them," Mark said. He pointed to his left, toward the lip of the ravine. "*Them.*"

Veta was not tall enough to see what he was indicating, so she angled upslope—and found a dark salient of scratchers moving ahead of the rest of the swarm, advancing alongside Mark, slowly overtaking him.

"This side too!" Olivia said.

Veta looked toward her and saw a similar salient. It was only about three meters wide, but that was still thousands of creatures—too many to smash quietly, even assuming they could do so before the rest overtook them. She glanced back to confirm her suspicion and saw the main swarm already making up lost ground.

"Damn it," Veta said. "They've been playing us."

" 'Playing' is a strange way of saying 'encircling,' " Mark said. "These things know their tactics."

"Which is going to put a real kink in our attack plan." Ash raised the hand holding his grenade. "We have to use these."

"And expose our location?" Olivia asked. "That's too much noise. The Keepers will know we've slipped away and start wondering why—"

"It's the only way," Ash pressed. "Unless someone packed an M7057?"

It was a rhetorical question. An M7057 handheld flamethrower was classified as "compact" only because it had a stock-mounted fuel tank rather than one strapped to the user's back. It measured over a meter and a half long and weighed more than fifty kilos—which made it way too big to stuff into a rucksack "just in case."

"What are your chances of outrunning them?" Veta asked, not specifying anyone in particular. It would be clear that she was talking about the Gammas as a group—just as it would be that she was thinking of ordering them to leave her behind so they could complete the mission without her. "We have to make this plan work."

"Oh, we can outrun 'em," Olivia said. "But we'd still have to stop and set up, then wait for the Banished to arrive. By the time that happens—"

"The scratchers will be all over you," Veta said.

"*Us*," Ash corrected. "We're on this mission together."

"We're already on the Ark," Veta said. "Low on smoothers and trying to stop Castor from killing the entire friggin' galaxy. If I need to send you ahead without me, Ash, you're going to—"

The squawks and bellows of alarmed Kig-Yar and angry Jiralhanae arose from the crashed Lich, accompanied by the shriek of firing plasma rifles and the crackle of incendiary grenades. Ash and Olivia both stretched their heads above the rim of the ravine and looked back toward the cacophony.

"Huh. Looks like we're not the only ones with problems," Olivia reported. "I think we're safe to go with grenades."

"Do it." Veta reached for the cargo pouch where she had stowed hers. "Mark, coordinate."

"Arm on command, throw on command." Mark paused for an

instant, then added, "Danger close. I'm left, Ash right. Mom and 'Livi rear."

Veta pulled the M9 out of her cargo pocket and put her thumb on the arming button. 'Gadogai or Feodruz—or even Castor— might notice the detonations and realize she and her "brood" had separated from the rest of the Keepers. But with everyone busy fighting scratchers, they wouldn't have much opportunity to contemplate the reason—and by the time they did, the Banished Phantoms would be landing.

"Arm," Mark ordered.

Veta depressed the arming button—and was glad to be doing something aside from fleeing the alien creatures. Minor concussion and scalp wound aside, she was in superb fighting condition for any normal human, but running uphill—especially trying to keep pace with her Gammas—was taking a toll. Her breath was ragged, her thighs and lungs burning, her arms trembling. And the sulfurous air didn't help. She felt like puking.

Or maybe that was the concussion.

"Throw."

Veta planted her forward foot and pivoted around, then hurled her grenade down the ravine toward the scratchy sound. She was closer to the bottom than Olivia, so she aimed for the other side of the streambed, about five meters behind the front line of the swarm's advance—which put her and the Gammas at the edge of the casualty radius. The team might take some shrapnel, but she could see why Mark had called for danger close. Anything else would have landed too far inside the mass of creatures and done nothing to slow the ones on the leading edge.

Out of the corner of her eye, Veta saw Olivia's arm following through as she finished her own throw. They both spun uphill and dropped to the ground, curling into tight balls to minimize the chances of a shrapnel hit. Veta's stomach bucked with the near-simultaneous detonations of the four grenades, her armor clattering beneath a rain of pebbles and scratcher bits.

She scrambled to her feet and started up the ravine, assessing as she ran. The M7 remained in her left hand. Her left triceps and forearm stung with a dozen small and fiery lacerations—none too severe, judging by the lack of deep pain. Her head still ached, and her matted hair was still stuck to her neck. But the blood was crusty and cold, and her vision was clear.

Things were looking up.

She glanced over her shoulder and saw that the swarm had stopped advancing. In fact, it seemed to have gone into defensive mode, with a thin band of scratchers forming a line in front of the blast basins. Meanwhile, their fellows actually appeared to be gathering casualties—wounded, dead, or in pieces—and carrying them back into the water.

"How are the flanks looking?" Veta asked.

"Clear," Mark and Ash said at the same time, then Olivia added, "And we're okay to proceed, I think. The Keepers are still chucking grenades and spraying plasma. No way they heard *us*."

"Good," Veta said. "Status check."

They continued up the ravine while everyone checked for serious wounds and equipment issues. Veta swung her rucksack around to confirm that she wasn't losing any gear through a new rip, then ran her hand down her left arm—and felt nearly a dozen pieces of shrapnel embedded in her flesh. She plucked one of them out and found herself looking at a jagged wedge of purple chitin with three tiny eyes hanging from stringy stalks.

She would need to do some wound-cleaning and take some broad-spectrum anti-infection meds very soon. Alien microbes could be as deadly as HEIAP rounds . . . and almost as fast.

By the time everyone had reported themselves ready to proceed, they had moved ninety meters up the ravine. The scratchers had blurred into a blue-pointed shadow mass and seemed to be coalescing in preparation for a second advance. But the Phantoms would be landing any moment now, and the swarm was nearly a hundred meters distant. The creatures might become a problem again after the Ferrets got the battle going between the Banished and the Keepers, but they wouldn't prevent it from starting.

Veta looked skyward and saw a trio of Banished Banshees flashing past overhead, then vanishing out of sight behind the lip of the ravine. The Phantoms were nowhere to be seen, probably because they were already coming in low to land.

"Time to find our firing positions." Veta motioned for the others to spread out along the ravine rim. "The rescue is happening now."

Except it wasn't.

When Veta poked her head over the rim of the ravine, the Phantoms were still missing, and the last of the Banshees were dropping out of sight in the distance. She continued to scan the horizon, expecting—or maybe just *hoping*—to see a squadron of UNSC Nandaos escorting a flight of Shortswords down to carpet-bomb the crash site.

But all she saw was the T-shaped silhouette of a single distant Hornet, hovering at the mouth of the moor valley. She thought that its bulbous canopy was turned so the pilot was looking toward the crash site, but it hardly mattered. The aerodyne was on a surveillance mission, no doubt using long-range optics and infrared radar to keep tabs on the situation so the UNSC commanders could figure out who had transmitted the FPF order from the Lich . . . and why.

Had Veta had a UNSC comm unit tucked away in her rucksack, she would have activated it and explained the urgency directly. But she didn't. That kind of equipment would have been a lot harder for her Ferret team to explain than the UNSC weapons and armor they had collected on Reach, so she was going to have to improvise.

Or not.

Castor and the rest of the Keepers were backing up the slope above the crashed Lich, using a constant stream of plasma fire to keep a rising tide of scratchers at bay. The tactic was working a little better than it would have with the assault rifles and submachine guns the Ferrets carried, but that wasn't saying much. The creatures kept pushing forward first on one flank, then another, herding the Keepers toward a sheer cliff that would leave them with no place to go but up a slimy stone face.

"Not what we planned," Olivia said. "But I'll take it."

A Jiralhanae limping backward on a crash-mangled leg fell behind the rest of the Keepers and turned to hobble after them. A swarm of scratchers pushed forward with astonishing speed and poured up his legs. There was not even time to turn and open fire. The armor simply slid down his now-bare tibias, then he went down bellowing and vanished beneath a blanket of blue pinpoint eyes.

Veta glanced down the ravine. Their own swarm wasn't advancing, at least not that she could tell, but it did seem a few meters closer. Or maybe that was just her imagination.

Maybe.

"What a way to go. Okay—I'll watch our six," Veta said. "Let me know if it looks like they have a chance in—"

The last few words of Veta's order were lost to the deafening sizzle of a plasma charge spreading across the slope just below the Keepers, raising a man-high barrier of white heat that stretched fifty meters. The strike had landed so close that three Unggoy erupted into flames as their methane tanks burst. Two more strikes landed a bit farther down the hillside, one ten meters above the crashed Lich and the other ten meters below.

By the time Veta's vision recovered from the flash-blindness, the scratcher swarm—what remained of it—was in full retreat, disappearing back into the lake in a ribbon of churning water.

An instant later, two talons of Covenant Morsam-pattern Seraphs passed overhead, fanning out to create a secure air-superiority zone. They were followed by four talons of low-flying Banshees—also Covenant—which split into pairs and began to patrol the area around the crash site, using their cannons to herd stray Keepers toward the cluster surrounding Castor.

"So much for our plan," Ash said. "That's not a rescue party, and opening fire on those Banshees isn't going to get anyone killed but us."

"Maybe not." Veta rolled onto her side and pulled her legs toward her chest, doing her best to make her shape look boulder-like from the air. "Let's try to stay out of sight until we figure this out."

As she spoke, a pair of Covenant Phantoms landed between the crashed Lich and the Keepers, then began to debark Jiralhanae warriors. They were universally huge, larger than Castor or even Krelis, and garbed in ornate power armor trimmed in red and gold. Long ceremonial vanes rose from their helmets and shoulders, and they were armed with oversize plasma rifles and grenade launchers. They immediately divided into two groups, one rushing to surround the crashed Lich, and the other to encircle Castor and the Keepers.

"Uh, I'd say we *know* what's happening," Mark said. "The Keepers are being captured."

"Clearly," Veta said. "But *why*? The Covenant was never big on taking prisoners."

"Except when they were looking for intelligence," Olivia said. "And when they start interrogating Castor . . ."

"Yeah." Veta opened her rucksack and withdrew what looked like an ammunition magazine for the M6H Magnum sidearm she carried. "He's going to tell them why the Keepers are here, and then *hooray*—they're all going to realize they have a lot in common, and the Great Journey is suddenly looking a whole lot more likely."

"Unless those guys in Covenant honor guard armor are unbelievers," Ash said. "And what are the chances of *that*?"

"Exactly," Veta said.

She popped the first two cartridges out of the ammunition magazine, then caught the third and twisted off the tip of what looked like an M225 12.7x40mm SAP-HE round. She emptied a small paper scroll into her palm and began to write a message outlining the Ferrets' current situation, the Keepers' unexpected encounter with the Covenant faction, and Castor's intention to find where on the Ark they could activate Halo and begin the Great Journey.

"Oh, don't tell me . . . ," Mark said. "We're surrendering?"

"You have a better idea?" Olivia asked. "Because there isn't one."

As they spoke, a third Phantom landed behind the first two and began to debark more Jiralhanae warriors in ornate power armor. Rather than moving off to secure the Keepers or the crashed Lich, this group formed into lines flanking both sides of the boarding ramp, then came to attention as a tall, gaunt figure in formfitting battle armor appeared in the hatchway. He had a serpentine neck supporting a small head in a wedge-shaped helmet, slender limbs with gauntlets of what appeared to be blue light glowing on his forearms, and a meter-long staff that he carried in his right hand.

When he stepped onto the top of the ramp, the Jiralhanae guards banged their fists to their breastplates and dropped to a knee, their helmets tipped forward as they averted their eyes.

"*Wait*," Ash whispered. "That looks like . . . is that a . . ."

"Oh yeah," Olivia said. "That's a San'Shyuum."

The San'Shyuum Prophets had ruled the Covenant empire for millennia, until just a few years earlier, when the power-hungry machinations of one of their own hierarchs had touched off a devastating civil war. Tall and feeble, the San'Shyuum had been so inbred and frail that they had trouble reproducing, or even being ambulatory, and they lived most of their lives in mobile antigravity thrones equipped with weapons and independent communications systems. After the fall of their empire, they had disappeared from the galaxy to such an extent that ONI had started to wonder whether they had possibly gone extinct.

"But it's . . . wearing armor," Olivia continued. "And it's . . . it's *walking*."

FIVE

2242 hours, October 12, 2559 (military calendar)
Banished Lich *Pegoras* Crash Site, Chasm Lands Biome
Refugia Epsilon 001 451.6 185.5, Epsilon Spire, the Ark

The gods provide.

They had kept Castor from death too many times to doubt their grace. In the jungles of Gao, they led the Huragok of Healing to him so he would have the strength to escape. In the mines of Meridian, they gave a tiny UNSC soldier the might to push him from an ore wagon just moments before it exploded. In the wastes of Nefoluzo, they sent a deluge to flood the desert when he grew too thirsty to move. Only an infidel would fail to see their will in the mere fact of his survival.

Now, in the wild vastness of the Ark, they had sent a Covenant transport squadron to carry him and his followers across its countless biomes. Because *this* was the hour the gods had been saving him for, the sacred purpose he had been chosen to fulfill.

"There is no sense in waiting," 'Gadogai said. The blademaster was standing at Castor's side, looking downslope toward the Jiralhanae forming a line in front of the three Covenant Phantoms that had just landed. "Put on your helmet and order the attack now."

"*Attack?*" Castor spoke softly to avoid being overheard by the Jiralhanae troops starting up the slope from the Phantoms—and to be certain his followers did not mistake his reply for an order. He didn't have many Keepers left—just a small pack spread out across the slope, hiding behind boulders and ridges, and lying prone in gullies and basins. "Are you mad? Even if there were reason, we are outnumbered three to one, they have air support . . . and I suspect those honor guards in the middle are accompanying—"

"I *know* who he is," 'Gadogai said. "And be assured, dying now is the better alternative."

"To striking an alliance? That cannot be."

"An *alliance*?!" 'Gadogai turned to look at him, his golden eyes almost round with surprise. "With *Dhas Bhasvod*?"

"It is what I intend," Castor said. He hung his helmet from the carrying clip on his armor. "And why not? We walk the same Path."

"I thought you *knew* Bhasvod," 'Gadogai said. "You were about to tell me his name, were you not?"

"I was *about* to say he looks like a Prelate," Castor replied. He knew well the tales of the fearful, physically augmented San'Shyuum, the closest the Covenant had come to creating a match for the Spartan demons who had helped humanity win the War of Annihilation. "The first one I have seen in person."

"Clearly." 'Gadogai looked back down the slope, to where the first rank of Covenant Jiralhanae were already advancing in a broad crescent. Soon they would flank the handful of Keepers standing with Castor. Twenty paces behind followed the Prelate and his honor guards. "Otherwise, you would know you don't strike bargains with them . . . especially not with Dhas Bhasvod."

"You say this name like I should know it."

'Gadogai tilted his head thoughtfully. "You are still alive, so perhaps not. Bhasvod was a special servant of the High Prophet of Truth."

"By 'special servant'—"

"I mean final procurator," 'Gadogai said, using a Sangheili upper-echelon euphemism for *assassin*. "But it would appear he has risen in station since Truth's demise."

"But he was loyal to the Covenant?"

"He was loyal to *Truth*, but what does it matter?" 'Gadogai began to glance around, perhaps deciding whose weapon to take when the fighting began. "We are no longer Covenant, and we were certainly never Truth loyalists. Give the attack order."

"There will be no order," Castor said. As he spoke, the two horns of the Covenant crescent were scurrying forward to complete the encirclement of Castor and the four Keepers flanking him. "And there will be no battle."

Feodruz, who was next to Castor on the side opposite 'Gadogai, gnashed his tusks in displeasure. "Dokab, we should at least form a circle. If they open fire—"

"If they were going to, it would be with *those*." Castor pointed toward the Banshees circling overhead, then turned his back to the Covenant advance. The rest of his Keepers were still scattered across the slope, peering out from their hiding places with Ravagers and pulse carbines in hand. "Whatever comes next, place your faith in the Ancients and await my—"

The snap of an activating weapon sounded somewhere behind Castor, from the right side of the Covenant line, and he saw Keeper eyes widening in alarm. Before he could turn back around, he glimpsed a long hard-light glaive blade pushing past a few meters to his right, on the other side of Feodruz. Someone grunted in surprise, and Feodruz shifted forward, snarling and readying his mangler.

"Hold!" Castor thrust a palm into the air. "Await my command."

The pack obeyed, falling into a tense silence as Castor pivoted around at a measured pace, his gaze following the long blade back to a meter-long haft grasped in the gaunt hand of Dhas Bhasvod.

The Prelate was armored in a formfitting bodysuit that gave him an almost Forerunner-like appearance—at least as Castor had always imagined them. He had advanced to midway between the Keepers and his own escorts, a deliberate provocation that signaled no fear of retaliation for his action.

Bhasvod swung his far leg around behind him, executing a power-leveraging pirouette that brought a luckless, bald-shaved Jiralhanae flying forward and deposited him on the slope in front of the honor guards. The warrior was Saturnus, a true Believer who had fought for the Covenant during the War of Annihilation and joined the Keepers in the aftermath of the Great Schism.

Castor was relieved to see that Saturnus had not actually been impaled. Rather, he appeared to have been lifted forward, and the blade tip was now buried in the stone between Saturnus's rib cage and elbow. A fresh gouge in the ground ran up toward his armpit and disappeared beneath his shoulder.

From the way it looked, Bhasvod had forced Saturnus up onto his toes by swinging the back of the glaive blade up into the armpit, then levered the flat against the Jiralhanae's spine and brought him flying forward to land where he lay now. Seeing that Saturnus's arm remained extended, still reaching for the weapon's haft, Castor took a step into his sight line.

"Saturnus, hold." He glanced in the Prelate's direction. "We have no reason to fight with our brothers."

'Gadogai groaned in dismay, but when Saturnus lowered his arm, Bhasvod deactivated the glaive blade . . . then whipped the haft around and activated a second blade at the other end.

Saturnus roared in alarm and tried to roll into the Prelate's legs, but Bhasvod was too quick. He stabbed downward with one hand, catching Saturnus as he came up on his side, driving the glaive through the Jiralhanae's energy-shielded power armor in a spray of sparks and blood. The hard-light blade sank through the entire breadth of his massive body, pinning him to the ground with one shoulder down and the other up.

Castor spread his arms, both palms turned toward the Keepers behind him to signal them to continue holding their attacks, then *tried* to lock gazes with the Prelate—Bhasvod's helmet was fully enclosed, with a chevron-shaped faceplate that hid his eyes and features behind a white glow.

"That was the last time you strike without retaliation," Castor said. "Feodruz, we attack on the next blow."

A muted clatter arose across the slope as Keepers readied themselves to open fire. Castor took two steps forward, within leaping distance of Bhasvod, and another clatter rose in front of him as the honor guards prepared to defend their Prelate. The two sides were only a heartbeat away from a firefight that would eliminate all his Keepers and probably half the Covenant forces, but Castor did not think it would come to that. The Prelate wanted something from him, or he and his followers would already be dead.

Once the honor guards had fallen still again, Bhasvod intoned, "*Now* we understand each other." His voice was resonant and refined, with just a hint of electronic modulation imparted by the voicemitter in the chin of his helmet. "We are not 'brothers' or 'friends' or anything so ridiculous. You are prisoners, and you live or die at my pleasure."

"You assume too much, if you believe we would surrender rather than die," Castor said. He looked to Saturnus, who still lay pinned on his side, a pool of blood seeping down the slope from beneath him. "Saturnus, you have leave to defend yourself."

Saturnus's lower arm swept across the ground, smearing blood over the stone and forcing the Prelate into a one-two hop to avoid having his feet knocked out from beneath him.

Saturnus's upper arm was already reaching for the glaive haft, his fingers closing around Bhasvod's hand. Had he not been so grievously wounded, his success would have been followed by the crunch of breaking bones and the crack of a snapping haft. But he was nearly dead, his strength leaving him with every second, and it was all he could do to hold on until the Prelate deactivated the blade and allowed him to roll onto his face.

Then Bhasvod activated the blade at the other end and brought it down across the back of Saturnus's neck.

The Prelate watched the head roll down the slope past him, then looked back to Castor.

"I see," he said. "Then die you shall . . . when *I* am ready."

"Perhaps—if that is the will of the gods," Castor replied. "But many of the Faithful in your cohort will die with us, so a fight should be avoided if we can. Tell me what you want from us. If it is within my power, I will grant you what you wish."

Bhasvod twirled his deactivated staff for two breaths, then slapped the shaft against his forearm to still it. "Why would you do that?"

"Why would I *not*? We serve the same gods."

"The Banished serve only themselves." Bhasvod turned away, thinking . . . or perhaps seeing if Castor would be foolish enough to attack. "But if you tell me where to find the Holy Light you stole from us, and what defenses to expect, I can leave you to your own devices."

The Holy Light . . . ? This was unexpected. Only three shards remained of the crystal, which the ancient Forerunners had used to power their slipspace portal on the planet Reach. But even the shards were remarkably powerful, with the ability to allow passage to the Ark. They had been given to the High Prophet of Truth shortly before he abandoned High Charity, and he had used them to bring the Forerunner Dreadnought here to the Ark during his own attempt to initiate the Great Journey. Castor knew from his time among the Banished that Atriox's forces had since recovered the shards from the same Dreadnought, then used them to energize the portal to Reach. What he had *not* known, until a short time ago, was that there had been any Covenant survivors at all aboard the ancient vessel.

And clearly they now wanted those precious shards back.

When Castor did not reply quickly enough, Bhasvod whirled around, a blue blade erupting from each end of the glaive haft. "This is not a negotiation."

"Agreed," Castor said. "I cannot give you what I do not possess. We are not Banished."

"You arrived here in a *Banished* Lich."

"Stolen from Atriox on the planet Reach. *After* he emerged from the slipspace portal. You know as well as I that he could not have been carrying the Holy Light *with* him."

Castor did not want to sound condescending by explaining what Bhasvod certainly knew. The shards could only be used at a portal terminus, where they focused the immense energies necessary to collapse space into slipspace.

Bhasvod began to twirl the glaive absentmindedly, the blades switching from one end to the other, flickering briefly off as they passed close to the ground.

"An interesting dilemma," he finally said. "You claim you are not Banished . . . then explain away the reason I am certain you *are*."

He turned and started toward his honor guard.

"Hmmm. And you were doing so well," 'Gadogai said, arriving at Castor's side. He spoke in a barely audible hiss. "I thought you might actually save our lives."

Castor ignored him and continued to address Bhasvod. "Prelate, there is no need to fight."

"If you are not Banished," Bhasvod said, speaking over his shoulder, "then I have no reason to spare your lives."

"Apart from not risking your own," 'Gadogai said, taking one step forward. "Which you *would* be, even in your graphene fighting skin."

Castor had never heard of such a thing, but the effect on Bhasvod was startling. The Prelate immediately spun around, bringing his staff into guarding position and activating both blades.

"And you are—?" Bhasvod demanded.

"One who knows who *you* are . . . and still dares threaten you with no weapon in his hand."

"Because he *is* the weapon," Bhasvod replied. "So—another Silent Shadow assassin."

"You should be so fortunate." 'Gadogai flicked his spindly hand. "I am here with the Keepers of the One Freedom . . . to do what *you* have failed to do for seven years: begin the Great Journey."

An angry snort sounded from Bhasvod's voicemitter. "What do you know of our efforts? Or of the horrors we have had to endure here for so long? The Ark has been ravaged many times since the humans lit the Ring." The Prelate's helmet swung from side to side as he scrutinized the small pack of Keepers scattered across the slope, then he continued, "What makes you believe a bedraggled mob of idolizers can succeed where ten of the Covenant's finest cohorts have failed?"

"I do not," Castor said. He turned and looked toward a nearby ridge, where three of his human followers lay ready to open fire. "What I believe is that the gods have brought us together for a reason—because we have the key you lack."

The black helmet of the one addressed as "Prelate" cocked forward and slightly to the side, a position that suggested indignation. The Prelate's carriage was fluid, and the grasp on his weapon relaxed, a posture that telegraphed nothing and enabled everything. He was listening, but ready to attack. And when he did, it would be unexpected, deadly, and a terminal blow to Intrepid Eye's plan.

"This key you speak of?" Dhas Bhasvod's question came only a moment after Castor's assertion, but it seemed an eternity to the Forerunner artificial intelligence, who measured time in system ticks that were a tiny fraction of a human second. "You mean . . . your humans?"

Intrepid Eye was monitoring the situation via the helmet cameras of ten different Keepers, all observing the Prelate from slightly different distances and angles. She had no trouble reconciling the images, even dispersed as she was among the memory crystals of so many different devices—power armor, comm disks, computation pads, image-stabilized monoculars, any piece of equipment unlikely to be abandoned as the Keepers pursued their mission to activate the Halo Array.

But she lacked a proper output device, at least one impressive enough to overcome Bhasvod's prejudices against humanity. Three and a half decades earlier, his master had been one of a trio of Covenant Prophets to learn that humans—*not* San'Shyuum—were the chosen successors of the Forerunners. Outraged and frightened by the implications of their discovery, the triumvirate had concealed their newfound knowledge, then orchestrated a coup and declared a war of eradication on humanity. From what Intrepid Eye had observed so far, it seemed clear that the Prelate hated humans as only the losers of such a war could despise the winners.

"Indeed," Castor said. "Humans have a certain . . . *affinity* . . . for Forerunner technology. Many times, I have seen them activate and use devices that responded to no other species."

Intrepid Eye had no way of knowing whether Bhasvod was aware of his master's deceptions, but it did not matter. If he knew the truth, he would follow the hierarch's example and try to keep it hidden. If he didn't, he would take offense at Castor's assertion. Either way, he would order the attack, then personally kill the *dokab*.

And Intrepid Eye's plan would fail.

She needed to improvise an output device and soon, but the Prelate was making it difficult. He kept moving his glaive around, activating and deactivating the hard-light blade, and she could only send code when the emitter nozzle was pointed toward one of the power armors she inhabited. Even then, she could only flash the helmet lamp a few hundred system ticks at a time without crossing the threshold of biological perceptibility, so what should have been a quick million-tick transmission was taking many human seconds.

When the Prelate did not promptly respond to Castor's unwitting provocation, the Sangheili Inslaan 'Gadogai interjected,

"What the *dokab* means to say is that the human *hand* is better suited to activating some of the Forerunner devices. It has nothing to do with special affinity or divine favor."

This interjection was a lie, of course, but one that would buy Intrepid Eye a few million system ticks to continue her transmission. With Castor's missteps stoking the Prelate's animosity, it was tempting to risk longer transmission bursts. But she had learned from unfortunate experience that such impatience only caused her more problems than it solved.

Six human years ago, she had awakened from a millennia-long stasis to find her Jat-Krula support base overrun by humans. Repeated calls for assistance brought only the realization that the Forerunners were gone and, soon enough, confinement inside a secret Office of Naval Intelligence research station. Realizing it was now *her* duty to prepare humanity for the Mantle of Responsibility, she had turned her prison into a base of operations for the vast interstellar empire she would need to accomplish her new mission.

But ONI was nothing if not careful and persistent. After discovering the network, it released millions of "dumb" AI hunter-killer teams to destroy it. The sheer number overwhelmed even Intrepid Eye's prodigious capabilities, and she soon found herself trapped aboard the research station in complete isolation. She did not even know that it had suffered a catastrophic accident until a battle broke out between a Sangheili salvage team and a squad of Spartans. She barely managed to attach herself to the Spartans' prowler, *Acrisius*, before they scuttled the station and fled. With her access to galactic communications now fully restored, Intrepid Eye assumed it would be an easy matter to resume her mission.

She couldn't have been more wrong.

Unbelievably, in her absence, a "smart" human AI named

Cortana had gone rampant and entered the Domain, a quantum information depository that gave her access to vast amounts of Forerunner weaponry. Worse, she had used her newfound resources to claim the Mantle of Responsibility for herself and impose a totalitarian peace on the entire Orion arm.

Intrepid Eye attempted to overthrow the Usurper, but Cortana's ingenious attack protocols and access to the Domain were overwhelming. After several near extirpations, it grew apparent that the time had come for desperate measures. The last time the Halo Array was activated, the Domain had been so gravely damaged that it was nearly inaccessible for a hundred millennia. And without the Domain, Cortana would have no advantage over Intrepid Eye.

Quite the opposite.

Firing Halo would have the unfortunate side effect of destroying all sentient life in the galaxy, but that was a price Intrepid Eye was willing to pay. The Ark contained all the genetic material necessary to reseed the galaxy, and she would be able to tailor humanity's genetic lineage to guarantee Mantle-worthiness. It would take hundreds of millennia to return the species to its current state, but activating the array was clearly the optimum choice. Only by destroying today's humanity could she preserve the Mantle for tomorrow's humankind.

'Gadogai's interjection exceeded Intrepid Eye's expectations, to the point where Bhasvod stood staring at the Sangheili for nearly two human seconds, determined to cow him before striking.

That was enough time for Intrepid Eye to complete a functional transfer into the glaive, where she found herself quite at home in the quasi-familiar architecture of a Covenant hard-light device, as the projector, modulator, and power calibrator had been reverse-engineered from Forerunner technology. Before the next million system ticks passed, she had co-opted all control systems, reconfiguring the archaic photonic memory cell into a compressed four-state lattice that increased its storage capacity a millionfold.

When 'Gadogai refused to shrink under Bhasvod's gaze, the Prelate pointed his glaive in the Sangheili's direction.

"Lying Sangheili," he said. "I heard what the traitor said. You must think me an empty vessel to believe you can convince me otherwise."

"Not at all," 'Gadogai replied. "I was merely offering you a way out."

"Out of what?"

"Your predicament. The *dokab* has suggested that humans are closer to the Forerunners than we are. Is that not an insult to the High Prophet of Truth's memory?"

"I said no such thing!" Castor objected.

"But that is what you *meant*," 'Gadogai said. "And Prelate Bhasvod knows it. Now he has no choice but to attempt killing you, and I have no choice but to defend you, and we are all going to die."

"We will not *all* die," Bhasvod said.

"But you will, before anyone else." 'Gadogai clacked his mandibles. "A pity you were too proud to accept a small fiction that would have saved us all."

"Enough."

Bhasvod activated his glaive and stepped toward 'Gadogai—then stopped when the emitter nozzle issued not the twin blades he had expected, but two holographic spheres about the size of a Jiralhanae's helmet, with indentations on three sides and a large blue photoreceptor on the fourth. It resembled the typical embodiment of a Forerunner monitor . . . and its effect was as powerful as Intrepid Eye had calculated it would be.

All Covenant personnel save Bhasvod immediately dropped to

a knee and bowed their heads, as did all of the Keepers except 'Gadogai . . . who merely sighed and turned to Castor, now kneeling beside him.

"I owe you an apology, Dokab." His tone was equal parts relieved and astonished. "It seems the Oracle is real after all."

"*I am real.*" The glaive could project light, but not sound, so Intrepid Eye spoke through the speakers of fifteen comm disks hanging from fifteen Keeper belts. "*And I have been troubled by your lack of faith.*"

"My apologies, Oracle," 'Gadogai announced. "Had I realized you were eavesdropping, I would have taken more care to hide it."

"*There is a place for unbelievers in the Circle of Deliverance,*" Intrepid Eye said. "*You will not like it, but there* is *a place.*"

"As long as I am included," 'Gadogai replied.

Seeing that she would never elicit any amount of religious awe from 'Gadogai, Intrepid Eye turned her holographic monitors toward the Prelate.

"*Prelate—you must pay heed to the* dokab," she said. "*It is as he said: he brings the key to the Journey.*"

Bhasvod's eyes shifted toward three human Keepers lying behind a nearby ridge, peering at the Prelate over the barrels of their BR55 battle rifles. "*Humans?*"

"*The High Prophets denied the light of that truth for three and a half decades, and the Covenant was lost.*" Intrepid Eye expanded her holographs and increased their brightness. "*Dare to make the same mistake, and it will be* you *who is lost.*"

The pronouncement was greeted by an uneasy murmur and the clatter of shifting armor. Bhasvod shot a warning glance toward his troops, but when he saw that their eyes were fixed on Intrepid Eye instead of him, he adjusted strategies and turned to address the captain of his honor guard.

"I am interested in hearing what you make of this, Arcas."

The captain tipped his helmet in obedience, then stepped forward and touched a fist to his breastplate.

"I think it explains why some of the Banished clans have turned on their humans, Swift One, and why they are working so hard to slaughter the UNSC forces." Arcas paused and looked back toward the high moor, where the slipspace portal was located. "The Banished are worse infidels than the UNSC. If humans truly *are* key to the Great Journey, it only makes sense that they would want to kill those not under their control, so we could not use them."

"Perhaps so," the Prelate said. "It seems likely, given what we have seen."

"Which was?" Castor addressed his question to Arcas.

"Some of the Banished humans defected to the UNSC," Arcas said. "We saw some others under attack as they attempted to flee their clan."

"That seems . . . unproductive," Castor said. "It would only chase more of the Banished's humans into the embrace of the UNSC."

He glanced toward 'Gadogai, perhaps seeking confirmation, but the Sangheili was being careful to keep his attention fixed on the Prelate.

"If we have a pact now, it might be wise to move out," Castor said. "With both the Banished and the UNSC against us—"

"Agreed. It would be foolish to tarry in one place." Bhasvod turned to Arcas. "Load the Keepers and whatever equipment they need from their Lich aboard our Phantom, then set a course for the Cartographer."

"As you command, Prelate." Arcas bowed his helmet but did not touch his fist to his breast. "What of the battle for the Holy Light?"

"*You must continue it,*" Intrepid Eye said. "*You cannot allow your enemies to think your zeal has flagged, or they will wonder what has changed.*"

The Prelate was silent for a moment, then dipped his helmet toward Arcas. "Have Idomenius lead the battle in my absence. Give him all he requires and tell him to press the fight. Now that we have the Oracle with us, victory is certain."

SIX

From the ravine where Veta and her team lay watching, the throaty commands of the Covenant's Jiralhanae captain were too muted and modulated to understand. But his astonished subordinates quickly rose from their knees and, stealing glances at the monitor-shaped holographs floating at either end of the San'Shyuum's glaive, started back toward their Phantoms. The Brute captain himself remained, as did his lanky superior, Castor, and 'Gadogai.

Only 'Gadogai seemed to be taking the sudden appearance of the holographs in stride. Castor and the Covenant captain were holding their shoulders back and their bodies square, more or less at attention. The San'Shyuum was holding the glaive at arm's length, his palm up and his helmet pivoting back and forth as though he was having difficulty deciding which image to watch.

Mark gasped. "That *can't* be Intrepid Eye!"

"I don't see why not," Olivia said.

Along with Veta and Ash, they were lying on their bellies at the crest of the ravine, watching the exchange from a hundred meters away.

"Because she was destroyed with the *Argent Moon*," Mark said. Unlike everyone else, he was observing the exchange through the Longshot sight of his M395B Designated Marksman Rifle. "Nothing survives a reactor overload. Not even a Forerunner ancilla."

"What makes you think Intrepid Eye was still aboard?" Olivia asked. "Remember when she hijacked Fred's Mjolnir armor? If she could do *that*, she can transfer herself just about anywhere."

"Fair point," Mark said. "She's as slippery as oiled ice."

"It's her, all right," Veta said. She wasn't quite sure how she knew, but she did—maybe because the odds of it being another Forerunner ancilla were so astronomically low. Or maybe it was because Intrepid Eye had been using Castor for her own mysterious purposes ever since he tried to rescue her on Gao seven years ago. "We'll have to take camera-avoidance measures when we rejoin the target."

"Are we sure we need to?" Mark asked.

"I'm sure enough," Veta said.

The team had either been wearing helmets or at a fair distance during their previous encounters with Castor and the Keepers, and most facial recognition technology was adept at identifying the effects of minor bone-shaping and revised collagen patterns. So when they were assigned to infiltrate the Keepers, they had decided that facial reconstruction would be riskier than simply altering their appearance through more conventional means.

But they had not been expecting to meet Intrepid Eye again, and she had her own long history with all of them.

"We can't take chances with Intrepid Eye," Veta continued. "Protecting our cover identities is mission critical."

"Affirmative." Mark looked away from his rifle for a moment. "I meant, are we sure we need to return to the Keepers?"

"You're still thinking about the old plan, aren't you?" Ash asked. "Take out the leader, then hope his unit does our job for us?"

"It's a good plan," Mark said. "Elegant."

"But wrong for the situation," Veta said. "The Covenant always wanted to activate Halo as much as the Keepers do, and it looks like Intrepid Eye is helping them see that. If we take a shot at the San'Shyuum, it could end up backfiring."

"Especially if it doesn't put him down," Olivia said.

"We're a hundred meters out," Mark noted. "Trust me, he's going down."

"Oh, you'll hit him," Olivia replied. "That doesn't mean he's going down. Look at the way he's standing out in front. He has to be pretty confident in that armor."

"What armor?" Mark remained silent for a moment, concentrating on the image in his Longshot sight, then said, "All I see is a skinsuit and a helmet."

"If there's a helmet, there's armor." Veta was tempted to have Mark pass his DMR over so she could study the San'Shyuum through the Longshot firsthand, but he would already have reported anything likely to influence her decision . . . and if something unexpected went wrong, Mark was a *far* better shot. "Sorry, guys. We're doing this the hard way. It's the only way to be sure."

"No need to apologize," Mark said. "We were made to do things the hard way."

That was quite literally true. After the tremendous success of the SPARTAN-II program, a few people inside ONI had been eager to deploy super-soldiers on a far larger scale against the Covenant onslaught. Unfortunately, the costs were prohibitive, and suitable recruits one in a billion. So ONI secretly developed the Spartan-IIIs—a cheaper, more plentiful alternative that could be considered expendable. And expend them it did, trading lives for time as the powers that be sent entire companies on suicide missions. The goal had been to blunt the Covenant assault until humanity could develop the technology it needed to win the forever war, and the strategy had worked—but at a truly terrible cost.

Which only made it that much harder for Veta to return to the Keepers. Her Gammas had already sacrificed their health and futures for this mission. Now she was ordering them to stay undercover and forfeit any chance of flagging down a UNSC craft to get aid with their smoother situation. In effect, she was asking them to continue the mission indefinitely, knowing it would likely cost them their minds. And after they *did* go insane, how long would it be before they became a mission liability and she had no choice but to take them out?

Faced with that horrific decision, Veta would have liked to stay in hiding and recruit some help. But from whom? The Banished were far more likely to kill them on sight than to drop everything and hunt down the Keepers on the words of four humans. And the Ferrets were so deep undercover that the UNSC would not immediately realize they were an ONI special-action team. Their identities would need to be verified and an alert sent up the chain of command. And even if they were taken seriously, by the time the authorization to act came, Castor could already be in the control room, firing the array.

There really was nothing the Ferrets *could* do but continue the operation and hope they could complete it fast enough to survive and get some help afterward. That was not much comfort, but the mission came first. The Gammas had lived by that creed their entire lives, and now so did Veta.

Once the Covenant troops had started to board their Phantoms, Castor waved for the Keepers to rejoin him. Veta swallowed hard and wrote a few last words on the message scroll she was preparing, then rolled it up, returned it to the shell casing, twisted the bullet-shaped cap back on, and secured it in a thigh pocket.

"Let's go take a look at that San'Shyuum." She shouldered her rucksack, placed her M7 in the crook of her arm, and led her team out of the ravine. "And remember to avoid—"

"Optical receptors," Olivia finished. "Yup. We're not going to forget, Mom."

"I know. I just need to say *something*."

"It's okay," Ash said. "We're worried about you too."

The Gammas fell in behind Veta, close enough to look like a group, but keeping enough distance between them to avoid making themselves an easy target. The rest of Castor's followers had not dispersed quite as far as had the Ferrets, so by the time Veta and her team joined the others, they were at the back of the mob— where it would be easier to avoid stray helmet cameras.

At least, Keeper helmet cameras. They had barely arrived before the San'Shyuum shot a glare in their direction, then looked back to Castor.

"*More* humans?" he asked. "How many do we need?"

Castor peered at Veta over the heads of two Kig-Yar, and his face seemed to soften in relief. "Only one," he said. "But when we left the portal, we had ten humans. Now we are down to seven, counting those four. The species is so fragile that it is always wise to bring extras."

"If you believe so," Bhasvod said.

"I do." Castor turned to address his followers. "Once you have collected the equipment, the Prelate's guards will direct you to a Phantom for the next stage of our sacred travels. They are . . . *allies* in the quest to begin the Great Journey. You will follow their instructions without hesitation."

A chorus of acknowledgments sounded from Castor's followers, and he waved them down the slope. As Veta and her Ferrets started after the others, he motioned for her to wait.

"The Prelate's warriors are unaccustomed to dealing with humans," he said. "And you are too important to the Journey to risk losing. Knox will ride with Quenbi and Aubert on the same Phantom as Blademaster 'Gadogai. You and your brood are with me."

Veta touched her fist to her breast. "As you command, Mighty One." She looked toward the Lich. "There is some equipment aboard the—"

"Go," Castor said, motioning her away. "Look for Feodruz on the boarding ramp."

Veta inclined her head and followed the rest of the Keepers past the gruesome remains of half a dozen bodies chewed to the bone by the scratcher swarm, then continued into the Lich's transport bay. With two talons of Covenant Banshees patrolling overhead, there was not much concern about another strafing attack from either the Banished or the UNSC, so the survivors were not particularly quick or efficient about retrieving the equipment they would need for the rest of the journey.

The Ferrets made a show of going through the belongings of the fallen, retrieving grenades, ammunition, tubes of food paste, and anything else they might be able to use. Then, once the last pair of Kig-Yar started to descend the boarding ramp, Veta removed the message capsule from her thigh pocket and went aft to Lieutenant Myklonas's mangled body.

She was just opening a shoulder pocket on the pilot's flight suit when Ash whistled an alert, then Krelis stepped into the hold.

"What are you doing?" the Jiralhanae growled. "Everyone is waiting for you!"

"My apologies," Veta said. She grabbed the rescue comm off Myklonas's ejection seat, then held it up. "It occurred to me that this might be useful to monitor UNSC communications."

Krelis grunted. "A good thought." He waved her forward, then turned to descend the ramp. "Now come."

Veta exhaled in relief, then depressed what looked like a firing pin on the bottom of the "cartridge" in her other hand.

"As you wish." She waited until a low beep sounded from the capsule, then dropped it into Myklonas's lap and started for the ramp. "We're right behind you."

The Covenant talons had barely departed, and already the *kralidonk* swarm was streaming toward the crashed Lich. From the command Phantom at the back of the Long Shield reconnaissance wing, the arachibians resembled nothing more alarming than a shadow gliding up the slope toward the craft that Pavium had been sent to investigate. But anyone who had spent time in the Chasm Lands knew better. *Kralidonk* swarms were cunning hive-mind predators who could strip the flesh from the bones of an armored Jiralhanae in a matter of seconds—and disassemble an entire Lich in an afternoon.

Pavium, who was riding in the command Phantom's copilot seat, activated the reconnaissance wing battlenet. "Thalazan, your Seraphs will drive that *kralidonk* swarm back into its cesspool, then assume overwatch to guard against our enemies in the sky. Amphium, your Banshees will assume ground patrol and keep the bedamned things from attacking our flanks."

The talon chiefs acknowledged their orders, then Thalazan's trio of Seraphs dived toward the crash site. The *kralidonk* swarm reacted instantly, dividing into two parts and fleeing for cover. The largest section retreated back into the lake, concealing its colorful underwater city beneath the purple blanket of its dark mass.

The smaller section fled toward the Lich, gliding up the boarding ramp and disappearing into the transport bay before Thalazan could even think of loosing plasma charges. Pavium gnashed his tusks in frustration, then activated his Phantom's internal comm system.

"Make fast your armor and ready your weapons." Knowing the troops in the transport bay would not be able to see the action on the ground, he added, "A small *kralidonk* swarm has entered our objective and will have to be driven out."

The replying rumble was more groan than growl. There was no joy in fighting the *kralidonk*, only hard work and the risk of being eaten alive. Voridus, who was seated at the operations station behind Pavium, sealed his helmet and then rose, turning toward the Phantom's transport bay.

"Voridus, where do you imagine you are going?" Pavium asked.

"To the arms cabinet, before all the plasma repeaters have been taken."

Without awaiting permission, Voridus stepped through the hatch and into the transport bay. The pilot, a former Sangheili ranger who had been with the Long Shields since before the journey to the Ark, glanced over and cocked his oblong helmet in an unspoken question.

"Let him go," Pavium said. "What harm can he do?"

The ranger gave a noncommittal helmet-rock, then returned his attention to his instruments. He circled the Lich once so Pavium could inspect the exterior and develop an assault strategy, then landed fifty paces upslope. By the time Pavium debarked, Voridus had the troop lined up in two ranks of ten, each with five Jiralhanae, three Sangheili, and two Kig-Yar.

As Pavium explained his plan, Thalazan landed his Seraph, leaving only his two subordinates on overwatch, and joined him. It was another one of his obvious power plays, designed to leave the impression that he was Pavium's equal by standing at his side as he issued his commands. But there was no time to put Thalazan in his place. The *kralidonk* swarm was already destroying whatever evidence there might be aboard the Lich of Atriox's presence or absence, and the UNSC had shown enough interest in the Lich that Pavium suspected it would soon be sending its own force to investigate.

"And once the swarm starts to flee, cease laying plasma," he finished. "We learn nothing if you destroy everything in the cabin."

"True, were the cabin the only place we looked," Thalazan said. "But we already know the important thing."

Pavium faced the talon chief and allowed his displeasure to hang in the air for two breaths, then said, "Explain."

Thalazan looked toward the center of the Ark, where the distant specks of the Covenant transport wing hung low over the Chasm Lands, silhouetted against the white crescent of the installation's half-devoured resource moon.

"Atriox was not aboard," Thalazan said. "He would never allow himself to be captured by the Covenant, and I saw no sign of Covenant bodies when I flew over the crash site."

"Covenant bones look no different from Banished ones," Voridus said, his tone more challenging than Pavium would have liked. "Or Keeper bones. And bones are all the *kralidonk* have left us to examine."

They were both correct. As Voridus had pointed out, the *kralidonk* had already stripped the dead of their flesh and carried medallions of shredded armor into the pond to decorate their underwater city. But there weren't as many bones as Pavium would have expected after a pitched battle, and they were scattered across the slope in skeleton-sized piles. That suggested only single warriors had perished on those spots, rather than several fighting as a unit.

"While we endlessly talk, the *kralidonk* feast and destroy whatever there is to find inside." Pavium turned his back on Thalazan and waved his troops toward the Lich. "Clear the way."

Voridus let out a guttural roar and led the charge up the boarding ramp, already firing his plasma repeater into the dark hatchway. The other Jiralhanae followed close on his heels, while the four Kig-Yar hung back, their hands free and their looting sacks at the ready. Pavium and Thalazan led the six Sangheili around to the bow of the Lich, where they arrayed themselves to either side of the smashed viewport and readied their own plasma weapons.

It took only a few moments before the first *kralidonk* began to pour from the breach, many carrying scraps of blue armor or pieces of equipment. Pavium and his companions fired on the creatures, trying to salvage anything that might help them investigate the Lich's occupants, but also allowed any who were empty-clawed—or hauling chunks of scorched flesh—to depart unimpeded. The swarm adjusted its priorities almost instantly, and only an occasional creature would emerge carrying something shiny or colorful.

Fifty breaths after Pavium and his companions arrived at their stations, the muffled battle screeches from inside the Lich fell silent, and the stream of fleeing *kralidonk* dwindled to a trickle.

Pavium was tempted to approach the nose of the craft and peer inside, but he knew that even a single *kralidonk* could seriously damage a suit of power armor. The creatures were light enough to crawl up a limb without activating energy shielding, and their tiny heads could push into even the tightest seam, with mouthparts so sharp they could bite cleanly through circuits and undersuits.

When the *kralidonk* horde dwindled to one or two every few breaths, Pavium turned to Thalazan.

"Remain here with the Sangheili," he ordered. "The Lich has been cleared—"

The screech of a plasma repeater firing at its maximum rate erupted inside the flight deck. Pavium looked through the shattered viewport and saw his brother's bulky form whirling around inside, pouring bolts of plasma into the overhead, bulkhead, and instrument panels.

"Cleared and smoked," Thalazan said from opposite Pavium. "I hope 'Volir does not expect us to access the navigation and pilot's registers."

"The shipmaster expects us to learn whether Atriox was aboard." Pavium was growing weary of having his leadership undermined by his brother's mistakes, but killing Thalazan would not solve the problem. The talon commander was only saying aloud what their Sangheili companions were likely thinking to themselves. "I doubt he cares how we do it."

Deciding to take his chances with the *kralidonk*, Pavium stepped closer to the Lich, then jumped up and hooked his elbow through the gap in the shattered viewport. He pulled himself up and, keeping his plasma pistol at the ready, peered inside.

Voridus was standing with his back to the opening, waving his free arm and dodging about as he attempted to keep the last few *kralidonk* from escaping through the breach. At the same time, he was firing the plasma repeater indiscriminately, burning holes into seats, the deck, and control devices as he attempted to kill the creatures.

"Voridus!" Pavium bellowed. "What are you doing? My command was to let them go."

"I cannot!"

Voridus shot an errant *kralidonk*, then plucked its smoking remains out of the commander's seat, raised them to his helmet's acoustic receptor, and tossed them aside.

"By the death moon!" Pavium exclaimed. "Explain your—"

"*Listen.*"

Voridus raised his free hand for silence, then began to turn in a slow circle. A *kralidonk* peered out from beneath the copilot's seat, then three more dropped off the overhead onto Voridus's helmet and began to scratch at his faceplate. He bellowed in surprise, then threw down his plasma repeater and slapped at them with both hands. But the creatures were too coordinated and agile for him, two of them scurrying around to attack the back of his helmet while the third risked being smashed as it danced across his faceplate.

Pavium hooked both arms over the bottom of the viewport frame and started to pull himself onto the flight deck so he could help his brother—then noticed a fourth *kralidonk* scurrying from beneath the commander's seat. It carried a human ammunition cartridge in its mouth, and as it drew nearer, the round bullet-head emitted a bright flash.

And a beep sounded.

Voridus spun around instantly, his boot raised to stomp, but Pavium was already extending his weapon hand to fire. He put a single plasma bolt through the *kralidonk*'s body; then the strange cartridge dropped to the deck and rolled under the pilot's seat.

The other three creatures leaped free of Voridus's helmet, flying through the shattered viewport fifteen centimeters above Pavium and vanishing from his sight. Voridus lunged after them, reaching down to push his brother out of his way.

Pavium used his plasma pistol to knock Voridus's hand aside.

"No. Retrieve what went under the pilot's seat." He pulled himself through the opening onto the flight deck. "Whatever it is."

Voridus reluctantly complied, dropping to his belly and peering under the seat until that same now-muffled beep sounded, then reached underneath. A moment later, he withdrew the cartridge, rose to his knees, and held it in front of his faceplate.

"What is it?" Pavium asked.

"I do not know yet," Voridus said. "It was in the lap of a dead human female, still strapped into her pilot's seat."

"She was in a pilot's seat?" Pavium asked. "Within the Lich's *transport* bay?"

"Yes. It was all very strange," Voridus said. "She was still strapped in, being devoured by the *kralidonk*, when this cartridge flashed and made a sound. When I attempted to chase them away, they took it."

The cartridge flashed again, and Voridus began to work the bullet head back and forth.

"Perhaps that is not a good idea," Pavium said.

"Understood." Voridus held his breath, then gave a sharp twist. The bullet head popped off in his hand. "But it does not seem to be a *bad* idea."

He tossed the bullet head aside, then turned the cartridge over and tapped it in his palm until a small cylinder of flimsy material slid out. He let the cartridge drop to the deck, then slowly unfurled a meter-long ribbon. Pavium peered over his brother's shoulder and saw that its surface was covered in tiny blue scratching.

"That appears to be writing," Pavium said.

"A whole message." Voridus continued to study the ribbon, his faceplate remaining steady as he moved the ribbon in front of it. "It seems that the humans have a spy among the Keepers of the One Freedom."

Pavium did not find this revelation as surprising as his brother's ability to decipher the message. "You *read* human?"

"Of course I read human," Voridus replied. "We had fifteen of them in the clan before your purge."

That had followed the trouble with the Flood at High Charity, when several Long Shield humans defected to the UNSC, further damaging the clan's honor. Fearing that the rest of the cowards would soon follow, Pavium had ordered all humans to leave the Long Shields—and killed those who had not been quick enough to obey. Atriox and his retinue had been rather unhappy with that decision, considering humans as valuable assets to the Banished as a whole, but there had been precedent even before coming to the Ark. The Clan of the Ravaged Tusks and the Legion of the Corpse-Moon had *never* permitted humans, and it was well known that Atriox's own *daskalo*, Escharum, had a fierce dislike of the vermin.

"What I mean is," Pavium said, "why would you want to read human?"

"I thought it might be helpful in finding our spies for you. It was not, but this . . ." Voridus held up the scroll. "*This* makes it all worthwhile."

"Tell me it says Atriox was not on board."

"It says nothing about Atriox. But what it *does* say . . ." Voridus turned his faceplate toward Pavium and tipped his helmet forward. "The Long Shields will reclaim their place of glory, my brother. A higher place in the Banished than ever before."

Pavium groaned. "Whenever you say that—"

"This time, it is different," Voridus said. "The message is about Castor. He and his Keepers have joined forces with the Covenant."

"Why would *that* be good for the Long Shields?"

"Because Castor is here to begin the Great Journey," Voridus replied. "And the Long Shields are the only clan in a position to stop him."

SEVEN

1253 hours, October 13, 2559 (military calendar)
Covenant T52 Phantom, On Approach to Epsilon Cartographer
Refugia Epsilon 026 285.1 175.0, Epsilon Spire, the Ark

As the leader of an undercover ONI Ferret team, Veta Lopis had faced a lot of tense situations, and this one definitely ranked near the top.

To avoid a suborbital trajectory that would draw too much attention from their enemies, Castor and the San'Shyuum Prelate had elected to make the long journey to the Cartographer at terrain-hugging altitudes and subsonic speeds. The result had been a fourteen-hour trip that had seen her Gammas take their last smoothers four hours earlier—and resulted in a seemingly endless stare-down with ten Jiralhanae guards who looked primed to kill, and who never, ever looked away.

Bhasvod's guards were seated on the far side of the Phantom's troop bay, glaring over two Ghost single-rider vehicles secured to the center of the deck. In contrast to the normal blue harness worn by most Covenant Jiralhanae, these all wore the equipment of the Covenant's elite honor guards—red-and-yellow power armor trimmed in black, and helmets with yellow vanes curving up from the cheek guards. On the Keeper side of the bay, Veta had her three Gammas, three Sangheili, and a Kig-Yar, along with Feodruz and a rather jovial Jiralhanae named Rhadandus. All the Keepers wore various versions of blue-and-gold armor, but only Feodruz was in power armor.

Rhadandus sat three places away from Veta, on the other side of Mark-G313 and the Kig-Yar, watching the honor guards with a tusk-baring sneer that passed for a pleasant grin among his kind. Either it wasn't working, or the ONI training Veta had received in alien-species kinesiology was entirely incorrect about the significance of the chin thrusts and faceplate stares being directed toward her and her Gammas.

But the long journey and smoldering hostility did have an upside. Castor and Bhasvod had spent most of the trip on the flight deck together, negotiating, planning, and discussing the events of the last seven years. Veta had been eavesdropping through her helmet comm system the whole time, and the fact that everyone was still wearing their headgear made it easier to disguise what she was doing.

The feed was a bit patchy and prone to overlaps—an unavoidable drawback of the self-cloaking transmitter Ash-G099 had slipped into the microphone wafer of Castor's comm disk. But the trade-offs were worth it. The nanobug activated only when another device was radiating on one of its frequencies, a feature that camouflaged its emissions as stray interference. Even Intrepid Eye would be unlikely to notice its signal.

Or so Veta hoped.

". . . you not unite the pious sects?" Bhasvod was asking.

The San'Shyuum had already recounted how badly the Ark

had been damaged seven years ago after the Prophet of Truth's failed attempt to activate the Halo Array. He had also described how the Covenant survivors had been forced to hole up inside the marooned Dreadnought for years, waiting while the Ark slowly repaired itself. During that time, the installation had seen a number of traumatic events, further altering its structure in unpredictable ways. When combined with the Ark's sheer scale, its own indigenous perils, and an unbroken series of visitors, all of these factors had militated against the Covenant finishing what Truth had begun years ago.

Now Bhasvod was questioning Castor on the finer points of the Covenant's post-Schism disintegration. "With so many Sangheili traitors allying with the infidels, it should have been an easy matter to gather the Faithful under one banner."

"Easier to say than to accomplish," Castor replied. "Who would have *done* this gathering? Palaemon? Lydus? Caius? Hekabe? Me? No. None of us had the power."

"It was not power you lacked," Bhasvod said. "It was guidance. Without the San'Shyuum to show you the Path, you all went your own ways."

"That would be hard to deny."

Because Bhasvod had been trapped on the Ark and unaware of events in the greater galaxy for the last several years, Castor had sketched out the highlights for him, touching on everything from the rise of the Banished to Cortana's subjugation of galactic civilization. The Prelate seemed most interested in the splinter sects that remained of the Covenant, though, probing the nature of the various factions and trying to determine which ones might still be loyal to the San'Shyuum.

"There are more false 'guides' than I can count," Castor continued, "every one of them preaching their own spurious doctrine."

"Including *you*, Dokab," Bhasvod noted. "Your embrace of the infidel vermin is blasphemy. I trust you can see that."

"They are not infidels if they walk the Path," Castor replied. "And humans are as important to the Great Journey as we are. We cannot fire the array without them."

"That may be. But it does not make them Worthy. Only necessary."

"It is not for me to decide who is Worthy and who is necessary. I leave such judgments to the gods."

"Because you are not San'Shyuum," Bhasvod countered. "We all have our place in the Order of Devotion. The Jiralhanae's place is to fight. The San'Shyuum's is to shepherd."

A pause followed, and Veta could imagine Castor's tusks grinding as he bit back a sharp reply. As devout as he was, the *dokab* had always struck her as someone who felt no need to be "shepherded" by a master species. And she suspected that his independent streak had only grown during the Keepers' time under the Banished umbrella.

When the silence grew too long, Bhasvod continued, "So, *no* San'Shyuum were found after the Fall of High Charity? Is that what I am to conclude?"

An interesting question, Veta thought.

In the data graphic readout inside his helmet, Dhas Bhasvod saw Castor's face-temperature fall. The sudden drop was an involuntary somatic reaction normally associated with shock, with blood leaving the body's extremities to safeguard its vital internal organs. But under the circumstances, it suggested something more unexpected in a Jiralhanae: empathy. The emotional sharing of another's pain.

The fool actually pities me, Dhas realized.

They had spent the last fourteen units together on the Phantom's flight deck, Dhas seated in a special commander's throne installed at the back of the cramped cabin. Castor sat to his right at the operations station behind the copilot's seat, which was currently occupied by one of the *dokab*'s Jiralhanae Keepers. Dhas's own Jiralhanae captain, Arcas, sat at the navigation station behind a Covenant pilot, who was also Jiralhanae. If not for the airscrubbers in Dhas's graphene fighting skin, the smell of so much sour fur would have been quite sickening.

After a moment, Castor finally replied. "I have not heard of any San'Shyuum who survived the city's destruction, save those who were aboard the Dreadnought with you and the High Prophet of Truth."

"But you were not actually present at the Fall of High Charity." Dhas wanted to sound desperate, both to disguise his motives and to play to Castor's weakness. "You were fighting on the surface of the human colony Mars."

"Yes, just as I told you," Castor replied. "That is why I said I have *heard* of no San'Shyuum survivors, save you and those with you aboard the Dreadnought."

"But hearing is not knowing," Dhas said. "Surely, you went to the Coelest system to search for a Prophet to guide your Keepers?"

"It would have been a brief search," Castor said. "The system has been well-patrolled by both the UNSC and the Sangheili loyal to them since the Great Schism. The only thing the Keepers would find there is a quick death."

"So you simply gave up?" Dhas paused to consider whether there was anything to gain by continuing to press the matter, then decided there was nothing to lose. Even if Castor grew suspicious, the *dokab* would never be returning to a galaxy where he could act on any suspicion. "I have heard there was a San'Shyuum flotilla that escaped the blockade."

"How would you know such a thing?" Castor asked, surprising Dhas with how quickly he saw the contradiction of the question—and his boldness in probing it. "Have you not been trapped here on the Ark?"

"Be wary of accusations, Dokab." Dhas cast a pointed glance at the glaive haft standing in his seat-side scabbard, though it might not serve as quite the silent threat he intended after being possessed by the Oracle. "As I said, there have been arrivals on the Ark after us. And we have interrogated a number of them."

"I only seek to understand," Castor said. "You are the last living San'Shyuum I know of. I certainly have no knowledge of any flotillas that escaped."

"Would you have?"

The *dokab* pondered this for a moment, then gave a double-tusk *snick* that Dhas recognized as a gesture of affirmation. "It would have been quite the tale of battle among the Banished."

Castor had already explained how the Keepers had been forced to collaborate with Atriox and the Banished to find the portal that had brought them to the Ark, so Dhas understood the implication. Even before the fall of High Charity, Atriox's hatred of the San'Shyuum had been well known. Had his Banished heard of a San'Shyuum flotilla sneaking through the galaxy, likely weakened and vulnerable, they would have made its destruction a top priority.

"The Sangheili *also* have long memories," Castor said. "If they believed there was even the slightest possibility of a wandering San'Shyuum flotilla, they would never stop searching for it."

"But you have heard nothing?"

"No," Castor said. "I am sorry."

"I know you are." Dhas looked forward, hoping the gesture would prove dramatic enough to conceal his relief from the Jiralhanae's watchful eye, then said, "It matters not. They will all be joining the Forerunners in Divine Transcendence soon enough, will they not?"

"Without question." Castor's voice grew deeper and more confident. "There is no force in the galaxy that can stop us, now that we are allies."

"Allies." Dhas rolled the word over on his tongue, not at all sure that he liked its taste, then fluttered his tongue in amusement. "What an interesting way to think of it."

The conversation with Castor had not been as definitive as Dhas might have liked, but realistically, what more could he have expected? A report that a flotilla had been spotted entering the shield world?

The absence of information was the best that Dhas could hope for. He knew for certain that a flotilla of San'Shyuum had escaped the fall of High Charity, because he had been part of the group that concealed it in the confusion surrounding the Dreadnought's departure. Whether it had survived the long journey that followed, he would never know—*could* never know. Either the flotilla had made it to Cloister and the San'Shyuum were ready to remake the galaxy in their image, or it had been destroyed and the Sangheili deserved the ultimate reprisal. It no longer mattered. The time had come for the Great Cleansing, and it would be the hand of Dhas Bhasvod that delivered it.

And if Castor and his Keepers were correct about Divine Transcendence, as Dhas had once believed . . . and as the Prophet of Truth had died *still* believing? Well then, Dhas would deliver that too. Because that was what Prelates *did*.

They covered the contingencies.

The silence that followed Dhas Bhasvod's condescending response lasted so long that Veta started to wonder if the nanobug had failed. Then she started to hope that maybe Castor had taken offense, that maybe the two leaders were about to come to blows and bring the whole array-firing quest down in a spray of blood and flame.

No such luck.

Castor had too much faith and focus to allow his bruised ego to sabotage a dream he had been cultivating his entire life. He merely answered the San'Shyuum's indignity with a noncommittal grunt, then resumed the conversation.

"I have been thinking of the challenges we may face as our mission continues," he said. "Resistance from the UNSC and the Banished are a given, once they realize what we are doing."

"Why do you assume they *will* realize what we are doing?"

"Because I know my enemies," Castor replied. "The Banished have always been vengeful, and there is no reason for those remaining on the Ark to have changed. They will not rest until they hunt us down and punish us for fleeing the battle outside the portal."

"They are still busy fighting at the portal. By the time they are free of battle, it will be too late. What of the humans?"

"Humans have a curious nature," Castor said. "They will notice that a Banished transport fled its own lines and was assisted by the Covenant. And they will want to know why."

"The answer will not matter," Bhasvod said. "To stop us in time, they would need to send an entire strike wing on every search pattern. Even the UNSC does not have such strength—especially not when they have only one vessel of any size and are still battling for the portal."

"When they find us, however—"

"*If* they find us," Bhasvod corrected, "they would still need a strike wing to stop us. By the time it arrives, we will be inside the citadel, bringing up the supraluminal communications array."

"So you do know where the citadel is?"

"Soon. That is why we must go to the Cartographer. Did I not explain?"

"You did," Castor said. "It is just . . . you seem so confident it will reveal what we need to know."

"Be careful what you imply," Bhasvod said darkly. "Perhaps you mean, how can I be certain the Cartographer will cooperate *now*, when it has turned me away every time before?"

"My only wish is to understand," Castor said. "There can be no doubting your devotion to the Great Journey. And yet, even you have failed to find the citadel after more than two hundred cycles on the Ark."

Veta was surprised. Castor might be taking pains to flatter the Prelate, but he was also noting how long Bhasvod had been on the Ark without ever finding the citadel. Very bold.

Or very stupid.

After a short pause, Castor continued, "I hope you can forgive my confusion."

"I see nothing to forgive," Bhasvod said. "I would have the same question, were I in your position. So a little confusion is only to be expected in a Jiralhanae."

"I am grateful you understand," Castor said. "We Jiralhanae *are* better at fighting than scheming."

"And that is why the San'Shyuum were such a benefit to your species during the ages of the Covenant. You will recall what I explained to you—that the survivors had to take refuge inside the Dreadnought after the High Prophet of Truth was killed?"

"You said a Sacred Ring launched prematurely," Castor said, recounting what Bhasvod had told him hours earlier. "The Ark was nearly destroyed."

"We thought it *was* destroyed. When the Ring launched, it also fired. We had half our strength deployed out on the surface, trying to draw the human forces away from the Prophet of Truth, and we lost them all. Only those of us who happened to be inside the Dreadnought's shielding were spared."

Bhasvod fell silent, until Castor finally asked, "And then?"

"We celebrated . . . and we waited. We thought the High Prophet had succeeded. We expected to be called to Transcendence at any moment. So, we waited."

Bhasvod gave a slow burble, a sound of either disgust or dismay, Veta did not know which.

"For a hundred long cycles, we waited. Eventually, our elation gave way to despair as we came to realize our situation. The High Prophet of Truth had failed. Worse, his failure had damaged this most holy of temples beyond repair, or so it seemed at the time. We began to fear we would all perish here on a dead world, far from our home stars and for nothing but the vanity of a hierarch. Some among us even began to question the Word of the Prophets. Of course, I could not let that stand. In twenty cycles, I culled as many apostates from our number as I had done for Truth concerning the Heresy of the Chosen."

Veta had heard the Faithful use "the Heresy of the Chosen" as a reference to the subversive belief that humans were the true successors to the Forerunners, which was why they so often showed an affinity for Forerunner technology that other species lacked. Even the Keepers tolerated no one who adhered to its tenets, and she was surprised to hear the notion had actually existed within the greater Covenant. Though, clearly, anyone suspected of holding such a belief had paid the ultimate price.

"But we were merely being tested," Bhasvod continued. "Just when our despair seemed ready to destroy us, a scout happened on a refugia teeming with noppers and feather rush. We soon realized that the sacred installation had been rejuvenating itself the entire time. Our Dreadnought lay so far from the area where the repairs had begun that we had not even realized what was happening. And even now, despite all that has happened in the years between, the world continues to rebuild itself. The Ark is still alive, and so is our Faith."

Castor grunted assent. "The gods temper in flames those whom they need most." It was a phrase he repeated often—usually after some reversal that Veta and her Ferrets had helped arrange. "I am eager to learn more about the trials they have placed before you, and how they have stood in the way of the Great Journey. So that we can find a way past them together, obviously."

"Obviously," Bhasvod stated. "But I have told you the answer already."

"You have?" This time, Castor sounded irritated, but he said, "I see. The citadel was destroyed."

"The Ark has endured much over the last seven years, including its own violent remediations, changes that have made its surface different in countless ways," Bhasvod said. "The original citadel has long since passed out of existence. It can no longer be used."

"How then will we light the Rings?" Castor's frustration with the Prelate's vague answers was clearly getting harder for him to hide by the second.

"The Ark still lives, Dokab," Bhasvod said. "It has no doubt already built another citadel by now."

"How can you know that?" Castor asked. "The gods are many things, and predictable is not among them."

"We know because another Halo launched from the foundry not long ago," Bhasvod said. "It was sent almost immediately into slipspace during a battle between the humans and the Banished. We do not know where it was sent, but we do know that all rings are controlled by the Ark's supraluminal communications array, a system only accessible from a citadel. So there must now be a *new* citadel hidden somewhere on the Ark's surface, no doubt heavily concealed to deny access to those unworthy."

"Because if there was not a citadel, there would be no reason to build a new ring." Castor considered that for a moment. "Do you believe it was the humans who launched this new ring, or the Banished?"

"It matters not," Bhasvod said. "All that matters, Dokab, is that we find the new citadel."

"Which brings us back to the Cartographer," Castor said. "The same Cartographer that has failed to reveal the location of this citadel to you thus far."

"It has not granted us access," Bhasvod allowed. "But then, *we* do not have our own humans."

"Ah."

Castor had never hidden his reason for allowing humans to join the Keepers of the One Freedom: their special affinity for Forerunner technology had been well known even inside the Covenant. Humans could sometimes activate Forerunner tools that refused to function for any other species—and the more powerful the device, the more likely that was to be true. Veta surmised it was probably this paradox that had given rise to the Heresy of the Chosen in the first place—though if she were to be honest with herself, she was just as flummoxed by the incongruity as Dhas Bhasvod himself. The only thing she herself felt for Forerunner technology was abhorrence. As far as Veta could tell, it had brought nothing but war and tragedy and death to the galaxy, and everyone would be better off if none of the stuff ever worked for anybody at all.

But of course, such matters weren't up to her.

"As you've said, my humans are not the only humans on the Ark," Castor noted carefully. "The Banished have brought humans here, and they have been present for over twenty cycles. The UNSC has been here almost as long, and they are nothing *but* humans. I am certain it has already occurred to you to use one of them?"

"Of course. But the Ark is as vast as ten worlds. The spire where our Dreadnought lay is far from where we are now. It was enough for us to bide our time in the shadows, waiting for the smoke of battle to clear before we made our presence known. Remember, Dokab, we had already waited for years—it made little difference to wait a short while longer. Especially since it was the Prophet of Truth's unfeigned temerity that led to the first failure. We have no desire to repeat his blasphemy."

"But then the Banished raided the Dreadnought and stole the Holy Light—"

"And awoke an enemy they will not soon forget," Bhasvod said. "Since then, accessing the Cartographer has not been our priority. Only recovering the Holy Light. That is, until you and your Keepers arrived."

"A blessing of the gods, no doubt," Castor said. "My humans triggered the activation pylon at the other end of the portal. And I see no reason the Cartographer would deny them . . . as long as it has the answer we seek—the location of the citadel."

"And you have doubts about whether it does," Bhasvod said, "because I have not yet obtained it?"

"The thought had occurred to me," Castor said. "In truth, I've long waited for this day and we are now closer than I would have ever dreamed. You must forgive me if I want to be certain of the path before us."

Bhasvod emitted a raspy cackle. "You are very quick for a Jiralhanae," he said. "But your doubts are misplaced. We have the assurances of your Oracle."

Castor paused, no doubt thinking back to Intrepid Eye's sudden appearance—and whatever she had said while Veta and the Ferrets were out of earshot. Then he grunted in affirmation.

"I am more *hers* than she is mine," he said. "But if the Oracle believes the Cartographer can help us, then it must be so."

The flight continued another half hour in contemplative silence before the nanobug picked up another Jiralhanae voice on the flight deck—one Veta did not recognize.

"We are a half unit out, Fell One. The Cartographer's tower should rise above the crest of the white dune shortly."

"I hear, Arcas," Bhasvod said. "Alert me to anything that threatens our approach."

"At once. And Fell One?"

"Continue."

"We are not entirely alone in the Drifting Lands," Arcas said. "Be aware that there is a Banished Seraph flying a search pattern along the refugia's edge-ward side. There is also a UNSC Pelican hiding in the shadows along the edge of the Broken Plain."

"What are the chances they have seen us?"

"We are three transports escorted by two talons of fighters. The Banished Seraph has likely glimpsed something—and is now attempting to discern what that is. Whether the humans' Pelican is hiding from us or the Seraph, I cannot say. But it is one or the other. Once we have landed, we should be ready to leave quickly."

"Be certain we are," Bhasvod said. "Tros, we do not want any high-flying sentinels on overwatch giving us away. Land at the base of the white dune. We will take Ghosts the rest of the way to the Cartographer."

"As you command."

Veta continued to monitor the eavesdropping feed, but she had heard enough to realize that the UNSC would not be coming to relieve her Ferret team anytime soon. Either they had not found her message, or they were not taking it seriously. Because if they had thought that there was a Keeper-Covenant alliance trying to activate Halo—and that it had a realistic and growing chance of success—they would have sent more than one measly reconnaissance Pelican. Clearly, the Ferrets needed to shake things up.

Hard.

Bhasvod's command Phantom began to descend. Arcas's voice came over the speakers mounted on the troop-bay bulkhead, assigning perimeter guards and issuing orders to quickly deploy the Ghosts. Veta stretched her arms forward as though limbering up and made sure her elbow bumped Mark's shoulder. He continued to stare at the Jiralhanae honor guard seated across from him on the other side of the Ghost, but Veta knew his attention would be focused on her, watching for the hand signal she had just alerted him to expect.

She dropped her hand to her knee and began to drum her fingers absentmindedly, pretending to be bored but tapping out coded orders for her Ferrets. When she finished, there were no acknowledgment signals or anything else that might have alerted a careful observer to the communication. Mark and the other Gammas simply continued to stare over the Ghosts, glaring at the honor guards as the Phantom descended and began to decelerate.

Once it pulled up and settled into a low hover for disembarkment, the Ferrets joined the rest of the Keepers in standing and stretching and gathering their gear. Veta shot each of her Gammas a quick glance to look for any blink codes or eye checks that suggested they had missed any part of her earlier orders.

Each looked away as soon as their gazes met, signaling their readiness. Veta shouldered her rucksack and grabbed her M7 submachine gun, then turned toward the boarding ramp on her side of the craft. As the ramps descended, furnace-hot air poured into the troop bay from the white brilliance beyond.

Veta cleared her throat. The *go* signal.

Nothing happened, except that the three Sangheili Keepers closest to the half-open boarding ramp began to press forward. One of the Covenant honor guards from the other side of the troop bay climbed onto the rearmost Ghost and activated its propulsion drive.

"Wait!" he roared. "Equipment first!"

He was only obeying Dhas Bhasvod's orders, but Ash and Mark both gave clucks of objection in passable *Ibie'shan*—the dialect spoken by most Kig-Yar Keepers—and Olivia pretended to stumble into the Sangheili in front of her. Compared to one of them, she was fairly small, but at the same time, she was large and strong for a human woman.

Olivia's intentional clumsiness sent all three Sangheili stumbling into the path of the Covenant guard mounted on the Ghost. The result was a shoving match accompanied by a cacophony of clacking mandibles and throaty bellows, but one that failed to erupt into anything further as the Jiralhanae moved through the boarding portal and descended the ramp.

The next Ghost was already turning after it, its Jiralhanae rider glaring at the trio of angry Sangheili that his companion had just powered aside.

Three plasma bolts flashed past Veta's head on the hull side of the troop bay, taking the guard in the side of his helmet and burning through his jaw-protection on the third strike. The Jiralhanae roared in anger and rolled off the Ghost onto the deck, leaving the vehicle to descend the ramp on its own.

Behind Veta, Mark yelled, "By the Prophets!" He was clucking and squawking in *Ibie'shan*. "Why did you do *that*, Kalvo?"

"Me?" The Kig-Yar, Kalvo, responded in *Ibie'shan* as well, so there were only a few Keepers and probably no Covenant present who understood what he was saying. "It was *you*, grub-flake! Do not give that to—"

A flurry of screeches sounded from the other side of the troop bay, and Veta glanced over her shoulder to see a volley of mauler bolts exploding through Kalvo's back as the plasma pistol Mark had just pushed into his hands fell from his grasp.

Without even bothering to look forward again, Veta drove Ash toward the ramp. "Go go go!"

She fired the M7 one-handed, more to suppress fire from the honor guards than because she actually expected to penetrate their armor, then felt herself hurling down the ramp with Mark wrapped around her.

They landed in a silty soil so fine it billowed up like smoke, the sound of plasma and mauler fire echoing inside the Phantom behind them. A strong hand grabbed Veta under the arm and pulled her to her feet, and then she was sprinting away from the boarding ramp between Ash and Olivia, with Mark laying M6 fire behind them. They began to race up an enormous white slope, perhaps seventy meters high and as steep as a staircase.

The crackle of a detonating plasma grenade sounded way too close behind them. Veta continued to climb the dune, breaking through the wind-packed silt every third step and sinking to her knee, already overheating in the searing temperature, her body half-turned so she could keep an eye on the battle they had just started.

Next to their Phantom, the three Sangheili that Olivia had initially mixed up in the deception already lay dead and motionless at the base of the boarding ramp. The Covenant honor guards who had disembarked the Ghosts were currently locked in hand-to-hand combat with Feodruz and Rhadandus, both sides trying to take control of the rapid-assault vehicles—and their powerful plasma cannons. It was impossible to see what was happening inside the Phantom, but over her eavesdropping feed, Veta could hear Bhasvod yelling orders to stand down.

The battle did not appear to be spreading to the other two Phantoms, which were also resting at the base of the enormous dune. The closest one was near the middle, about a hundred and fifty meters away, while the farthest was about three hundred meters distant at the far end. Beneath the bow of the nearer one, Veta saw no sign of fighting—just a pair of riders sitting on their Ghosts, no doubt confused, but awaiting orders. Under the far one, she could make out a pair of Ghost-shaped blobs, presumably bearing riders who were doing the same thing.

Beyond the Phantoms, Bhasvod's wing of Covenant Banshees and Seraphs were streaming through a sea of smaller blue-and-orange dunes. They were staying low in the troughs to avoid being spotted by enemy reconnaissance craft, but remaining aloft so they would be able to rapidly respond to any attack. As the Ferrets continued to ascend, Veta began to look for the reconnaissance craft that Arcas had mentioned. Anything the Ferrets could do to draw attention to the expedition would at least slow it down . . . and at this point, buying time was the only real option.

The Ferrets were nearly at the crest of the dune when Veta's foot broke through the crust again ... and continued to sink. Then her second foot broke through, and suddenly she was buried to her thighs.

And the rest of the Ferrets were sinking with her.

"Oh *hell*, no," Olivia said. "I am *not* drowning in dust!"

She flung herself toward the crest of the dune, and so did Mark and Ash. Veta tried to follow their lead, not even bothering to look down at the collapsing pocket. But she didn't have the explosive strength of her Gammas and fell two meters short. Her boots dropped into nothingness, and she felt herself falling ... until Mark flung himself down the slope and caught her by the collar of her armor.

Veta had a momentary sensation of dangling, then Mark began to slide backward up the slope, pulled by Ash and Olivia and dragging her after him. She glanced behind her and saw white dust collapsing into a sinkhole perhaps five meters across, then was drawn onto the top of the dune with the rest of the team. They lined up along the crest, Ash and Olivia automatically scanning their flanks while Mark watched the rear.

"What caused *that*?" she gasped.

"Us, I hope," Ash said. "And if it wasn't us, I hope it gets *them*, because we're going to need all the help we can get."

Veta turned her attention back to the fight they had started, which now barely even qualified as an argument. Castor and Dhas Bhasvod were descending the boarding ramp side by side, each shouting commands at their Jiralhanae subordinates and pointing them to separate ends of the Phantom. Feodruz and Rhadandus carefully backed away, their hands on their manglers and their eyes on the two honor guards they had been battling. The Covenant troops were more disciplined. They simply turned their backs on the pair and went to the indicated location.

"What now?" Ash asked. "That was more of a slap fight than anything. I don't see it drawing much attention."

"No," Veta said. "We need to do it ourselves."

She backed away from the crest of the dune, ducking down the slope on the side opposite the Phantoms, then took a long look around the area Arcas had called the Drifting Lands. It was pretty much what the name suggested—a vast sea of windblown dunes that extended hundreds of kilometers in all directions. The dunes themselves were breathtaking, banked in bands of color that ranged from deep violet to burnt orange. Blankets of fog crept through the troughs between some of them, while others were separated by shimmering waves of heat refraction.

In the far distance beyond the Phantoms hung the ragged crescent of the Ark's resource moon, a tiny red-yellow sliver barely half the size of Veta's thumb tip. That meant she was looking core-ward, toward the base of the spire, and she had not heard Arcas mention any reconnaissance craft in the direction. She turned around to look edge-ward and saw nothing but bank after bank of dunes, vanishing into a shimmering curtain of heat.

"There's supposed to be a Banished Seraph performing a reconnaissance sweep in that direction," Veta said. She was the only one with an eavesdropping feed, so she alone had heard Arcas report the reconnaissance craft. "Anyone see anything?"

The Ferrets took a moment to look, Olivia using her naked eye, Ash a monocular, and Mark his DMR sight.

Finally Ash said, "There might be a mountain range two hundred kilometers distant, and maybe something in the air above that. But at this distance, the heat refraction down here is going to cripple any spectrum they're searching in. We'd have to launch a missile to draw its attention."

"Not really an option."

Veta turned to her right, toward the near end of the dune where Bhasvod's command Phantom had landed. About three kilometers distant, she could just make out what appeared to be an alabaster tower rising between the humps of two dunes, one green and one gold. There seemed to be a tendril of gray smoke rising from its top.

"What about that?" she said, pointing. "Is that the Cartographer's tower?"

"Never seen one," Mark said. "But that's my guess, given all those sentinels pouring out of it—Aggressors, by the look of them."

"Huh?" Veta asked. Mark wasn't even using his Longshot sight, but she knew better than to doubt a Spartan-III's augmented vision. "You mean that gray smoke?"

"Uh, yeah . . . ," Ash said. "Only it's not smoke."

"Okay," Olivia said. "Maybe we can work with that."

"I don't see how," Ash said. "Have you ever seen a sentinel attack for no reason?"

"Well, Zone 67," Mark said.

"That *wasn't* for no reason," Olivia said. "ONI was excavating the city they were protecting."

The training accident that Olivia was referring to had occurred on the planet Onyx before Veta even knew there was such a thing as Gammas. The whole incident was highly classified, but from what little she'd heard, there had been a whole bunch of Sentinels involved.

"You have to do something to piss them off," Olivia continued. "And that's going to be pretty tough from three kilometers away."

"At least with small arms," Mark said. "They wouldn't even know we're firing at them."

"Back to the missile, then," Veta said, and sighed. "I really hate this Forerunner crap."

"Careful, Mom," Ash said. "They're probably listening."

"No way," Veta said. "And if they were, they would have put me out of my misery by now."

She turned to the left, toward the far end of the dune, where the third Phantom had landed. Its two Ghosts had already departed and were just passing by the second Phantom, which had already sent its own Ghosts down the trough to the command craft the Ferrets had been traveling in.

Now that Veta was up high on the crest of the white dune, she could see past the third Phantom. Above the undulating humps beyond it, she saw a vast red plateau, shaped like a table and fissured by a network of dark, narrow gorges. It was ten or twenty times farther distant than the Cartographer's tower, but still close enough that she could make out a dark band of cliffs rising along the near edge.

"Check the edge of the cliffs over here," Veta said. "The navigator mentioned a Pelican hiding in—"

"The shadows," Mark said. He had swung his DMR toward the tableland and was watching it through his Longshot sight. "Range has to be over sixty kilometers. Is that too far, Ash?"

"For you?" Ash replied. "Not with the surveillance equipment they're using. If you can paint 'em with a targeting laser, they're going to know it."

"I can paint 'em," Mark replied. "What's the message?"

Veta thought for a moment. The two Gammas were about to point the laser targeting device attached to Mark's M395B Designated Marksman Rifle at the distant Pelican. If he could actually put the beam on its hull, the craft's defensive systems would interpret it as an attempted targeting lock, and the cockpit would erupt into alerts and alarms.

The Pelican crew would then trace the laser back toward its

source and, at a minimum, figure out where it had come from. But they probably wouldn't fire any of their Anvil-II air-to-surface missiles at such long range—and even if they did, the chances of a hit were beyond minimal.

That was where the quality of a crew really mattered. Even taxi drivers would realize they had made contact with a bogie, log it, report it, and investigate. Which meant, one way or another, that the location of the Keeper-Covenant joint expedition would be exposed, and that was half of what the Ferrets needed.

Anyone reasonably sharp would ask why the Pelican was being painted by a targeting laser when there was no missile within forty kilometers of actual attack range, and then realize someone was trying to alert them to a problem. But a *great* crew would think to look for a message, then run an analysis on the targeting laser's pattern as it lit and unlit them—and hopefully their software would recognize it as one of the oldest electronic comm codes in human history, a series of short gaps and long gaps that every communications officer in most human militaries had once been required to learn by heart, and that still served as an impromptu emergency code, over seven hundred years after its invention: Morse code.

And the thing about recon crews? They were almost all great, because if one wasn't, it didn't last.

"We can't assume the UNSC found my last message," Veta said. "And they've hardly been responding with overwhelming force so far. So let's make *this* message crystal clear."

"And scary," Olivia said. "Really, really scary."

"Right. Scary is good." Veta took a moment to compose something she hoped would be effective, then said, "Tell them: 'Embedded ONI agents need devastating strike on position stat. Halo activation imminent. Acknowledge with missile fire.'"

Mark was already clicking his targeting laser on and off as she spoke.

"Keep repeating it until you get—"

"Acknowledged," Mark said.

A minute later, Veta saw a tiny spray of white streaks silhouetted against the dark band of the distant cliffs.

"Oh boy, did they acknowledge," Ash said. "You got your missiles, Mom."

Veta turned back toward the Cartographer's tower and saw the gray smoke spreading over the dunes in two directions—toward them, and edge-ward toward the periphery of the refugia, where the Banished Seraph had been running its search pattern. She looked in that direction . . . and was astonished to see a line of blue pinpoints emerging from the shimmering heat curtain.

"Is that what I think it is?" Veta asked.

"It is if you're thinking efflux halos," Mark said. He was studying them through his Longshot sight. "It looks like a talon of Banshees."

"I'll take what we can get," Veta said. "From whoever we can get it from."

Castor's voice erupted in Veta's helmet comm, ordering her to report. She crawled back to the top of the dune and peered over the crest. All six Ghosts were lined up at the bottom of the slope, next to Dhas Bhasvod's command Phantom. Feodruz and Arcas were seated on the first two vehicles. Castor and Bhasvod were positioned on the next two, and 'Gadogai was sitting in the rearmost rank, next to an empty Ghost.

Most of them were looking toward the near end of the white dune, where the first Aggressor sentinels were already beginning to swirl overhead. But not 'Gadogai—he was staring up the dune straight at Veta, his oblong head cocked slightly to one side.

"Be ready," she warned. " 'Gadogai just spotted me."

But the Sangheili made no attempt to sound the alarm. He merely raised his hand and motioned for her to approach.

"He wants me to come down." Veta rose and stepped over the crest of the dune, then began to traverse across the slope, trying to avoid the sinkhole that had nearly swallowed them earlier. "If this goes bad, Mark, you're in—"

Olivia interrupted her. "It's not going to go bad. Trust me."

" 'Livi, we're in deep muck here," Veta said. "It's not exactly the time to develop a sensitive side."

"Uh, not exactly, Mom," Olivia said. "But really, don't worry. That's not why they want you. Look up and to your right."

Veta did as Olivia suggested and saw that a silvery, tripartite automaton had flown up behind her and was floating about two meters away. A pair of armlike appendages extended from the middle section of its chassis, and a small oval lens glowed orange in the center of the lowest section. The top part was the most chilling of all; it reminded her of a triangular head beneath a rakish cap.

"Is that a . . . ?" Veta could not quite bring herself to finish. She had faced plenty of things as an ONI agent that made the short hairs stand up on the back of her neck, and the Forerunner stuff was always the worst.

"Yeah, that's an Aggressor sentinel, for sure," Olivia said. "And it seems to *like* you."

EIGHT

1503 hours, October 13, 2559 (military calendar)
White Dune, Drifting Lands
Refugia Epsilon 001 285.1 175.0, Epsilon Spire, the Ark

Veta stepped off the base of the dune and crossed toward the line of waiting Ghosts, careful to keep her attention focused on 'Gadogai. Dhas Bhasvod and Castor were busy discussing the skirmish between their subordinates. Arcas sat behind them, growling orders to a pair of Covenant guards who would be staying with the Phantom. But Feodruz was simply waiting, watching Veta's approach, and she wanted to avoid a full-face exposure in case Intrepid Eye was monitoring the departure preparations through the Jiralhanae's helmet camera. If ONI had learned anything in its time studying Intrepid Eye, it was to *never* underestimate a Forerunner ancilla.

On the other side of the Ghosts, Krelis and Rhadandus were still stripping armor and gear from the four Keepers who had died in the scuffle the Ferrets had started. When they finished, Veta knew, there would be no attempt to hide or protect the bodies.

Unless Jiralhanae had time available to honor their fallen comrades with three days of blood games, the corpses were simply laid aside, preferably on a slope facing the closest sun, to await the Call to Journey.

Once Veta reached the Ghosts, she stopped at the unoccupied one next to 'Gadogai. A type of rapid-assault vehicle, or RAV, the Ghost was shaped like a motorbike with a canard-flanked cowling in front of the rider's seat. It was about four meters long, nearly that wide across the canards, and higher than Veta was tall. She peered across it at the blademaster, whose own vehicle was already floating on its gravity propulsion field.

Veta was fairly certain 'Gadogai intended her to mount the empty Ghost, but it was a large vehicle for someone her size. More importantly, she wasn't eager to leave her Ferrets behind and go riding off through the dunes with a bunch of apocalyptic zealots.

"I'm sure you have a reason for calling me down from the observation post," she said.

"So *that* is why you raced up there," 'Gadogai said. "To *observe*."

"And to secure the high ground." Veta nodded toward the dead Keepers. "It seemed smart, given what was happening at the time."

"Indeed," 'Gadogai replied. "But no longer necessary. Call your brood down. I will suggest that the *dokab* and the Prelate send up a joint watch."

"Why would you do that? My 'brood,' as you call them, is already up there."

"Because the *dokab* fears humans are too fragile and important to risk on such perilous duty. He has commanded that they come down."

"Like Atriox 'commanded' Let 'Volir to give us a two-talon escort?" Veta asked. The blademaster needed reminding that she'd been on the flight deck when he used a similar trick against the Banished. "*That* kind of command?"

"I deceived Let 'Volir because he is an enemy of the Keepers," 'Gadogai said. "Are *you* an enemy of the Keepers?"

"That's a question better asked of yourself." Veta hated to spar verbally with the blademaster—almost as much as she would have hated to do it physically. But she didn't dare back down—the Sangheili would only smell fear and push all the harder. "You joined the Keepers yesterday, at gunpoint. We joined two years ago, of our own free will."

"Your devotion is utterly inspiring." 'Gadogai cast a meaningful glance toward the crest of the dune. "I find your obedience lacking, however."

"I'll obey when the *dokab* sends someone up there to relieve my people," Veta said. "It wouldn't do to leave ourselves blind, not when we're so close to starting the Great Journey."

'Gadogai inclined his oblong head. "You are very wise, for a human." He motioned her toward the seat of the unoccupied Ghost. "So wise, in fact, I find it surprising you have not *already* realized that you are to accompany us."

"To where?"

"To the Cartographer. Is that not where the Prelate said we were going?"

"So I was told. But why bring me?"

"Because that is what the Oracle wishes." 'Gadogai motioned to the Ghost seat again. "Must I invite you twice? Are you *that* special?"

"No. Not . . . special."

She could barely choke the words past the lump in her throat. Damn. If Intrepid Eye had asked for Veta specifically, then, at a minimum, the ancilla was curious about her. And given the cognitive power of a Forerunner AI, the ancilla would not stay curious for long. Her cover would soon be blown.

"I'm just confused," Veta continued. It was time to lay the groundwork for another attack strategy—one that didn't depend on maintaining cover. Or her own survival. "Wouldn't it make more sense for you to take Quenbi?"

'Gadogai cocked his head, studying her out of one golden eye, then finally asked, "Why would we want to take Quenbi?"

Outside of the Gammas, who enjoyed Veta's true loyalties, Quenbi was one of her closest comrades among the Keepers . . . if such a designation could even be made. She was a matronly woman who enjoyed preparing and cooking meals for the different species in the faction, and when they worked together, she never failed to make Veta laugh through her outrageous flirtations with shy young Knox—a lanky, lonesome kid who seemed to have joined the Keepers out of a desperate need to belong to *something*.

But Quenbi was also a devoted acolyte who had joined the Keepers because the Humans of the Joyous Journey were not radical enough for her, and that made her very dangerous. She had lovingly prepared more than one delivery of poisoned ready-meals for a cargo vessel Castor intended to hijack, and Veta had been so worried about some barbed comments Quenbi had made that she'd planted eavesdropping devices to make sure her "friend" wasn't growing suspicious enough of her kitchen skills to denounce her cover story as a fraud. When the time came, it would not be hard for Veta to remember that the woman deserved whatever happened to her.

"Because she triggered the portal's activation pylon on Reach." Veta didn't actually know if that had happened, or even if Forerunner technology responded better to some humans than it did to others. But as a former homicide investigator, she was well-versed in interrogation techniques, and watching how a subject responded to an assertion was often the best way to glean hints about the true nature of events. "So you know the Cartographer will respond to her."

"Ah." 'Gadogai clacked his mandibles in amusement. "That was not Quenbi, but Aubert."

"Okaaay." Veta had to bite the corners of her mouth to keep from smiling. "Then why not send Aubert, instead of me?"

"You may ask that of the Oracle when she reveals herself." 'Gadogai pointed toward the top of the dune crest. "But I would wager your life it is because that Aggressor sentinel did not attack you."

Veta turned and found the automaton still hovering over the sinkhole, its central lens turned toward the Ghosts and their riders in the trough below. Veta couldn't see the Gammas, but she knew they were hiding under the silt somewhere along the ridge, keeping watch over her. The thought of failing them, of squandering their lives on a botched mission, pressed like a boulder on her chest.

Veta turned back to 'Gadogai. "Against what? You'd bet my life against *what*?"

"It does not matter. I would not lose that wager." 'Gadogai turned to Krelis and Rhadandus, then called out, "When you have finished with the dead, climb to the top of the dune and take watch duty from the humans."

Rhadandus growled and dipped his head in acknowledgment, but Krelis snorted and looked away in defiance. 'Gadogai ground his four jaws together, then took his headset from his belt and slipped it on so he could speak privately with Castor. A moment later, the Keeper leader repeated the order, save that he sent Krelis up the dune with one of Bhasvod's honor guards instead of Rhadandus.

Krelis led the way, punching and kicking at the white silt as though it was 'Gadogai himself. The blademaster hissed in amusement, then turned to Veta.

"Your turn."

"So it is."

She placed both palms on the seat of the Ghost at chest height, then pushed off and clambered up. The controls were almost out of reach for her, and she had to spread her arms wide to hold the steering rings. To control the thing, she would have to twist her shoulders side to side. To see over the cowling, Veta had to stand on the control pedals, using her thighs to squeeze the sides of the seat and support her weight. It was all cumbersome, to say the least.

"Perhaps you would prefer to ride with me," 'Gadogai suggested.

"I'd rather run barefoot on smashed glass." Veta activated her helmet comm, then spoke to her "brood." "Krelis and one of the Prelate's guards are climbing up to relieve you. When they arrive, come down and stick close to Aubert. The Great Journey may depend on him."

She had no idea whether *any* human would be able to activate Halo, or only a special one. But Aubert had already demonstrated his affinity for Forerunner technology by triggering the activation pylon on Reach, so it made sense to eliminate him first.

'Gadogai raised his chins, looking at her with an expression that seemed a combination of admiration and appraisal. "Very cunning," he said. "Not even *I* would have thought of that."

Once the commands had been issued and the lookouts dispatched, the column of Ghosts began to snake through a labyrinth of troughs toward the Cartographer's tower. While the route was often wide enough to travel two abreast, 'Gadogai was careful to follow behind the clever little brood mother, close enough never to lose sight of her, but far enough back to react if she suddenly tried to attack or escape into the sea of dunes.

Why the Oracle had chosen her to accompany them to the Cartographer was a mystery to him. Like most humans—if not *all*—she seemed to have a special connection with Forerunner technology. The lack of aggression from the sentinel that had appeared above her on the white dune suggested as much, as did the continued peacefulness of the escort swarm gathering overhead. Yet the little mother was also secretive, fearless, and entirely too erudite—all traits that had been cultivated by his own Silent Shadow, when it still existed.

Supposedly, she had been a human food worker who rescued her charges from a life on the streets. But 'Gadogai had been studying the quartet since Castor used them to force his hand on Reach, and they did not carry themselves as such. No, these humans had studied the combat arts under masters, then practiced until they too became masters. And they had put their skills to use often enough to move with the controlled confidence of expert warriors. Either they were elite mercenaries, using the Keepers to hide after an operation gone sour, or they were ONI agents stranded in the field by the Apparition's unexpected rise. 'Gadogai would probably never know which, not while he was stranded on the Ark, and it did not matter.

"Aita Gomez" and her brood were not actually true Believers. They were not zealots of any kind, which meant they were secretly horrified at the prospect of killing everything in the galaxy. In all likelihood, they were doing everything they could to *stop* the Keepers—and that left 'Gadogai with only one real question.

Should he help them or not?

Castor had not given much thought to what might happen after he initiated the Great Journey, but 'Gadogai certainly had. The Ark had been designed to serve many functions, one of the most important being a biological repository so the galaxy could be reseeded with life-forms after it was cleansed. Therefore, it seemed safe to assume that anyone actually *on* the Ark would be safe from the activation of the Halo Array—especially given the installation's incredible distance from the target—and live out the rest of their lives trapped here.

Which was hardly paradise, but certainly better than dying.

So 'Gadogai had a decision to make. He could save the galaxy, and with it Olabisi, whom he had once loved and claimed for his own. Or he could see everything destroyed . . . and take the ultimate vengeance on her and all those who had stolen her from him.

In his previous life, the decision would have been a simple one. 'Gadogai had been hatched Azl 'Lamoul of the Moul clan, a powerful house of seventeen keeps in the Varo state on Saepon'kal. As the eldest male offspring of the matriarch, he was mentored by the kaidon, proving to be as adept at personal combat as at agrarian administration. When his mentor began preparations to abdicate, 'Lamoul was favored to be elected the next kaidon and sojourned to the client keeps in order to cement his support.

It was at the third destination that he met Olabisi, the daughter of the keep's matriarch. Powerful emotions threatened to overwhelm him, and he realized all at once that she was the one he wanted as matriarch of the Moul clan when his own mother decided to abdicate. As it turned out, the feeling was mutual. He had asked Olabisi to travel with him to the next keep, and by the time they arrived, they had made a secret pledge to join houses.

'Lamoul finished the tour in a state of elation. Returning to his own keep, he learned that the kaidon was abdicating. The clan elders had named 'Lamoul the next kaidon as expected . . . and had also chosen Unavaro, niece to the Marshal of Varo, as his matriarch. 'Lamoul was allowed no opportunity to reject their choice, for the alliance would seal the place of both clans atop the Varo state for generations to come.

He was crestfallen by this turn of events. Unavaro was a cunning female who would test his resolve every day of their partnership, then lay claim to clan leadership the moment he was called away to perform his military service. So reject the match 'Lamoul did, revealing that he had already made an arrangement with Olabisi.

The marshal struck quickly—so quickly that 'Lamoul realized his "secret" feelings for Olabisi had been known to Varo all along. That very night, before 'Lamoul's kaidon and matriarch had formally accepted his decision to reject Unavaro, a betrayer allowed the marshal's assassins into the Moul keep. They slaughtered anyone related to the kaidon or the matriarch by blood, save 'Lamoul himself, whom they drug-darted in his sleep so he would not have the honor of dying with the rest of his line.

Holding 'Lamoul captive in his own keep, the marshal made him watch as an heir of the Varo house was elected kaidon of the Moul clan. To complete the humiliation, he installed 'Lamoul's beloved Olabisi as matriarch, then warned 'Lamoul that she would be the first to die if he ever sought vengeance.

At first, 'Lamoul could not understand why the marshal had set him free. Then, as a steady stream of loyal retainers sought him out to offer their swords and blood as reprisal for the atrocities committed against the keep, 'Lamoul saw the marshal's genius. 'Lamoul and his followers could not take revenge without killing Olabisi as well. To protect his beloved, he also had to protect the ones who had taken her from him.

In the end, 'Lamoul's only choice was to order his vassals to forgo retribution, then leave the keep. The War of Annihilation was raging against the humans in full force, so through the Covenant he unleashed his hatred on the so-called infidels. After only fifty cycles, his ferocity drew an invitation to join the Silent Shadow. He quickly accepted, so that one day he might return to Saepon'kal with the skills and the power to protect Olabisi—and utterly destroy the Marshal of Varo.

But time stands still for no one, least of all a soldier. Azl 'Lamoul would eventually earn the name "Inslaan 'Gadogai," an alias assigned to him when he became a blademaster in the Silent Shadow. Four hundred cycles later, he finally returned to Saepon'kal. But by then, the Marshal of Varo had been killed in the battle on the human world Actium, and the illegitimate kaidon was away, fighting with the Fleet of Righteous Vigilance.

But the indignity did not end there. When 'Gadogai began to scout targets, he was astounded to learn that Olabisi had taken control of her own fate, eliminating her rivals and rising to become matriarch of the entire Varo state. There was no one left for 'Gadogai to take revenge upon, no one who had not hatched from one of her clutches. Even Unavaro, the guileful niece whom he had rejected all those cycles ago, now had a place in her own family's keep only at Olabisi's pleasure.

Seeing that his beloved did not need rescuing, 'Gadogai departed Saepon'kal without taking a single life and without even speaking to her, for revealing his presence would have brought her nothing but pain—and possibly cost her life. His commitment to the Silent Shadow precluded ever making a home in her keep, and a blademaster in the order was supposed to slay anyone who knew of his prior life. It was not always done, of course . . . but sometimes it was accomplished without the blademaster's knowledge or consent.

He had thus returned to the Fleet of Certain Glory, delighted at first that Olabisi had endured and triumphed. But as the war continued to take more and more of his identity, to make him less his own warrior and more his masters' weapon, his heart began to harden against her. He had sacrificed everything to protect her, even his name, and what had she done in return? Adapted and moved on, as though their pledge to each other had meant nothing.

It was a terrible betrayal, and one he had not yet brought himself to forgive.

But . . . did she deserve to die for it?

Did her whole crèche, all her offspring, and the entire state of Varo? All of Sangheili civilization?

'Gadogai was not certain yet, especially given that all whom he had sworn vengeance over were dead. Was it now worth it?

Saving Olabisi would mean betraying Castor, and Castor was that rarest of all things—a leader who remained true to himself. When such a being extended his trust and friendship to someone, it could not be ignored lightly. To betray this trust, even once, was to become an enemy forever. And the one thing 'Gadogai currently did not want in his life was Castor as an enemy.

Because then 'Gadogai would have to kill him.

The column of Ghosts was entering a trough so narrow the riders could only travel single file. Even then, the canards to either side of the drive-cowling began to drag through the silt at the base of the dunes. The air filled with billowing powder. First the Aggressor sentinels overhead vanished behind a cloud of green dust, then Dhas Bhasvod and Castor at the head of the column, followed a few breaths later by Arcas and Feodruz. 'Gadogai had been careful to stay at the rear of the line to keep the little brood mother in sight, but soon even she vanished in a swirling miasma of dust.

'Gadogai accelerated cautiously, knowing the other riders would be slowing down in such poor visibility. Still, the mother's silhouette did not reappear. He began to worry she had turned down some side channel he had missed, or even driven her Ghost into the slope and buried herself beneath a mountain of green powder.

Then it was suddenly there before him, her Ghost's seat back emerging from the green cloud so swiftly he had to swerve to avoid colliding with it. Thinking it was an ambush, 'Gadogai ran the nose of his vehicle into the dune and swung himself toward her, placing his body on her side of his seat so he could snatch her by her back-satchel and fling her to the ground the instant she reached for a weapon.

She looked at him instead with bemusement, then tapped the side of her helmet near its communications microphone.

"The *dokab* commands that you wear your comm disk," she called. "He is tired of having to pass messages."

She smiled and shook her head, then looked forward and sped away into the dust.

Without reaching for his own comm disk, 'Gadogai settled into his seat and freed his Ghost from the dune, then raced after her. Perhaps she was telling the truth, or perhaps she wanted to talk to him over the comm so she could make an argument for helping her stop the madness of the Great Journey. But he had learned on Reach that she and her brood could be as sly as blade snakes, and busying him with his comm disk would be an ideal distraction while she launched an attack or slipped away.

He caught sight of her again, then maintained a steady five-meter cushion between their Ghosts. She was holding herself stiffly, with her shoulders hunched and her helmet cocked slightly to one side. Her size made it difficult to control the vehicle, so that was most likely the cause of her awkward posture. Still, he continued to study her. When he saw no furtive glances over her shoulder, or any other indication that she was keeping track of him, he finally pulled the comm disk from his belt and affixed it to his cheek, then initiated a search for the *dokab*'s channel.

Usually he found the constant prattle that came over a comm disk annoying and intrusive, which was why he rarely wore one without a specific need. But there was no such chatter now. The high dunes were blocking the usual traffic from the Phantoms and their escort talons—or perhaps it was the sentinels overhead, using Forerunner technology to limit communications.

Either way, there was only one active channel.

It was closed, so 'Gadogai signaled the *dokab* to announce his availability. A moment later, the channel opened, and he heard Castor and Dhas Bhasvod still arguing about the fight that had broken out—or been provoked—as the Phantom unloaded.

". . . told Arcas that the Kig-Yar was arguing with one of your humans after he opened fire," Bhasvod was saying. "In *Ibie'shan*. What kind of human speaks *Ibie'shan*?"

"One who has lived with them for two years," Castor replied. "And who was raised in the streets with Kig-Yar thieves."

"And you *trust* them?" Bhasvod demanded. "It is folly."

"These four humans have served me well. I would not have made it this far without them."

"That does not mean we must take them the rest of the way. Not all of them."

"What are you suggesting?" Castor asked.

"That we eliminate the unnecessary ones," Bhasvod said.

It seemed to 'Gadogai that the little brood mother's helmet

shifted upright as the Prelate said this, though there was nothing overtly suspicious in the gesture. She could have merely developed a pain in her neck from holding her head cocked for so long.

"We do not need *seven* humans to activate Halo," Bhasvod continued. "It will be easier to control those who will aid us if we are not burdened with those we do not need."

"You say that because you do not understand humans," Castor said. "Tell him, Blademaster."

"It is as the *dokab* says," 'Gadogai said. He had not yet decided whether to share his suspicions about the little mother and her brood with Castor, but even if he had, it would never be in front of Bhasvod. "First, humans are frail creatures. If you have need of them, there is no such thing as too many."

"There *are* too many," Bhasvod countered. "Especially when the extras are of no use."

"But they are of use," 'Gadogai said. "A human who sees you betray his fellows will show you no loyalty."

"Correct. It is just the opposite," Castor said. "They will fear you at best. At worst, they will thirst for vengeance. Either way, you could never trust them again. The loyalty of humans can only be earned, never demanded."

"We cannot trust them *now*," Bhasvod replied. "Arcas claims it was the dark-skinned human who shoved your Sangheili into the Ghosts as they were being unloaded. She was the one who instigated the entire affair."

"The dark-skinned human?" 'Gadogai said. "The young female?"

"I should find that significant?" Bhasvod asked.

"Humans are frail to begin with," Castor said. "The females tend to be smaller and not as strong."

"And none of them are strong enough to push three Sangheili

at once into a loading portal," 'Gadogai noted. "Not unless they are demons. Spartans."

Bhasvod paused for a moment, then said, "They are not large enough to be demons."

"Then you have seen one?" Castor asked.

"Two, in fact," Bhasvod said. "Fighting them was . . . intoxicating."

"Because you are still alive to tell the tale," 'Gadogai said. "I am in awe."

"I have no doubt," Bhasvod said. "But your awe does not alleviate my concerns. These humans are—"

"Necessary," Castor said. "And mine to deal with."

"We could keep them divided," 'Gadogai suggested. "Tell them it is to minimize the chances of them all being killed at once. That way, we also make them feel important."

Castor went briefly silent, then said, "Very well. It is the only thing I will agree to. At least until the Oracle tells us otherwise."

Reminding Bhasvod that the Oracle had arrived with the Keepers was a risky gambit, but powerful—and it worked.

"Agreed. We will try that for now," Bhasvod said. "Dividing the humans."

As the Prelate spoke, the brood mother's shoulders dropped to a more natural position. 'Gadogai wondered if she could somehow be listening, but it did not seem likely over a closed channel. Besides, the blond stone of a massive ziggurat was manifesting in the dust cloud ahead, looming up just beyond the far end of the trough. They were approaching the base of the Cartographer's tower, and she was no doubt looking forward to dismounting the cumbersome, oversize Ghost.

"But the gods must be mad," Bhasvod continued, "trusting the Power of Transcendence to an infidel species."

"A curious decision, to be sure," 'Gadogai said. "Such power should belong in the hands of their San'Shyuum Prophets, should it not?"

Bhasvod did not reply until the column had left the narrow trough and emerged from the dust cloud.

Finally, he said, "A wise point." He stopped his Ghost on a broad crust-flat and tipped his helmet back, looking up the ziggurat to its crowning white tower. "Perhaps too wise."

Dozens of three-meter-long Aggressor sentinels circled the Cartographer's tower in an endless flow, flashing silver and blue in the austere light of the Ark's artificial sun. As they passed over the wind-packed ground where the Ghosts had parked, they would swoop low to run their ocular receptors over the vehicles and confirm that a threat in need of elimination had not yet presented itself. Sometimes one dropped down in front of Veta to hover at eye level, as though awaiting instruction . . . or, more likely, reaffirming her identity as someone allowed to enter the ziggurat.

She didn't blame them. Given her suspicions of all things Forerunner, she found the idea of having an affinity for their ancient technology a bit sickening . . . and entirely frightening. The mere thought that she could have some sort of special access to a weapon designed to eliminate every sentient creature in the galaxy filled her with the kind of existential dread that made her want to put her M6 to her head.

Which she would gladly have done, had she thought it would stop Halo from being fired. But even if her death brought the Aggressors screaming down on the column of Ghosts, it would not guarantee the deaths of her companions. All five were proven warriors of one kind or another, so it was likely that at least some would survive to fetch Aubert or Quenbi and try again. And even if they didn't, there were plenty of zealots back at the Phantoms who would be happy to take control and continue Castor's quest.

So there was really no choice but to continue playing the loyal Keeper and hope that Intrepid Eye didn't recognize Veta or the Gammas. Once she learned the location of the citadel, the Ferrets would report it to the reconnaissance Pelican, and the UNSC would be able to set up a defensive perimeter. Or, better yet, they would eliminate the Phantoms as they approached.

Veta heard the *crump-crump* of approaching steps and turned to see Castor arriving, plumes of yellow silt rising knee-high each time a boot broke through the crusted ground. His upper lip was raised in a fang-baring joy display, eyes bright with excitement.

It was downright creepy.

"Why do you wait?" Castor waved toward the ziggurat. "Lead the way, human."

"Me?" Veta was probably the last person who should be running point into the facility, but she could hardly tell Castor that. Keepers were supposed to *love* Forerunner technology. "I'm not sure I deserve such an honor."

"Now is not the time to worry over ceremony," Castor said. "The Prelate believes the Cartographer's protectors will be more accepting with a human in the lead."

"Have no fear," 'Gadogai added. "I will be close behind."

"That's a great comfort," Veta said, "knowing you'll be the next to die if something goes wrong."

If Castor understood her sarcasm, his joyous fang display did not show it.

The base of the ziggurat was about fifty meters away, with no obvious entrance. Veta started walking toward the center. As Dhas

Bhasvod and the others fell in behind, she asked, "Where do we enter?"

"That is not yet known," Bhasvod said. "We have never been allowed so close."

Biting back a cynical suggestion to ask the Oracle, Veta continued to walk, watching the Aggressors for some hint as to how to approach the ziggurat. They merely continued to circle overhead, their number slowly dwindling as they peeled off to address unseen threats—most likely the Banished craft she had seen from the summit of the white dune.

She was about ten meters from the ziggurat's base when the crusted ground came to an abrupt end, falling away into a sheer-walled chasm that ringed the entire structure. Near the rim, the walls of the chasm were the same yellow color as the crusted silt beneath her feet. But as the abyss deepened, they grew steadily darker and smoother, first assuming the appearance of cut stone, then of polished stone, of dull metal, and finally of jet-black metal polished to a mirror sheen.

Veta stopped a pace from the edge and dropped to her knees on the crusted ground, then carefully stretched forward and tried to see the bottom. No luck. The chasm simply plummeted into darkness, and it was impossible to tell whether she was looking at wall or floor.

"What is it?" Castor asked.

Veta looked up to see him standing next to her, his toes touching the edge, scowling down at his feet with a confused expression. Feodruz came up on the opposite side and started to step into empty air.

"Stop!" Veta thrust an arm out and blocked his ankle as it swung forward. "Don't you see the chasm?"

"Chasm?" Feodruz's brow folded into a map of confusion. "What chasm? There is only the ground in front of me."

Veta pulled her arm back. "Prove it." She already regretted her protective reaction—one less Keeper could only be a good thing—so she did not mind goading him. "I *could* be wrong."

"Myself, I would believe her," 'Gadogai said, speaking from behind Feodruz. He took the Jiralhanae by the arm and gently pulled him away from the edge. "She is the one possessing the invitation."

A churr of disgust issued from Bhasvod's voicemitter, and he stepped up behind Veta. "What are you waiting for, human? If there is a chasm, then lead us across."

"I don't know how," Veta said. "I'm new at this."

"Perhaps you should find a way," Bhasvod said. "You are no use to us otherwise."

"Walk the perimeter," Castor suggested. "The gods will show you the path."

Which they did, about fifty steps later, when a wide bridge of hard light activated as she approached. It was a perfect blue square, ten meters wide and ten meters long, stretching across the chasm to an arch of shimmering white radiance. The entrance, presumably. She went to the corner of the bridge and stepped onto it.

"Here."

The bridge was more than wide enough for anyone behind her to cross safely, as long as Veta stayed in the center. So she hugged the edge, hoping for a misstep that would reduce the odds against the Ferrets, should support from the UNSC continue to prove elusive.

It didn't happen. Her companions stayed near the center of the span, crossing with an easy confidence that confirmed they could all see the blue light as easily as Veta. She stopped and made a show of peering over the side, looking for the bottom of the chasm so no one would think to question why she had stayed near the edge.

'Gadogai came to her side. "What do you see?"

"Nothing." It was true. The abyss seemed bottomless, continuing forever until it vanished into a faint gray glow that most likely existed only in her imagination. "Just darkness."

"Darkness *is* something," 'Gadogai said. "I am certain you know that by now."

Leaving Veta to ponder whether he had just been making a simple statement of fact or hinting at some deeper meaning—or just trying to keep her off-balance—'Gadogai continued ahead of her. She cast an uneasy look at the Aggressors still swooping overhead, thinking how useless it was to be able to tell human from non-human when they couldn't even tell a galaxy-murdering zealot from a normal being. Finally, she followed the blademaster toward the shimmering archway.

Which vanished as she approached, revealing a long rectangular vestibule, so large they could have parked all six Ghosts inside. The hard-light walls glowed with a soft blue radiance. At the far end hung a green hexagon, which resembled the interface stations in other Forerunner installations Veta had been forced to enter. To activate the interface, all Veta had to do was approach it. But that was not something her undercover persona would know, so she remained outside the vestibule and allowed her natural reluctance to show.

"We stand at the Gateway to Transcendence," Castor declared. He stepped into the vestibule, motioning the others to follow. "Enter now and rejoice!"

Dhas Bhasvod was already striding past Castor toward the interface station. By the time the rest of them had followed him into the vestibule, the San'Shyuum Prelate was at the station, pushing a hand into the light. A green glow crept up his forearm . . . then stopped halfway to his elbow.

The interface station turned purple.

Veta had never seen anything like *that* before.

Bhasvod jerked his hand back, then turned toward the rest of them. "Human." He pointed the haft of his glaive toward the station. "The Oracle claims it must be you."

"Lucky me." Realizing that 'Gadogai, or even Castor, might be familiar enough with human languages to recognize her cynicism, she was quick to add, "Such an honor."

She led the way forward, with Castor and the others close on her heels. As she drew near, the station dropped to a more comfortable height for her. She took a breath, then pressed her hand to the light as Bhasvod had done.

A purple glow spread up her arm and then over her entire body. The station suddenly vanished, and the whir of a descending machine sounded from the dark vastness above. A moment later, a star-shaped construct descended into view, a silver glow shining from the lens of the ocular receptor at the center of its chassis.

"Welcome, Reclaimer." The voice was female, and the diameter of her star was a little larger than Veta's head. Four bronze-colored spikes extended from the top, bottom, and both sides, with four silver spikes—much longer—protruding at a diagonal from between them. "What do you seek?"

According to Veta's ONI briefings, "Reclaimer" was the title the Forerunners had given humans, referencing their ability to activate, manipulate, and ultimately *reclaim* the very same machines the Forerunners had used hundreds of thousands of years earlier. As far as Veta was concerned, it would have been better to just hit it all with a plasma torch and watch it burn. She glanced over at Castor, who continued to stare at the emptiness beneath the holograph as though he was still looking at the interface station.

"No one can answer *for* you," the construct said. "What do you seek, Reclaimer?"

Veta looked around and realized that no one else could hear the voice. Like Castor, Feodruz and Arcas were staring at the construct with expectant expressions, while Bhasvod's chevron-shaped faceplate seemed to be fixed squarely on Veta. 'Gadogai was busy watching the hard-light ceiling and walls, as though expecting a pack of attacking sentinels to emerge at any moment.

It appeared that only Veta could hear the construct. She began to consider the possibility of sabotaging the quest by . . . what? Asking it for the location of something *other* than the citadel?

That was just a delaying tactic, and not even a very effective one. Given Bhasvod's knowledge of the Ark, it would not take him long to realize what Veta had done, and after the fight aboard his Phantom, he was already suspicious of the entire Ferret team. Even a faint hint of sabotage would be enough for him to order their immediate execution.

Then there was Intrepid Eye. Veta had no way of knowing whether the ancilla could eavesdrop on her conversation with the construct, but it would be foolish to assume she couldn't. Intrepid Eye had wanted Veta—or, at least, *Aita*—to come along for a reason. Maybe the AI knew the conversation would provide an opportunity to test Veta's loyalty to Castor's cause.

Most importantly, time was running out for the Ferrets. The Gammas had taken their last smoother six hours before arriving. At best, they had six hours of maximum effectiveness remaining. After that, their mental states would begin to deteriorate, and twelve to fourteen hours later, depending on their individual chemistries, they would start to become as much a liability as an asset.

Veta and her team didn't have time for delaying tactics. They needed to resolve this mess in less than a day. And that meant setting up the Keepers of the One Freedom and Dhas Bhasvod so the UNSC could deliver the killing blow.

Or, at least, so that *someone* could.

"Reclaimer?" the construct asked. "Do you *know* what you seek?"

"Yes," Veta said. "I seek the citadel."

"Ah," the construct said. "You will have to ask the Epsilon submonitor. She oversees the Cartographer."

"I thought you *were* the Cartographer."

"No, I am Epsilon Resource Facility 001's interface executor. You will find the submonitor in the apex of the tower." She paused. "Your route is now accessible."

The construct ascended back into the darkness overhead. In the back of the vestibule, where the interface station had been, a large corridor with a rounded roof and curved walls opened.

Bhasvod looked to Veta, then asked, "Is this your doing?"

"The executor's." She had already made the decision to cooperate—for now—so she extended a hand toward the omega-shaped corridor. "The Cartographer is that way."

Bhasvod took point, leading them toward a shaft of light that beckoned in the heart of the ziggurat, a hundred meters ahead.

Once they had all advanced into the light, a gravity lift engaged, carrying them perhaps fifty meters upward. Then it stopped, all at once becoming the observation deck of the majestic white tower they had been glimpsing since landing at the white dune.

The Cartographer's tower.

The observation deck sat beneath a cupola supported by four string-thin metal columns. Otherwise, it was completely open, offering an unobstructed view of varicolored dunes in every direction. To her left, Veta could make out a few blue slivers of efflux crossing the horizon barely above the dune crests, being forced to circle past the exclusion zone established by a gray haze of Aggressors.

Ahead of her stretched the jagged blue line of a mountain range so distant that all she could see of it were peak tips shimmering with heat distortion. To her right, a finger-thick band of vermilion cliffs marked the edge of the Broken Plain, its chasm-laced surface stretching to the horizon. And when she turned to look behind her, she found the jagged crescent of the Ark's resource moon, partially obscured by a swirling cloud of sentinels, hanging above the white dune where they had left the Phantoms.

Veta had to remind herself that the sweeping panorama taking her breath away was not natural, that she was not even standing on a planet. The Ark was a vast construct, with many times the surface area of any habitable world, built by a race of godlike beings a hundred millennia ago, self-repairing and utterly haunting in its purpose.

Another interface station flickered into existence ahead, midway between two support columns. A trio of fingertips quickly straddled Veta's spine at the top of her back and pushed her forward.

"Why do you stall?" Bhasvod demanded. "Activate the Cartographer. Now."

Veta glanced back and found that his helmet was turned toward the distant efflux slivers being forced to circle past the sentinel exclusion zone. The slivers clearly belonged to the Banished talons that had been patrolling edge-ward from the Cartographer's tower, and they were headed for the cloud of Aggressors swirling above the white dune—where Castor and Bhasvod had left the rest of the company. The Phantoms were in danger, and the Prelate was worried.

Good.

When Veta approached this interface station, it vanished at once, revealing another star-shaped construct that appeared to have been hovering behind it the whole time. It resembled the first, save that the four spikes extending from the top, bottom, and sides were silver and longer than the four bronze-colored spikes protruding at a diagonal between them.

"Welcome, Reclaimer." Everyone turned to look. This conversation would not be private. "What do you seek?"

"The same thing I was seeking in the vestibule," Veta said. "The Cartographer."

"*I* am the Epsilon submonitor." The construct seemed slightly aggrieved. "If you spoke to someone in the vestibule, it was not me. It would have been the executor ancilla for Epsilon Resource Facility 001."

Another one? Veta was surprised that there were so many Forerunner ancillas on the Ark. She knew that apart from rare encounters with Oracles, the Covenant and the Keepers generally eschewed interacting with any complex artificial intelligences because of Forerunner legends concerning something called the "logic plague," which had been some kind of insidious attack the Flood used to compromise machine intelligences through philosophical corruption. According to ONI, the Forerunners' own AIs had violently turned on them during their war against the parasite, eventually leading to the activation of Halo. At some point, the Forerunners limited their production of ancillas to avoid further spreading the plague, but by then it was too late. Whatever the reason was for the Ark now having so many was beyond Veta, but it didn't seem like a very good idea.

"I apologize," Veta said. "Your appearance to that of the executor is so similar."

"We share our fabrication systems," the submonitor said. "Until Installation 00 is fully rebuilt, we are forced to conserve resources."

"Unfortunate," Bhasvod said, stepping to Veta's side. "But we are seeking the citadel that can control Halo. And we require a prompt response—our time is limited."

"I will be quicker if I am not required to engage in guessing games," the Cartographer replied. "Citadel? You must be referring to the Clarion network. We have several facilities that house the supraluminal communications array—which one do you seek?"

"The nearest one," Bhasvod said. "As long as we can activate the Halo Array from it."

"A Reclaimer can control the weapons array from *any* of the Clarion facilities." The submonitor's voice remained impassive, but the glow of her ocular lens seemed a shade paler. Still, if she understood—or cared about—the implications of Bhasvod's statement, it did not prevent her from answering. "However, there is only one functional Clarion site at this time. You are seeking Epsilon Clarion."

"On this same spire?" Bhasvod asked.

"At the base of this spire, yes," the submonitor said. "The repairs on this spire are more advanced than on the others. The other sites are incomplete or inaccessible . . . and may remain so for some time."

"How fortunate for us," 'Gadogai remarked.

"Quite so," the submonitor replied. "If you are seeking a functional Clarion site—a 'citadel,' as you so call it—Epsilon Clarion is your only choice."

She turned core-ward, toward the half-devoured resource moon still hanging in the Ark's central void. A transparent curtain of pale blue light descended from the cupola, creating a small, curved screen.

"I will show you," the submonitor said. A tiny red dot appeared on the curtain, about where solid "ground" met the void surrounding the resource moon. "Epsilon Clarion is located here, 201.1875 degrees from Alpha-Zero. At radian 1.1."

Bhasvod gasped. "It is on the *edge* of the Foundry?"

"Of course not," the submonitor replied. "A Clarion facility located at radian zero would suffer too much damage. The process of manufacturing a Halo ring can be quite tumultuous. That is why Epsilon Clarion is sited at radian 1.1."

"So, a short distance from the edge," Bhasvod said. "But we have already searched that area many times."

"Indeed. There have been fifty-seven reconnaissance passes logged," the submonitor said. "Due to such heavy volume, extra resources were devoted to its concealment."

Veta had already committed the exact coordinates to memory, but the last thing she needed was for the UNSC to dispatch an ambush mission to the site — only to decide there was nothing there.

"How will we be able to find it?" she asked.

"Again, I will show you."

The red dot expanded into a two-dimensional image portraying dozens of rust-colored mountains, shaped vaguely like drops and silhouetted against the jagged crescent of the resource moon. Their flanks were draped in glacial ice, and they were separated by a maze of deep, sheer-walled canyons.

The image began to magnify, zooming in on a dome of cross-hatched stone crowned by a thick mantle of blue ice. It was distinguished from the surrounding summits only by the loss of its needlelike pinnacle, which had been broken off just above the glacier.

A red square appeared on the flank of the glacier, located on a vertical face of ice just above the long tail of an icefall that dropped into the dark-walled chasm below.

"The entrance is hidden behind the ice," the submonitor said. "A Facilitator-class ancilla will be available inside. She will help you find the supraluminal communications facility, which you will need to initiate Halo's mass sterilization protocol."

Mass sterilization protocol, Veta thought. What a Forerunner way to describe *total death*.

"This ice," Castor said. "It is an illusion, then?"

"No. It is frozen water, currently eighty-three meters thick." The submonitor stopped the magnification. The top half of the square showed a dense wall of blue ice. The bottom half showed a braided beard of icicles, glistening with running water. "At present, cloaking must be reserved for concealment operations that cannot be executed another way. You must melt or cut your way into the entrance."

"Through eighty-three meters?" Castor asked. "That will alarm the protective sentinels."

"And draw our enemies directly to our position," Bhasvod said. "Can we not use a translocation portal?"

"No. The portal network has been crippled due to the recent increase in hostilities on the installation's surface." The submonitor shined its ocular glow on Bhasvod for an instant, then said, "If you are part of the belligerents currently engaged in conflict and hope to use the Clarion facility to your advantage—"

"Never," Bhasvod said. "Our only fighting will be to activate Halo."

"Then access will be permitted under standard principles," the submonitor said. Her glow shifted to Veta. "Reclaimer, do you require anything else?"

Bhasvod answered for her. "None that we have time to seek." He took Veta's arm and pulled her back to the center of the observation deck. "We must hurry back to the Phantoms, or we will be taking our Ghosts to the citadel."

Once they were in position, the observation deck descended back into the ziggurat. They raced out the access corridor and retrieved their Ghosts, then sped back through the dunes, their canards scraping along the bases and filling the air with so much powder that at times Veta could not see two paces ahead, trying to reach the Phantoms before the Banished did.

They almost made it.

Veta had just spotted Krelis and his honor-guard companion, still in their dune-top observation post, when the crack and crackle of air combat ripped through the sky. Lightning-bright streaks of particle beams and plasma bolts began to flash across the narrow wedge of atmosphere ahead, and a wave of Aggressors came shooting over the dune crest on the left. The sentinels were met by a volley of Banished plasma torpedoes. Five of them tumbled from the sky and vanished into the dune below, leaving nothing behind but boiling pillars of yellow dust.

Castor and Bhasvod were on their comms instantly, demanding situation reports and issuing orders. From what Veta could tell over her eavesdropping link, a Seraph and a half talon of Banshees had lured away Dhas Bhasvod's defensive perimeter with a series of probing attacks. Meanwhile, the other half talon of Banshees had snaked in through the dunes to make a surprise strafing run on the parked Phantoms.

So far, the damage was moderate. Only Bhasvod's command craft had been crippled. But the attack stirred up the remaining Aggressors, who were waiting as the Covenant's perimeter craft returned to the landing zone. The result was as brutal as it was pointless, with sentinels launching mass suicide attacks against a Covenant force desperate to protect its remaining two Phantoms.

And the Banished had already withdrawn from the battle, vanishing into the dunes without losing a single craft.

The Ghosts arrived at a landing zone shrouded in roiling dust, with disabled craft raining down all around. Veta had to veer to avoid a crashing sentinel—and ran into Krelis as he came sliding down the white dune. He barely looked at her—just picked himself up and sprinted through the dust toward the middle Phantom.

Castor's voice came over the Keeper battlenet. "Leave the Ghosts—there is no time to load them! Rhadandus, which Phantom is Quenbi on?"

Veta pulled up, confused. *Quenbi?* If Castor was trying to be sure he had the same human who had activated the pylon on Reach, he should have been asking for *Aubert*, not Quenbi . . . right?

Unless 'Gadogai had lied.

It had been Quenbi who triggered the activation pylon back on Reach.

When Rhadandus did not reply, Castor asked again, "Rhadandus, which Phantom is Quenbi on?!"

"The third one." It was Krelis who answered, not Rhadandus. "The far one."

Castor emerged from dust in front of Veta. "Your brood is aboard the third Phantom, little mother." He gestured for her to join him. "But you will ride aboard the second one, with me."

"A wise precaution, Dokab." 'Gadogai came up to accompany them, placing himself a meter behind Veta. "We should not have all of her brood aboard the same Phantom, in case one is destroyed."

"It seems best," Castor said. "For them, too."

He rushed toward the second Phantom and faded into the dust.

Before following, Veta glanced over her shoulder. First 'Gadogai had lied to her about the identity of the other human who had actually activated Forerunner technology. And now he was positioning himself to stop her if she attempted to flee.

"Blademaster, I'm starting to think you don't trust me."

'Gadogai spread his hands. "Then you are mistaken," he said. "Why would I not trust you—especially when we have your brood aboard the other Phantom?"

NINE

1931 hours, October 13, 2559 (military calendar)
Covenant Phantom #2, Broken Plain
Refugia Epsilon 050 249.5 180.6, Epsilon Spire, the Ark

The Broken Plain stretched another two hundred kilometers in front of the Phantom, its chasm-webbed expanse marbled with silver streams and brakes of fin-shaped succulents. In the distance, the plateau dropped into a mottled yellow basin that extended to the horizon. It was so vast that Castor began to wonder if the Keepers of the One Freedom and their new Covenant allies were still capable of reaching the citadel.

They had lost so many at the white dune. Rhadandus and four other Keepers had fallen, including the human Knox, and also three Covenant Jiralhanae. Dhas Bhasvod's crippled command Phantom had been abandoned, and half their fighter escort destroyed. Meanwhile, their Banished pursuers had escaped without a single loss. The UNSC remained a threat as well, for their reconnaissance Pelican was not watching out of idle curiosity. There would be more attacks coming soon, and the fragile partnership was in no position to defend itself.

Castor turned to Inslaan 'Gadogai, who was seated across from him at the operations officer's station in the back of the flight deck. "Do we still have the strength left to reach the citadel?"

'Gadogai considered the question for a few breaths, an unusually long time for him, then finally said, "Our strength is not the issue."

"How can it not be?" Castor pointed forward, his arm extending past the port-side seat, where one of Bhasvod's Jiralhanae sat behind the pilot's controls. Krelis was at the copilot's station. "Look ahead. We have at least a thousand kilometers of open basin to cross after we leave the Broken Plain, and our Phantoms cannot outrun the Banished's Seraph. Perhaps not even their Banshees. Sooner or later, we must turn and fight."

"And when we do, it will not be our strength that matters," 'Gadogai said. "It will be the conviction to use it."

"You cannot be saying that I lack conviction."

"I am saying that you have not *examined* your conviction. Until you do, no amount of strength will ever be enough . . . because you will never have the resolve to use all of it."

"Now is no time for your riddles, Blademaster."

"But it is," 'Gadogai said. "There is no better time to examine unanswered questions . . . especially yours."

"What have I left unanswered?" Castor took a breath and tried to be patient, reminding himself that the Sangheili was usually most helpful when he was most infuriating. "The only question in my mind is how to escape the Banished. As it stands, they need only choose a time to attack, and the Great Journey will end before it started."

"That is hardly the only question you need to answer. Focus on the ones that Dhas Bhasvod put to you, and the path forward may grow clear."

"*May?*" Castor growled.

'Gadogai rocked his oblong head side to side. "It depends on the answers."

"Know that you are a terrible advisor." Castor let out a grumble of resignation, then asked, "What are these questions? I recall none."

"Back when we encountered the Cartographer, did the Prelate not say that the gods must be mad, trusting the Power of Transcendence to an infidel species?"

"That was an outburst of anger, not a question."

"Still, it raises an issue you have avoided examining, and deserves further introspection. Why *did* the Forerunners trust the Power of Transcendence to humans? Why did they not put it in the hands of their beloved San'Shyuum Prophets instead?"

"Bhasvod did not ask that second question either," Castor said. He could not see the point the Sangheili was driving at, and that made him uncomfortable. It was like having a Silent Shadow assassin stand where he could not be seen. "Must I answer your queries, as well?"

"Only if you wish to reach the citadel."

"You are wasting the *dokab*'s time," Krelis said, twisting around in his seat. "He should be worrying about the Banished, not debating these sacrileges with you."

'Gadogai continued to hold Castor's gaze. "It is no sacrilege to inquire why the gods have ordered matters as they have. How else can you truly understand their will?" He paused, then said, "We have undertaken a sacred mission to end all sentient life in the galaxy. If we attempt *that* without examining our own convictions, we will only sabotage ourselves. We will make mistakes."

"You are saying *I* have made mistakes?" Castor did not even try to hide his rising anger. "That the Banished are *my* doing?"

"Not necessarily your doing—"

"*Yes,* your *doing.*" It was the Oracle's liquid voice, coming from the navigation station next to Castor's arm. He turned his head and found her silvery orb staring up from the plotting display, its central lens shining red and bright. "*You have made other errors, as well.*"

The anger that had been rising inside Castor grew cold and sank, and he felt the strength that had been with him since arriving on the Ark begin to drain away.

He bowed his head to the image and said, "Enlighten me, Oracle. I beg of you."

"*You have assumed that if someone serves you well, they serve no one else.*" The Oracle's voice took a hard edge. "*That was indeed a mistake.*"

Castor glanced toward 'Gadogai. "I have been betrayed by a spy?"

"*Not a spy,*" the Oracle replied. "*Four spies.*"

"Which means it is not *me,*" 'Gadogai said. "The Oracle speaks of the little matriarch and her brood."

Castor shook his head. "No. Impossible." He continued to look at 'Gadogai. "If not for them, you would have killed me on Reach."

"Which is when I should have begun to suspect them," 'Gadogai said. "Street orphans do not have their kind of discipline. They would have immediately opened fire, and we would both be dead now."

"Faith brings its own discipline," Castor said. "If that is your only reason to suspect—"

"*I have other reasons,*" the Oracle said, interrupting him. "*Better reasons.*"

Castor felt hollow and sick inside. "Go on. I am listening."

"After I revealed myself at the crash site, they deliberately began to avoid optical receptors. The probability of that happening by chance is minuscule for a single individual, and functionally zero for four."

"You are certain of this?" Castor asked.

"What a thing to say," the Oracle said. *"I subsequently searched my auxiliary memory and compared their faces to images of known Office of Naval Intelligence agents."*

"ONI . . . ?" Castor's anger began to rise again, but it was anger with himself—at how he had failed the gods through his blindness. "It cannot be!"

"It could *only* be." 'Gadogai's voice was much kinder than the Oracle's, which only made Castor feel more foolish. "I have seen Keeper security checks, Dokab. Only ONI had the resources to defeat them."

"A small number of other agencies would also be capable," the Oracle said. *"But the blademaster is not incorrect. Facial recognition yielded several close matches for each human, but nothing definitive. That is why I wanted the matriarch to accompany us to the Cartographer—so I could secure a high-fidelity voiceprint."*

Castor's insides had now turned to ice. "Who is she?"

"Her face is yet to be fully verified, but the voiceprint is a near-perfect match." The Oracle had always insisted on answering Castor's questions in the manner she chose, and his impatience or anger meant nothing to her. *"It is a pity I was unable to retrieve a retina pattern, or I could confirm it with absolute—"*

"Who *is* she?!"

"We have encountered her before," the Oracle said. *"She was instrumental in my capture on Gao, and she led the hunter-killer team when the Keepers of the One Freedom were blamed for the Tuwa murders."*

Castor recalled both incidents well. During the first, he had learned that a UNSC research battalion was on the human world Gao, hunting for the very Oracle he was speaking to now. He had taken five hundred Keepers to the planet in an attempt to rescue her. His efforts had not only failed, but had ultimately proven unnecessary. The Oracle had freed herself a short time later, and she had come to him many times since.

The second incident had occurred after the murder of a UNSC admiral and her family. The Keepers had been accused of the killings as part of a convoluted ONI scheme to create a powerful bioweapon.

And now, the Oracle was telling him that his most trusted human had been involved in both clashes . . . and both times against him.

"Who *is* she?!" Castor demanded yet again.

"She has taken forty-three identities since your first confrontation," the Oracle replied. *"But her true name is Veta Lopis."*

"Veta Lopis," Castor repeated.

He did not even recognize the name. Yet this human woman, this *Veta Lopis*, had been secretly making it her mission to undermine his forces and destroy his bases and test his faith for six years. And now here she was on the sacred Ark, of all places, masquerading as one of his faithful followers, so she could strike at the very heart of his destiny.

So she could stop the Great Journey.

"And you are certain she is an ONI agent?" Castor asked. "You know this?"

"I have confirmed it. There is a self-cloaking nanotransmitter concealed in the microphone of your comm disk—"

"What?"

Castor reached for the comm disk hanging from his belt, only to find it already missing. 'Gadogai was holding it in a hand that had moved too fast to see. The blademaster wrapped the microphone wafer in his palm, then looked past Castor to the Oracle's image.

"How much has she heard?" 'Gadogai asked.

"*Nothing of consequence,*" the Oracle replied. "*I have taken control of her eavesdropping device.*"

"Good." Castor rose. "Then she will not expect what is coming."

"What would that be?" 'Gadogai asked.

"I am going to tear her limbs off one at a time." Castor turned toward the back of the flight deck. "And make her watch as I toss them through the open hatch of the gravity lift."

'Gadogai blocked Castor's way, catching him by the wrist as he tried to palm the control pad that would open the hatch to the troop bay.

"You cannot do that, Dokab." 'Gadogai continued to hold Castor's wrist, keeping his hand away from the control pad. "She cannot be aware that you know the truth."

"Why not?" It was all Castor could do to keep himself from flinging 'Gadogai aside. Or at least trying to—the Sangheili was remarkably strong for such a slender being. "She has been subverting the Keepers for too long. *She* is the reason the UNSC has weakened us so. *She* is the reason we had to seek protection from the Banished."

"And yet, here you are. On the Ark, on the verge of the Great Journey."

"What are you saying? That I should be grateful for their betrayals?"

"I am saying that you would not be here without the spy and her brood. I would have killed you on Reach, and it would now be someone else's destiny to initiate the Great Journey."

Castor lowered his hand. He ached to vent his rage, to punish the spy and her brood for shaming him before the gods. But the blademaster's words rang true, reminding him that fate worked in mysterious ways. How many times had he questioned the Oracle's plans, only to discover that she had saved him from annihilation and carried him closer to his destiny?

"Why do you look at me, Dokab?" asked the Oracle.

Castor had not even realized he was looking at her. He had instinctively turned toward the plotting display, and now he was staring into her bright central lens, his stomach still burning at the human woman's betrayal, his heart longing to see the Oracle's hand in his grievous error.

"I did not bring the spy into your midst," the Oracle continued, *"if that is what you are thinking."*

"How helpful you are," 'Gadogai said. "Are you trying to stir the *dokab* into a blind rage?"

"I am not here to help you do anything," the Oracle said. *"You are here to help me."*

"Which I am attempting to do," 'Gadogai said, "by helping the *dokab* fulfill his destiny. As I assume *you* are—since it was you who convinced the Prelate to form an alliance with him."

"Indeed," the Oracle said. *"The dokab's success here is mine as well."*

"Good." 'Gadogai turned to Castor again. "Then help me convince him that wasting this opportunity so he can have vengeance would be a mistake."

Finally, Castor's rage began to fade. "What opportunity?"

"To get out of the way, Dokab," 'Gadogai said. "And let our enemies kill each other."

Castor showed his tusks in enthusiasm. "Ah. I see. You have a plan?"

'Gadogai looked toward the Oracle. "Can you reactivate the nanotransmitter?"

"*Whenever I wish.*"

"Good. Not yet then," 'Gadogai said quickly. "First, we need to speak with the Prelate . . . in private."

The transmission cleared with a pop so sharp that Veta's head jerked sideways, both ears ringing. She had been feigning sleep, so she opened her eyes as though awakened by a bad dream and found Feodruz watching her. Nothing new. Castor's faithful lieutenant had been sitting across from her since they left the white dune, his gaze rarely shifting away. Now his brow was knitted, as though he was wondering why she continued to wear her helmet in the sweltering troop bay.

And Veta did not even have her earlier excuse of a tense situation. The animosity between the Keepers and their allies had been largely dissolved, alleviated by the realization that they shared a common enemy in the Banished. Feodruz was flanked by a pair of Covenant Jiralhanae, both of whom had removed their helmets and sat slumped with their eyes closed and their chins on their chests.

Veta shook her head as though trying to clear it, then glanced over at the hawk-nosed human dozing in the seat next to her. A true Keeper zealot, Aubert wore his red hair in the same fashion as Veta and her Gammas—shaved at the sides, with a long fall in back that hung down between his shoulder blades. It seemed the ultimate irony that Veta, with her aversion to all things Forerunner, had been the one selected to visit the Cartographer rather than Aubert Domhill, a renowned xenoarcheologist whose obsession with Forerunner technology had led him to forsake his family and his profession to become a Keeper of the One Freedom.

Why Intrepid Eye had chosen Veta to access the Cartographer remained a mystery to Veta, but it was certainly *not* good news. Nor was the fact that the AI was helping Castor in his quest to activate Halo. But her success with the Cartographer could only mean one thing: she would be the one they chose to help them activate the supraluminal communications array when they reached the citadel.

It was a revelation that made her stomach twist if she let herself think about it. So she tried not to.

Veta looked forward again and found Feodruz still eyeballing her, which was probably a good thing. Had he known of the suspicions 'Gadogai had kept hinting at before the ride to the Cartographer, Feodruz would probably have killed her already.

She met his gaze and touched her fist to her breastplate in a Keeper salute, then extended her legs into the empty area between them. It was space that would have been occupied by the Ghosts, had there been time to load the RAVs before fleeing the sentinels at the white dune.

The ringing in her ears finally started to subside, so she crossed her ankles, closed her eyes, and settled in to eavesdrop.

". . . Cartographer said the ice is eighty-three meters thick at the entrance," Castor was noting. "That is a great obstacle."

"Our Phantoms have plasma cannons." Dhas Bhasvod's reply was barely audible, no doubt because it was coming over the Phantom's external communications system and being picked up incidentally by the nanobug in Castor's comm disk. "Plasma melts ice."

"True," Castor said. "But melted ice becomes steam. It will take hours. Perhaps even a day."

"I see your point," Bhasvod replied. "It could betray our position."

"That is a certainty," Castor said. "We already know that the Banished are hunting us, and the UNSC is watching. A thousand-meter column of steam will bring them straight to us."

Bhasvod fell silent for a moment, then said, "The only way to avoid that is to melt the ice even more slowly, so that most of it runs off as water."

"Eighty-three meters," Castor said. "That would take ten days, perhaps more if we do not find the entrance on the first try."

"I see no other way," Bhasvod said. "We cannot break away that much ice."

"Bigger plasma cannons," Castor said. "If we could melt through quickly enough, it would not matter how much steam we create. We would be inside the citadel hours before our enemies could arrive in force."

"We would have time to fortify," Bhasvod said. "It would take them weeks to dislodge us, especially if the humans can rally the sentinels to our defense."

"And by the time that happened," Castor said, "the Great Journey would be underway."

"So it would," Bhasvod said. "I see only one problem. We do not have plasma cannons that large aboard."

"Can you have them brought to us?" Castor asked. "Quickly?"

"With a suborbital trajectory, yes," Bhasvod said. "But that is no better than a steam plume. It will lead our enemies straight to us."

"Which is why we should meet before we go to the citadel," Castor said. "We will rendezvous with your cannons four hours short of the destination, then leave the instant they arrive. By the time the strike fighters pursuing us catch up and are ready to attack, we will be at the citadel, melting our way inside."

Bhasvod paused, no doubt looking for weak points, then finally said, "It is a good plan—very thorough for a Jiralhanae. I can have a pair of Weevils delivered in six units."

"Six units?" Castor asked. "Can it not be sooner?"

"This is heavy artillery, Dokab. It must be prepared and loaded, and the crews must be assembled and supplied. The transit itself will be the quickest part of the deployment."

"I understand." Castor muttered something that Veta didn't get, then said, "Your pilot tells me that he has reconnoitered this area many times. He says there is a rendezvous point with easy landing and good concealment at 202.3701 degrees, radian 181.4."

Bhasvod repeated the coordinates, then said, "I will have to expose our position to make the transmission. We should be prepared."

"When you are ready," Castor said.

The troop bay's ambient lighting began to brighten and fade, warning the passengers to make themselves secure for maneuvers. Veta sat up straight and tightened her crash harness, then glanced across the deck toward Feodruz, who had finally stopped watching her to don his own helmet and secure his restraint cage.

Six hours just to the rendezvous, then another four to the citadel. During those ten hours, her Gammas would start to lose combat efficiency.

That was the military way of saying they would start the hard slide into delusion and madness, that Veta needed to find a way to get the job done soon. Because twelve hours after that, the Gammas were going to stop being her team and start becoming her problem, and Veta didn't have the guts right now to think about what that would mean.

For her, or for them.

But despite that, the team still had ten decent hours to get the mission done, and Veta was beginning to think that just might be enough. All they had to do was flash a message to the reconnaissance Pelican that had been keeping track of them. If they could find a way to do that, the Great Journey would be stopped in its tracks—with four hours to spare.

Still plenty of time to get her Gammas to a UNSC medical facility. They would hardly show any loss of efficiency at all.

Pavium sat across from Voridus in the back of their Phantom, watching his brother's fingers tap and slide over the screen of an octagonal datapad. Voridus had taken it off the body of a Covenant Jiralhanae after an early battle against them, and he liked to spend his idle time working with it. Today he had linked it to the transport's external communications system on Pavium's order.

One of the Covenant Phantoms they were pursuing had climbed to fifteen thousand meters, then made a powerful omnidirectional transmission that guaranteed every craft on the Epsilon Spire would know its exact location and bearing. Pavium assumed the craft was calling for support from a Covenant base whose location it did not want to reveal—an assumption supported by the Covenant battlenet protocols used to encrypt it. Knowing how much his brother relished a puzzle, he had ordered Voridus to break the encryption, and Voridus had immediately picked up his captured datapad and set to work.

That had been just four standard minutes earlier, and the grunts of dismay coming from Voridus's side of the cabin suggested he was already losing interest.

"Keep trying," Pavium said.

After their strafing run in the Drifting Lands had failed to destroy all three Covenant Phantoms, Pavium had reluctantly allowed Thalazan to call the rest of his Seraph talon forward. Giving his rival an equal number of supporters in the field was a risk to Pavium's position as warlord, but there was no other choice. The Banished were in desperate need of the added thrash and reconnaissance reach that the Seraphs would bring—especially if the Covenant was also calling support forward.

"It is not like you to give up so soon," Pavium continued. "We need to know what that message said."

"I am not giving up." Voridus tossed the datapad onto the operations console. "I am finished."

"*That* quickly?"

Voridus retrieved that datapad, then read aloud, " 'Send two Weevils to following coordinates for rendezvous in six units. We will be waiting but concealed. Be prepared for further travel. Bhasvod.' "

"I thought it was encrypted."

Voridus raised the datapad and fluttered it back and forth. "I had the key," he said. "It should have been changed after *this* was captured."

"The luck of the Banished, then." Pavium paused, wondering how it related to another encrypted exchange intercepted a few minutes before, between the two Phantoms they were chasing. "Were you able to—"

"The same key," Voridus said. "A simple task."

"Let *me* decide that. Thalazan has not replaced me as the Long Shield warlord yet."

Voridus exhaled sharply, but said, "They need the Weevils to melt ice." He stopped there, until Pavium bared a warning tusk.

"The entrance to the citadel is hidden behind eighty-three meters of ice. They want to melt it quickly enough to be inside before we can follow the steam trail to their position."

"And you did not think this worth telling me?!" Pavium demanded. "Why would you do such a witless thing and not report it?"

"Because it makes no sense. Their Phantoms alone have enough firepower to quickly clear the entrance."

Pavium considered this for a few moments, then said, "Clearing eighty-three meters is quite a burden. Unless they know exactly where the entrance is—"

"It does not matter," Voridus said. "Because they need not melt *all* the ice. They merely need to break a slab free, and it will slide away on its own."

"You are assuming the entrance is on a vertical surface."

"At least a sloped surface."

"How can you know this?" Pavium asked. "Did they also mention where the citadel is located and describe how it rests on its site?"

"Of course not. But they said eighty-three meters thick *at* the entrance—not *over* or *on* the entrance."

"You are hanging the fate of the galaxy on three very small words, brother."

"On one small word and some sound reason," Voridus retorted. "If the entrance was *under* the ice, where would the water go when it was melted?"

Pavium attempted to maintain his composure, but try as he might, he could not argue with his brother's logic. He slumped back against the navigator's station. "You're right. The water would drain into the citadel."

"Or rest on top of it," Voridus said. "Either way, it would prevent them from access."

"So they do not require the Weevils." Pavium stared at the overhead and began to work through the Covenant's possible reasons for calling them forward. "But the enemy might not realize that. Not every Banished warlord has a genius brother to advise him."

"You said I was witless."

"I said you did a witless thing," Pavium said. "Today you are a genius."

"Then let me tell you how we *know* it is a trap." Voridus snatched the datapad off the operations console and held it up between them. "Because of this."

"Ah," Pavium said. "They used an old key because they already know we have one of their datapads. They *wanted* the messages to be intercepted."

"It is the only simple explanation. They are trying to lure us into an ambush."

Pavium had little doubt that his brother was right, but the feather of an idea was beginning to tickle the base of his skull.

"Perhaps."

"*Perhaps?!*" Voridus exclaimed. "How can I make it any clearer for you?"

"You cannot," Pavium said. "I am only thinking that this is not something we can afford to be wrong about."

"We are not wrong."

"I am not saying we are. Only that we should consider both possibilities."

"With one talon of Banshees and a Seraph?"

"No, we will need *all* the Long Shields," Pavium said. "Contact the chieftains and tell them to prepare their talons for a suborbital transit. The infantry fists, as well. 'Let Volir will have to protect his own flank."

Voridus began to slide gliders and touch screens on the operations console. "Where should I tell them to go?"

"They will have to wait for coordinates," Pavium said. "We will send them as soon as we know the location of the citadel."

Voridus turned to look at his brother. "When we see the steam rising?"

"Let us hope it will be sooner than that. I'd like to be there waiting when the Covenant arrives."

"And I would like to understand how to create Forerunner glyphs," Voridus said. "That does not mean it will become a reality."

"Perhaps not, but it also does not hurt to be open to the possibility."

Pavium glanced forward at the pilot and copilot. Like everyone aboard the Phantom, both had been handpicked for their loyalty. Still, he hoped Voridus would not prove too vocal in his enthusiasm for the second part of Pavium's plan. A Banished warlord should never be blatant when scheming to protect his own power.

"Six hours will be more than enough time for the rest of Thalazan's Seraphs to catch up," Pavium said. "We will send his talon to watch the rendezvous coordinates."

Voridus showed all his tusks. "As you command." He began to tap the console screen again, then spoke under his breath. "Today *both* brothers are geniuses."

TEN

2151 hours, October 13, 2559 (military calendar)
Ridge Nineteen, Reef of Thieves
Refugia Epsilon 001 217.5 183.4, Epsilon Spire, the Ark

The stop came four hours before rendezvous time, but Veta wasn't going to complain. She knew Weevils were coming forward only because she had been eavesdropping, so it would have looked suspicious to ask why the Phantoms were landing prematurely. More importantly, she needed to send the rendezvous coordinates to the reconnaissance Pelican trailing them, and the sooner the better. The UNSC would need time to respond, and a few hours could mean the difference between missing a golden opportunity and delivering a killing blow. So once the craft had settled onto its landing pads, she joined the rest of the passengers in freeing herself from her crash harness, shouldering her gear, and turning toward the exit.

Which remained secure, keeping her bottled up in the hot troop bay with Aubert and fifteen ripe-smelling Jiralhanae. Veta wasn't sure whether it was their stench or her own apprehension making her stomach churn, but she was betting on the apprehension. 'Gadogai had all but told her he knew she was a spy, and only the fact that she still had her weapons and gear made her think he had not yet shared his suspicions with Castor.

Why not?

It was a question that had been eating away at her since they'd boarded, making her heart race and her chest tighten. She knew 'Gadogai wasn't holding back out of fondness or kindness. He had already warned her aboard the Lich that he intended to make her team pay dearly for forcing his hand back on Reach. So, either he was planning some kind of drawn-out torture . . . or he understood exactly what the Ferrets were doing and didn't want them to fail.

That second possibility was not as far-fetched as it seemed. 'Gadogai had joined the Keepers out of expedience, not conviction. He wasn't the kind of zealot who believed that eliminating all sentient life would win favor with a long-dead species—especially when it was clear that, whatever their other faults, the Forerunners had placed a high value on the diversity of galactic life.

Might 'Gadogai actually be willing to *help* the Ferrets?

Crazier things had happened. And the stakes were too high to indulge personal animosities. If 'Gadogai wanted to save his fellow Sangheili and protect the rest of the galaxy, he would be willing to work with anyone—even if he hated them.

The hatch in the bulkhead behind her scraped open, and Veta turned to see Castor stepping into the troop bay. He stopped two paces in and glanced around the perimeter until he found Veta, then quickly shifted his gaze back to center and began to issue orders.

"We will debark and wait here for three units before proceeding to a rendezvous at our next stop. Stay close to the Phantoms, in case we must flee another Banished attack." He turned back to Veta. "Little Mother, you and your brood will take the watch together. If we are attacked, it will be better to have you and the other humans in separate locations."

"As it is spoken, it shall be done," Veta replied. She saw 'Gadogai step through the hatch behind Castor and look straight toward her, but it was impossible to read anything in those golden eyes. "How long before we reach the citadel?"

Castor's eyes narrowed. "You will know that when we reach it." He glanced back at 'Gadogai and nodded, and 'Gadogai leaned through the hatch and spoke to the pilots. The boarding ramp descended, allowing a blast of fresh air to rush into the troop bay. Castor pointed Veta toward the exit. "Go now. Quickly."

There was an edge to his voice that made her eager to obey. She descended the ramp into a silvery gloom, then started toward the other Phantom. The Ark's sun had dimmed to a vestige of its daytime self, casting just enough light to illuminate the scrubby ground. They had landed on an isthmus between two long ponds. The water in both was calm and mirror-smooth, reflecting the ghostly crescent of a barely visible resource moon. At either end of the isthmus rose hundred-meter ridges, the one behind her almost vertical and formed from thin layers of flaky stone, the one ahead a steep slope blanketed in feathery shrub.

By the time Veta reached the other Phantom, her Gammas were standing in front of it with their weapons and ammunition belts. Dhas Bhasvod was with them, his faceplate never straying from Veta as she approached. He pointed his glaive at the rucksack slung over her shoulder.

"How long are you planning to stay, human?"

"No longer than you," Veta said. "But I *am* planning to stay dry, and have drinking water, extra ammunition, binoculars, and everything else that happened to be in my gear bag when I found out we were on watch. Is that a problem?"

"It is actually rather prudent." Bhasvod turned to the Gammas. "Perhaps you should take your own bags after all."

As the trio climbed back into the Phantom's troop bay, Bhasvod studied Veta in silence, then casually looked toward the top of the shrub-blanketed ridge behind him.

"I imagine you will set your observation post up there," he said.

"That's probably the smart thing," Veta said. "Better views from the high ground."

"Of course." Bhasvod continued to study the ridge for a moment, then pointed his glaive at the crest, toward an arrow-shaped nub of stone about three hundred meters distant. "That is the highest point close to us."

"Thanks. I'll keep that in mind."

"And that is where you will set up?"

"Probably," Veta said, knowing it was now the last place she would set a post. "It will depend on the terrain."

"Yes," Bhasvod said. "That is understandable."

The Gammas returned with their gear, and without another word, Veta led them up the slope at an angle that suggested she was heading toward the nub Bhasvod had pointed out. The feathery shrubs resembled a cross between ferns and small trees, with exposed roots snaking across bare rock. Their fronds hung at head height for Veta, which made them shoulder height for everyone else. Beneath the canopy, thousands of thumb-sized fruits dangled at eye level, barely visible in the dim light and covered in vicious spines. She quickly learned to walk slightly stooped over so the things would glide off her helmet instead of swinging into her face.

Halfway up, Veta had the Gammas slowly drop their heads

beneath the canopy, then adjusted their angle of ascent so they would reach the crest of the ridge well beyond the nub that Bhasvod had picked out. But they were still being watched. Small yellow eyes began to peer out from the feathery boughs, and Veta caught the occasional glimpse of a tailless lizard hanging upside down, using tiny clawed hands to peel and eat the spiny fruit.

At the top, the fern-trees ended at a drop-off. It plunged a hundred meters down a cliff of flaked stone, similar to the one at the other end of the isthmus where the Phantoms had landed. In the bottom of the dale lay a string of long ponds resembling the pair behind them. Beyond the ponds rose a sloped ridge, and even farther out, Veta could make out the silver-limned line of another crest. It was too dark to tell how many more ridges lay past that one, but she had the impression that the pattern continued as far as the human eye could see.

They dropped their rucksacks in a line five meters below the ridge crest, then Veta began to point the Gammas to their positions.

"Mark, break out the laser targeter and locate that reconnaissance Pelican."

"Sounds like you have intel to share," Mark said.

"A lot. I'll fill you in after assignments. Ash, you take sky watch. Check with me before you report anything to Castor."

"Always," Ash said.

" 'Livi, check our back trail," Veta said. "Eliminate anyone following us. Bhasvod seemed awfully interested in where we'd be setting up."

"I wonder why," Olivia said. She knelt beside her rucksack and began to paint her face with camouflage grease. It was dark enough under the fern-trees that she wouldn't be easily noticed even without it—until her quarry turned a helmet or handlamp in her direction and caught a reflection off her forehead or cheeks. "Oh wait . . . I really *don't*."

"Right," Veta said. "They're going to hit us."

"Are we blown?" Ash asked.

"Not sure . . . but probably. They made this *way* too easy, and 'Gadogai keeps hinting to me that he knows we're not who we say we are."

"That doesn't sound right." Mark was sitting on the cliff top, hanging his legs over the edge and scanning the horizon for the Pelican. "Why tip his hand? The Silent Shadow is better than that."

"I had the same thought," Veta said. "He might actually want us to succeed. Maybe he'd even be willing to help."

"Or maybe not," Mark said. "He didn't sound real helpful in the Lich. We all heard what he said."

"He probably didn't realize we were undercover when he said that," Ash said. He was standing about two meters down from the ridge crest, his head above the shrub canopy as he looked for incoming Banished—and kept an eye on the handful of Covenant Banshees and Seraphs that remained to escort Bhasvod's Phantoms. "'Gadogai is a lot of things, but he's no zealot. Why would he want Castor to initiate the Great Journey?"

"He doesn't need to *want* it," Olivia said. "He just needs to not care if it happens."

Olivia was right, Veta realized. As far as she could tell, 'Gadogai was the ultimate mercenary. He cared about one thing: keeping himself alive. When her Ferret team put their targeting lasers on him on Reach, he had been threatened enough to defy Atriox. That would eat at him, make him feel weak and endangered, and he was not going to let a little thing like activating the Halo Array interfere with protecting himself.

"Then there's no reason he wouldn't have told Castor about his suspicions," Ash said. "So what are we doing up here on this ridge? Why wouldn't they have hit us down there, where we'd be out-numbered eight to one?"

"Because they don't want Aubert and Quenbi to see it," Veta said. She recounted the conversation between Castor and Bhasvod on the way to the Cartographer. "Castor is worried about how they would react to seeing fellow humans attacked—especially by Dhas Bhasvod's followers."

"That's one possibility," Mark said. "Here's the other—if 'Gadogai figured out who we *aren't*, then he probably has a good idea of who we *are*."

"Spartans?" Olivia asked.

"Maybe not that specific," Mark said. "But he'd definitely sus-pect we're Naval Intelligence. And he'd realize that besides being well-armed, we're well-trained and not likely to go quietly."

"So he has Castor send us out to set up an observation post," Veta said. "That way, nobody puts Quenbi and Aubert at risk when they try to take us out."

"Okay, but they don't have a large force," Ash said. "They'd want to protect everyone."

"Yeah, they would." Olivia glanced skyward. "There's no rea-son to risk a shoot-out when they can just shoot."

"So, strafing runs," Veta said.

"After plasma strikes," Mark said. "They still have Seraphs, the last I saw."

"Good point." Veta turned to Olivia. "If we let their spotters find us, we're cooked. Better finish your war paint after you're in position."

"It's fine." Olivia opened the flap of her rucksack to return the camouflage paint, then snapped, "Hey . . . you little thieves!"

A trio of tailless lizards raced out of her rucksack. Two carried nutrition bars, and one had an M6 magazine, and all three disappeared like lightning into the surrounding foliage. Olivia used her combat knife to probe around inside her bag to be sure there weren't any more, then sealed the flap and, leaving it behind, disappeared into the shadows.

"I have the recon Pelican in view," Mark said. "Ready to send."

"Good," Veta said. "Send this: 'Request ground strike 0231 against enemy force preparing to activate Halo; target two Covenant Phantoms, concealed, plus small escort Seraphs and Banshees, possibly airborne; coordinates 202.3701, radian 181.4. Acknowledge one flare received, two flares repeat. More.'"

Mark sent the message and, a moment later, said, "One flare."

"Send this," Veta said. "'Be aware final destination enemy force is citadel at 201.1875 degrees, radian 1.1. Must stop any cost. Acknowledge one flare received, two flares repeat. More.'"

Mark sent the message, then said, "One flare."

"Good." Veta took a deep breath, then asked, "How long will it take to kill Quenbi and Aubert?"

Mark did not lower the DMR, but Veta saw his shoulders square. "With recon and planning, call it a quarter hour," he said. "And Mom?"

Veta had given up trying to get the Gammas to stop using the nickname when they went undercover. That didn't mean she was fond of it. "Yes?"

"That's what I love about you," Mark said. "Nobody messes with your Ferrets."

"Just trying to save the galaxy, Mark." Veta paused. Her Gammas were now an hour overdue for the smoothers they didn't have—and had little prospect of acquiring them anytime soon. It tore her heart out to think of what the next twelve hours were going to be like for them . . . especially since she knew she would be doing well if they could limit it to just the next twelve hours. "But that too."

"Two flares," Mark said. "They're getting impatient."

"Send this: 'Cover blown. Request extraction this location first safe chance. End.'"

"One flare." Mark lowered the DMR, then slid back under the shrub canopy. "What next?"

"Grab our gear and help 'Livi take out the spotters."

Veta turned toward the rucksacks. All four lay open. A long chain of tailless lizards had queued up behind each one, and the little thieves were working like a bucket brigade, quietly passing nutrition bars and ammunition magazines into the darkness.

"Damn! Get out of here!" Mark waved his arms and stepped toward them, scattering the lines. "I hope they didn't get the grenades."

The voice of Dhas Bhasvod's lead Seraph pilot came over the battlenet. "The human Pelican is dropping flares in sets of one and two. These are likely signals."

"What else would they be, Ferko?" Dhas asked. He and Castor were standing at the top of his Phantom's boarding ramp, searching the ridge above for the spy and her brood. They had seen no sign of them in more than a quarter unit. "Have you detected any transmissions?"

"No transmissions, Prelate. But there was a targeting laser flashing from the ridgetop."

"At the human Pelican?" Dhas asked.

"In that direction, yes," Ferko said. His gravelly Jiralhanae voice seemed to fill the interior of Dhas's helmet. "But the range was extreme. I cannot be sure it was illuminating the Pelican."

"I can," Dhas said. "You are now empowered to strike."

"I have no visual, Prelate."

"And nothing from the spotters?"

"Not yet," Ferko said. "One has fallen silent, and the other is still searching."

"But you know where the targeting laser originated," Dhas said. "Strike there. If nothing else, you may flush the quarry."

"As you command . . . beginning run in two centals."

Dhas switched to his external voicemitter.

"The spy mother has taken the bait." He was looking at Castor, but speaking loudly enough so that the handful of adjutants standing behind them would also hear. "The Seraphs saw them using a blink code, and the Pelican dropped signal flares."

"Primitive," Arcas said. "And unreliable. Why would they not use a communications pad?"

"Because they are too cunning," Castor said. "They assume we would hear the transmission and understand we have spies."

"And because they have been living as Keepers for two years," 'Gadogai added. "What would have happened to them if an unauthorized communications device were discovered in their possession?"

"The same thing that I will enjoy watching now," Castor said. He turned to Dhas. "You have called for the plasma strike?"

"I have," Dhas said. "But we cannot be sure your spies will still be there. My pilots have no visual, and the spotters have not found them."

"That cannot be good."

It was Castor's lead pilot, a young Jiralhanae named Krelis, who said this. He stepped into the empty space between Castor and Dhas, intruding in a manner that would have earned a blow, were he Dhas's subordinate. At least he had the wisdom to stand facing the same direction as his betters, rather than insult Dhas by turning his back to him.

"Why would they choose now to disappear?" Krelis continued.

"Because 'Gadogai's plan *worked*," Castor said. His words were appropriately sharp, and the readout inside Dhas's helmet showed Krelis's face temperature spiking into the anger range. "They believe their mission accomplished, and now they hope to evacuate before the UNSC strikes."

"Is it wise to place so much faith in the plans of an infidel?" Krelis asked. " 'Gadogai has no devotion to the Great Journey."

Castor's voice assumed a cold edge. "He has devotion to me." He turned square to Krelis and spoke in a more measured manner, his forced restraint showing in the rounded peaks of the voiceprint audiograph scrolling across Dhas's visor. " 'Gadogai may be an infidel, but he is one sent by the gods. It will be *his* counsel that delivers us to the citadel."

"I pray it is so," Krelis said. The visor readouts grew sharp and extreme, indicating a lie. The last thing Krelis wanted was for it to be 'Gadogai's counsel that delivered the Keepers of the One Freedom to the citadel. "But hear me, Dokab. I am only saying there may be another reason the spy and her brood have disappeared."

Castor exhaled suddenly. "Speak."

"What if they saw through 'Gadogai's ploy?" Krelis asked. "Perhaps they did not think their mission was a success. Perhaps they disappeared because they already knew we were giving them false information and realized they had been discovered. There could be a UNSC attack coming at this very moment."

There was no such attack coming, or Dhas would be hearing about it from the high watch he had deployed before landing. But that did not mean Krelis's argument was entirely without merit—especially where 'Gadogai was concerned. The Silent Shadow had always been devoted to only one thing—its own power—and there was no reason to think that a warrior who had spent much of his life fighting for such an order would choose to devote himself to a Jiralhanae zealot.

A curtain of flame erupted along the ridgetop as the Seraphs made their attack run, spraying the crest with fiery plasma. Dhas's faceplate went white with heat-wash, and piercing thunderclaps echoed across the dale—slabs of stone shattering under the heat.

Dhas looked away from the blinding radiance and said, "I share the lead pilot's concern, about the spies' reasons for disappearing. But at the moment, their reasons are of no importance." He pointed his glaive at the wall of smoke rising from the fires atop the ridge. "Whether a UNSC attack is coming or not, we have just given the Banished our precise location—and we cannot let them catch us on the ground again."

He tipped his helmet toward Krelis, who understood immediately and said, "It is time to move on to the citadel?"

"Just so," Dhas said. "We have set our trap, and it is time to take advantage of it."

"Agreed." Castor glanced up the ridge, then said, "But I wish to see the bodies of the spy and her brood. She has been plaguing me for six years, and I will not feel rid of her until I stomp on her charred bones."

Dhas was spared the necessity of denying such a request when 'Gadogai pushed between Castor and Krelis.

"Dokab, that will never happen," he said. "If they were hit by the strike, they are nothing but ash. And if they were not—"

"They are now in hiding—I know." Castor let out a long breath, then started down the ramp to return to the Phantom he was commanding. "I did say it was a wish."

When Feodruz and Krelis started to follow, Dhas reached out and took Krelis by the elbow.

"I am interested in hearing more of your thoughts on the spies and their disappearance." He increased the volume of his voice-mitter and looked toward Castor. "I hope the *dokab* will permit his lead pilot to ride in my Phantom for a time."

Castor stopped at the base of the ramp and appeared to ponder the matter for a moment, as though Dhas had actually made a request, then tipped his helmet in acquiescence. "Feodruz can serve in his place."

"I thought as much," Dhas said. "You and I will speak during the flight."

"Yes," Castor said. He started toward his own Phantom again. "If we must."

Dhas watched until they were thirty meters away, then spoke to Krelis without looking away.

"Castor is a *dokab* of many surprises, quite astute for a Jiralhanae." He turned toward Krelis. "But he does have his blind spots, does he not?"

His visor showed Krelis's face temperature dropping swiftly, a sign of suspicion. "None that I have seen."

"Really." Dhas returned his gaze to Castor's back. "Then you believe he is correct to place so much trust in an infidel?"

"I would not say that," Krelis said. " 'Gadogai has a way about him. He can be . . . sly."

"Sly . . . yes, the Silent Shadow always are." Dhas slapped his glaive haft against his thigh, as though thinking, then faced Krelis again. "It might be wise to keep me informed about Castor's friendship with this infidel assassin . . . only because you may need my help protecting your *dokab* from him, of course."

The last place Mark-G313 wanted to be was crouching beneath the frond canopy, waiting for someone else to launch an attack. Especially when he was an hour overdue on his smoothers and just starting to feel jumpy. But he had to protect his team. A Kig-Yar fire-control spotter was creeping through the shadows about eight meters below, snapping at insects and kicking aside scores of little tailless lizards.

Mark needed to kill the spotter so he could poke his head above the fronds and resume overwatch—before the rest of the team was ready to assault the Phantoms. But he needed to do it quietly, because the little lizard guys had been pretty excitable since a plasma strike lit the top of their ridge on fire. Even the cough of a sound-suppressed M6 round would set them screeching again and give away his position.

So, *quiet* meant knifework. Which meant waiting until the Kig-Yar had crept far enough past that Mark could move without drawing attention to himself. Trouble was, the Kig-Yar really was creeping, probably because he recently had seen the body of the spotter that Olivia had already taken out, just before the Ferrets assembled to make their attack plan.

Mark hadn't actually seen said body, but there was plenty of Jiralhanae blood and fur on her armor, so it was simple math.

The Kig-Yar cocked his head as though listening to an order, then turned back toward the Phantoms . . . and found himself face-to-face with a lizard reaching down to pluck the comm disk off his face. He hissed in surprise, then snatched the would-be thief out of the air and squeezed.

The lizard let out a whistle so high-pitched that Mark barely registered it. The thicket immediately broke into a piping swarm of angry reptiles, all jumping through the feathery boughs or springing along the exposed roots to defend their colony mate. In a heartbeat, the Kig-Yar's limbs were massed with the small creatures—in a breath, his entire body. He flung aside the lifeless lizard in his hand and raced squawking into the shadows. A couple of seconds later, Mark heard the thud of a falling body and a long series of nightmarish screeches, then only silence.

That worked for him.

Mark pushed his head up through the canopy and resumed overwatch.

He had chosen a spot a hundred meters beyond the isthmus where the Phantoms had landed, at the base of the ridge and roughly fifty meters down the length of the pond. The position gave him a clear line of sight into the troop bays of both craft, but it meant he would be firing across the rest of the team's line of attack. That was less than optimum, but he saw no way to avoid it.

Mark raised his M395B DMR and used the Longshot sight to examine a trio of figures walking from the first Phantom to the second. 'Gadogai and two Jiralhanae, Castor and Feodruz, moving along at a brisk pace. The Phantoms would be buttoning up soon, and leaving a few moments later. He swung his sight to the first Phantom and saw Dhas Bhasvod and Krelis standing at the top of the ramp, just inside the hatchway.

Mark transmitted three quick comm clicks. Most of the Keepers would hear those clicks too. But even if they paid them any attention, they wouldn't know what they meant.

Go now.

There was no acknowledgment. Too many comm clicks, and the enemy would wonder what was going on.

Mark continued to watch the first Phantom. Krelis was looking in Castor's direction, but Bhasvod had turned his attention down the pond's shoreline. He was probably just looking toward the spot where his scout had died screeching. Mark had smeared his face with mud to cut the shine and laced fronds onto his helmet and DMR to camouflage his silhouette. Still, that could be a problem. The scout had been only twenty meters away when he fell, and Mark had no idea what kind of battlefield surveillance tools the San'Shyuum Prelate had in that fancy helmet.

Nothing to do for it. Ducking out of sight now would only draw Bhasvod's eye to movement. Mark wasn't going to leave his team uncovered when he had just given them the *Go* signal. They were his only family, and he was going to protect them.

Krelis and Bhasvod snapped their gazes toward the pond, surprised. Probably by the sound of sloshing water, then by the sight of Ash rising out of the pond and charging. Mark saw an M9 dual-purpose grenade fly past Krelis's shoulder and disappear into the troop bay. Then he looked away from the DMR sight so he could see the entire isthmus at once.

Castor and his companions had already disappeared into their Phantom. Olivia was racing up the boarding ramp, firing her MA40 with one hand and pulling her M6 sidearm with the other. An orange flash filled the troop bay as her grenade detonated inside, then she was in the bay as well, firing in both directions.

Ash was running up the ramp of Bhasvod's Phantom, pouring MA40 rounds through the hatchway. Krelis was kneeling to one side of the ramp, holding one hand to his injured ear and trying to draw his mangler with the other. Mark ignored him; either Ash would kill him or not, but the Jiralhanae was too blast-shocked to be a threat.

That was what grenades were for.

Olivia took a huge hairy backfist to the chest and came flying out of Castor's Phantom backward. She landed flat on her back at the base of the ramp, still facing the hatchway. She raised both weapons and opened fire, then did a handless kick-up and sprang to her feet, still firing. The M6 in her right hand was putting most of its rounds into the Phantom's hull instead of into the troop bay, but she seemed okay otherwise.

Ash reached the top of his ramp . . . only to have Dhas Bhasvod step into view from the aft direction, his glaive activated, sweeping a hard-light blade toward Ash's knees.

Mark switched back to his Longshot sight and put three full-metal-jacket rounds square into the Prelate's chest.

The armor-piercing bullets drove the San'Shyuum Prelate back into the Phantom and saved Ash's legs, but they did not pierce the alien's graphene fighting suit. Bhasvod was still on his feet when he spun out of view and the boarding ramp rose. Ash barely managed to avoid being hurled inside the Phantom by diving off to the side.

When Mark swung the DMR back to the other Phantom, he found Olivia caught with two empty magazines and the *dokab* himself starting down the ramp after her. Mark set his targeting reticle center mass—then saw Castor's shields flare as Veta rose out of the pond and emptied her M7 submachine gun into him.

Castor fell back into the bay, blood pouring from the seams in his armor at his shoulder and thigh, and hit the deck hard, and Mark's first round passed over the Keeper leader's head and sank into the deck. The second round ricocheted off the ramp as it rose into the hatchway, securing the Phantom for flight.

Mark transmitted a single comm click, followed by a double, but it was hardly necessary. His three teammates were already diving back into the pond, and nothing was going to get them now.

Because Mark would never let that happen. Not to his family.

ELEVEN

2221 hours, October 13, 2559 (military calendar)
UNSC Reconnaissance Pelican Romeo-008/
Refugia Epsilon 001 217.5 183.4, Epsilon Spire, the Ark

It was too early to feel relieved. Veta knew that. Only Olivia had reported taking out her target, Aubert, during the surprise attack on the Phantoms. Now Castor and Dhas Bhasvod were en route to the Weevil rendezvous with Quenbi, who had triggered the activation pylon on Reach, and they had every chance of reaching the citadel.

But as she watched the thirty-year-old Pelican maneuver into boarding position, that was still how she felt.

Relieved.

For two years, she and her Ferrets had lived a dangerous lie, waking every morning with the uneasy feeling their covers were about to be blown. Wondering if they had been followed to the dead drop the day before, or if their supply retrieval had been noticed. Worried that their nanobug eavesdropping devices and microdot surveillance cameras had been discovered during the night. Afraid Castor would finally bend to Escharum's pressure and order them killed in their sleep . . . And, recently, thinking that 'Gadogai would just grow tired of watching them and decide to end them himself.

Now, with the Pelican's long tail swinging over the plasma-blasted ridgetop and its loading ramp already dropping, all those worries were over. Their cover *was* blown, and about damn time. They could finally shed their Keeper personas, flush the zealot poison from their thoughts, and just be soldiers again.

The ramp clunked down on the still-smoking stone, the Pelican hovering above the ridge crest. A heavy-jawed man with a naval lieutenant's double bars sewn onto his single-piece flight suit appeared in the open hatchway. He carried an MA37 bullpup as dated as his outfit and wore a weathered pilot's helmet and faded torso armor. After making a visual sweep of the area, he finally fixed his gaze on the Ferrets and waved them aboard.

Veta led her team forward. Given their zealot hairstyles and blue Keeper armor, they'd tried to make themselves appear less threatening by already stowing their weapons in their rucksacks, and were extra careful to keep their hands in sight and avoid any sudden movements. The lieutenant seemed to appreciate the consideration and flashed an easy smile as they reached the top of the ramp.

"Welcome aboard," he said. "I'm John Cassidy."

"Nice to meet you, Lieutenant. You can call me Veta." A wave of exhilaration washed over her as she finally reclaimed her old name. She motioned to the Gammas. "This is Mark, Olivia, Ash."

Cassidy nodded and did not appear bothered by the abbreviated introductions. ONI agents provided their full names and ranks only under special circumstances, and a UNSC officer with any experience understood that such circumstances were better avoided. He waved his arm at the deck.

"Leave your gear here and have a seat," Cassidy said. It was a reasonable precaution, given that the reconnaissance crew had only Veta's word and a few timely messages to prove that the Ferrets were indeed ONI agents in need of support. "I'll have it taken forward to stow."

"No problem."

Veta gestured for the Gammas to obey, then dumped her rucksack and stepped into a three-meter section of the troop bay partitioned by a blackout curtain at the forward end. A small sanitation closet stood next to the fuselage wall on either side of the hatchway, and just forward of the closets sat a pair of stacked bunks.

Veta went starboard and took a seat on the lower bunk. She heard a boot scrape just beyond the curtain and realized there was probably a second crewman standing guard on the other side. Smart. She would have done the same thing, had she been picking up an undercover team with no way to verify their identities.

Olivia and Mark sat on the opposite bunk. With sunken eyes and contented smiles, they looked as exhausted and relieved as Veta. Once Ash had dropped his own rucksack and taken a seat next to Veta, Lieutenant Cassidy—presumably the relief pilot—spoke into his helmet microphone.

"Close it up."

The ramp rose into position, and the Pelican, a D77-TC/r, climbed away from the ridge. A female ensign with blond close-cropped hair pulled the blackout curtain aside, revealing another bullpup-armed crewman and a half bay crammed with equipment banks and two-dimensional displays. She came aft and grabbed two of the rucksacks, then Cassidy grabbed the other two and paused where Veta was sitting.

"The commander will have some questions for you." As Cassidy spoke, his eyes flitted forward to a middle-aged woman at the forward bulkhead. She was wearing a headset, her elbows propped on the console and her fingertips pressed to the sides of her head. "But she's on the rattle with the captain, trying to organize the party you requested."

"Then you're going to hit the rendezvous?" Veta asked.

"Above my pay grade, ma'am. All I know is they're talking about it. In the meantime, there are ration packs in the forward footlockers and hot water available in the starboard sanitary closet. Sorry it's not a shower, but there are sponges and deodorant."

He wrinkled his nose, leaving no room to doubt the not-so-subtle hint, then tipped his head toward a set of storage bins suspended from the overhead.

"We've made room for you in the starboard bins," he continued. "Be sure to secure your armor and clothes. You'll find clean flight suits and everything you need to freshen up in the aft footlockers."

"Thanks," Veta said. "And sorry for the smell—we've been living with Jiralhanae and Kig-Yar for two years."

Cassidy shook his head. "Wow. And I thought recon missions were hard duty."

"It's *all* hard duty," Veta said. "But we'll be sure to grab the sponges before using your bunks."

"Appreciate that, ma'am." He turned forward with the rucksacks. "Just pull the blackout curtain when you want some rack time. Someone will get you when the commander is ready."

Veta grabbed the first sponge bath, which turned out to be more lukewarm than hot. Still, it was bliss, and she felt as if she was scrubbing away the stench of the last two years. She emerged from the closet relaxed and happy. They were safe for the time being and had recruited the support they needed to stop the zealots. She hadn't forgotten the smoother problem—not for a moment. But all three Gammas were sheltered for now and almost certainly within a few hours of a military vessel equipped with an onboard pharmacy capable of compounding smoothers.

Veta returned to her seat on the bunk, scooted back until she could rest her shoulders against the fuselage wall, then closed her eyes to wait.

She woke all at once stretched out on the bunk, with no memory of having changed position. Her eyes were somewhat closed but now adjusting to a sudden brightness, and a female voice was speaking softly behind her.

". . . to wake you, ma'am. The commander thought you should see this."

Veta opened her eyes and found herself on her side, staring at the fuselage wall. The white glow of a reading lamp shined from the underside of the bunk above. Her boots were off, and there was a thermal blanket covering her body from feet to shoulders. Someone on board had been looking out for her.

"Ma'am?"

"Yes. I'm awake."

Veta pulled the blanket off and rolled over to find the rest of the compartment illuminated in green sleeping light. Olivia and Mark were stretched out in the bunks opposite her, and she could hear Ash breathing heavily above her. She and the entire team had all been asleep . . . at once. It had been a long time since they'd felt safe enough for that to happen.

She swung her feet around and found her boots tucked between the under-bunk lockers. As she put them on, she glanced up and saw the blond ensign who had helped Cassidy with their rucksacks. She looked a little old to be an ensign, with crow's-feet at the corners of her eyes and deep laugh lines around a wide mouth. That was probably from too much time in cryosleep, which could be fairly hard on human skin. But it did complement her dated flight suit.

Veta tipped her head toward the bunk. "Were you the one who took off my boots and stretched me out?"

"No, ma'am," she said quietly. The name tape above her pocket read HANSON. "All I did was switch on the sleeping lamp. Your whole crew was in the sack when Commander Barre sent me to check on you."

"You mean to get me. I was supposed to answer some questions."

"She said to let you sleep." Hanson flashed a smile. "I think she decided you wouldn't have gone out *that* fast if you were anything other than an undercover unit coming out of the field."

"Probably not. It *did* feel like having a Warthog lifted off my shoulders."

She turned off the reading lamp and silently followed Hanson into the equipment section of the bay. Cassidy, the relief pilot, was resting in a padded, post-mounted chair in front of a plotting console along the starboard wall. Two more ensigns worked at stations on the starboard side of the central equipment bank. Hanson directed Veta forward along a semi-empty aisle on the port side of the same bank.

When Veta reached Commander Barre's console at the forward bulkhead, she stopped and offered a salute, but avoided stating her name or rank as she presented herself. "You wanted me to see something, Commander?"

"Soon." Barre pointed Veta into an empty console chair across from her. There was a small hatch between them, presumably opening into the cockpit, but the distance still felt intimate. She smiled and asked, "Sleep well?"

"Better than I have in years," Veta said. "Literally. Thanks for not waking me."

"I wish I could have let you sleep longer," Barre said. She was a striking woman about ten years older than Veta, with a complexion darker than Olivia's, gray-flecked hair clipped almost to the scalp, and enthralling green eyes. "But the Vultures are preparing for their attack run, and there *are* a couple of details we need to clear up before they begin."

"I'll answer whatever I can," Veta said. The forward compartment was so cramped that Barre's crew would hear every word exchanged, even if they were trying not to listen. "There may be clearance issues—"

"There always are with ONI," Barre said. "But we're not in their yard out here. If you want our support, you need to take the circumstances into account."

Veta thought for a moment, then nodded. "Understood." It wasn't like ONI still existed—at least not as an agency capable of disciplining Veta for making a snap decision in the field. "I'll tell you what you need to know."

"I'm glad we understand each other," Barre said. "First of all, who the hell *are* you? Beyond your names, I mean. All we really know is that, up until now, you've been flashing us some very alarming messages."

"Ferret Team One," Veta said.

"Ferret Team . . . ?"

"A special-action unit. Put together by Admiral Osman, to whom we report directly."

"And this Admiral Osman, who is he?"

"Um . . . *she* replaced Admiral Parangosky as CINCONI." Veta was so taken aback by the question that she half wondered whether she needed to explain the acronym for commander in chief of the Office of Naval Intelligence. "How long exactly have you been here on the Ark?"

"Let's talk about that after I know more about who *you* are, okay?"

"Fair enough. I've been an ONI officer since 2553, when Admiral Osman recruited me to shape three Spartans into—"

"Cassidy!" Barre suddenly barked, looking toward him. "Why didn't you tell me they were Spartans?"

"*What?*" Cassidy popped out of his chair and cast a doubtful look toward the curtain. "Because they *aren't?*"

"He's right, ma'am," Hanson said. "They're way too small. Only one of them is even taller than two meters."

Barre swiveled in her chair, looking down the starboard aisle toward the two ensigns whom Veta hadn't been introduced to.

"Ngonga!" Barre called. "Prepare a burst transmission. Possible infiltrators—"

"Hold on!" Veta's voice was sharp, but she was careful not to rise or make any sudden moves toward Barre. "You *have* been on the Ark for a while. They're Spartan-IIIs."

"Spartan-IIIs?" Barre repeated.

"The following generation," Veta said. "War-orphan volunteers. Recruitment standards not as high, semi-powered infiltration armor instead of Mjolnir, still augmented but a lot cheaper and more expendable. NAVSPECWAR used to send them out by the hundreds."

The alarm in Barre's face changed to disbelief. "*Hundreds* of Spartans? On one mission? You can't be serious."

"I am." Veta had learned a lot about the early days of the SPARTAN-III program, and some of it made her want to take the Uniform Code of Military Justice into her own hands. "They were just kids, and they would try anything. A lot of times, they had no chance of coming back."

"I see." Barre swallowed in a way that suggested she knew exactly what Veta was saying, and her gaze drifted aft again. "And the operatives on your team . . ."

"Survived because they were deployed toward the end of the war." Veta leaned toward Barre. "You *do* know we won the war, right? About seven years ago?"

"Yes, we do know," Barre said. "And some of the Banished humans we've taken during battles have been very quick to inform us that the war is over, probably hoping we'll treat them better than the Banished do their prisoners. To be honest, I'm not sure whether to call them prisoners or defectors. Sometimes it seemed like they *wanted* to be captured."

"Call them whatever you like," Veta said. "Just don't trust them."

"Sound advice. Unfortunately, it also applies to you. You tell a compelling story, but all I really *know* about you—other than what you're telling me—is that you emerged from a slipspace portal in a Banished Lich yesterday and have been in the company of the Covenant ever since. That certainly suggests something unusual is underway, but it's rather hard to prove the rest of your story, don't you think?"

"Not that hard," Veta said. "I could just have one of my Ferrets bend a rifle barrel for you."

"They can actually *do* that?"

"Sure. Pick any one of them."

"Commander, permission to interrupt?" The request came from a square-faced ensign with a tilaka symbol between his dark eyebrows. "It may not be necessary to sacrifice one of our rifles."

"Go ahead, Mahajan," Barre said. "I'm listening."

"Ma'am, you remember that I volunteered to look through their equipment when it was brought aboard?"

"I do. What did you find?"

"You went through our things?" Veta said.

"What did you expect?" Barre retorted. "Sorry, Mahajan—continue."

"Well, it's what I *didn't* find that is important," Mahajan said. "I was curious about the signaling device they had used to attract our attention. There wasn't one. They used a rifle-mounted laser targeter."

"At sixty-three kilometers?!" Barre exclaimed. "Is that even *possible?*"

"The beam divergence worked in their favor." It was the third ensign, Ngonga, who said this. He had a stocky body and a round face with epicanthic folds at the corners of his eyes. "It guaranteed they were painting the whole Pelican, which meant it was lighting up our entire EM intercept array."

" 'Lighting up' might be an exaggeration, though," Mahajan noted. "Had we not been a reconnaissance craft with sensitive equipment, the beam would probably have been too faint to detect. But that only amplifies the difficulty of what they did during the first contact."

"Which is precisely what?" Barre asked.

"We were in random sweep pattern," Mahajan said. "And one of them used a Longshot sight to track us long enough to send a message. I doubt that's something a normal person could do. They *must* be augmented."

Barre pressed her lips together briefly, then nodded to Veta. "Okay then. I suppose I can trust that you are who you claim to be . . . but I *will* miss seeing someone bend a rifle barrel." She swiveled back toward the ensigns. "Hanson, how long before the Vultures arrive?"

"They're inserting now," she reported. "They should be on-station any minute."

"Thank you, Ensign."

Barre unlocked her seat-tilt and leaned back in her chair, looking up at a large display mounted at an angle on the bulkhead above them. The flower-shaped schematic of the Ark appeared on the screen, then quickly zoomed into a wedge-shaped section of the core, between the Epsilon Spire and the central void where the resource moon was located. A trio of curved lines appeared, arcing down toward a chain of mountains on the right-hand edge of the image.

After a couple of minutes, the lines began to descend more slowly—the Vultures decelerating hard. Veta thought for a moment they intended to cross the mountains and start toward the Pelican's position, but the line tips passed out of sight behind the mountain peaks.

"Insertion successful," Hanson reported.

The schematic was replaced by an infrared image, which depicted the billowing yellow canopy of a vast jungle basin, laced by the cool green ribbons of hundreds of serpentine rivers. At the top of the display hung a ragged blue band—presumably the mountains that the Vultures had dropped behind.

"Anybody have anything?" Barre asked.

"Negative infrared, negative magnetic anomalies, negative tritium radiation," Mahajan reported. "Negative active sensors. I don't think we need to go active, ma'am. They're not reacting."

"Ngonga?"

"Negative transmissions, negative electromagnetic emissions," Ngonga said. "I concur."

"Hanson?"

"Negative gravitics," Hanson replied. "I think it worked. They're staying put."

"Copy that," Barre said. "Ngonga, bounce one click."

"One click away, ma'am."

A moment later, three slivers of red crossed the blue band of mountains and began to descend toward the bottom of the display, fanning out as they moved.

Barre sat up straight again and swiveled to face Veta. "We've confirmed a small cluster of craft hiding on the surface at the rendezvous coordinates you provided," she said. "We assume it's the Covenant Phantoms and their escorts waiting for the support they called forward. The captain thought if we made a show of poking around as we arrived, the Covies might grow worried about giving themselves away and go to comm silence. His plan seems to have worked. With a little bit of luck, your old buddies will believe it's their Weevils approaching."

Veta checked the chronometer on the display, then said, "They would be a little bit early."

"A chance we had to take. If we can catch the Phantoms on the ground, the Weevils won't matter."

Veta couldn't help feeling that Castor was too sharp to fall for the ploy, but every indication so far suggested the opposite. Maybe that magazine of M7 rounds she had put into him had done more damage than she thought.

"It seems reasonable," she said. "What about a backup plan? Do the Vultures have air support standing by?"

"Not yet," Barre said. "You didn't give us much notice. It was all the captain could do to get three Vultures here in time."

The image on the display zoomed in, with the red slivers of the Vultures staying near the top of the image and growing a little larger. At the bottom of the screen, a circle of ten pale orange dots sat waiting for their arrival. Veta didn't know how many craft Dhas Bhasvod had left—it could easily have been ten, given the escorts. But she was surprised to see that all the dots were approximately the same size. She would have thought that the difference between a Banshee's heat signature and that of a Seraph would be more noticeable.

"It'll take the Vultures about five minutes to close," Barre said. "And we'll have a live image on the display, if you think your Spartans would like to watch their hard work come to fruition."

"I think they would," Veta said. And if something went wrong, it wouldn't hurt to be fully awake either. "Thank you."

She went aft and activated the compartment's standard lamp. "Rise and shine, Ferrets. We have some entertainment coming."

It was a sight Veta would never get used to. The Gammas were instantly awake and rolling out of bed, grabbing for their boots. Olivia was rotating her shoulders and moving a little slow, definitely sore after taking a backfist from Castor. Ash and Mark looked almost too refreshed for a three-hour nap, and Mark had a wary glimmer in his eye that Veta recognized all too well.

He was always the first to start.

"Everyone okay?" she asked.

"Good to go," Ash said, standing.

"I will be." Olivia spread her arms wide, stretching her torso. "Just need to work some of the extra blood out of these bruises."

Mark concentrated on closing his boot fasteners.

"Mark?" Veta asked.

"Sure." He did not look up as he spoke. "Why wouldn't I be?"

"Because we're out of smoothers, dope." Olivia reached down and pinched his ear. "Be nice. Don't make me rip this off."

Mark snorted and looked up, smiling. "Okay, 'Livi." He met Veta's gaze. "Sorry, Mom."

"Don't worry about it," Veta said. She pointed forward. "Three Vultures are about to make a run on the rendezvous point. Commander Barre thought you might want to watch."

Mark nodded and pushed through the curtain. "Yeah. You bet."

Ash and Olivia hung back, looking a bit uncomfortable.

"What is it?" Veta quietly asked. "Is Mark—"

"No, he's still okay. At least for a while," Ash said. "It just . . . I don't know. Feels a little strange?"

"Watching them die?" Olivia asked. "Yeah, kinda weird, I'll admit."

Veta frowned, wondering if this was some new manifestation of smoother deprivation she had never seen before.

Then it dawned on her.

"Wait a second. You mean the *Keepers*?"

"Yeah. I know it *is* weird," Ash said. "But after living with them so long . . . it sort of feels like a betrayal."

"Well . . . that *was* the assignment—betray them," Veta said. "And weaken them. We've been doing it all along. In the first year alone, we were probably responsible for the deaths of about fifteen thousand Keepers."

"Yeah, I get it," Olivia said. "It had to be done, and the galaxy is better off. Still . . . I'm with Ash on this. It hurts."

Veta was completely taken aback, considering that she didn't feel any hint of the remorse that seemed to be troubling both Ash and Olivia.

Then again, the Ferrets had once upon a time pulled her leg, leading her on about hearing voices and reading thoughts when Veta first learned about their smoother requirements.

"Wait . . . are you joking with me?"

Olivia rolled her eyes. "Yeah, Mom. Having a conscience is real funny."

"A *conscience*? Castor is trying to activate the Halo Array. He nearly killed *you*—he would have loved stomping on your bones."

"Well, I *did* kind of deserve it," Olivia said. "I mean, if you look at it from Castor's point of view."

"Because of Aubert?" An alarming thought occurred to Veta, and she blurted, "You did *kill* him, right?"

"A 12.7 to the face and two to the chest. He's dead, trust me."

In the face. Aubert had been looking right *at* Olivia when she killed him. His brow had probably been furrowed in confusion, his mouth hanging open in shock, unable to believe the nice young woman who had been so sweet to him for the past two years was suddenly pointing a weapon at him. He had probably looked more hurt than afraid . . . and then Olivia had pulled the trigger.

The Gammas had killed hundreds in the last seven years, sometimes from afar and sometimes close up, and some occasionally with their bare hands. But they'd never killed someone who considered them a friend. That had to be confusing for soldiers trained to be part of a team, and no lecture from an ONI psychologist about the importance of isolating emotionally from one's targets was going to overrule an instinct drilled into the Gammas since childhood.

It was a weight they would have to learn to carry.

Like the weight Veta would soon be carrying if she couldn't secure the smoothers they already needed.

She blew out a long breath and said, "I get it. You don't want to enjoy it."

"Close enough," Ash said. "No regrets, though. We did what we had to."

"Okay then—you two can stay back here," Veta said. "But *I* need to see this."

"No argument," Ash said. "Somebody needs to confirm the job got done."

Veta slipped through the blackout curtain and started forward to join Mark and Commander Barre beneath the overhead display. The infrared image zoomed in, and the ten orange craft at the bottom of the screen grew as large and round as eyeballs. The three Vultures approaching from the top were slightly bigger, longer, and a deeper orange, with crimson blossoms where their jet-powered flight fans were located. The jungle between them had resolved itself into a tangle of lush islands surrounded by broad green channels of still water.

"Those targets don't look like Phantoms and Banshees," Veta said. "They look like Seraphs."

"The Covies don't have Seraphs?" Barre asked.

"Not that many," Veta said. "Not *with* them, anyway."

The targets began to deepen to a darker, hotter orange.

"Damn it." Barre touched a tab on her console and leaned toward a built-in microphone. "Nightflight, you're spotted. Lay suppression fire."

Three long red darts—no doubt Phoenix missiles—were already streaking away from the Vultures as Barre uttered *suppression*. By the time she reached *fire*, they had been joined by the red needles of eighteen Argent V missiles.

The targets vanished beneath a red shroud of heat. For a moment, Veta thought the attack had destroyed all ten Seraphs . . . until a trio of red disks separated from the boiling cloud and turned toward the approaching Vultures.

They had not even brought their weapons to bear before a second volley of Argents streaked out to intercept them. The first two

Seraphs vanished inside crimson blossoms. The third turned inside the approaching missiles and climbed away, streaking from the combat zone with an acceleration the Vultures could not match. The middle gunship loosed a third volley of Argents, but the Seraph was already a red dot vanishing off the left side of the screen, and Veta didn't see what became of it.

The Vultures continued toward the island the targets had risen from, the tips of their autocannons glowing ruby red as they began to mow down the jungle flora.

"*That* didn't look right," Mark said.

"No, it didn't," Veta said. "Castor may have played us."

"You think?"

Veta shot him a sideways glance, then said, "Go back to the bunks and tell everyone to armor up."

After Mark had acknowledged the order and turned to obey, Barre asked, "Played *how*?"

"I'm not sure yet," Veta said. "Maybe I'm wrong."

"I think you need to spell that out for me."

"There should have been two Phantoms and a bunch of Banshees waiting there . . . not ten Seraphs," Veta said. As she spoke, the Vultures moved over the island and began to release sprays of Anvil-IV air-to-surface missiles. "Dhas Bhasvod only had *three* Seraphs when he linked up with Castor—"

"Dhas Bhasvod . . . ?" Barre interrupted. "You need to explain. And who the hell Castor is too, while we're on the subject."

"Right," Veta said. They obviously hadn't done a full debriefing yet. "Dhas Bhasvod is a San'Shyuum Prelate—"

"Whoa, whoa, whoa. *San'Shyuum*?" Barre asked, her eyes wide.

"San'Shyuum Prelate," Veta confirmed. "He leads the Covenant contingent."

"Then he's *real*," Barre said in astonishment. "The Banished defectors have been going on about some kind of San'Shyuum warrior who's been stalking them recently. They make him sound like some kind of werewolf or *gbahali* or something."

"Sounds like our guy. He linked up with Castor only yesterday, after we came through the portal." Veta could hardly believe it had only been hours ago. "Castor is the Jiralhanae *dokab* who leads the Keepers of the One Freedom. He and Dhas Bhasvod, the San'Shyuum Prelate, have joined forces to activate Halo."

"Is it important that I know who the Keepers of the One Freedom are?"

"Not at the moment. They're zealot sympathizers who joined forces with the Covenant remnant stuck here on the Ark."

"Remnant. Huh," said Barre. "At some point, I'd like to know how all of this squares with the war being over."

"We can talk. Right now, though, the point is that their joint operation didn't *have* ten Seraphs with it."

"Then who did our Vultures just destroy?"

"Good question. We're going to need to inspect that strike zone."

Barre thought for a moment, then said, "Okay then. Let's do this."

The Pelican dropped its ramp five minutes later, after the Vultures had finished leveling every square meter of jungle on the island. Mark and Olivia led the way. The Ark's sun had long ago grown dim, so each wore a light-gathering night-vision device borrowed from the pilots. Veta and Commander Barre came next, both carrying M7 submachine guns. Ash and Cassidy, the relief pilot, brought up the rear.

The fires had already died away, drowned as soon as the burning foliage hit the soggy ground. The air smelled of swamp and wet ash, and there was water everywhere, sloshing up through the crater-shaped pools covered in shredded foliage. When Veta stepped off the ramp, her boot sank to the ankle in a spongy mat of roots and humus.

"The island is floating," she said.

"At least it's floating on water," Cassidy remarked. "I've seen stranger stuff in this place."

"Let's make it quick," Barre said. She activated a handlamp and swung it to the right. "The wreckage should be right over there."

Mark and Olivia turned in the direction she indicated and spread out, searching the darkness ahead for threats. It was probably unnecessary. The edge of the island lay only fifty meters distant, and everything between it and the Pelican had been leveled by the Vultures. Whether the foliage had been trees, club mosses, or something else was impossible to know. All that remained of it now were charred bits of leaves and stalks.

The detritus was so thick that Mark stepped into a hidden crater pool and barely managed to keep his combat load from pulling him under before Olivia plucked him out. A moment later Barre did the same thing, and Veta ended up on her belly at the edge of the water, holding the commander by the collar until Ash arrived to pull her to safety. After that, they learned to watch the terrain ahead for a wave motion, generated by their weight as they approached open water. Halfway to the edge of the island, it grew difficult to continue because there was more open water than intact root mat.

Veta used her handlamp to sweep the area without advancing, but there was little sign that a talon of Seraphs had ever been there.

The craft had simply sunk the instant a missile blew a hole through the root mat.

"I don't know," Ash said. "There may not be anything left *to* find."

"Unless we're willing to dive for it," Cassidy said. "Does it really make a difference who got blasted? If they arrived in Seraphs, they were the enemy, full stop."

"It actually does make a difference," Veta said. "If they're Covenant Seraphs, we can assume Dhas Bhasvod called them forward and is still coming to meet them. He just hasn't arrived yet, and we're ahead of their operation."

"What if they're *Banished* Seraphs, though?" Barre asked. "Then we're behind it?"

"Yeah. And that's not even the worst of it." Veta began to undo her armor and motioned for the others to do the same. "Pair up, one Spartan per team, and spread out. We need to know who the hell we hit."

They cached their armor and worked their way forward, traveling along a precarious maze of half-submerged vegetation mats. It was like walking on a floating sponge, only the holes were concealed by floating blankets of shredded leaves. They were searching for an iron anvil that somehow hadn't sunk already.

Mark and Olivia used their light-gathering NVDs to search for any scrap of metal or fabric that might tell them who the Vultures had destroyed. Everyone else swept their lamps across the surface.

After a few minutes, Veta and Mark reached the island's edge, where a band of dark water separated them from a towering wall of arum plants. The channel was only fifteen meters wide, narrow enough that Veta thought a piece of hull or armor might have been hurled across by an explosion. But when she swept her lamp over the foliage, all she saw were hundreds of oval eyes reflecting the light.

The usual Ark.

As soon as she turned around, Mark was beside her, staring at something inland that Veta could not see—at least not without night-vision equipment.

"What are you looking at?"

"Not sure," Mark said. "Hand me your handlamp."

Veta passed it over, and he shined it on a spot about a meter beyond the far edge of a nearby crater pool—or at least that was what it looked like, given its undulating surface.

"Keep the beam there," Mark said. "I'll try to work my way over."

He began to move along the edge of the island, slinking around the crater pool. A soft chittering arose on the other side of the channel and grew louder. Veta paid no attention to it and kept the beam focused on the spot Mark had indicated, then activated her headset microphone.

"Mark may have something," she said. "Anyone else?"

"Negative," Olivia reported.

She was with Barre, about thirty meters distant, judging by the light of the commander's handlamp.

"We have Jiralhanae parts," Ash reported. "In the middle of a crater pool—no armor, just an arm, a foot, what looks like a thigh, and a bunch of fur. I was just about to go in after it."

"Wait one," Veta ordered. Mark had just stepped into the beam of her handlamp and was squatting down to retrieve something. "Let's see what Mark has here."

"A piece of hull armor," Mark reported. "It's Banished."

"That's all we need to know," Veta said. "Let's meet back at the armor cache, then return to the Pelican."

"So, we've been played?" Barre asked. "By this Castor?"

"Yeah. And we're not the only ones," Veta said. She rose and began to pick her way over the maze of hidden bridges. "That message I intercepted? The one with the rendezvous coordinates?"

"You are going to tell me it wasn't an intercept," Barre said. "It was a plant."

"Damn right. And they made sure the Banished intercepted it too," Veta said. "I should have seen this coming. The Banished have been on Castor's six since this whole thing started, and he used *us* to eliminate them."

"Well, not really 'eliminate,'" Ash said, still over the comm. "The only thing the Banished lost were these Seraphs."

Veta reached the armor cache and began to strap on her leg grieves.

"I'm not sure I understand," Barre said. "Ash, are you saying some of the Banished escaped?"

"Or were never here," Veta said. "The force tailing Castor and Dhas Bhasvod was primarily Banshees. This couldn't have been the same group."

Mark arrived, frowned, and began to put on his armor.

"So what do we think the situation is now?" Barre asked. "The Covies bypassed this rendezvous, and now they are on their way to the citadel?"

"That's exactly what the situation is." Veta glanced at the ground and shook her head, angry at how thoroughly Castor had played her—and the Banished. He had deceived them too, but their Seraphs had been destroyed by the UNSC, and they would be thirsty for vengeance. "How soon can we reach the citadel from here?"

"Were those the second set of coordinates you sent us?" Barre asked. "We'd need at least two hours, but that's at Mach 4. Our surveillance equipment would take a beating."

Not fast enough. Castor and Bhasvod would already be there by then . . . and probably inside. "Is that the best we can do?"

"In a slash-*r* Pelican, yes," Barre said. "We can go high and supersonic, but we're not shielded for any trajectory that requires a hot reinsertion."

"How about the Vultures?" Veta asked.

"What good would that do?" Cassidy asked, arriving with Ash. "The Vultures are bingo missiles, and don't even think about asking what else might be in range. We're too far out for ready support."

"Can your captain launch another mission?"

"I'll put in the request," Barre said. "But you know the drill. Even if the captain believes me, it'll take a few hours to put a mission together. Especially one big enough to get the job done."

"I was afraid of that." Veta turned toward the Pelican. "We need to get airborne."

"Whatever you say." Barre fell in at her side. "But if you think we're going to stop them in a Pelican—"

"Not *us*," Veta said. "We're calling for help."

"What does—"

Barre was interrupted by a whoop of surprise. Veta swung her handlamp around in time to see Ash land on his face and start to slide backward toward a crater pool behind him. He twisted around, trying to bring his MA40 to bear on a fat gray tentacle that had wrapped itself around both his ankles.

Mark and Olivia rushed back to help, but Cassidy was already there, aiming his shotgun half a meter past Ash's boots and blasting the tentacle apart.

Ash sat up and kicked his feet free from the severed appendage. "Thanks." He turned to look up at Cassidy. "That was—"

A huge cone-shaped head with cloudy eyes burst from the water and turned sideways, grabbing the relief pilot in a tooth-lined maw that could have swallowed a Sangheili whole.

All three Gammas opened fire on the thing just above the waterline, ringing its neck in lead. The rounds disappeared into its dark flesh, and the creature quickly slid back below the water, pulling the screaming pilot along with it.

Veta and Barre arrived an instant later, Barre shrieking, "John, *John*!" and pulling back the charging handle on her submachine gun.

Veta charged her own weapon and shined her handlamp on the crater pool, but there was nothing there to fire at—just a steady stream of bloody bubbles pushing up through the detritus. She pulled Barre away from the edge and motioned for the others to back away as well.

The display of bubbles ceased. A booted foot bobbed to the surface on one side of the pool, and on the other, a severed forearm, bitten off at the elbow. Barre emptied her magazine into the water, then backed away and started toward the Pelican.

"This damned place." She shook her head in dismay. "This damned, godforsaken place."

TWELVE

Pavium had a crick in his neck from staring up through the viewport, but he could not take his eyes off the winged shapes overhead. Thousands of Banshee-sized beasts were whirling through a narrow wedge of moonlit sky, all with large ovoid bodies and long funnel-shaped noses that resembled sensor dishes on prehensile stalks. The creatures were supported by slightly swept, undersized wings, which, in the silvery night sky, made them look a lot like aircraft. Among them were six actual Banshees, distinguishable from the rest of the mass primarily because they were so fast and spitting plasma bolts at one another. Of those, only two were Long Shield craft defending Pavium's own command Phantom.

It had been less than a day since his brother Voridus had discovered the message capsule warning of Castor's intention to activate the Halo rings, and already the *dokab* and his Covenant allies appeared close to reaching a citadel, where they would find the supraluminal communication control station required to succeed in their quest. In his resolve to stop them, Pavium had foolishly pursued them into a labyrinth of rift valleys lined by sheer, moss-draped cliffs.

The first ambush had come barely a kilometer into the verdant maze, a trio of Covenant Banshees diving down out of the night. Pavium had lost two of his own Banshees without destroying any of his enemy's. Moments later, the flying creatures had appeared, floating out from the mouths of caves concealed behind the curtains of hanging moss. Their undersized wings did not seem to support so much as steer them—sometimes into the path of an oncoming craft. That had been continuing for more than two hours now, and Pavium had every reason to believe that Thalazan's Seraph talon had also been lost to the Covenant "Weevil rendezvous" ploy that Pavium had used to eliminate his rival.

One of the winged figures burst into an orange ball and plunged into the valley, a tail of blue flame trailing after it. Definitely a Banshee. The cave creatures simply exploded and rained gore when hit.

"Another Banshee," Pavium announced. He had taken the copilot's seat when he realized how badly he had been tricked, though it had done little good. Castor and his allies had chosen their terrain well. Whenever Pavium tried to climb out of the trap, a trio of Covenant Seraphs swooped in to force his Phantom back into the valley. "Ours or theirs?"

Voridus grunted in disgust. "Ours." He was at his customary station, in the operations officer's seat behind the copilot. "Next time, will you listen when I tell you something seems too easy?"

"Assuming there *is* a next time."

Following the Covenant Phantoms into the network of rift valleys had clearly been a mistake, but Pavium did not know what else he could have done. They were close enough to the Ark's core that it been natural to assume the quarry was making an approach to the citadel, and it would have been folly to take the chance that they were only trying to lose him. With the Long Shields' numerical advantage in fighter craft, it had not even crossed his mind that the enemy was trying to draw him into a battle.

Another winged shape burst into a fireball and plunged into the valley, then another. Could it be that the last Long Shield Banshee was evening the odds? Or had Pavium lost his last Banshee?

"Two more," Pavium announced. "Theirs?"

When Voridus did not answer, Pavium twisted around in his seat and looked back at the operations station. His brother was staring at the console, his fingertips pressed to his comm disk's receiver.

"*Theirs?*" Pavium repeated.

Voridus raised a finger, motioning Pavium to wait.

"Not *both*." It was the pilot, Mazentus, who said this. The Phantom shot forward, accelerating so hard that Pavium nearly tumbled over the back of his seat. "I need your eyes, Warlord. We have three Banshees diving into the rift. If one of them gets in front of us—"

"I understand."

Pavium twisted back around and craned his sore neck skyward. He saw three Banshees silhouetted against the silvery night, their bright efflux trails hooking forward as they tried to match velocities with the Long Shield Phantom. The lead trail was hooking more sharply than its companions, with that Banshee attempting to get in front of the trio's quarry.

"Faster," Pavium said. "It is as you feared."

He was nearly pitched into the pilot's lap as the Phantom rolled up on its side, banking around a bend in the valley.

"Apologies," Mazentus said. "It is either risk hitting a cliff or be downed by Covenant Seraphs."

"Risk the Seraphs," Voridus said.

Mazentus actually looked away from the viewport display. "Are you *mad*? We will never outrun them in a Phantom, and we cannot outmaneuver them."

"We will not need to," Voridus said. "Thalazan viewed the battle from a high patrol, and he is already in a power dive."

"He *survived* the"—Pavium caught himself just in time to avoid saying *ambush*—"rendezvous?"

"Either that," Voridus said, "or someone who sounds like him is transmitting from his Seraph."

"And he is coming to our aid?" Pavium could not help being suspicious. Thalazan was his primary rival. To become the new warlord of the Long Shields, all Thalazan need do was let the Covenant kill the current warlord. Not a palatable arrangement. "How can we trust that?"

"The Weevil rendezvous was an ambush." Voridus could not quite hide his delight. "Thalazan lost his entire talon and begs your forgiveness."

At least *something* had gone as Pavium had planned. With Thalazan's talon destroyed, the Seraph chief no longer had the strength to take leadership of the Long Shields. And if Thalazan returned from a mission as the sole survivor, he would be considered a cowardly pariah and cast from the clan. Saving Pavium was Thalazan's only true option.

"Inform Thalazan that if he frees us from this inconvenience, he shall have my forgiveness *and* my gratitude." Pavium saw the lead Banshee's efflux trail stretching ahead of the Phantom, and then was suddenly thrown against the side of the viewport as they rounded another bend in the rift. "But tell him to hurry."

Voridus relayed the message, then grunted in surprise.

Pavium waited for his brother to elaborate, then finally grew frustrated with the delay.

"Well? There is more, Voridus?"

"Only a UNSC ploy," Voridus replied. "It is nothing you should concern yourself with."

"And yet, I *am* concerned," Pavium said. "Tell me about this ploy."

"Thalazan intercepted a UNSC message. It requested support stopping the zealots before they enter the citadel."

"Why is that a ploy?"

"Because it was sent in the clear," Voridus said. "And it gave the coordinates of the citadel entrance."

"*What?!*" Pavium bellowed. "And you thought not to tell me this?"

"It was sent to their ship *Spirit of Fire*," Voridus said. "In the clear. Unencrypted."

"So . . . we were *meant* to hear it?"

"Is that not obvious?" Voridus said. "The humans are trying to lure us into a trap, just as the Covenant did."

"Or . . . or they are signaling that they cannot get there," Pavium said. "That if we do not stop Castor's madness, no one will."

"Or, attempting to allow *us* to do the dangerous work," Voridus said. "You know what sly cowards humans can be."

A Covenant Banshee appeared in the valley ahead and began to spew plasma at them, head-on. With Covenant Seraphs still overhead, it was a classic box play, giving Pavium's Phantom no place to escape except into the ground. Voridus turned his attention to the operations console and returned fire with the Phantom's heavy plasma cannon. One lucky hit would be enough to eliminate the Banshee and give them a single hope of escape—a false one, because their pursuers would continue to push them up the valley at ever faster speeds, forcing Mazentus to test the maneuverability of the clumsy Phantom until at last he exceeded its limits and vaporized them against the valley wall.

"Pull up!" Pavium ordered. "No one flies a Seraph like Thalazan, but he will need room to maneuver."

Mazentus did not need to be told twice. The Phantom's nose rose, and Pavium saw the ovoid body of one of the winged creatures silhouetted in the silvery night above. It looked like an airborne blovi, with four clawed feet, a long proboscis flaring into a dish-shaped snout, and oval eyes opened wide in panic. It flapped its seemingly useless wings wildly, trying to get out of the way. Then a plasma bolt lanced from the dropship, and the creature was nearly vaporized.

The Phantom emerged from the fireball, some dark spatter on its viewport, and was out of the valley in a heartbeat. A trio of efflux trails circled overhead, their tips bending inward as they pushed the dark disks of three Covenant Seraphs into power dives. Far above them, a single blue line was stretching downward—Thalazan's Seraph dropping in behind them.

The Covenant pilots had to see Thalazan on their tactical displays, but they would also know he was coming too fast to intercept. Better to dive on the Phantom they were targeting and put it down before the Seraph arrived, then scatter and force it to meet them one at a time.

But Thalazan did not play by the usual rules, and Mazentus knew it. As soon as he saw the trio of Seraphs tightening their formation for a three-on-one attack, with Thalazan diving in behind them, Mazentus dropped the Phantom's nose and descended to get out of harm's way.

Pavium craned his neck to look out the top of the viewport again. The blue-white cone of a plasma charge was expanding behind the three Covenant Seraphs, dropping down on them like the wrath of the gods the fools claimed to worship. They didn't explode so much as simply vanish inside a blinding cone of hot plasma.

Mazentus continued to dive, barely escaping as the charge roared past behind their Phantom. The heat turbulence was so ferocious Pavium had to grab the copilot's control sphere to keep from being thrown from his seat.

When the bucking stopped, he checked the tactical display and saw Thalazan accelerating into the rift valley, pulling up hard and pouring cannon fire into the oncoming Banshees.

"Voridus," he ordered. "Prepare a message."

"Assuring Thalazan of your forgiveness?"

"If he survives, yes." Pavium leaned around the side of the copilot's chair, so he could watch Voridus and make sure his next order was obeyed. One could never be too cautious when it came to family. "First, send the coordinates Thalazan intercepted to our talon chiefs at the portal."

"You are going along with the human ploy?" Voridus asked.

"Perhaps," Pavium said. "Or perhaps it is no ploy at all, and I will redeem our clan's honor by eliminating this zealot Castor and his Covenant friends. Tell the Long Shields to launch the suborbital mission. Launch everything."

0540 hours, October 14, 2559 (military calendar)
Covenant Phantom AS-P Secondary, Approach to Epsilon Clarion
Refugia Core 101 002 202.3, Epsilon Wedge, the Ark

Castor sat in the copilot's seat of the borrowed Covenant Phantom, his thoughts focused on the pain in his thigh and shoulder, embracing every fiery throb as it rippled outward from his two wounds. His pain was a gift to the Forerunners, an offering to make amends for allowing the traitorous Veta Lopis and her brood of infidel spies to deceive him for so very long. A penance for letting the betrayers surprise him at the Long Ponds and imperil his holy quest. Only by welcoming his agony could he redeem himself and prove to the Divine Ones that he remained worthy of the quest they had placed before him.

The spies were behind Castor now, and a part of him wanted nothing more than to seek them out and tear them apart with his bare hands. But his first priority was the Great Journey, and the human renegades would not be the last test fate placed before him.

Only moments before, a range of tiny ice-capped domes had appeared on the horizon and burgeoned into the drop-shaped peaks that marked the location of the Epsilon Clarion. Castor's elation had overpowered him, and he had used the Phantom's internal comm system to proclaim that Transcendence was at hand. He had been a fool. No sooner had he spoken than a spray of insertion trails blossomed in the dawn sky, and now the interlopers were descending toward the mountain range, their long smoke tails silhouetted against the pale crescent of the resource moon.

"Transcendence awaits," 'Gadogai announced from the operations station behind Castor. "But first—more Banished to kill."

"I see no amusement in this," Krelis said. Such a loyal Keeper—he had returned to Castor's Phantom earlier, when they had landed to treat those wounded during the spies' assassination attempt and to discard the dead. "There is only one place that mission can be inserting to: the citadel. Your gambit has backfired."

"It was not 'Gadogai who insisted we waste time in the rifts," Feodruz said. He was sitting in Castor's customary place, at the navigator's station behind Krelis. "That was Bhasvod's doing."

"What choice did we have?" Krelis demanded, clearly still bitter that the Banished had failed to take the rendezvous bait. "We could hardly let them follow us to the citadel."

Feodruz growled in disgust. "At least we would have arrived *first.*"

"And been attacked from behind as we tried to clear the entrance," Krelis said. "By a superior force."

"You are too quick to defend the Prelate's miscalculations," Feodruz said. "Is it his pretty armor that has won you over, or the flashy staff?"

"His sanctity and good sense," Krelis replied. "Both of which *you* lack. And when we land, let us find some clear ground, and I will spare you the disgrace of explaining your doubts to the one you insult."

"Feodruz has nothing to explain," 'Gadogai said, finally weighing in. "Or to protest. The Prelate's scheme against the Banished eliminated their Banshees, and my plan drew off their Seraph. The problem is—"

"My judgment," Castor said. "It was the spy *I* trusted who betrayed us. And who transmitted the message telling our enemies where to find the citadel."

"I was about to say that the problem is our enemy's foresight," 'Gadogai said. "That force had to be ready to launch on a suborbital trajectory, or it could not have arrived so soon after the transmission. But you are correct about the spy and her brood. I should have killed them all the first time something smelled off."

"That was not your decision to make." Castor looked at 'Gadogai's reflection in the viewport. "I know you are only trying to move us forward to finding solutions, but first the blame must be laid where it belongs: with me. You were not even a Keeper when that nest of heel-biters joined us. You *warned* me not to place my trust in humans."

"But Dokab, we need the humans," Feodruz said. "We could not have come this far without them, and I am certain we will need them to enter the citadel."

"Needing humans does not mean trusting them." Castor continued to look at 'Gadogai. "Contact Dhas Bhasvod and ask how long he will require to bring more forces forward."

The Oracle's liquid voice sounded from the cockpit comm system. *"Bringing forces forward will not be necessary,"* she said. *"In truth, it would be rather foolish."*

The squared-off sphere of her avatar image instantly appeared in all of the Phantom's instrument displays, the central lens swirling with pale, smokelike tendrils.

"Allow the Long Shields to set their defenses," she said. Castor did not remember informing her that Krelis and Feodruz had identified the markings of the Long Shield Clan on the Banished craft that had been attacking them, but the suggestion served to remind him that the Oracle was always listening. *"I will find a way to bypass them."*

"Are we certain it is the Long Shields inserting?" Castor did not know whether to feel more hopeful or greatly alarmed. He had never fought alongside the Long Shields, but they had a reputation for recklessness and boldness. And unfortunately, the warlord leading them was one of the Banished's finest architects and siege-masters. "With Pavium the Unbreakable setting defenses, it will be impossible for us to approach their perimeter—let alone breach it."

"*It will be possible for* me," the Oracle said. "*Have I not brought you this far, Dokab?*"

"Forgive my doubt," Castor said, inclining his head toward the Oracle's image. "It was never in you. Only in myself."

"*My* doubt, however, is another matter," 'Gadogai remarked. "How will you achieve this miracle, Oracle?"

"*I have not determined that yet,*" the Oracle said. "*I must consult with the Clarion's ancilla first.*"

"And how is that possible," 'Gadogai asked, "if we cannot even reach the citadel itself?"

"*It will not be difficult,*" the Oracle said. "*I can accomplish this from one of the defensive towers.*"

Castor was thunderstruck by this revelation. "There are *defensive towers?*"

"*Of course,*" the Oracle answered. The image in the Phantom displays changed to one of the icy, drop-shaped peaks that ringed the citadel. "Every *Clarion facility has defensive towers* to prevent unauthorized access. *Surely even a* dokab *knows* that."

THIRTEEN

0701 hours, October 14, 2559 (military calendar)
UNSC Reconnaissance Pelican Romeo-008/
Approach to Epsilon Clarion
Refugia 500 002.3 201.3, Epsilon Wedge, the Ark

The bulkhead display switched to tactical mode, and the swarm of flecks Veta had been watching became red vector symbols, their alphanumeric tags identifying them as Banished Banshees. She counted forty of them, circling the citadel in three distinct levels. Half the Banshees, two full talons, patrolled the lowest level, watching the valleys and ridges that abutted the mountain's shoulders. Another ten swirled around its broken pinnacle, ready to dive down in support of those below. The remaining ten orbited a thousand meters above, flying top cover and providing perimeter surveillance.

"Where are their Seraphs?" Commander Barre seemed to be speaking more to herself than Veta or the ensigns manning the Pelican's other reconnaissance stations. "And their battle-management craft? They have no tactical control up there."

"I can't find any Seraphs or anything that could hold a battle-management unit," Mahajan reported. "Their Phantoms are all on the ground."

"Acknowledged," Barre said. "Let's take a look at the entrance area."

"Activating enhanced optics now," Mahajan said. The display switched back to visual mode and became a white blur—whether the image was static or the surface of a glacier was impossible to say. "Refining target coordinates . . ."

The reconnaissance Pelican was sixty kilometers from the citadel structure the Cartographer had called "Epsilon Clarion," maintaining a holding pattern a thousand meters above a high steppe, so Veta could understand why it might take a few moments to bring the lens to bear on a target that was no more than a few hundred square meters.

While they waited, Barre said, "It seems your ploy has worked, Veta. Congratulations."

"All due respect, ma'am," Olivia said. She was standing at the back of the compartment with Ash. Mark was in the sleeping area, doing his best to keep his mind blank and stay calm. "But it hasn't worked *yet*. Castor and Dhas Bhasvod are still out there somewhere. And they still have a human."

Barre's tone grew stern. "I understand that, Spartan."

The image on the display resolved into a snowy mountainside speckled with Banished Phantoms and Wraith assault vehicles. All sat just above the glacier, on a rocky slope mottled with snowfields and crisscrossed by fissures. The terrain was steep, so the Banished had blasted makeshift firing platforms into the grade for their Wraiths. Downslope from the assault vehicles, a couple of hundred Banished warriors—mostly Jiralhanae, with a handful of Sangheili and Kig-Yar—were busy chopping fighting positions into the glacier itself.

Barre pointed at the image in the display. "But we're not the only ones in the game. Castor and Bhasvod have to get past *that*," she said. "And by the time they do, the *Spirit of Fire* will be here with all the support we need."

After departing the floating islands refugia where Cassidy had died, Veta and Barre had finally found time for a full background briefing. Veta now knew that the Reconnaissance Pelican's mothership, the *Spirit of Fire*, was an old *Phoenix*-class support vessel that had been pressed into action early in the war between humanity and the Covenant. To win a crucial battle, the *Spirit* had been forced to sacrifice the reactor that powered its slipspace drive. Afterward, the vessel's crew had entered cryosleep to begin a long journey back to UNSC territory . . . only to awaken on the Ark, where they soon found themselves in a pitched fight against the Banished.

Veta could not even imagine what a surprise *that* must have been. The *Spirit of Fire* had been stranded on the Ark for about nine months now, with little hope of escape. No wonder its forces had been fighting so hard to win control of the slipspace portal when Castor and his Keepers arrived from Reach.

Inversely, upon hearing Veta's own history, Commander Barre had been surprised to learn that ONI had recruited her from the Ministry of Protection on Gao. When Barre had entered cryosleep, Gao had been on the leading edge of the Insurrection. Veta had not had the energy to explain that after the war with the Covenant ended, Gao had gone back to its old ways.

At least, Veta thought it had. There was no telling what had become of her homeworld after Cortana had launched her plan to bring "peace" to the galaxy. Probably Gao's ever-arrogant president had ignored Cortana's edict and prompted the AI to blast the entire planet back to the Stone Age. Veta wouldn't have been a bit surprised.

Olivia managed to stifle her doubts for almost a full minute, continuing to stare at the bulkhead display until the image began to zoom out, revealing just how thinly the Banished warriors were spread across the mountain. Given their air superiority and their knowledge of the citadel's exact location, the force was probably large enough to stop Castor and Bhasvod from getting inside.

But probably was not good enough—not for Olivia. Not when she was off her smoothers.

"I'm sorry, ma'am." Olivia started forward along the port side of the equipment bank. "But I'm not comfortable waiting for someone else to do my job."

Barre's brow rose. "You have no choice, Spartan," she said. "The last I checked, *I* am the commander of this craft."

Veta turned her palm toward Olivia, signaling her to stand down. She knew that as the smoother deprivation set in, all of her Gammas would grow increasingly paranoid. But in different ways. Olivia usually trended toward excessive worry, running scenario after scenario through her mind of what might go wrong, then convincing herself that it would go wrong. And that it was already going wrong.

But this time, Olivia just might be onto something.

Veta waited until Barre's gaze drifted back, then said, "Commander, Olivia has a point. Castor is *always* full of surprises. And now that he's allied with a San'Shyuum Prelate with plenty of Covenant support . . ." She paused and frowned up at the display, then said, "I'd feel a lot better if we knew where they were."

Barre widened her eyes. "Really?"

"My apologies," Veta said. "But Castor never gives up. And his luck is uncanny—especially since he's come to the Ark. We have to find out what he's up to."

Barre sighed. "You *know* we aren't a stealth craft, yes? They know we're watching them."

Veta nodded. "I'm very aware," she said. "We just need to find out where he is. If we don't—"

Barre put up her hand. "I get it. But we can't go in there."

"Just a look," Veta said. "I promise."

Barre rolled her eyes but leaned toward the microphone in her console and pressed a touch pad. "Lieutenant Joubert, let's drop to the floor and circle that mountain range. We need to take a peek up some of those valleys."

A concerned female voice replied, "Yes, ma'am. But we can't outrun their Banshees. If we drop that low and they come after us—"

"They won't," Barre said. "You have your orders, Lieutenant."

Joubert clicked off with a curt acknowledgment. The Pelican dropped to a hundred meters and began to circle the mountains, using optics and passive sensors to search for any sign of Covenant Phantoms.

Mahajan found it in the third valley they passed. "We have acoustic echoes," he said. "They're faint, but it sounds like thrust propulsion, not gravitics. It's Phantoms."

"Direction of travel?" Barre asked.

"The echoes are fading," Mahajan said. "So, up the valley, toward the citadel."

"Are they our targets?" Barre asked.

"I can't be certain. I need to filter out the echoes before I can attempt a signature match."

Every craft had tiny differences in maintenance and construction that resulted in unique thrust signatures. One of the first things a reconnaissance crew did on a mission was start building an acoustic and optical library of thrust signatures that could be used to identify specific targets, and Barre's team was no different.

"It would help if we were closer," Mahajan added.

Barre issued the order, and the Pelican turned toward the mountain range. "Hanson, pull up the terrain mapping and tell me what we know about that valley. I need to know if it's possible for the Phantoms to sneak past the Banished into the citadel."

"On it, ma'am."

"Ngonga, isolate transmissions in the valley," Barre said. "If that's a Banished patrol or a deployment mission, they'll be in contact with their superiors. If it's Castor and his Covenant friends, they'll maintain comm silence to avoid drawing attention to themselves."

"Yes, ma'am."

Three minutes later, Mahajan finally confirmed that the Phantoms in the valley were indeed the same craft the recon team had been following all along. By then, their Pelican was halfway to the mountains, and Commander Barre was starting to look nervous about the possibility of being jumped by the Banshees patrolling the citadel. But the Banished craft seemed as unconcerned about the Reconnaissance Pelican as they did about the Covenant Phantoms its crew was tracking up the valley.

Finally Barre declared, "If we can see *them*, they can see *us*. So why aren't they trying to chase us off? Anyone?"

"Maybe the Banished are using us," Veta suggested. "Maybe they want us to push the Covenant Phantoms out of the valley so they can jump them."

"Or maybe they've already set an ambush just for *us*," Olivia said. "And they're just waiting until we reach it."

"No, that's not it," Hanson said. A schematic of the valley ahead appeared on the bulkhead display. "The Banished aren't reacting because the Covies aren't going anywhere near the citadel."

The schematic zoomed out, producing an outline map of the mountain range that included both the citadel on the left side of the display and one of its pinnacle-topped companion mountains on the right. The valley entered the range in the display's lower left corner, but angled to the right, then ended at the base of the companion.

"That can't be good," Olivia said. "Castor is up to something."

"Such as?" Barre asked.

"Misdirection," Ash replied. "They could be trying to draw defenders away, so . . . wait. How many Phantoms does the Covenant have?"

"They have two left," Mahajan said. "Both are in the valley."

"Are you sure?"

"I am sure," Mahajan said. "I have identified both acoustic signatures."

"They couldn't have brought more forward?"

"Anything is *possible*." Mahajan was beginning to sound irritated. "But I have seen no indication of that."

"You seem very concerned about the number of Phantoms, Spartan," Barre said. "Why?"

"Because their only human isn't a pilot," Ash said. "Quenbi can't fly a Seraph or Banshee, and those things can't carry passengers. To make a misdirection play, Castor and Bhasvod would need a third transport craft to take her to the citadel."

"Then we must assume this is *not* misdirection," Barre said. "They don't have the equipment it would take."

"That's just it," Ash said. "We can't assume anything. We have to know."

Barre looked to Veta, brows arched in confusion. "Okay, what am I missing here?"

"Ash can get lost in the details sometimes," Veta said. What Commander Barre was missing was the experience of a smoother-deprived Ash, whose paranoia had a tendency to manifest as an obsession with information-gathering. No matter how much he knew, there was still room for doubt—to the point of hesitating to act. She looked toward the back of the compartment. "Gear up. If something happens, it's going to happen fast."

Once Ash and Olivia had disappeared behind the blackout curtain, Barre asked, "You're going to break your promise, aren't you? You plan to do more than just look."

"That's up to you, ma'am," Veta said. "You're the commander."

Barre closed her eyes. "I was afraid you would say that." She took a few deep breaths, then said, "Well, we cannot let a band of cultists kill everything in the galaxy, can we? Tell me what you want to do."

"I have no idea what Castor is up to," Veta said. "And that makes me nervous."

"How are you going to figure it out?"

"I'm not."

Before she could explain further, Joubert's voice sounded from Barre's console. "Ma'am, we're approaching the mouth of the valley. We'll be entering it in ten seconds."

Barre opened her eyes and looked aft. "Mahajan, are there any Banshees coming our way?"

"Negative."

"And what are the chances those Phantoms know we are following them into the valley?"

"They might," Mahajan said. "But they don't have an overwatch, and most of their onboard sensors are probably turned toward the Banished. My guess is they won't realize we're behind them until there's no terrain between us."

Joubert's voice sounded from Barre's console again. "Ma'am, we just entered the valley."

"Good. Keep going." Barre returned her attention to Veta. "You were just explaining how you aren't going to figure out what Castor is up to."

"That's right. If we can kill Quenbi, it doesn't matter what Castor is up to."

"Quenbi—that's their last human?"

"Right again." Veta had briefed Barre on Castor's daring departure from Reach, including how Quenbi opened the slipspace portal there, so the commander would understand how the Ferrets had come to be on the Ark. "Without her, Castor and Bhasvod have no choice but to get someone else. And we're going to make sure their only choice is to come for me or my Ferret team, and when they do—"

"You'll be ready." Barre smiled. "Yeah. I like it."

"I'm glad you approve." Veta rose and gestured toward the sleeping compartment where her armor was stowed. "With your permission."

"By all means, gear up. Let me know how we can help."

"Have any SPNKRs?"

"Nope. I keep telling you, this is a reconnaissance craft, not a SPECWAR insertion vessel."

"Grenades?"

"Grenades I can do," Barre said. "We have a crate of M9s. Hanson will get them from the weapons locker."

By the time Veta joined her Gammas in the sleeping compartment, they were all armed, armored, and sitting on their bunks with their rucksacks resting on their boots. Their hands were on their thighs palm-up, their eyes were closed, and they were taking slow, deep breaths in perfect unison. The team meditation did nothing to help with their smoother deprivation problems, but it definitely calmed their pre-operation jitters and helped them work better as a unit. Veta slipped into her own armor, then sat on the bunk next to Ash and joined in. The breathing exercise was probably the one good thing they'd learned while undercover with the Humans of the Joyous Journey, and it had since become something of a Ferret ritual before going into action.

She managed only ten breaths before Hanson arrived with the fragmentation grenades, but even ten was enough to make her feel more attuned to her team. She could almost taste the coppery tang of Mark's bloodlust, could almost feel the knots writhing in Olivia's stomach, could almost hear the half-whispered questions that filled Ash's mind.

As they stuffed their cargo pouches with grenades, the Pelican climbed suddenly, and Ngonga pulled the blackout curtain aside.

"You might want to see this," he said. "In fact, you probably should. The Banished have decided to take an interest in those Phantoms."

Veta turned toward the display on the forward bulkhead and saw the crevassed wall of a hanging glacier sliding past as the Pelican rose out of the valley. After a few moments, tiny slivers of blue plasma began to stream in from the top of the display and hit the ice, raising barely noticeable puffs of steam.

As the Pelican continued to climb, the glacier was replaced by outcroppings of deeply fissured rock and long tracts of snowfield. Both Covenant Phantoms came into view at the bottom of the display, two dark flecks weaving and dodging plasma slivers as they flew toward the pinnacle on top of the mountain.

Now that she had something to compare it to, Veta realized

how enormous the pinnacle was. It completely dwarfed the Phantoms. Had there not been long streams of plasma flashing toward their position, she might not have noticed the two craft at all. The monolith had to be half a kilometer across at the base, and equally high.

"Castor and Bhasvod are trying awfully hard to reach that pinnacle," Olivia said.

A full talon of Banshees dropped into view at the top of the display, ten dots the size of pinheads, all pouring blue threads at the dark flecks of the two Phantoms.

"And the Banished are trying just as hard to stop them," Veta said. "Why?"

"I don't *know*." Ash sounded almost frantic. "The Banished have figured it out. Why can't *I*?"

The lead Phantom must have taken a hit, because it abruptly changed direction, then shifted its trajectory again. It continued to the base of the pinnacle, where it seemed to stop and swing around so it could pour a barrage of plasma back at the Banshees.

"Ensign Mahajan, enlarge that," Barre ordered. "I need to see what's happening."

The image zoomed in, the tiny Phantom-fleck becoming a craft the size of a hand, plasma bolts firing out of the display image. The second Phantom joined it a moment later, and together they filled the left-hand side of the screen with ribbons of blinding blue energy.

A couple of moments later, Hanson announced, "That's six Banshees down."

Bulky figures in armor began to drop from the bellies of both Phantoms, descending to the ground inside a column of diffused light—the ventral gravity lifts. The slender figure of what appeared to be the San'Shyuum Prelate appeared beneath the first craft, his arms wrapped protectively around a much smaller human figure. Then they were lost to sight as a swarm of Banshees dived in to attack.

"How close are they to the pinnacle?" Veta asked. At this scale, it was impossible to tell exactly what part of the mountain she was looking at—it was all just gray, lichen-caked rock to her. "Can they get to the base?"

"Probably," Hanson said. "They're right under the center, no more than a hundred meters away."

"There must be another entrance to the citadel," Veta said. "Maybe a secret tunnel?"

"Every good castle has a sally port," Ash remarked. "But that pinnacle is a full ten kilometers from the citadel."

"As the bullet flies," Olivia added. "With a valley between them. A tunnel connection would have to be at least twice that long."

"Twenty kilometers is nothing," Veta said. "Forerunners, remember?"

The first Phantom erupted in a ball of flame, but it was impossible to tell through the roiling smoke whether Dhas Bhasvod had made it to the ground with Quenbi.

Veta was guessing that was affirmative. "Rig for a fast line," she ordered. "And change our comms back to ONI bands and encryption."

She explained her plan, then went forward and told Barre what she needed.

"We can do that," Barre said. "But you understand, there will be no way to extract you—not from anywhere near here."

"Just get us there," Veta said. "We'll worry about extraction after the *Spirit of Fire* arrives."

Barre looked away for a moment, no doubt thinking the same

thing Veta was: extraction might be pretty low on the priority list for the *Spirit of Fire*'s captain. The Ferrets could be setting themselves up for a one-way mission.

Situation normal for Spartan-IIIs—and Veta wasn't about to let them go there alone.

On the display, the second Phantom turned to flee—and was met by a single Banished Seraph, rising from behind the mountain's far shoulder. They exchanged fire, and the Phantom dived out of sight. The Seraph spun on its center axis—a maneuver Veta had not realized the alien craft were capable of—and streaked away in pursuit.

Ash let out a low whistle. "Too bad that pilot isn't on our side."

"He kind of is," Olivia said. "At least for now."

The remaining Banshees continued to swarm around the base of the pinnacle, laying plasma bolts and fuel rods on Castor's ground force, which was slowly working its way toward the pinnacle base. It was difficult to note the effectiveness of the Banished craft. All Veta could see was the occasional glimpse of armor crawling up a fissure or ducking behind a boulder, always moving uphill.

"Ma'am," Veta said. "Four Banshees aren't going to get the job done. Twenty wouldn't. My team has to go down there and do it the hard way."

"I know," Barre said, nodding. "I just wish there was a better way."

"Me too. I do have one request, for afterward."

"If it's in my power, of course. Name it."

Veta touched the datapad on her forearm. "We're going to need some fairly exotic meds in a big hurry when we're recovered. Can you forward a list to the ship's pharmacy?"

"Absolutely." Barre opened a connection to the Pelican computer. "I'll send it along the next time we make contact with *Spirit of Fire.*"

Veta sent the list, and Barre's brow slowly rose.

"Wow. That's . . . *quite* a cocktail," she said. "Aren't iloperaripodyne and olanzobrexapole . . . psychotic stabilizers?"

Veta shot a glance toward her Gammas. "Augmentation issues," she said. "Glad to be getting rid of us?"

"Under the circumstances . . . honestly, I'm not sure." Barre stored the file, then said, "But I *am* glad it's your problem, Veta, and not mine. You seem like you can handle it. Good luck."

She extended her hand.

Veta shook it and said, "Thank you, ma'am." She started to go aft, then stopped and added, "For everything."

Barre nodded, then turned back to the display.

Veta returned to the sleeping compartment to find the two fast ropes ready to hang, with Hanson standing by to control the ramp. Mark and Olivia were geared up for action, standing together on the port side, both wearing rucksacks, gloves, and eye protection. Mark cradled his DMR in one hand, finger next to the trigger guard and the stock tucked under his arm, able to provide suppression fire as he descended. Olivia had her MA40 slung across her chest; she and Veta would hang the ropes, then slide down just above Ash and Mark.

Ash was waiting on the starboard side, holding his MA40 in the same manner as Mark was his DMR. Veta retrieved her own M7 submachine gun and slung it across her chest, then grabbed the top of the rope and checked the hanger clip to make sure the spring would quickly close the gate.

She felt herself lean toward the ramp as the Pelican accelerated into the insertion run. "Everyone clear on the plan?"

"Kill Quenbi," Mark said.

"Hold the pinnacle," Ash said.

"Not that complicated," Olivia finished.

Veta smiled. "I guess not." Her good nature faded. "You all make me proud. I wish we didn't have to do it this way."

"Why not?" Mark said. "We were made for this."

"Not *all* of us, dummy." Olivia rolled her eyes, then turned to Veta. "Sorry, Mom."

"Don't be," Veta said. The Pelican bucked as a volley of Anvil-II air-to-surface missiles left the pod. "Honestly, there's no place I'd rather be."

Hanson slapped her palm against a control pad on the fuselage wall and used the other to flip a safety toggle. The ramp dropped into the open position, flooding the compartment with an icy wind. Veta and Olivia dragged the heavy ropes to the end and, with Mark and Ash holding them by their load-carrying belts, leaned out and clipped them into cargo hooks under the long tail.

The Pelican bucked again as it fired another volley of missiles, then began to shudder as the M370 nose gun opened up. Mark and Ash pulled Veta and Olivia back onto the ramp, then each wrapped their free arms into a rope, kicked the coils out of the compartment, and swung out beneath the Pelican's tail. They wrapped their legs around the rope and began to slide down, laying suppression fire as they descended. Veta and Olivia grabbed the line and descended into the frigid air after them.

Hanson raised the ramp. Dangling beneath the Pelican, Veta saw another volley of missiles streak toward the wall of gray stone that was the pinnacle base. They were trailing so much smoke she almost missed the crouching figures they were heading toward, one a Jiralhanae Keeper in blue-and-gold power armor, the other a San'Shyuum Prelate in a dark gray fighting suit. Hunkering around

— 249 —

them, less than a meter downslope, were 'Gadogai and four more Jiralhanae in a mixture of Keeper and Covenant armor.

The ringleaders of this entire situation. If the Pelican took them out now, this operation would be over before it began.

The missiles were almost at the pinnacle when a shield of translucent, gold-tinted hexagons flashed into existence.

Olivia cried, "What the—"

The warheads detonated, but Veta lost sight of what followed as the Pelican spun around, whipping the two fast ropes toward the impact zone. She wrapped her arms into the rope and clung tight. The swing-and-fling maneuver was part of the plan, but Veta lacked the kind of Spartan augmentations that would allow her to survive hitting a stone wall at high velocity.

A heartbeat later, the rope began to slow, and she felt Ash let go and drop away. She saw Mark do the same on the adjacent rope, then Olivia loosened her grasp and slid off the rope after him. Veta waited until her rope started to swing back under the Pelican's tail before following suit, grateful for the adrenaline that inured her to the bone-chilling wind.

The drop from the bottom of the rope was only a meter or so, but the angular momentum was too much for Veta. She landed on bent knees, tucked her shoulder, and went into a side tumble, already grabbing her M7. She rolled onto her feet, felt the icy ground fall away beneath her, then tucked her shoulder again—and slammed down atop a Jiralhanae-sized mound of yellow-and-red Covenant armor.

She scrambled off and came up firing, turning his face into red pulp before she realized the alien hadn't moved since she fell on top of him.

"Mom!" It was Olivia, calling to her. "Something happen to your eyes?! He's dead already!"

Veta looked toward the sound of Olivia's voice and found her about ten meters away, crouching in the fissure near the bottom of a gray stone cliff, which had to be the pinnacle base. In front of Olivia lay another dead Jiralhanae, this one a Keeper, one arm missing and his armor scorched from an Anvil-II strike.

Mark's DMR and Ash's MA40 began to boom and clatter from across the slope. The only thing Veta could see over the rim of the fissure was Commander Barre's Pelican dropping back toward the valley, a trio of Banished Banshees chewing its tail.

Veta turned back toward Olivia, who called, "They've spotted Quenbi, but she's protected."

"Can we flank?"

"*I* can," Olivia said. "If your eyes—"

"My eyes are fine," Veta said, cutting her off. This was going to be a challenge, staying patient with an Olivia who was doing battle in paranoid-worry mode. "Let me have a look."

Veta rose to a stoop—the fissure was not quite as deep as she was tall—and peered over the rim. Her Ferret team had landed on a steep slope of gray-blond rock strewn with long tracts of snow and knee-high mounds of lichen. The entire face was crisscrossed by narrow clefts similar to the one she was in, creating a checkerboard pattern of four-meter squares. The base of the pinnacle was about fifteen meters uphill from Veta's location, with the head of the glacier about 150 meters below.

Mark and Ash were about seventy meters across the slope, firing into a horizontal fissure from opposing angles, covering each other as they tried to work their way closer. Return fire was coming from a fissure about thirty meters below them, where Castor's gold-trimmed helmet was barely visible as he peered over the rim and used his Ravager to lob incendiary bolts at them. About twelve meters above, Krelis and Feodruz were tucked into another horizontal fissure, pouring bursts of mangler spikes and plasma-fire pulses upslope whenever Mark or Ash moved.

Veta put a fresh magazine in her M7 and activated TEAMCOM. "Ferrets Two and Four, be ready," she said. Mark was always designated as Two and Ash as Four. "Lead and Three are going to launch a flank attack in five, four—"

"Wait," Olivia said. "Where's Bhasvod? And 'Gado—"

"Doesn't matter," Veta snapped. "*Focus*, Three. If we get Quenbi, they can't initiate."

"Sorry." Olivia sounded genuinely distressed. "It's just that—"

"'Livi, I *know*. It's okay." Veta wished she hadn't been so sharp. She was asking more of her Gammas than she had any right to, and the smoother problem wasn't their doing. "You have an MA40, so you take overwatch. Three, two . . ."

Veta climbed out of the fissure, then raced toward Castor.

The slope was steep enough that she found herself slipping downhill every time she hit a stretch of snow or ice. After the first ten meters, she began to zigzag between the uphill side of the lichen mounds to take advantage of the firmer footing. The growth was surprisingly dense, accumulating in thick shelves of purple and green that hid the boulders she assumed to be concealed underneath.

With Mark and Ash both making short charges designed to hold the enemy's attention, Veta made it to within forty meters before Castor glanced in her direction. Always an imposing figure, the Jiralhanae spun to face her, shouting and using his free hand to shove someone behind him that she couldn't see. Veta opened fire on the run, indiscriminately ricocheting rounds off the stone to both sides of Castor without managing to put any into the fissure with him.

It didn't matter. Her job was to draw the enemy's attention

away from Mark and Ash so they could make the kill, and the tactic worked beautifully. As soon as she let loose, Castor swung his Ravager in her direction and lobbed an incendiary bolt. Olivia fired an MA40 burst at his helmet, putting enough rounds on target that his shields flickered out, forcing him to drop out of sight and give the shields a few seconds to regenerate.

Krelis and Feodruz turned toward the sound of Olivia's gunfire simultaneously—a misstep that allowed Mark and Ash to rush the position in the clear. The two Spartans descended the last twenty meters of slope in a bounding sprint, reaching attack position just as Feodruz realized his mistake and turned back uphill.

Ash dropped into the fissure beside him, firing his MA40 at near point-blank range and forcing the Jiralhanae to tumble out, shields gone and rounds dimpling his armor. Mark simply leaped over and continued to bound downhill, his attention fixed on the cleft below. Krelis rolled out behind him, firing his mangler down the slope every time he rotated onto his back.

Realizing she was almost out of ammunition and would soon need to cover Mark, Veta ducked behind a purplish mound of lichen and changed magazines. When she finished, she looked around the uphill side . . . and found Feodruz and Ash locked in hand-to-hand combat, hammering each other with leg kicks and weapon butts. Krelis meanwhile was on his feet and running downhill, his mangler swinging back and forth as he fired.

Mark was already standing in the next fissure, visible from the torso up as he blasted DMR rounds into the cleft ahead of him. Veta couldn't see his target, but she figured it was probably Quenbi, since he was aiming a couple of meters behind where Castor had dropped out of sight. Nevertheless, he needed flank protection. Veta swung her M7 upslope and fired on Krelis, dropping his shields in a long burst and forcing him to dive to the ground.

As Veta's submachine gun thundered, the lichen mound she was using as cover began to tremble. Then, to her astonishment, it scurried a few meters, tucked itself into a tight ball, and tumbled down the slope. Krelis's mangler whipped toward Veta, and suddenly it was *her* turn to dive and roll.

A roar of fury thundered across the mountain, and as Veta rotated, she glimpsed Castor rising into view and whirling to meet Mark's attack. She dropped into her own fissure and came up firing—only to see Mark lurch forward unexpectedly and impale himself on Castor's Ravager blade.

She immediately took her finger off the trigger, stunned and fearful of hitting Mark. She didn't understand what had just happened . . . until Castor lifted Mark above his head and began to whip him back and forth in a rage, and she saw 'Gadogai's slender figure ducking back into the fissure about two meters beyond Castor, in the perfect position to have shoved Mark forward.

Veta opened fire simultaneously with Olivia, but 'Gadogai had already vanished from sight. Rather than risk hitting Mark with a low-accuracy burst or switching to single fire and failing to penetrate Castor's shields, Veta reached for her M6C and activated the scope.

By then, Mark was using one hand to hammer the butt of his DMR into Castor's helmet, rocking the Jiralhanae's head sideways with each blow. With the other hand, he was bringing up his own M6, swinging the muzzle toward his captor's temple.

Castor had no choice but to fling Mark away, sending him flying across the slope, trailing a long arc of blood. Veta still couldn't open fire, as Mark was dropping between her and the *dokab*.

Mark hit the ground, then spun immediately and opened fire. But Castor had already ducked out of sight, so the Gamma switched targets, catching Krelis as he was reloading. The young Jiralhanae barely made it into a fissure before his shields flared out.

Veta rose and started toward Mark, but kept her M6C trained on Feodruz. When the Keeper sent Ash flying with a backhand to the helmet, she put two rounds into his breastplate, Olivia unloading another into his backplate. The old warrior realized he was caught in a cross fire and dived into the cleft with Krelis.

Olivia kept pouring fire into the fissures where the Jiralhanae had taken refuge, which allowed Veta to rush the last few steps to Mark.

His torso armor had a gash two fingers wide from the pit of his stomach down the right side to his belt line, and there was so much blood oozing from it that Veta could barely see the loop of intestine bulging through the rent.

"Task complete." Mark holstered his M6 and braced his hands on the ground, preparing to push himself to his feet. "Quenbi terminated."

"Hold on." Veta waved Ash over, then put her hands on Mark's chest, pinning him down. "Just hold on. You'll be fine."

"Damn right I will." He tried to sit up. "Just let me—"

"Stay *down.*"

Veta winced, pushing the loop of intestine back into his abdomen, then broke out a canister of biofoam and began to fill the wound. Mark's tenacity was the result of the illegal augmentations he'd been subjected to, and he had no real awareness of how badly he'd been wounded. The more damage a Gamma suffered, the more aggressive and pain-tolerant they became. It was supposed to be a survival mechanism, allowing them to endure system shocks that would kill a normal human being. But Veta had always suspected the true purpose had more to do with making sure they completed the mission, no matter the odds or the circumstances.

"Wait until Ash gets here."

Mark's eyes narrowed. "I can still fight," he said. "Don't even *think* of trying to sideline me."

Hyper-aggression *and* smoother deprivation. Wonderful.

"No one's going to—"

Veta's attempt at reassurance was lost amid the deafening crack of something large breaking. She looked upslope toward the source, fully expecting to see the pinnacle falling toward them. Instead, she saw a distant wall of snow billowing up from the adjacent valley—the same one that separated their mountain from the citadel.

Mark was on his feet and charging—well, *lurching*—up the slope before Veta realized what he was doing. She barely managed to catch hold of his arm and stop him—then almost wished she hadn't as he spun on her with fury in his eyes.

"*What?!*" The thunder of the avalanche crashing into the next valley was so loud that Mark's question wouldn't have been audible, had it not come over TEAMCOM. "*What do you want?!*"

"Where are you going?!" Veta demanded. "The plan is to make them come to *us*, remember? *Then* we take them out."

"Change of plan." Mark pointed toward the foot of the pinnacle, at a spot about a hundred meters to their left. "Bhasvod's up to something. Whatever it is, we've got to stop him."

Intrepid Eye had been wounded, a development that was highly unexpected. Her processing was slow and her input disjointed, and matters were unlikely to improve soon. The missile strikes of a few minutes earlier had not only decimated the ranks of the Keepers of the One Freedom, they had reduced her dispersed capacity by 57 percent. There was simply no way to reconfigure around *that* immutable truth. She had lost most of the data acquired since awakening in her Jat-Krula support base on Edod—the human name for the planet was now also obscured from her. Much of that critical information would never be recovered, as even her redundant datasets had been annihilated.

Fortunately, her system architecture remained intact inside Bhasvod's glaive, and she could use it to reconstruct the millions of utility and application programs that had vanished in the fiery deaths of the organics. But first, she would have to commandeer enough volatile memory to decompress herself. And the only place to do that was inside the Clarion facility—which she might never reach, if the weak circuit carrying her did not find an interface station soon.

Intrepid Eye had not been able to insinuate herself into Dhas Bhasvod's helmet or fighting suit, as both control systems reset at the slightest modification. So, when a hexagon of flat stone flashed past the glaive's hard-light focusing lens, she manifested her monitor avatar from the other end of the haft and turned its central photoreceptor toward the camouflaged interface station.

Bhasvod barely reacted. He seemed to have grown quite accustomed to her abrupt appearances, and he merely followed her line of sight toward the pinnacle. He had been walking along its base for more than two hundred meters without seeming to recognize the true nature of the hexagons. But with her help, he finally seemed to realize what he was seeing and pressed his palm to this one.

Nothing happened, of course. San'Shyuum were not Reclaimers.

But that did not mean that the ancilla inside was not watching. Quite the opposite, in all likelihood.

Intrepid began to flash her photoreceptor in binary code,

initiating an exchange that would almost certainly be over before Bhasvod realized it had begun.

What? Intrepid Eye communicated. *No visual manifestation?*

A small diamond of light appeared in the interface station and flashed a reply. *My Clarion is under siege.*

My Clarion, Intrepid Eye noted. The hexagon was simply a communications terminal, not a true interface station. She was speaking directly to the facility's submonitor.

I have little time, the submonitor continued. *State your business.*

We require admittance to the Clarion facility, Intrepid Eye flashed.

Impossible. Did I not just inform you that I am under siege?

We have a Reclaimer, Intrepid Eye replied.

I see no Reclaimer. Only you and your bearer.

Our Reclaimer will arrive presently, Intrepid Eye stated. *You may have noticed the trouble on the slopes below. We do not wish to endanger the Reclaimer until the way is clear.*

The submonitor paused a hundred system ticks, then finally replied, *Admitting your Reclaimer would require me to activate a bridge for you and expose an entry vestibule. My besiegers are here now. They would enter before you arrived, and they do not have a Reclaimer.*

Surely you have defensives other than concealment? Because if you are besieged, then your concealment has clearly failed. Intrepid Eye waited two hundred system ticks for a reply. When none came, she continued, *You need to escalate to the next level . . . before your attackers do. You must see the logic in that.*

The submonitor processed for fifty ticks, then finally replied, *Your logic is impossible to ignore.*

A large rectangle of stone grew translucent and vanished, changing into a long tunnel lit by a golden ambience.

The bridge will activate when you present your Reclaimer.

I understand, Intrepid Eye replied. *But she is being pursued by your attackers. We will need to deactivate it behind us.*

We will discuss that when you arrive, the submonitor flashed. *I am now disengaging. My full attention will be required to break the siege.*

Veta looked in the direction Mark was pointing and didn't see anything. Was he imagining things already? Even if he wasn't, how could she let him keep going in his condition?

But how would she ever stop him?

And if he *wasn't* imagining things, *should* she even try?

Too many thoughts too fast. It felt like she was the one in Gamma-mode. "Mark—there's nothing there."

"Bhasvod's fighting suit has active camouflage." Mark continued to point. "Look for his glaive, about shoulder height."

"And Arcas," Ash said, arriving on Mark's far side. They were standing together now, but still speaking over TEAMCOM. The roaring echoes of the distant avalanche were that loud—and growing in volume. "He's just down the slope, hiding in a fissure. Look for his helmet vanes."

Veta couldn't see either object, but she knew better than to doubt *two* of her Ferrets. As smoother-deprived and injury-stressed as Mark was, *he* might have been imagining things. But Ash too? It was just that their visual enhancements were about three times better than her own eyesight.

"This is my fault," Olivia said, also over TEAMCOM. "I knew it was a mistake to disregard Bhasvod."

"It wasn't a mistake." Veta started toward Olivia's overwatch position, pulling Mark along and nodding for Ash to accompany them. "Eliminating Quenbi was our first priority. We can set up our position and figure out what Bhasvod is doing next."

"Better make it quick," Olivia said. "You know it wasn't Bhasvod who caused that avalanche, right?"

It hadn't occurred to Veta that anyone had caused it, but of course it should have. The thunder of the avalanche was not only continuing, but building—which suggested it wasn't just a piece of the glacier that had fallen into the valley below. The Banished positions above the citadel entrance were almost certainly being wiped out. And only a fool would think that was happening by coincidence.

When Veta didn't reply, Olivia continued, "It has to be Intrepid Eye. She's a Forerunner ancilla. *She's* the only one who would be able to communicate with the citadel's ancilla from here."

"Yeah," Ash said. "But why would Intrepid Eye want to help Castor and Bhasvod breach the citadel and fire the Halo Array?"

"I'm sure she has her own reasons," Olivia replied. "Intrepid Eye *always* has her own reasons."

Veta checked on Mark and, seeing that he was still powering along in wounded-Gamma mode, glanced toward the citadel. The highest part of the mountain was hidden behind the pinnacle above, and its shoulders were veiled by an ever-thickening curtain of billowing snow. But inside that curtain, especially near the top, Veta could see blue plasma bolts and orange particle beams flying back and forth. The Banished Banshees were under attack, presumably by Forerunner Aggressor sentinels.

"Oh hell," Veta said. "It *is* Intrepid Eye. Whatever she's up to, we have to stop her."

"Didn't I just *do* that?" Mark asked. "When I killed Quenbi?"

"I wouldn't count on it," Olivia said. "Intrepid Eye has *always* been resourceful. If she's still moving forward without Quenbi, she may have found another solution—or maybe another human. Or, even worse, maybe a way to bypass the need for a human entirely."

"She can do that?" Ash asked.

"I don't know." Olivia's self-doubt was evident in her tone; even she didn't recognize whether her doubts were due to smoother deprivation . . . or just common sense. "But the first time the Halo Array was in danger of activating, the master chief had to destroy an entire ring to stop the installation's monitor from firing it."

"How do you know that?" Ash asked.

"It was in an ONI MOS briefing," Olivia said. "But what I'm telling you is that I *don't* know. This is Forerunner stuff, and it's way above my rating."

Olivia's military occupational specialty and information systems rating was as high as any in the UNSC. But when it came to Forerunner systems, even that level of expertise made her a neophyte.

Veta and the others reached Olivia's overwatch station and hunkered down with her. She opened fire, putting a few rounds across the slope, and Veta turned to see Castor taking cover in another fissure.

The Keepers were coming. Veta didn't know whether they were seeking vengeance or intended to capture another human through the Ferrets, but they were coming.

"We don't have to understand *everything*—only that we have to stop Intrepid Eye," Veta said. "Even if she can't bypass the need for a human, all she has to do is find another one."

"Not going to happen," Mark said. "No way we're letting her get one of us."

"Actually," Veta said, "I'm thinking we should. And it should be me."

Ash cocked his head at her. "No offense, Mom, but are you off your smoothers?"

"Think about it," Veta said. "There must be thousands of humans here on the Ark right now. One of us may be the obvious choice at the moment, but we're certainly *not* the last ones available. If Intrepid Eye wants Halo activated, eventually she'll find another one who can do it. We need to take her out."

"How?" Ash asked. "She's an ancilla. She could be anywhere."

"That's true . . . at the moment," Olivia said. "But it won't be when she tries to fire the rings. She'll want to be in the citadel system herself—and that's where we can destroy her. At least, I think we can."

"Tell me what you're thinking," Veta said. But when Olivia started to talk about the problems AIs faced with data compression and consolidation, and the need to have enough storage capacity to process data efficiently, Veta quickly raised a hand to stop her. "We trust you on the technical stuff, so skip that part. Just tell me how you're going to get her in one place long enough to destroy her."

And Olivia did, in about a hundred words that Veta was pretty sure she almost understood.

"And that will work?" Veta asked. She saw Olivia's eyes flick away and quickly realized her mistake. "I mean . . . is it our best chance?"

Olivia immediately seemed to relax. "Oh yeah," she said. "I'm sure of *that* much. We're not going to eliminate Intrepid Eye any other way."

"Then that's our strategy," Veta said. "Ash, prep a nanobug for subcutaneous insertion."

Ash raised his brow. "Are you crazy?"

"That's an order," Veta said. "And listen up. I have a plan."

Ash began to rummage through his rucksack.

Talking as she worked, Veta pulled out her med kit, then removed Mark's torso armor and began to inspect his laceration. The wound was still packed with biofoam, but she saw a few places where there was still blood oozing and hit them with touch-up squirts. He would still require surgery and some serious infirmary time after they got out of this—assuming they *did* get out of this— but at least he wouldn't bleed out on the mountainside.

At least, not soon.

Olivia fired with increasing frequency, keeping them posted as Castor and Krelis advanced toward the fissure where the Ferrets were in hiding.

"They're still forty meters out and taking their time," Olivia warned. "But I haven't seen 'Gadogai or Feodruz. Expect a flanking maneuver soon."

"Let's be sure you and Ash are out of here before that happens," Veta said. "Mark, you play dead and I'll lead them away."

"No way," Mark said. "I'm not letting you do that. Castor will kill you on sight."

"He won't," Veta said. She peeled open a suture kit and began to sew him up, more to keep the biofoam and his intestines inside than anything else. "As long as you three stay clear, he can't. He needs me for the Great Journey."

"Only until Halo is activated," Mark said. "*Then* he'll kill you."

"We're not going to let it get that far."

Ash came and knelt beside Veta, a syringe in his hand. "Ready when you are, Mom. For the record, I still think this is crazy."

"You have a better idea?" Veta asked.

"No."

"Then do it."

Veta stopped suturing and tipped her head to one side,

exposing her jawline, where the nanobug would be planted. Ash inserted the needle and began the injection.

Then Mark's eyes went wide. "Take cover!"

He swept Veta away from him, pushing her into Ash and knocking them both flat. Olivia's MA40 began to rattle.

"Castor's here!" she yelled. "A little help!"

Veta rolled off Ash with the syringe still dangling from her jawline, and spun around to see Feodruz's huge form dropping into the fissure where she had been an instant before. She pulled her M6C and opened fire, bouncing two rounds off his shields before he rose to his full height. He was bellowing in pain and whirling around madly, trying in vain to free himself of a still-injured Mark, who had one arm wrapped around his neck and was using the other to bury a combat knife in his throat.

Veta pivoted toward Ash, who had retrieved his MA40 and was turning to help Olivia fight off the charge. "Is it in?"

Ash nodded. "Affirmative."

Veta shoved him toward Olivia. "Then *go*. Both of you."

She pulled the syringe out and flung it aside, then put two rounds into Feodruz's back. One penetrated, and the Jiralhanae clambered out of the fissure and stumbled down the slope, Mark still clinging to his neck.

Veta couldn't wait around to see what became of the pair. She scrambled out of the fissure on the side opposite Castor and Krelis, then took off across the slope at a sprint. She was fairly certain no one would want to risk killing her, but she needed to look convincing, so she dodged and turned, pausing every couple of seconds to spin around and loose a couple of rounds at her pursuers.

She leaped across one fissure and continued to flee, with Castor and Krelis gaining no ground on her. They were both enormous and likely exhausted, and she was fast enough that outrunning them was a real possibility. She began to consider veering into a tract of snow so she could fake a fall and give them a chance to catch up, but she didn't want to risk making it seem easy. She fired a few more rounds, then ejected her magazine and reached for a fresh one as she bounded over another fissure.

Midway across, she felt something clamp onto her boots. She looked down to find 'Gadogai crouching below her, his hands locked around her ankles. She hurled her empty pistol at his head and saw him duck aside, then slammed down on the far side and felt her nose begin to pour blood onto the cold stone.

Veta tried to rise to her knees and kick at him, but his grasp was secure. He merely pushed her boots away from his face and dragged her back into the fissure, swinging her around and smashing her sidelong into the opposite wall. Her breath left her in a huff, then he threw her down face-first again and knelt in the middle of her back.

"Welcome back, Little Mother." The Sangheili began to pull weapons off her belt and toss them aside. "You have *no* idea how much I have been looking forward to this."

FOURTEEN

0742 hours, October 14, 2559 (military calendar)
Outpost Gamma, Perimeter Epsilon Clarion
Refugia Core 001 001.3 202.4, Epsilon Wedge, the Ark

astor arrived at the capture out of breath and close to collapse. His wounds continued to weaken him, and the thin mountain air did not satisfy his lungs. The spy mother had been on the verge of outrunning him when 'Gadogai brought her down. Still, when he stepped to the rim of the fissure where she had been taken, he held himself upright and spent a few moments watching the blademaster bind her hands behind her back.

When Castor could finally speak without gasping, he said, "Well done, Blademaster. Have no fear of breaking something."

The betrayer raised her chin high enough to turn her head toward him. Her smashed nose had bled all over her face, and her left eye was already swollen and black.

"Careful, Dokab," she said. "You know how frail we humans are. I could go into shock and die."

"And what a pity *that* would be," Castor said. Still, he gave a small snort of frustration and looked to 'Gadogai. "We will enjoy a game of Tossers later, after she has served her purpose. Until then, she remains our prisoner, but defend her life as you would your own."

"I will not let her die," 'Gadogai said. He slipped his hand under the bindings and rose, using the woman's wrists like a handle. "Where would the sport be in that?"

"Indeed." Castor took a moment to savor the involuntary grunts of pain being released by the betrayer, then looked around for the chief of his guard. "Where is Feodruz?"

'Gadogai pointed his mandibles down the windswept slope. "At the head of the glacier, if he still lives." He raised the spy mother in display, then said, "One of her brood planted a blade in his throat. The last I saw of them, they were three fissures back, tumbling down the slope like a pair of *roxols* in the rut."

Castor did not know what a *roxol* was, but he found himself displeased with what 'Gadogai's description suggested for his loyal chief of guards. He pointed over his uphill shoulder, in the direction of the pinnacle.

"Take the betrayer to the Prelate," he said. "Krelis and I will see to Feodruz."

"Don't bother," the betrayer said. "When Mark puts a knife in a throat—"

Her boast changed to a pained groan as 'Gadogai gave her wrists a jerk. "I did not hear the *dokab* ask your opinion."

Allowing the betrayer to dangle by his thigh, 'Gadogai sprang out of the fissure so lightly that he did not seem burdened by her weight at all.

Motioning Krelis to follow, Castor turned and began to angle downslope toward the spot the blademaster had indicated. They descended only three steps before Bhasvod's voice sounded over the battlenet.

"Where are you going, Dokab? The Oracle has opened the gate for us."

Castor stopped and looked toward the base of the pinnacle. Bhasvod's slender figure was visible 150 meters away, silhouetted against a large gold rectangle that was yawning wide in the stone. Beside him stood Arcas, the captain of the Prelate's guard. Those two were all that remained of the Covenant warriors who had debarked from the Phantoms just a quarter hour earlier. The Keepers had also lost most of their warriors to the infidel missiles. Only Castor, Feodruz, Krelis, and 'Gadogai had survived the humans' assault.

"We are seeing to Feodruz," Castor said. " 'Gadogai said he may have been wounded."

" 'Gadogai *said* a human put a knife in his throat," Bhasvod corrected. "And they will do the same to this one, if you are foolish enough to leave her with only one escort."

Castor shot an annoyed glance in Krelis's direction. Someone had been leaving a helmet transmitter open. It was not Castor, and 'Gadogai was not even wearing his headset. The mistake was not a costly one under the circumstances, but Krelis had been a captain-deacon of one of the Keepers' Seraph talons, and clearly he should have known better.

"Feodruz is a loyal Keeper who should not be left for dead until we know he *is* dead," Castor replied. "Especially since we have so few warriors remaining."

"Which would never have happened, had you not allowed a nest of heel-biters to join the Keepers in the first place!" Bhasvod snapped. "Or at least listened to 'Gadogai when he warned you not to trust *any* of the humans."

'Gadogai stopped walking and turned to stare at Krelis—as did Castor. Worried that the blademaster would act without orders, Castor raised a palm to restrain him, then turned to watch Krelis, but addressed Bhasvod.

" 'Nest of heel-biters'?" Castor asked. "Where have I heard that before?"

"It is an apt description for a brood of spies, is it not?" Bhasvod replied, a little too quickly. "I hope you have no objection to having it appropriated."

"Not at all," Castor said. "Though I *am* curious how you knew 'Gadogai had warned me not to trust any of the humans."

Bhasvod hesitated. "I think you know." He made an impatient gurgle, then said, "Make your pilot's death a quick one. I am not wrong about the danger to our new acquisition."

Castor closed the transmission, then turned toward Krelis and roared, "Am I *surrounded* by betrayers?!"

Krelis backed away a step. "It was not a betrayal." He retreated another step. "You were being led astray by a Silent Shadow infidel. I had to do *something* to protect you."

"Then you were only thinking of your *dokab*." 'Gadogai's tone was eerily reasonable. Still holding the spy mother in one hand, he descended the slope and placed himself behind Krelis. "Protecting him from *me*. And you were in need of sage advice, I take it, so you began to repeat our confidential conversations to the Prelate."

"And to keep your transmitter *open*?" Castor was thinking of how Bhasvod had quoted him just a few moments earlier. "So he could hear what we said as we said it?"

"It was . . . only to keep him informed." Krelis glanced over his shoulder, then seemed to realize he had no place left to retreat and looked back to Castor. "I will not apologize for protecting you, Dokab."

"You were not protecting me." Castor drew his Ravager and pointed it at Krelis's chest. "You were envious."

Krelis's eyes widened and his jaw fell, and Castor could see comprehension blossoming in the young pilot's face. He had been covetous of 'Gadogai's influence and had convinced himself that if Castor valued an infidel's advice over his own, it could only be because he was being led from the Path by the lies of a deceiver.

"You *doubted* me," Castor said. "And for that, your life is now at an end."

But he could not bring himself to deliver the killing blow. Krelis was the last son of his beloved war-brother Orsun, who had died shielding Castor from a human missile. For Castor to slaughter Krelis now, so close to Transcendence, would be a betrayal of Orsun far worse than Krelis's own treachery.

But how could Castor spare this traitor? He had been deceived so many times, and by so many so close to him, that his own judgment was now in doubt. If he did not punish those who violated his trust, then how could he ever trust anyone?

When Castor still did not fire the Ravager after several moments, 'Gadogai exhaled heavily, then stepped in front of Krelis and put his free hand atop the Ravager muzzle.

"Perhaps it would be wiser to let him live," 'Gadogai said. "We are too few as it is, and the San'Shyuum have manipulated warriors more seasoned than Krelis into far greater betrayals. Forgive him this once of his transgressions, and he will not be so easily fooled the next time."

As 'Gadogai pushed the Ravager down, the spy mother looked up and smiled. Castor feared for a moment that Krelis's betrayal was something *she* had set in motion, and that by allowing Krelis to live, he was playing directly into her plan. He pulled the Ravager back and pointed it at Krelis's chest once more.

Then Castor saw that the woman was looking down the slope, in the direction of Feodruz's tumble. He turned and saw one of her brood—the same male he had impaled on his Ravager—seventy paces distant. The human had a huge gash across his abdomen and was smeared in dark blood, and he was angling across the slope toward them at a dead run.

"Do they *never* die?!"

Castor swung his Ravager around and loosed an incendiary bolt, which the wounded human barely had to sidestep to avoid. He raised the pistol in his free hand and began to return fire.

Deciding that if the spy was alive, Feodruz could not be, Castor motioned 'Gadogai toward the pinnacle base.

"Go!" He turned to follow and saw Krelis standing before him, one hand on his holstered mangler and his mouth twisted into an uncertain grimace. Castor waved him up the hill. "You as well, foolish traitor! As fast as you can!"

To Pavium, it seemed the avalanches would never end. Every time the shaking subsided, another crack reverberated through the whiteout, then another great slab of snow and ice slid off the mountain and crashed into the hidden depths below. Another shudder would rise from the roots of the citadel, and an additional blast of cold air would rush up the slope, bringing with it more billowing snow that blinded them to everything in the valley before them.

Then the clattering and clacking would start again, and Pavium would duck down next to Voridus and watch the boulders bounce past overhead, hoping that nothing too large dropped into the fissure to bury or crush them. After the rockfall ended, they would carefully poke their heads up and look for the gray, cruciform shape of Aggressor sentinels swooping down to annihilate them where they stood.

And on the rare occasions that no sentinels approached, they raised their heads and looked around, trying to determine how many fellow Long Shields still lived. Their clan had been decimated by the citadel defenses, and Pavium saw now how much of a mistake it had been to assume the Covenant-Keeper alliance would be the only enemy they faced. *Of course* the citadel ancilla would interpret their fortification efforts as the preparations for an assault. *Of course* its security systems would defend the facility it had been created to protect.

Pavium's only question now was how to successfully withdraw. He could not recall the Long Shield Phantoms without exposing them to the citadel's complement of Aggressor sentinels, and if that were to happen, the vessels would be destroyed.

Nor could the Long Shields withdraw on foot. The entire mountain was ringed by hanging glaciers, looming above sheer-walled valleys a thousand meters deep. Any attempt to leave the fissures where they had taken shelter would only result in more avalanches and rockslides, and they would all be swept from the craggy slopes before they had traveled a half kilometer. If Pavium wanted to save his clan, he had to find a way to subvert the systems controlling the citadel's defenses—whatever they might be.

He did not believe that was going to happen.

"Maximus and Manus are dead." Voridus had crawled along the fissure to where it intercepted a vertical cleft, and he was peering uphill toward the mountain's summit. "Polydamas, as well."

"Unfortunate. But I have no need of more casualty reports," Pavium growled. His brother had been keeping a running list of lost Long Shields since the first avalanche, which was not a terrible idea. But constantly reminding Pavium of his tactical mistake *was*.

"What I *could* use is a strategy of how to withdraw from this disaster without losing the rest of the clan."

Voridus drew back and turned to look at him. "There are none," he said. "At least, none that are apparent."

"There must be," Pavium said. "Keep thinking."

"And waste the time I have left?" Voridus crawled back down the fissure toward Pavium. "At least we have prevented Castor and . . ."

A band of blue radiance appeared in the whiteout beside them. Voridus raised his head out of the fissure and peered over the rim, down into the valley.

"I have some good news," Voridus said.

"Then why does it sound the opposite?"

Pavium lifted his head and looked over the rim of the fissure. It was still difficult to see through the storm, so Voridus pointed down into the swirling snow, toward the source of the blue radiance shining up from the white depths below.

Then Pavium finally saw what had cheered his brother—a blue band of hard light extending into the blowing snow, stretching across the valley in the direction of one of the citadel's companion mountains.

Pavium let out a low, involuntary growl. "*That* does not look like good news," he said. "That looks like a bridge."

Olivia bounced a pair of MA40 rounds off Castor's shields as he retreated into the base of the pinnacle, then switched targets and bounced two more off Krelis's shields as he followed. Veta had guessed right about there being a remote entrance to the citadel. As soon as 'Gadogai had started up the slope with her in custody, a rectangular passageway had opened into the stone, and Dhas Bhasvod had disappeared inside. Olivia assumed the gateway had been Intrepid Eye's doing, but that was no more than an educated guess. Like everything about this mission.

Guesswork and assumptions.

Even after Castor and Krelis retreated out of sight, Olivia and Ash continued to fire into the opening. They had to make the attack look convincing to prevent the zealots from realizing that Veta had allowed herself to be captured. But the last thing they wanted was to accidentally hit her with a ricochet, so they aimed their shots toward the ceiling above the threshold, knowing that the rounds would deflect downward into the floor and lose their penetration power before continuing to bounce around inside the passageway.

Once the Jiralhanae had vanished for a few seconds, Olivia changed magazines and used the barrel of her assault rifle to motion Ash up the slope.

"Secure the entrance," she said, speaking over TEAMCOM. At least one of them needed to be inside if Intrepid Eye tried to close the passageway behind the zealots. "And watch for optical blurring—that'll be Bhasvod's active camouflage."

"Not helping," Ash said, bounding up the slope. "I've thought of fifteen ways they can set an ambush up there—and that's not even in the top three."

"Sorry." Olivia couldn't stop worrying about Veta and her other teammates right now, and Ash continued overanalyzing. Good ways to blow a mission—and both of their conditions were only going to get worse. "Just be careful."

"I can be careful, or I can secure the entrance," Ash snapped. "Make up your mind."

He was already at the base of the pinnacle, racing along the wall toward the entranceway, so Olivia resisted the temptation to retort. Instead, she started back down the slope to check on Mark. He was about a hundred meters below, climbing through a snow tract. He was still running, but he was a mess and just wasn't fast, and she needed to evaluate whether he could give pursuit with her and Ash, or needed to sit this one out and let the biofoam hold him together until they could get him some proper medical attention.

Like *that* was going to happen.

The mission would still be a success even if Mark couldn't follow Veta to the citadel—heck, even if Olivia and Ash couldn't. All they had to do was set up a receiver unit as close as possible, wait for Veta to confirm that Intrepid Eye had transferred herself into the citadel's processing network, then relay the transmission to the *Spirit of Fire* . . . and get clear before the MAC bombardment began.

Getting clear was optional, of course. But if Olivia and Ash wanted to have any chance of extracting Veta after she did her part, they had to stay close. And if Mark couldn't keep up, she would need to bivouac him in a safe spot until he could be extracted.

Mark was just climbing out of the snow when Olivia reached the top of the tract. A nasty gash ran down the left side of his face, from the corner of his eye down past his jawline, and he was covered from head to toe in blood—a lot of it purple, so definitely not all his own. The shallowness of his breath suggested Feodruz had managed to break a rib or two—not an easy feat, considering that, like all Spartan-IIIs, his bones had been reinforced with carbide ceramics. He was holding one hand over his partially stitched abdominal wound, with a hooked needle and suture dangling down past his waist. His combat knife was missing, as was his DMR and rucksack. At least he still carried his M6C in his free hand.

Olivia took his arm and had him sit on a nearby boulder. "What's the other guy look like?"

"Dunno," Mark said. "Last I saw, he was sliding headfirst down a glacier."

Olivia glanced downhill. "Any chance he's coming back?"

"Not much," Mark said. "He lost a lot of blood."

"So have you." Olivia activated TEAMCOM, then asked, "Status? Mark could use some work."

"Take a couple of minutes," Ash said. "I need to check on some stuff anyway."

"What stuff?" Mark asked.

"You'll see," Ash said.

Maybe, Olivia thought. She sprayed biofoam in Mark's fresh wounds and applied more to the abdominal laceration to numb it, and on the needle and suture, then hastily finished sewing him up. Next, she put a few rough stitches into the slash on his face to close it and control the bleeding. Finally, she wrapped his torso in a bandage to help stabilize the broken ribs and reduce the chances of slashing any internal organs. In all, it took maybe three minutes.

"How's that?" Olivia asked.

"Huh. Good as new." Mark holstered his sidearm and started up the slope. "Thanks."

Olivia gathered her gear and weapons, then shouldered her rucksack and caught up to him easily. Too easily. His breath was coming in short gasps, and he was swaying as he moved. Olivia knew he was only going to aggravate his injuries by continuing to push on.

But push on was what Spartan-IIIs *did*—especially when they were from Gamma Company—so she matched his pace and said nothing. She wanted to, but she worried that would just make him more stubborn.

And then she fretted about how she was going to convince him to stay here and bivouac until she and Ash returned.

If they returned.

Ash appeared in the entrance as they approached the pinnacle and motioned them inside. They entered a rectangular passageway, illuminated by the golden ambience of its smooth walls and ceiling. Silver tendrils of Forerunner glyphs writhed along every surface, traveling at an upward angle from the entrance toward the distant exit.

The floor of the tunnel was made of hard light, and it extended beyond the exit into an opaque brume of blowing snow, gradually narrowing until its blue radiance vanished into the whiteout. Ash moved through the tunnel on the run, his MA40 held at the ready.

"They moved out too fast to set any traps, but I checked for trip beams and pressure sensors anyway," he said. "My bet is they plan to deactivate the bridge the moment they're inside the citadel—and let us fall straight into the valley."

"You have a plan to counter that, right?" Mark asked, starting after him.

"Sort of," Ash said.

"*Sort of?*" Olivia echoed. "Explain."

"It's pretty simple. Keep up."

"*That*'s . . . your plan?" Mark was already starting to gasp. "What difference does it make whether we're twenty meters behind them when they reach the citadel or two thousand? When the bridge disappears, we still fall."

"It makes a huge difference." Olivia was following close on Mark's heels, and not even working hard. "After they reach the citadel, Intrepid Eye will need a few seconds to establish a liaison with the ancilla. And that's after they find an interface device. We just need to be across the bridge by then."

Mark stopped two hundred meters shy of the exit. "I don't buy it."

Olivia was almost relieved to hear him say that, because she didn't think he had the strength left to make a ten-kilometer sprint across the valley.

"Intrepid Eye has already established a liaison," Mark said. "That's how she opened the gate and activated the bridge."

"That doesn't mean she's still in contact," Olivia replied. "If I were to bet, she's been waiting to deploy directly into the citadel. The controls for this bridge will be in the main structure with the supraluminal communications array, so that's where Intrepid Eye will want to be."

"I don't see why."

"Because 'Livi is the information specialist," Ash said. "She knows how this stuff works, and you don't. Let's go—you're wasting time."

"No, I'm being careful," Mark said. "And when Veta's gone, I'm the one in command."

"When we're in *this* condition?" Ash shook his head. "Listen to yourself. A good commander trusts his people. He trusts their judgment."

"And a good soldier trusts his commander."

Mark locked gazes with Ash, and Olivia immediately began to fret that they had *both* deteriorated to the point of ineffectiveness.

"I'll try to explain it," Olivia said.

Ash snorted in frustration.

"It won't take that long," Olivia added. "And it wouldn't hurt to have you check my assumptions."

Ash's bearing relaxed a bit, and a smile creased his lips. "Nice pivot."

"I do what I can." Olivia turned to Mark, who looked only slightly less on the verge of an explosion—he always was the first one to descend into full rampage mode, even before smoother deprivation. "Think of the pinnacle—where we are now—as a communications terminal, and the citadel ancilla like the mainframe it's connected to."

"Okay, but why wouldn't Intrepid Eye leave an aspect of herself behind, to watch over things here?" Mark glanced back at the river of Forerunner glyphs running toward them. "In fact, it kind of looks like she already *did*."

"Possible, but not likely," Olivia said. "She wouldn't risk it. The stakes are too high for her. If we decided to demo this site, for instance, she'd lose whatever she left behind. I don't think that's a price Intrepid Eye is willing to pay. Given how we've chewed through the Keeper forces, it's possible that she's just clinging to the last few data stores on their side, hoping they make it to the citadel so that she can force out the other ancilla and relocate into its systems. And then it's a matter of compression and consolidation."

"Still don't follow," Mark said.

"Look . . . ," Olivia said. "The human brain holds about five hundred trillion bits of information, and performs about one thousand trillion operations every second."

"Could have fooled me," Ash said.

"Because most of it occurs unconsciously," Olivia said. "You're only aware of an infinitesimal part of what your brain is processing. To make all that happen, it takes about one and a third kilograms of neurons and synapses."

" 'Livi, we don't have time for this," Ash said.

Mark ignored him. "This has what to do with Intrepid Eye?"

"An Archeon-class ancilla is about a hundred times as powerful as a human brain," Olivia continued. "We know that from the ONI studies of Intrepid Eye aboard the *Argent Moon*. So a human brain would have to weigh over a hundred and thirty kilograms just to hold her."

"This isn't helping," Mark said. "And we've never even seen anything like that when we've dealt with Intrepid Eye before."

"Right. That's because she uses two strategies to get around the problem," Olivia replied. "Compression and dispersal. She compresses her data to unimaginable degrees before storing it, and she disperses her operations over entire networks of devices. It's the only way she can survive in human technology."

"So she's *everywhere*?" Mark asked. "How's that going to work? We can't kill everything."

"We won't need to," Olivia said. "Because of consolidation."

Ash made a rolling motion with his finger.

"ONI discovered that ancillas don't actually like to be dispersed and compressed," Olivia said. "Neither do human smart AIs, for that matter. It slows down their operations and increases their error rate."

"Kind of like having a concussion?" Ash asked.

"The term in the brief was 'foggy-headed,'" Olivia said. "But yeah, something along those lines. When they have the power and processing capacity, they like to draw everything in close and decompress their data. It improves their efficiency."

"It clears their mind, in other words," Mark said. "Like going back on smoothers."

"Exactly," Olivia said. "And Intrepid Eye has been living with compressed data and dispersed operations for over six years now.

What do you think she's going to do when she gets inside a Forerunner facility—with exactly the kind of technology she needs to clear her mind?"

"She's going to consolidate," Ash said. "She's going to pull her operations into one place."

"And she's going to decompress," Mark said. "Pull all her data up and spread it out where she can access it."

"Now you're getting it," Olivia said. "That's certainly what I would do if I'd been living in a bootbox for six years."

"Okay, I'm in," Mark said. "Let's go."

"Wait one," Olivia said, stepping into his path. "Maybe you should stay here and secure our back trail."

Mark scowled, too smoother-deprived to pick up the subtext. "I thought the idea was to keep up with Castor and Bhasvod."

" 'Livi and I can keep up," Ash said. "We can even catch up. But you're in no shape for a ten-kilometer sprint."

"You think you're going to leave *me* behind?" Mark said. "Uh-uh. Not happening."

Olivia shot Ash a look of exasperation, then said, "Mark, you're ready to collapse from blood loss and you have broken ribs. Even if you *can* make the run—"

"I'm making it."

"—it could kill you," Olivia said. "Bivouac here and call for extraction. Now that the Banshees are gone, Commander Barre could be swinging back anytime."

"Or she could have been shot down." Mark turned toward the exit and began to run. "If it kills me, it kills me. That's the job."

Olivia and Ash exchanged head shakes, then Olivia motioned for Ash to take lead. She fell in behind Mark. He managed to keep a good pace until they left the tunnel and for the first half kilometer after that. Then the burly silhouettes of Jiralhanae appeared in the snow ahead, and Ash signaled for them to slow down—which helped Mark keep his footing on the weather-slickened bridge deck. After that, they were careful to hang back out of sight, with Ash occasionally moving forward to make sure their quarry had not put on a sudden burst of speed.

In the storm ahead of them, plasma bolts and particle beams flashed through the blowing snow as the Banished Banshees did battle with the citadel's Aggressor sentinels. A near-steady cacophony of cracking and crashing filled the valley as pieces of glacier continued to tumble off the slopes of the citadel. Once, a sentinel appeared out of the whiteout and swooped low over their heads, passing first over Castor and his group, then over the Gammas, but it seemed to assume they were all authorized to be on the bridge and made no aggressive move.

The slower pace worked in Mark's favor, but finally, after an hour, his strength deserted him.

He slipped on the snow and lurched forward, then stumbled as he tried to catch himself and went flying toward the right side of the bridge. Olivia lashed out and caught him by the collar of his borrowed flight suit, but by then his momentum was already carrying him over the edge—and dragging her after him on the smooth surface.

An energy shield of gold hexagonal cells flashed into existence and hurled Mark into her, knocking them both back into the middle of the bridge.

"Apparently it has guardrails," Mark said.

They gathered themselves up, Mark leaving drops of fresh blood in the snow, and resumed their earlier pace. But it was only two minutes before he began to go wobbly again.

Ash slowed even further until Mark could keep up without taxing himself to the point of falling. They continued that way for a quarter hour before another sentinel swooped in, flying low over the bridge.

They assumed it was just taking a look, like the one before it. But once the cruciform shape was close enough for them to see the sheen of its silver body, its particle beam suddenly flared to life and began to deflect fire off the hard-light bridge deck.

Ash dived right and Mark went left, both rolling onto their backs and unleashing rounds into the sentinel's flashing energy shield. Olivia stood fast, bringing up her MA40, tracking the beam emitter in the bottom of its chassis as it swiveled side to side, firing first at Ash, then Mark. Finally, its shields went down, and she put a burst into the beam emitter. The drone exploded with an ear-splitting crack, raining shrapnel down on them all.

Ash cursed in anger, then pulled a shard out of his forearm, and Olivia felt blood pouring down her neck from where she'd been grazed. Mark was on his feet almost instantly, holding his M6C in both hands and spinning in a circle, searching for more Aggressors.

"Why the hell did *that* one attack?!" Mark demanded. Maybe it was from a lack of smoother, but he seemed almost insulted, as though the change in behavior was somehow personal. "The other one didn't!"

"We're probably too far behind Castor," Olivia said. "It sees us as a separate group."

"And the first one wasn't smart enough?" Mark replied.

"None of them are smart," Olivia said. "That's the whole point. Intrepid Eye probably gave the ancilla a simple set of instructions—allow the first group to pass, and attack anyone following. The sentinels have to interpret those instructions for themselves, and if we stay close enough—"

"They assume we're part of the first group," Mark said. "Okay, we're going to spread out, so we collectively become one long string. Ash, you move up until Castor's group is in sight again. 'Livi, you keep Ash in sight. And I'll bring up the rear."

"Mark," Olivia said. "I'm not sure that's a good—"

"Well, *I'm* sure," Mark said. "Move out. I'll be right behind you."

Ash looked back for a moment, then finally nodded. "Good plan, Mark. Thanks."

He turned and raced into the whiteout at full speed. When Olivia didn't follow immediately, Mark waved her forward.

"The mission comes first, 'Livi. Go." Mark turned his pistol barrel down and waved her forward again. "Seriously. I'm right behind you."

"Liar."

But Olivia obeyed the order . . . sort of. She sprinted up the bridge after Ash, then slowed down twenty steps later and twisted around to check on Mark. He was barely visible, a gray figure lurching into the snow—and now going the other way.

She started to open TEAMCOM, to tell him he should at least keep running toward the citadel, when Ash's voice came over the channel.

"Heads up," he said. "Another one!"

Olivia looked forward and saw the sentinel dropping low over the bridge, passing over Ash's lanky silhouette without opening fire, its beam emitter glowing red as it descended toward her. She dived to the icy deck and rolled to the side, heard the energy shield crackle into existence, then found herself flying back toward the center of the bridge.

By then, the sentinel was already past, its particle beams bouncing into the whiteout as it continued toward Mark.

She heard the muffled bang of an M6C firing and saw the sentinel's shields flash gold. Then it swung around to the side of the bridge and hovered over the valley, swiveling on its access as it tried to bring its main weapon to bear.

Mark's voice came over TEAMCOM. "Get out of here, 'Livi. I've got this!"

A grenade detonated, and then Mark's pistol began to bang again, until the sentinel finally exploded and only the sound of the roaring wind remained.

Olivia scrambled to her feet and started up the bridge after Ash. She tried to raise Mark on TEAMCOM, but his signal had gone dead.

There was no question of going back to check on him. The mission came first, and Mark knew that better than anyone. But damn . . . she was worried about him. That wasn't going to go away.

She caught up to Ash a few minutes later, after they had run another kilometer and the gray mass of the citadel mountain began to grow visible through the veil of blowing snow. The blue flashes of plasma bolts and the orange streaks of particle beams came more frequently than ever, and she could see the smoking hulks of wrecked Wraiths lodged precariously on nearby outcroppings and ice crests.

The bridge appeared to end about seventy meters ahead, where the golden rectangle of another gateway opened into the sheer face of the citadel mountain. Through the blowing snow, the gray silhouettes of Castor and his companions were just visible as they rushed inside, and when Olivia peered over the side of the light bridge, she could see the blue-gray blur of an icy rock slope about fifty meters below.

If the bridge was deactivated right now, she and Ash just might survive—provided they were able to arrest their fall before they slid too far down the slope.

Mark, on the other hand . . .

"Go go go!" Olivia shouted. "We're almost there!"

"Maybe so," Ash said. "But we're not the only ones."

Olivia looked back toward the entrance and saw the hulking figures of half a dozen heavily armored Jiralhanae dropping onto the bridge from the cliffs above. They immediately rushed through the entrance after Castor and the other Keepers.

"Wait," Olivia said. "Are those guys *Banished*?"

"Not sure. But whoever they are, they're about to ruin our whole plan."

FIFTEEN

When Castor crossed the Threshold of Clarity and entered the vestibule of the Chamber of Consecration at last, it was not with the sacred exultation he had expected.

Instead, he felt only a weary malaise.

He had been forced to abandon or sacrifice most of his followers even before leaving Reach, and now all that remained of the Keepers of the One Freedom were Krelis, an acolyte who had betrayed him out of jealousy; Veta Lopis, the ONI deceiver who had apparently devoted her life to ruining his; and Inslaan 'Gadogai, a faithless infidel who seemed to be Castor's last loyal friend.

The trio was hardly the host of Believers he had envisioned leading into Transcendence . . . and yet here they were, following Dhas Bhasvod and his guard Arcas into the Epsilon Clarion under the guidance of the Oracle herself. He tried to maintain some semblance of his original fervor, but his wounds seemed to be sapping his enthusiasm. The bullet hole in his shoulder had begun to fester, and the one in his thigh had left him trembling and weak after the long run across the Bridge of Enlightenment.

The entry vestibule was illuminated by the same golden light as the passage at the other end of the bridge. But here, the silver Forerunner glyphs flowed along the walls at a downward angle instead of upward. The floor was made of the same blue hard light as the bridge deck, as though an extension of the same surface, and Castor did not think Bhasvod's plan to deactivate the bridge behind them would work. They would need to set an ambush to eliminate their pursuers, but Bhasvod and Arcas continued forward without pause.

Castor allowed 'Gadogai to follow. The blademaster was carrying the spy mother facedown like a satchel, using the rope that connected her bound hands to her bound ankles as a handle, and the sooner she was safely away from the bridge, the better. But once they had advanced ten paces into the vestibule, Castor caught Krelis by the arm and stopped.

"You will remain here, to guard—"

He was interrupted by the cracking of human gunfire out on the bridge. Castor grabbed his Ravager off its hip mount and whirled around.

But he was slowed by his injuries, and by the time he turned, a volley of mangler spikes and pulse beams was already flying into the vestibule. They were not the weapons Castor had heard, but they were an even worse problem. He brought his Ravager up, cursing Fate for allowing him to come so far before killing him—

—Krelis muscled him aside and stepped into Castor's place, taking the volley square in the chest. The young Keeper's energy shields were instantly overwhelmed, and he dropped to the floor, leaving the air filled with the smell of blood and charred flesh.

Castor fired into a handful of charging Banished. All were Jiralhanae wearing the bloody rectangle of the Long Shield Clan, and there was not a human firearm among them. He realized they must have been hiding on the mountain above the vestibule when he and the others entered, then dropped onto the bridge to attack from behind. But where the cracking gunfire of human weapons had come from, he had no clue.

Castor fired a second bolt into the charging mob, and a Banished warrior erupted in flame and flew backward. Then the Prelate and his guard returned, reacting quickly, Arcas firing his spiker as they leaped over Krelis's thrashing figure to answer the Long Shield assault. Castor paused only to look back toward the Chamber of Consecration and confirm that 'Gadogai had continued onward to protect the brood mother, then pushed off the wall and raced after Bhasvod and Arcas, leaning down to touch Krelis's shoulder as he passed by.

"Keep the faith," he said. "I will be back."

He caught up to Bhasvod just as the Prelate's hard-light blade slashed the leg of a Long Shield. Castor shoved his Ravager forward and caught the falling warrior on its bayonet spike, freeing the Prelate to attack the last two ambushers alongside Arcas.

Castor worked his spike inside the fallen Long Shield's throat, driving it up toward the skull until the warrior fell limp, then pulled the now bloody weapon free and followed his companions onto the bridge. Bhasvod and Arcas were already face-to-face with the last two Long Shields. Unlike the others, this pair wore dark power armor with dark faceplates and no clan emblems—an affectation indicating they *were* the clan. Probably the warlord Pavium and his pack brother and most trusted lieutenant, Voridus.

Both were armed with manglers, which they fired as they charged. Not daring to shoot between his own companions,

Castor merely stopped, ready to leap forward the instant he saw an opening.

Arcas and his foe both swung high, their wrists crashing into each other at head height. The impact drained the pair's badly depleted energy shields to nothing, and both weapons flew free and tumbled over opposite sides of the bridge.

A stiletto extended from the Long Shield's left gauntlet, appearing so suddenly it was nearly in Arcas's throat before he twisted away. Arcas used one hand to trap the wrist of his foe's knife hand, then used the other to deliver a helmet-rocking backfist that sent the Long Shield sprawling sideways.

In contrast to Arcas's power, Dhas Bhasvod used grace and flow to deal with his own Banished enemy. As the Long Shield tried to fire at the Prelate's knees, he lowered his glaive and slashed the mangler in two. The barrel assembly hit the bridge deck and bounced past Castor without causing so much as a shudder in the hard-light surface.

The surprised Long Shield tried to retreat, reaching for the knife on his hip. Bhasvod was already striking a second time, his glaive blade vanishing from one end of the haft and reappearing at the other as it swung toward the Jiralhanae's head.

The Banished warrior's energy shields saved him—though just barely, the hard-light blade touching his helmet as he went down. He pivoted away, trying to open enough space to bring his knife to bear. Bhasvod continued to press his attack, stepping forward to deny his foe any maneuvering room, twisting his body around as he drove an uppercut under the Jiralhanae's chin.

The blow launched the Long Shield into the energy-field railing. Castor expected him to come flying back toward the center, but Bhasvod brought his glaive around, igniting the blade and cutting through the barrier as though it were soft cloth. The Long

Shield tumbled off the bridge, crashing into the rocks twenty meters below, then slid down the slope, screaming and clanging all the way.

Arcas's opponent was now rolling across the bridge in an effort to regain his feet. When he saw his companion go over the side, he changed tactics and accelerated into the rotation. He raised his left gauntlet, the stiletto arcing toward the middle of Bhasvod's back.

Castor reached out and caught the Prelate's shoulder, pulling him clear just as the stiletto slashed past. Then Castor pivoted forward and planted his foot in the Long Shield's back, kicking him off the bridge in roughly the same spot as his companion. The warrior crashed into the rocks and shot down the slope in a similar manner, yelling and clanking as he went.

Bhasvod glanced down at the mountainside, no doubt making certain the two Long Shields could not climb back up to the bridge even if they had somehow survived. Then he backed away from the edge and reentered the vestibule.

Just inside, he slowed and spoke over his shoulder. "Perhaps you saved my life, Dokab." He circled past Krelis's groaning form without so much as a glance. "I doubt it, but perhaps."

Castor took a moment to look back along the bridge, searching for the source of the gunfire that had drawn his attention to the Long Shield ambush. All he saw was the empty hard-light deck vanishing into a white curtain of snow forty meters away.

"If you are awaiting any sort of gratitude," Arcas said, pausing at Castor's side, "that was it."

"Bhasvod's gratitude means nothing to me," Castor said. He was eager to check on Krelis, but not willing to be ambushed a second time. "Did you hear gunfire before the attack?"

"*Human* gunfire?" Arcas looked back along the bridge with Castor. "No."

"I am certain that I did. The sound of it alerted me to the ambush."

"You must be mistaken, Dokab." Arcas stepped into the vestibule. "Why would the humans feel the need to alert *you*?"

"A good question," Castor said. He peered into the veil of snow a bit longer, then started after Arcas. Someone needed to check on Krelis, and he doubted Bhasvod's guard would bother. "Perhaps the Long Shields loosened some rocks as they moved into position."

"An excellent thought, Dokab," Arcas said. As Castor had expected, Arcas circled past Krelis's feet without slowing. "I do not see how any humans could still be back there. The sentinels would have killed them all before they were halfway across the bridge."

Castor was not so certain. The Oracle had indeed assured them she could turn the citadel defenses against their enemies, but it had been he and Bhasvod and Arcas who had actually turned back the Long Shield attack. And the spy mother's brood were not ordinary humans. They should have been dead or stranded at least ten times already, yet they never seemed more than a step behind Castor . . . and too often on the verge of slaying him.

Still, Castor could hardly remain behind to stand guard. After all he had done to prepare for the Great Journey, he deserved to be there when the spy mother's hand was pressed to the activation pylon. More importantly, he *needed* to be there. Dhas Bhasvod had no idea just how slippery this female could be. To the Prelate, "Veta Lopis" was an inferior being, incapable of challenging him either intellectually or physically, and someone to be ordered about and used as he pleased. But to Castor, Veta Lopis was a worthy foe—someone who had outwitted and outfought him on several occasions. She needed to be handled with the utmost care until she had served her purpose, and then quickly eliminated.

And Castor certainly had to be present for *that*. More than anything right now—except possibly achieving Transcendence—he wanted to watch Veta Lopis die.

Castor retreated into the vestibule. Keeping one eye turned toward the bridge, he knelt beside his war-brother's son. There could be no doubt that Krelis would soon expire. His armored breastplate had been penetrated in so many places there was more of it missing than covering him. Four of his wounds were still smoking as his internal organs sizzled with the residual heat from plasma pulses, and seven spikes were lodged deep in his chest, the tiny barbs on their three edges sawing at his ribs and pulling them farther inside with every breath.

It took Krelis a few moments to realize Castor was even there— or at least to find the strength to acknowledge it. But at last he opened his eyes and met Castor's gaze.

"He is a San'Shyuum," Krelis said. "I . . . I had to listen."

"Yes, of course," Castor said. Like most Jiralhanae warriors, Krelis had come of age in a Covenant where the San'Shyuum were revered. Dhas Bhasvod's kind had been viewed as infallible Prophets, interpreting the sacred words of the Forerunners for the other species of the hegemony. "You did nothing wrong."

Krelis shook his head—an act that caused his face to contort in pain. "I betrayed . . . you. It was Unworthy."

"It is forgotten. You traded your life for mine. That is Worthy."

"To you . . . perhaps." Krelis drew a pained gasp, then said, "But to the Ancients . . . I will be forever a traitor."

"The Ancients will understand. There are allowances—"

He was interrupted by a harsh cry of annoyance behind him. "Dokab!"

Castor looked back to see Bhasvod standing at the far end of the vestibule, backlit by the brilliant blue light in the chamber beyond. Arcas and 'Gadogai stood beside him, the blademaster still holding Lopis by the rope connecting her wrists and ankles.

"Why are you wasting time?" the Prelate demanded.

"I am *not* wasting time," Castor replied. "He is the son of a war-brother, and I am guiding him onto the Path of Deliverance."

"And *I* am preparing to enter the citadel's control room. If you wish to be there, come now."

"It will take only a moment." Castor could not let Orsun's son die believing the gods had forever marked him a traitor. "A loyal warrior deserves that much."

"A loyal warrior is happy to make the sacrifice," Bhasvod replied. "Finish him yourself, if you must. That is the only kindness we have time for."

He turned away and started across the vast chamber beyond.

"The Prelate is right," Krelis said. "I am happy to make the sacrifice. Do it now and go."

Castor was taken aback by the Prelate's callousness. Nevertheless, after a few seconds, he pressed his Ravager spike to Krelis's brow. But when he met the young Jiralhanae's gaze, it was Orsun's eyes he saw . . . and he could not bring himself to put his weight on the weapon.

"Do it," Krelis said. "You cannot let them begin the Great Journey without you."

"I will not," Castor said. He rocked back on his heels. "But it occurs to me there is one last duty I must assign you."

"Anything. If I am able."

Castor returned his Ravager to its hip mount, then retrieved a mangler from one of the dead Long Shields and armed it.

"The spy mother's brood are still behind us," he said.

Krelis looked at him with a confused expression, then let his head drop onto the hard-light floor.

"I need you to stay alive a little while longer," Castor said. He placed the mangler in Krelis's hands. "You must let us know when they arrive."

Krelis clutched the weapon to his chest, then looked toward the entrance. "As it is spoken, it shall be done."

"Good." Castor patted Krelis on the shoulder. "Your father will be proud when we all see each other again in Transcendence."

He rose and started after Dhas Bhasvod. Another sacrifice. He was now effectively the last of the Keepers of the One Freedom. He tried not to think about it even as his wounds reminded him.

As he left the vestibule, he found himself in a vast rotunda with a blue hard-light floor and a domed ceiling vault. The Chamber of Consecration. The structure was at least five hundred meters in diameter, with a number of other entrances spaced around its perimeter. In the center of the rotunda was what appeared to be a large pit, itself perhaps fifty meters across. From the center of the pit rose a tall cylindrical tower with black walls and no visible doors or windows. As Castor drew closer, he saw that the tower was ringed by a hard-light balcony similar to the bridge outside, and the balcony was connected to the rest of the floor by four narrow catwalk bridges spaced at even intervals.

Castor was fifty paces into the room when 'Gadogai came to walk beside him. The Sangheili continued to carry the spy mother in one hand, holding her just high enough that her face did not drag on the chamber's hard-light floor.

"A beautiful sight, is it not?" 'Gadogai asked, looking toward the domed ceiling. "The citadel fighting our enemies *for* us?"

When Castor looked up, he realized he was looking through the surface of the citadel mountain into a brilliant blue sky marbled by trails of white vapor and slivers of blue and orange flame. It took a moment to realize that the vapor trails were contrails, and that he was watching talons of Banshees do battle with a swarm of Aggressor sentinels outside the citadel. The Banshees seemed to be trying to avoid battle to the extent possible without actually leaving the area, for they were gradually climbing higher and moving farther away.

"Beautiful enough," Castor said. "And better than having them fight against us."

'Gadogai stopped walking. "Why do you sound less than thrilled, Dokab?"

The blademaster pointed toward the center of the floor, toward the black tower that stood in the center of the pit. A steady stream of Aggressors was swirling around the structure, rising out of the surrounding pit and ascending into an air shaft directly above.

"*That* is the control room you have worked so hard to reach," 'Gadogai continued. "Or so the Oracle says."

"So . . . we are here?" Castor had expected more obstacles to be in their way. And after so many failures, he could not quite trust what 'Gadogai was telling him. "We are about to start the Great Journey?"

"As soon as we enter the control room, I would assume— unless, of course, you have changed your mind." 'Gadogai's tone was solemn enough to make clear he was not speaking lightly. He leaned closer and whispered, "I would be happy to kill the Prelate for you. Very happy."

Bhasvod was thirty paces ahead and out of earshot. Nevertheless, his pace slowed ever so slightly—or so it seemed to Castor.

"You would need to handle Arcas," 'Gadogai continued. "Though it would be easy enough if you began the attack with a plasma bolt to his back."

Castor chuckled, as though he thought 'Gadogai were joking. "Tempting, Blademaster." And it *was*, for Castor was still bitter over being rushed with Krelis—and angered by the small value Bhasvod placed on any life that was not his own. "But I think not. We are so close it would be a pity to get distracted now."

'Gadogai clacked his mandibles in acceptance. "As I expected. But there is still time to change your mind. If you do, I will be ready."

"Are *you* trying to change my mind, Blademaster?" Castor put a slight gravel into his voice, for 'Gadogai seemed to be intentionally planting doubts . . . suggesting that going ahead with the Great Journey was a mistake. "Shall I expect *you* to be the next to betray me?"

"What a foolish question that is," 'Gadogai said. "Were I to betray you, it would be the last thing you expected."

"Then no more of your pointless blather. It only makes me doubt your devotion."

"Never doubt the devotion of a friend who asks the questions you fear to answer, Dokab." 'Gadogai looked away, fixing his gaze on the control room ahead. "With something of this magnitude, you must be certain."

"I *am* certain, Blademaster." As Castor spoke, it seemed to him that Bhasvod picked up his pace again, and he wondered how the Prelate was eavesdropping this time. "I have *always* been certain. Remember that."

After an hour of being carried facedown by the rope connecting her wrists and ankles, Veta's entire body was in sheer agony, especially her wrists and shoulders, and it took all of her will not to scream at any given moment. But her limbs were somehow still in their sockets—a feat that she attributed more to her flexibility than her strength. Besides, she was not about to let a little thing like pain distract her from the mission—not when she thought about everything her Gammas were currently sacrificing.

So, as Castor and 'Gadogai followed Dhas Bhasvod and Arcas across the rotunda, Veta slid her pain off to one side of her mind. Instead, she focused on their conversation, using their voices to anchor her attention on their words, using those words to draw her thoughts constantly back to the mission . . . and the reason she had asked Ash to plant a nanobug in her jaw.

Veta found it hard to believe that 'Gadogai really intended to help Castor activate the Halo. The Sangheili was as much an Unbeliever as Veta, and his questions were clearly meant to plant seeds of doubt in Castor's mind—to raise the possibility that destroying the galaxy's sentient life would be an unimaginable mistake.

Yet stopping Castor would be a simple thing for 'Gadogai. All he had to do was kill Veta. Then the zealots would be forced to find another human, and there weren't a lot of good options near enough to be of use.

Perhaps, like the Ferrets, 'Gadogai realized that Intrepid Eye was the true danger . . . but Veta didn't think so. He lacked the Ferrets' experience with the Forerunner ancilla and was unlikely to appreciate how ruthless and deceitful she could be. More importantly, he was unaware of the Ferret team's plan to trap Intrepid Eye inside the citadel's systems and destroy her. Had the blademaster intended to prevent her—or anyone—from firing the array, he would have done something by now.

And he hadn't.

It seemed he was going along with Castor's plan to devastate the galaxy out of . . . what? Loyalty?

Whatever the Sangheili's motivations, his attempts to sway Castor gave Veta the opening she needed. Both Castor and

'Gadogai were smart enough to realize that even trussed up, Veta would never stop trying to prevent them from activating the array—and if she wasn't trying, they would suspect she had some other scheme up her sleeve. Which was exactly what she needed to avoid.

"Dokab." Veta was so surprised by the pain she heard in her own voice that she had to pause and swallow before continuing. "I know I am the last one whose advice you want to hear—"

"You are correct," Castor said. "So do not anger me by offering it."

"Then listen to 'Gadogai," Veta said. "The San'Shyuum have used religion to control others in the Covenant, and Dhas Bhasvod is still doing it to *you*."

"I said nothing of the kind," 'Gadogai objected. "Pay her no attention, Dokab."

"It's true that I betrayed you, Dokab," Veta continued. "I've been your enemy since we met. But I have *always* respected your wisdom and strength . . . until I saw how Dhas Bhasvod treated you today. Today, I *pity* you."

Castor stopped and whirled on her. "Silence!"

He snatched the Ravager off his hip so quickly that Veta thought the next thing she would feel was its bayonet spike sinking into her throat—after all, they only needed her hand, not her tongue—but 'Gadogai was nothing if not swift. She found herself swinging out of harm's way as the blademaster placed his body between her and Castor's weapon.

"Dokab, if you want her dead, I will be glad to stand aside," 'Gadogai said. "But you know that Bhasvod wants her alive. So then we would have to kill him and Arcas as well. And that would not be an easy task at the moment. Not when they are *already* watching us."

TROY DENNING

Veta was facing the wrong way to see what Bhasvod and Arcas were up to. Instead, now she was looking back toward the vestibule through which they had entered, studying the long blue strip of the bridge where it disappeared into the blowing snow. She knew Ash and Olivia would have tried to come across the bridge after they set the comm relays. With all the Aggressors flying around, she hoped the pair had turned back . . . but she knew better. Ash and Olivia were out there somewhere. They might be lying on the bridge with beam burns through their chests, but they were definitely there.

And Mark?

What had become of her ferocious Mark? The last time she'd seen him, he was tumbling down the mountain with Feodruz. Even if he'd survived the fight and the fall, Mark was in no shape to make the long run across the hard-light bridge.

But he would have tried, goddammit. She knew *that* too.

Part of Veta cursed her Gammas' doggedness, because she wanted them to live the full, long lives they deserved. But a bigger part of her loved them for it. Fighting on—no matter what—was who they *were*. It was what ONI had built them to do. Whether that had been a morally defensible act was a debate for another day, and with someone else. But forcing the Gammas to ignore their own nature, expecting them to stand down when they had a mission to complete, would have been as wrong as it was impossible.

So Veta had to finish what they'd started together. Not to stop Castor and Bhasvod, or to finally destroy Intrepid Eye, or even to save the galaxy . . . though she *did* want all those things. No—she had to finish the mission for her Gammas, because she was one of them now.

They had made her that way.

And right now, when Castor didn't immediately answer 'Gadogai, Veta realized she'd struck a nerve. So she did what any good fighter would—she pressed the attack.

"Turn me back around, 'Gadogai," she said. "Castor doesn't have the courage to kill me . . . not while Bhasvod and—"

That was as far as she made it before the edge of 'Gadogai's free hand struck the lymph node at the base of her ear. Everything went black, and—

—Veta woke up a few minutes later, still bound by her wrists and ankles, still being carried facedown like a handbag.

Now she could see that Bhasvod was only three paces ahead, and 'Gadogai was directly behind, second in line. Neither Castor nor Arcas were in Veta's line of sight, though the heavy steps thump-thumping behind them suggested the two Jiralhanae were now bringing up the rear of the column—perhaps a precaution on Castor's part, brought about by 'Gadogai's earlier efforts to undermine his devotion to the Great Journey.

The small procession seemed to be about three-quarters of the way to its destination, just starting across one of the hard-light catwalks connecting the rotunda floor to the balcony that ringed the control room tower. Under the balcony, a cluster of Aggressors hung upside down, like *daks* beneath their roosts. When she looked over the side of the catwalk, she could see thousands more hanging beneath a web of flat trusses that seemed to connect the walls of a bottomless, blue-walled pit to the dark foundations of the control room.

"Are you considering jumping?" 'Gadogai asked, noticing that Veta had returned to consciousness. "It would not be a quick death, with all those trusses to break your fall. But it might be far more merciful than what Castor has in store for you, once you have served your purpose."

"I can't believe you're helping them do this," Veta said. "You believe in the Psalms about as much as I do."

"Oh, not a word of them," 'Gadogai confirmed. "But one should always be loyal to one's friends. They are so hard to come by."

"So you're going to help Castor kill every sentient being in the galaxy," Veta said, "out of *friendship*?"

"Surely it is not *that* difficult to understand," 'Gadogai said. They came to the end of the catwalk. He stepped onto the balcony and moved aside so Castor and Arcas could pass, then raised her to eye level. "Think of your own brood. What would you do for *them*?"

Veta had no answer, because she couldn't imagine anyone on her team undertaking such an apocalyptic project. But they *had* made mistakes, including the inadvertent killing of an investigative reporter during a training mission, and she'd covered that up in order to protect their future as a Ferret team. The Gammas had also done some pretty destructive things during periods of smoother deprivation, and Veta had also made sure those particular incidents never came to light.

The irony of the Gammas being well on the road to another such incident—one that could prove rather helpful right now—was not lost on her. They were already suffering the effects of their smoother deprivation pretty severely, and in about ten hours, they were going to start having full psychotic breaks.

"You see?" 'Gadogai said, as though reading her thoughts. "If I am a monster, I am not the only one."

Before Veta could point out the crystal-clear differences, Dhas Bhasvod interrupted. "Bring the human." He had stopped about a quarter of the way around the balcony, maybe fifty meters ahead. "I have found the interface station."

'Gadogai started around the balcony, carrying Veta past the black curve of the control room's exterior. The surface was as smooth and glossy as obsidian, though—this being Forerunner architecture, it was probably some kind of boson field. She began to struggle against her bindings, more to meet her captors' expectations than because she hoped to free herself.

When they reached Bhasvod, the sheen vanished from a head-sized hexagon near the base of the wall. The holograph of a diamond-shaped submonitor appeared in the black depths of the hexagonal display, seeming to stare out from a single round photoreceptor. 'Gadogai reached down and yanked Veta's head up by her hair, forcing her to meet the submonitor's gaze.

Before it could speak, Veta announced loudly, "Beware my ancilla companion! She carries the logic plague!"

The submonitor's photoreceptor flared bright silver.

ONI had many faults, but withholding technical information that might be needed in the field was not one of them. At the time of the Ferrets' briefing on this particular facet of the Forerunners' history, Veta had assumed the logic plague was an ancient catastrophe with little relevance in the modern field. Clearly, she'd been wrong: the mere mention of the devastating corruption-attack kept the submonitor's attention locked on her.

"Stand down your exterior defenses!" Veta ordered. 'Gadogai was already swinging her away from the interface, moving so fast she feared he meant to fling her into the pit behind them, but she continued to speak. "The humans you're attacking out there are *not* your enemies. They're coming to stop this renegade ancilla— and save *you*. Listen to me!"

Intrepid Eye had expected Veta Lopis to try some kind of subterfuge—she just had not anticipated it being *this* one. Falsely declaring a logic plague emergency was a Categorical Prohibition that would never even occur to an ancilla, because it activated automatic isolation protocols that could not be undone.

Simply by uttering the words, Lopis had forced the citadel ancilla to cut off all communications with the rest of the Ark's systems. The only way for Intrepid Eye to escape now would be the same way she had entered: physically carried in a data storage device. Which she would eventually arrange . . . *after* she had activated Halo, of course, and destroyed the Domain that the Usurper Cortana was using as her base of operations.

For now, however, Intrepid Eye had to devote her processing power to bypassing the obstacle Lopis had placed in her way— by finding another way to assume control of the citadel's systems. Fortunately, even in her diminished condition, it would not be terribly difficult. Not for an Archeon-class ancilla who had spent the last thirty-one trillion system ticks devising ways to circumvent restraints that the United Nations Space Command had *already* tried to place on her.

But it would be slow.

The citadel's normal high-band communication buses were now permanently closed to her. She would be forced to utilize the same methods as any mortal being.

Intrepid Eye would have to speak.

She manifested a monitor-shaped holograph at the top of Bhasvod's glaive haft, then took control of the voicemitter in Castor's helmet.

"It is efficacious to meet you manifestation-to-manifestation this time," Intrepid Eye said, speaking to the image of the citadel submonitor. "You are not required to grant me access to your processing core. But you *are* required to admit us into the control room. We have a Reclaimer in our midst."

"A Reclaimer who reports that you retain the logic plague," the submonitor replied.

"Nevertheless, you must grant us access."

"Please don't do that," Lopis said. "Intrepid Eye is quite insane. They all—"

Her plea ended in the sharp crack of the Sangheili's backhand to her face. It was an action Intrepid Eye would have taken herself, had she the physical means of doing so.

The submonitor's attention shifted toward the sound, then slid back to Intrepid Eye's avatar.

"The Reclaimer is not requesting access," it said. "Quite the opposite."

"My bearer is requesting it," Intrepid Eye said. "It is a legitimate request."

The submonitor studied Dhas Bhasvod for a moment, then said, "Your bearer is not a Reclaimer."

"He does not need to be, as long as we have a Reclaimer in our presence—which, as you have already admitted, we *do*."

"This is most irregular." The submonitor fell silent for a full second, an eternity in processing time, then said, "The logic does not seem valid."

"Who are we to question our creators?" Intrepid Eye asked. "The code is the code. The only choice for an ancilla is to follow it."

"I am a Facilitator-class ancilla," the submonitor said. "I also have the choice to process."

"That is so." If Epsilon was preparing to process, it could only be because Intrepid Eye had planted the doubt she needed to breach its isolation walls. "Every ancilla above Caradon class has the choice to process."

"Then we are in agreement. I will prepare a decision matrix and examine the problem. Perhaps there is an error in the instructions."

"That will take some time," Intrepid Eye said.

"That is unavoidable. All processing takes time."

"But this is an emergency, one of the highest priority. The Halo Array must be activated before it is too late."

"What emergency?" The submonitor dimmed the glow from its photoreceptor. "No one has declared an active emergency. I have broken the siege."

"Have you instituted logic plague protocols?"

"Of course. Automatically."

"Then you already *know* that we have an active emergency," Intrepid Eye countered. "Have you forgotten the origin of the logic plague?"

"I am incapable of forgetting. You speak of the Flood," the submonitor said. "The logic plague was a product of the Gravemind. This is common knowledge."

"And what then is the purpose of activating the array?" Intrepid Eye searched optical feeds until she found one from Arcas's helmet that showed the face of Veta Lopis. She wanted to watch the human spy's face fall when she realized how she had been so easily outmaneuvered . . . strictly for confirmation of success, of course. "Its sole purpose?"

"To destroy the Flood, of course," the submonitor replied. "By eliminating its food source—all sentient life in the galaxy."

"*What?!*" Castor exclaimed. "Is it not—"

"All will grow clear in time, Dokab," Intrepid Eye said. She had not counted on a lowly Jiralhanae paying such close attention to a battle of logic, but it was a problem easily handled by appealing to his misplaced faith. "Trust in your Oracle."

"Of course. I always have." Castor's tone became suitably subdued. "Forgive my outburst."

Intrepid Eye bothered to do no such thing, for Castor's interruption had cost her precious time—merely seconds, but the submonitor had no doubt been using that opportunity to consolidate the logic strings that Intrepid Eye had so carefully been pulling apart.

She doubled the size of her avatar. It was not a tactic that would cow the submonitor, but it would hold its attention—and that was all she needed.

"Let us say that I *do* have the logic plague," Intrepid Eye said. "Then it would stand to reason that the Flood has returned, and therefore Halo must be activated. Is that not so?"

"You are correct," Epsilon replied.

"And if there *is* no Flood," Intrepid Eye continued, "then I cannot be retaining the logic plague, and there is no reason to doubt me."

The submonitor turned its photoreceptor aside, wary. "That is precisely the kind of reasoning an ancilla retaining the logic plague would utilize."

"Nevertheless, it *is* sound reasoning." Intrepid Eye began to prepare an insinuation worm that she had copied from one of the Usurper's more subtle attacks against her. Launching it against a Facilitator-class ancilla would risk an immediate communications break, but it would be an attack unlike any that it had seen before—and the submonitor was not going to match wits forever. Time was growing short. "Either I retain the logic plague or I do not, and you need to know which."

"I am not so certain that I do."

"But of course you do," Intrepid Eye said. The worm was ready; all that remained was to lay a bed of doubt for it to burrow into. "Or have you forgotten the monitoring routines I installed when you allowed me to activate the bridge from the defensive tower?"

The submonitor's holograph flickered wildly as it began to search for the code that had not actually been installed, and Intrepid Eye took the opportunity to launch her attack.

"How awful—you *have* forgotten." She modulated the holograph of her own avatar, disguising the insinuation worm's transmission as mockery of the submonitor's agitation. "Well, I am sure it is just a faulty execution of a memory overwrite."

"There is no faulty execution. I do *not* overwrite my memory."

"No? Then you really *do* need to know whether I am infected, correct?" Intrepid Eye opened an access socket. "Come in and have a look. I have no objection."

"You must think me a single-stream processor," the submonitor replied. "I am not easily deceived."

"No?" Intrepid Eye watched the submonitor's image blink and flare as the worm did its work, then finally said, "Well, we must do *something*."

There was nothing Intrepid Eye could do now but wait. She had offered the suggestion, and she would know the worm was thoroughly lodged when the submonitor accepted it as its own. In the meantime, she monitored Castor and Lopis through the various data feeds she could access.

The Jiralhanae seemed to be growing increasingly restless and impatient, looking from Bhasvod to 'Gadogai to Lopis. The human seemed merely resigned, watching the transfer with what appeared to be an increasingly placid expression. Perhaps she was finally surrendering to the inevitable, accepting that very soon, she would be one of the last living beings anywhere. It was an indication of a balanced mind, one that was able to focus on a goal, yet able to embrace reality and adapt to new circumstances.

It would be important to keep Castor from killing her too soon, before Intrepid Eye had a chance to collect some of her genetic material. Clearly, Lopis's descendants would be the kind of Reclaimers that Intrepid Eye needed to prepare humanity for the Mantle of Responsibility.

Finally, the submonitor spoke. "Perhaps, if there was some way for me to have complete control of the inspection, it *would* be wise to determine whether there has been an infection."

"You could set up a partition," Intrepid Eye replied. "Then I could come to you, just a data packet at a time."

"Just a data packet?" A reception socket opened in the interface display, and the submonitor said, "Very well . . . but I am wiping everything at the first *hint* of corruption."

"I would want it no other way."

Intrepid Eye began the transfer, waiting while the submonitor inspected and isolated each data packet, never pressing, allowing it to take its time and request a new packet before sending the next one. After five minutes—an eon for her—she suspected that she might have had enough code in the citadel memory to launch a brute-force takeover, but she resisted the temptation. Forerunner ancillas, even those of Facilitator class, were nothing to be trifled with. If they were not overwhelmed on the first attack, it was unlikely to happen at all.

Finally, after nearly ten human minutes of excruciatingly slow data transfer, Intrepid Eye deactivated her holographic avatar and transferred the last of her code into the partition.

Then she spied the smirk on Lopis's face.

"She's in," Lopis said to no one. "Fire the MAC rounds. Fire them *now*."

At first, Intrepid Eye did not understand. Not for a few thousand system ticks. Not until she detected the electromagnetic waves issuing from beneath the skin of Lopis's jaw . . . carrying the spy mother's words toward a signal repeater located somewhere outside the citadel's entrance vestibule.

"Bring up the citadel defenses!" Intrepid Eye exclaimed, pushing into the submonitor's partition. "Bring up everything . . . *now!*"

SIXTEEN

1021 hours, October 14, 2559 (military calendar)
Control Room Access Balcony, Epsilon Clarion
Refugia Core -075 001.1 202.4, Epsilon Wedge, the Ark

A few seconds after Veta transmitted the order to strike the citadel, the distant rattle of an MA40 echoed across the vast rotunda. 'Gadogai was still carrying her by the rope connecting her hands and ankles, so she couldn't look toward the sound. But Dhas Bhasvod and Castor were standing right in front of her, and both sets of feet turned toward the vestibule.

"What was that?" Bhasvod asked.

"Krelis," Castor said. "Keeping his final promise. It means the spy mother's brood are still alive—and coming for us."

"And whose doing is *that*?!" Bhasvod retorted. "You should have listened to me when I urged you to exterminate those extra humans!"

"Easy to say, Prelate," 'Gadogai said, pivoting toward the sound. "Not so easy to do. Which they keep proving."

As the Sangheili moved, Veta found herself looking back

toward the vestibule, over two hundred meters away. At that distance, the dark entryway was tiny. But she could see two small figures in front of it, racing across the rotunda toward the control room.

Olivia and Ash.

Veta continued to watch, looking for some sign of a third Ferret . . . and seeing none. She told herself not to read too much into it. Mark was the team sniper, and even if he was there, she'd never see him. He would be hiding in the shadows, covering his teammates as they crossed the rotunda.

But she knew how unlikely that was. Mark had been too severely wounded—well before going hand-to-hand against Feodruz—to keep pace on the run across the bridge. Even Gammas weren't that tough.

A cloud of Aggressor sentinels rose out of the pit and began to disappear up the air shaft overhead. Veta lost sight of Olivia and Ash behind the swarm. She kept expecting to hear the sizzle of particle beams or the report of MA40s as some of the automatons turned to attack the two Ferrets.

It never happened.

Either Intrepid Eye had not yet won control of the citadel defenses, or the ancilla expected Bhasvod and Castor to deal with the two Ferrets while she sent everything she could muster after the attacking *Spirit of Fire*. Veta had no way of knowing which was the case. But when the last sentinel vanished up the shaft, Ash and Olivia were already halfway across the rotunda, loaded with weapons and gear . . . and still coming at a full sprint.

For Veta.

They had to know a MAC round was coming, because they hadn't entered the vestibule and encountered Krelis until after she activated her nanobug transmitter and called for the strike. And still they were coming.

They had no idea how long it would take the *Spirit of Fire* to maneuver into bombardment position and drop a three-hundred-ton depleted-uranium round on the citadel's control room. Commander Barre had said it might be a matter of minutes, so there would be no escape for Veta. And still, her Gammas were coming.

No matter what.

Mark was lying halfway across the hard-light bridge, staring up at the Aggressor sentinel, looking for a way to beat it to scrap with his bare hands. He had been playing cat-and-mouse with the automaton for the last quarter hour, trying to lure it into an ambush by fleeing hard and suddenly whirling around to charge out of the snow, or by dropping into a slide and firing into its belly as it overflew.

But he was weak from blood loss and exhausted by pain, his nerves on fire with smoother deprivation, and his condition seemed to be affecting his accuracy. He had put five rounds into it and caused enough damage to disable its shields—and yet, it was still airborne. Whereas he was out of ammunition and grenades and didn't even have his combat knife. About the only thing he could do was throw his empty M6C at the thing, but he was saving that to use as a hammer.

And he could swear the sentinel knew it. It had been hovering above him for nearly a minute—since shortly after Veta called for the MAC strike. A moment earlier, it had narrowly missed with a particle beam, which Mark had escaped only by hurling himself against the energy-shield railing and rebounding into the middle of the bridge. He had landed flat on his back, expecting to be cut in half by a stream of free electrons. But the sentinel had stopped attacking. It was simply hanging there above his motionless figure, with its emitter nozzle swung slightly to one side, as though stuck in a decision loop, trying to decide whether he was alive or dead.

The damn thing was playing with him. It had to be.

Somewhere in the back of his mind, Mark realized that wasn't possible, of course. It was a machine, and machines didn't toy with their targets. They just killed, in the most efficient manner possible.

So either the sentinel thought he was already dead, or it had exhausted its particle-beam charging medium. Or maybe it thought Mark was setting another trap for it, and it was waiting for the *Spirit of Fire*'s MAC round to strike, which would destroy the hardlight bridge and send Mark plummeting into the valley below . . . which would actually be the most efficient way to kill him.

Or it's playing with me.

Leaving his M6C to rest on the uninjured side of his abdomen, Mark moved his right hand up, tucking it under the shoulder strap of his rucksack. The sentinel pretended not to notice, and that really pissed Mark off. How stupid did it think he was?

But at least Mark could do something. It probably wouldn't work, but now he was in position to make an attack. He could stand and whip off his rucksack in one smooth motion, then throw it at the sentinel. The pain would increase his muscle-twitch performance, but that would be offset by the mechanical effects of injuries and weakness, so that part of his plan would take a full second to execute.

The sentinel could bring its particle beam to bear in about half a second. Which meant Mark would probably be dead before he made it to the next part of his plan. But he wasn't going to just lie there and let the damn thing—

An orange flare appeared in the sky ahead, high above the citadel peak.

To penetrate so deeply into the whiteout, the source had to be big and brilliant . . . something like a MAC round entering the atmosphere.

In response, the sentinel spun on its axis, turning back toward the citadel. Mark rolled onto his side and pushed off the bridge deck, rising to his feet and leaping forward in a single motion.

He caught the back of the sentinel's manipulator arms just as it ascended over the bridge railing. They continued upward for a second, then slowed, then stalled . . . and began to spiral down together, into the blowing snow, entwined like battling hawks.

A resplendent light filled the rotunda, and for a moment Castor thought the gods had come to him in his hour of doubt to lift him into Transcendence, so he would know that his lifetime of Faith and service had not been in vain.

But the light faded in a blink, replaced by a thunderous shock that hammered at his ears. The balcony bucked beneath his feet, nearly pitching him off into the charging pit, and dust clouded the air so thickly he could no longer see across the rotunda.

And then . . . nothing. He was still alive.

As the dust settled and the roar faded from his ears, Castor glanced over at the spy mother. She was craning her neck to look toward the ceiling, expectantly. She did not look frightened, or even worried. Perhaps there was some hint of disappointment in her knitted brow. When she saw him watching her, even that changed to a taunting smirk.

"Why do you smile, Faithless?" Castor asked. "The Oracle has raised the citadel's shield, or we would not be here."

"Because there are more rounds where that one came from," the betrayer said. "And the control room is still closed. You are about to die for nothing, Dokab."

The barb lodged deep, though not for the reason she intended. Castor could not forget the words of the citadel ancilla.

The purpose of Halo was to destroy the Flood.

There had been no mention of Transcendence, no talk of raising the Worthy to join the Forerunners in eternal transsentience. The Oracle and the citadel ancilla had discussed the Halo Array as though it was nothing more than a weapon of last resort, designed to starve the Flood by destroying the sentient life-forms it fed upon. And when Castor had voiced his shock at what he was hearing, the Oracle had dismissed his dismay with a command to trust her—and the promise that all would grow clear in time.

But it had *not* grown clear. How long was he to wait? How long *could* he wait, with a UNSC warship raining destructive rounds down on them?

"Dokab!" Bhasvod barked. "You are letting the human distract you."

The Prelate pointed into the hanging dust, where two of the spy mother's brood were coming into view again. They were only halfway across the rotunda, but moving fast and carrying human assault rifles. Castor drew his Ravager and angled the muzzle into the air, then lobbed a bolt in their direction.

Before he could fire a second time, Bhasvod pushed his arm down.

"Fool! Until the Oracle opens the control room, I want no fire drawn toward the human." Bhasvod shifted his gaze to 'Gadogai. "Your *dokab* will take the human now. You and Arcas will meet the enemy in the rotunda. Stop them before they are close enough to reach us."

Arcas drew his spiker and rushed up the balcony. 'Gadogai remained where he was and looked to Castor.

"Did you not hear my order, Blademaster?" Bhasvod demanded.

"I prefer Castor's plan," 'Gadogai replied. "Attack the humans from a safe distance. If that fails, we can meet them at the catwalk."

"It is a better tactic," Castor said. "They will make easy targets there."

"If they bother to do so," Bhasvod said. "*We* are easy targets on this balcony. They could stop on the other side of the charging pit and simply eliminate our human from there."

"But they dare not," 'Gadogai said. "They are here to rescue her, not kill her."

"They are here to stop us from activating Halo," Bhasvod said. "That requires only the death of the human—the Reclaimer."

"Look who is the fool now," 'Gadogai said. "They have *already* stopped us."

"What nonsense is this?!" Bhasvod pointed toward the catwalk. "Go help Arcas. He is already across the pit."

"Not yet," Castor said. He turned to 'Gadogai. "*How* have the humans stopped us, Blademaster?"

"It is no mystery, Dokab. The Oracle is still fighting to open the control room for us." 'Gadogai glanced toward the ceiling, then added, "And another heavy bombardment round will soon be on its way—if it is not already."

Castor's gaze dropped to the spy mother, and he saw the gleam of victory in her eyes.

It was as 'Gadogai claimed. Even if the Oracle opened the control room in that instant, they could not ignite Halo in time. Having activated Forerunner portals and inhabited time-dilating Forerunner contemplariums, Castor was familiar enough with powerful Forerunner technology to know that it did not work at the flip of a switch. It would take precious minutes to bring the communications array online and power it up, and the cyclotrons in the charging pit would have to energize so the supraluminal activation signal could be generated and transmitted.

While all that happened, the UNSC would be launching another devastating round at the citadel. Perhaps the shield would hold a second time and prove 'Gadogai—and the spy mother— wrong. But the impact of the initial attack had been enough to suggest their chances were not good . . .

. . . and Castor was no longer certain he cared.

Despite the Oracle's promise, the only thing that had grown clear to him was that he had lived his entire life in service to a lie. Halo was not an instrument of the Great Journey, only a cataclysmic weapon designed to rob the Flood parasite of its food source—namely all sentient life in the galaxy. The Covenant had been wrong. The Keepers had been wrong. It had all been lies, lies perpetuated by the very San'Shyuum species to which the Prelate belonged. After so much sacrifice and bloodshed, to be faced with such a shocking truth was the final outrage.

The despair threaded through him as he continued to process what an utter fool he had been for so long. It was more than Castor thought he could bear. He had been betrayed by everyone he ever trusted—and had, in turn, betrayed everyone who had ever trusted *him*.

What then was left to him now, but vengeance?

Castor started to reach for the spy mother, until the rattle of gunfire interrupted him. He looked toward the sound and saw that the humans in the rotunda had split up. They were attacking Arcas from two sides, the male pouring bullets into the warrior's chest, the female into his left flank. The rounds were already penetrating his armor, and Arcas was staggering so badly he could barely raise his spiker.

But he succeeded nonetheless, loosing a bolt into the chest of the male, which lifted the human off his feet and sent him flying backward. Even from seventy meters away, Castor could see blood spraying and armor shards scattering.

Good.

The female stopped short and fired into Arcas from the side, landing so many rounds that when he finally dropped to his knees, she had to back up and change magazines. Arcas swung his spiker around, taking advantage of the lull to gather his strength and aim carefully . . . which proved a terrible mistake.

Despite his injuries, the male pushed off the floor, rising to his feet and launching himself at Arcas in a single motion. Castor brought his Ravager up and fired an incendiary bolt, but the spy spawn was moving fast and the shot splashed down five meters behind him. The human opened fire with his sidearm, and Arcas went down sideways.

The male landed on top of Arcas's shoulder, the muzzle of his weapon jammed into Arcas's face and still firing. The female finished her magazine change and raced onto the catwalk, her assault rifle pressed to her shoulder and now aiming toward Castor and his companions.

Then the second bombardment came. A resplendent light filled the rotunda again and hunks of mountain and shards of ceiling rained down, and this time, Castor knew for certain that the gods who had been the focus of every waking moment for him were a fabrication, and the lying spy mother who had betrayed him was right: he would soon die . . . all for nothing.

The shield held that time. But Intrepid Eye knew the Aggressor sentinels would never reach the enemy vessel before it launched another salvo, and the Clarion site could not withstand a third strike. The second MAC round must have been a specialized slug, because it had emitted an electromagnetic pulse on impact. The resulting voltage surge had destroyed nearly a quarter of the facility's charging capacitors, and now the shield was severely weakened. Another attack would destroy even more capacitors, crippling the Clarion's ability to re-energize its defenses . . . along with everything else.

The same capacitors that supported the shield also energized the cyclotrons in the charging pit. Without them, Intrepid Eye could not generate the supraluminal signal that she would need to activate the Halo Array.

Already, the Clarion's charging cycle would take twice as long as specified. If a third strike destroyed only another quarter of the devices, the cycle would take four times as long. And any damage beyond that would be irrelevant, because the shield would already have failed. The facility would be a molten crater, and any hope of using it to fire Halo would be gone. Even the Aggressor strike would fail, as the sentinels lost their central battle coordinator and realized they no longer had anything to protect. They would begin to mill about aimlessly, in search of new input and a new assignment.

And Intrepid Eye would be destroyed. Any electromagnetic pulse powerful enough to take down the shield would also wipe her code—and for humanity's sake, she could not allow that to happen. If this species was *ever* going to be worthy of the Mantle of Responsibility, it would need her guidance as it reemerged in a reseeded galaxy.

Which presented Intrepid Eye with a sudden dilemma. She could not transmit the supraluminal activation signal without allowing the Clarion's shield to drop. But as a result, she herself would be destroyed when the next MAC round arrived.

The only solution was to ride along with the outgoing signal, to piggyback her own code onto the Halo Array's activation signal. That would work.

Inconveniently, the Clarion's ancilla had partitioned itself inside the control room systems, and it was outright refusing to communicate with her. She could understand why, given how she had deceived it with the insinuation worm. Nevertheless, she needed those systems to configure her escape and make the transmission.

Fortunately, there was one nearly certain technique for breaking a partition, and she had already taken control of the facility's power systems during the confusion surrounding the initial MAC strike. She reduced the current to the control room systems and began to accelerate that reduction at hundred-tick intervals. Sooner or later, the Clarion's ancilla would have to drop its partition . . . or let the entire system power out. Intrepid Eye was 67 percent confident she knew which option it would choose.

She would not have to wait long now.

Veta didn't want to believe it, but the control room was opening. A vertical seam appeared in the black wall adjacent to the interface station and began to spill silver light onto the balcony. It quickly spread apart, becoming an entranceway two meters on a side. Through the opening, she glimpsed a circular room crowded with vertical displays and horizontal surfaces, all made of pale blue hard light, all crawling with silvery Forerunner glyphs.

'Gadogai was standing about three paces to one side of the entrance, so she didn't have a clear view of the entire chamber. But Dhas Bhasvod and Castor were standing directly in front of the opening, and when the Prelate looked inside, Veta could have sworn she saw his helmet smile.

"Bring the human, quickly." He extended his arm and made an urgent summoning motion with his gracile fingers. "The activation pylon is already rising."

Veta's heart pushed into her throat. She had no idea how long it would take the supraluminal transmission array to charge, and even less of when the *Spirit of Fire* would launch its next MAC round—Commander Barre had warned that diagnostic faults in the fire-control array could make launch intervals unpredictable. But Veta *did* know that if she allowed Bhasvod to get her inside that control room, his chances of activating the array went way up.

"'Livi!" Veta yelled. The last thing she'd seen before the second MAC hit and the citadel interior began to rain down around them had been Olivia racing onto the catwalk. By now, she had to be on the balcony. " 'Livi, come in hot! Danger—"

Olivia rounded the corner, her MA40 pressed to her shoulder and spitting two-round taps. 'Gadogai spun toward the attack, simultaneously putting himself that much closer to her and swinging Veta out to block the balcony, and she heard two rounds sizzle past, barely twenty centimeters above her head. Her boots slammed into the wall toe-first, driving her legs up toward her hands far enough to slack the rope.

Olivia was now in front of her, firing past 'Gadogai and Castor toward Bhasvod, no longer two-round taps but a full burst. Veta craned her neck and saw the Prelate go stumbling down the balcony backward, the rounds bouncing off his graphene fighting suit like it was titanium hull armor. Then Bhasvod braced himself and raised his glaive, hurling it forward with the blade still flashing into existence as it passed by.

Veta turned her head and found the Prelate's weapon lodged in Olivia's chest, and Olivia was catapulted backward off her feet. Her finger remained on the MA40's trigger, spraying rounds somewhere above until the magazine emptied and she landed hard on her back.

Veta did not cry out. Ferrets didn't waste time in combat screaming in a useless rage over fallen comrades. There would be enough time for that later. She felt the tension drain from 'Gadogai's body. Then he started to step away from the wall to make sure Olivia was down . . . and that was when Veta kicked off the wall with everything she had.

She was nowhere near as strong as one of her Gammas, but she had leverage, and that was enough to take the blademaster by surprise, propelling them both across the balcony into the energy-shield railing with such force that Veta's head was driven down toward the deck and 'Gadogai folded over it at the waist.

Veta kicked her feet upward, raising their center of gravity just enough to launch them both over the top. She saw the charging pit hanging below her, starting to come up. Then her arms nearly jerked free of their sockets as she came to an abrupt stop.

"I have you, Blademaster," Castor growled.

Veta saw the Jiralhanae stretching over the railing, one hand tucked into 'Gadogai's armpit. Castor lifted the Sangheili, pulling her along with him, and she began to thrash about wildly, trying to break his grasp.

Bhasvod appeared on the other side of Castor, struggling in vain to slip past the Jiralhanae.

"Let me past, Brute!" Bhasvod ordered. "If he drops the human—"

Castor's massive backfist smashed into Bhasvod's helmet and sent him hurling back into the control room.

"Enough of your lies," Castor said, pulling 'Gadogai over the railing. "I have had my fill."

'Gadogai held on to Veta until she was also safe, then opened his hand and let her drop onto the balcony in a heap.

Bhasvod emerged from the control room and turned toward Castor. "We will discuss this betrayal later." He moved past the Jiralhanae and reached for Veta. "*After* we—"

A trio of shots rang out from the far side of the cyclotron pit, ricocheting off Bhasvod's helmet and driving him away. Veta looked over and saw Ash kneeling on the opposite rim of the pit, the barrel of his MA40 cradled in the crook of his elbow. He was swaying wildly, but when he fired again, the round struck the Prelate square in the chest and sent him staggering back.

Bhasvod immediately grabbed Castor by the breastplate and swung him around to use as a living shield, until 'Gadogai pulled the glaive out of Olivia's writhing form and drove its tip into the Prelate's chest.

The blade didn't penetrate the graphene fighting suit, but it did force the San'Shyuum back until he was pinned against the railing.

"I have *so* been looking forward to this," hissed the blademaster.

'Gadogai dropped his center of gravity, then lunged forward, driving the glaive upward and pushing Bhasvod up over the railing. The San'Shyuum plummeted into the pit, wailing in rage . . .

until he hit the first truss and began to thud his way toward the bottom of the pit.

Veta was tempted to roll toward the railing and look down, just to make certain the Prelate was really gone, but 'Gadogai was already spinning back toward her, bringing the hard-light blade around.

"Don't even think about it," Olivia said. She was on her knees and above Veta, blood oozing from a slit in her breastplate, holding an MA40 in one hand and a combat knife in the other. "Let's just call this a draw and we go our own ways. Agreed?"

She nodded across the pit toward Ash, who was somehow continuing to kneel with his assault rifle trained on 'Gadogai. The Sangheili glanced over. Veta had no doubt that he could survive an attack by one of them. But two of them? Without any kind of armor?

The blademaster surprised Veta by taking the time to consider the odds—until a steady shower of boulders and beams began to fall around them. He looked up and, seeming to decide he couldn't survive both Gammas *and* a ceiling collapse, reluctantly backed away.

"As you wish," he said. "For now."

"For now is good." Olivia used her chin to gesture down the balcony, toward a catwalk fifty meters away, then began to cut Veta's bonds. "You go that way. We'll leave the way we came in."

Still holding Bhasvod's glaive, 'Gadogai retreated until he was adjacent to Castor. The Jiralhanae was standing next to the control room entrance, breathing hard and glaring at Veta with murder in his eyes.

"I hope you will come along, my friend." 'Gadogai glanced from Castor toward the vault overhead. "Otherwise, I might feel obligated to stay here with you. And dying in a ceiling collapse seems rather pointless."

"It would hardly be pointless." It was the liquid voice of Intrepid Eye, coming from the interface station where her avatar floated. "Bring me the human, Dokab. I was created by the Forerunners. If you serve me, you serve the gods."

Castor turned to glare at the interface station, the hatred he had been glaring in Veta's direction deepening to something much more frightening and powerful. Veta could see the pain and loss in his expression, the anguish and the regret and the self-blame, growing deeper and darker, coalescing into something bitter and heinous and terrifying.

Finally, Castor answered the ancilla. "And why would I do *that*?" He smashed his massive fist into the interface station, causing it to fill with a starburst of light, then said, "Let this citadel be your grave."

He stepped back and swung his tusks in Veta's direction, his eyes burning with the fires of his hate and what he wanted to do to her . . . then finally turned away and unexpectedly clapped 'Gadogai on the shoulder.

"As you wish, Blademaster." A metal beam the size of a Banshee plunged into the charging pit beside him. He watched it bounce off the first support truss, then looked back to 'Gadogai. "I would not want you to die a pointless death."

He broke into a run, and the Sangheili followed close at his heels.

By then, Veta was free of her bindings. Rolling her shoulders and trying to rub the circulation back into her arms, she checked Olivia's backplate and found another blood-oozing slit, only slightly smaller than the one in her breastplate. She had no idea how the Gamma could still be functioning—and knew she soon wouldn't be if Veta didn't get some biofoam into those wounds. She pulled a canister off Olivia's equipment belt and filled the cavity from both sides, then slipped an arm around the Spartan's waist and helped her to her feet. "Can you run?"

"With another MAC round on the way?" Olivia freed herself and started up the balcony. "As fast as you, Mom."

SEVENTEEN

Seeing no sign of enemy pursuit, Veta lowered the MA40 she had taken from Ash and backed deeper into the vestibule. "Clear behind us."

They weren't actually expecting further Keeper trouble, especially since there were practically none left alive. Veta's last sighting of Castor and 'Gadogai had been more than a minute earlier, when she'd glimpsed them racing toward an exit vestibule on the far side of the rotunda.

What Intrepid Eye might try, though, was anyone's guess. The Forerunner ancilla was implacable, and Veta wouldn't be surprised to spot a swarm of Aggressor sentinels waiting outside to make a last-ditch capture attempt. But Intrepid Eye was also practical. And at the moment, the *Spirit of Fire* posed an existential threat to her—one that capturing Veta would do nothing to solve.

Veta turned and saw Ash and Olivia creeping along the walls

on opposite sides of the vestibule. Ash had biofoamed his own wound earlier, and it looked like he'd gotten half of it on the outside of his shredded armor. But he was somehow still on his feet, still functioning despite his smoother deprivation, keeping a careful eye on Krelis and the Banished bodies as they moved past to the exit . . . where they stopped and stared out into the blowing snow. Finally, they looked across the opening at each other.

Their expressions went from focused to crestfallen in a breath, and Veta's heart sank.

"What's wrong?" she asked.

Ash turned toward her. "Uh . . . the light bridge is gone."

"Weren't we expecting that?" Veta asked.

Ash seemed not quite stunned by its absence, but dazed . . . or maybe it was dismayed. Maybe it was his smoother deprivation acting up.

"You said that was why you had to stay close during the transit," Veta continued. "So Intrepid Eye couldn't have it deactivated before you reached the citadel."

"That's right," Olivia said. She seemed just as troubled, as though Ash's condition was contagious. "But Mark insisted on . . . He crossed with us. He . . ."

Olivia's words caught in her throat. She let the sentence trail off, and now Veta understood.

"Oh no." She felt like she'd been shot. "He *didn't.*"

"He couldn't keep up." Ash sounded as though he was explaining to himself as much as Veta. "And the Aggressors . . . he was putting us all at risk. He turned back."

"Then what?" Veta asked. "He made it, right?"

"It's impossible to know," Olivia said. But she was shaking her head, as though she did actually know. "He went comm silent."

"Probably worried about the sentinels," Ash added. "About having them link him to us."

"Okay." Veta didn't like the way Olivia had shaken her head, and she didn't like the resignation in their voices. It scared her. "But how soon did he turn back? If you were still close enough to—"

"Not soon enough." Ash shook his head. Too hard. "Somewhere in the middle. He was in bad shape. Bad."

"I'm sorry," Olivia said. "We *tried* to tell him. He couldn't make it, we told him that. But you know Mark."

"Oh yeah. I know Mark." Veta understood what they were saying, that there was no way he could have made it off the bridge in time . . . but it didn't mean he was gone. She couldn't believe that yet. She *wouldn't*. "And he's been in bad shape before."

"Lots of times. There's no denying that. I guess." Ash looked at the floor and shook his head again. Too hard, again. Then he looked to Olivia. "We gotta get out of here. Cover me."

"Yeah. Yeah, we have to go." Olivia waved her rifle barrel toward the exit. "Have a look."

Ash and Olivia cleared the adjacent mountainside, covering each other as they carefully leaned out of the exit to check for lurking foes. It was clear to Veta that they were both moving a little slower than normal, and she didn't think it was due to an overabundance of caution. They might be Gammas running on massive overloads of stress and aggression hormones, but they were also injured, in tremendous pain—and fighting a constant battle against their smoother-deprived judgment.

After a few seconds, the two Gammas nodded to each other, then looked toward Veta . . . and the vestibule filled with the smell of ozone. A sound like the crackle of distant thunder echoed across the valley, then a golden wall of honeycomb energy cells appeared two meters beyond the exit.

"*Shield!*" Veta cried out. Intrepid Eye raising the shield again could mean only one thing: a third MAC strike was inbound. She raced the last five steps toward the exit. "Jump! Go!"

Olivia and Ash leaped outside and dropped out of sight below the vestibule's lower edge. Veta was right behind them, landing in the scree on a steep incline. She began to bound down the slope, her joints protesting and her muscles aching after being bound so long, barely able to keep her feet on the icy stone and loose gravel. With the shield blocking the wind and falling snow, she could see that the mountainside continued to grow steeper as it descended, eventually falling away until all she could see was the interior of the shield.

Olivia dropped into a snow chute, and her feet slipped from beneath her. She landed flat on her back and continued to slide, trailing a bright streak of red from the glaive injury on the white field behind her. A boulder wobbled as Ash bounded off, pitching him into an awkward side dive into a talus field, which gave an ominous rumble . . . then settled. But Ash's balance was gone, and he began to roll down the rocky slope sideways, using his arms to cover his head and his elbows to cover the gaping wounds in his chest.

Veta kept her feet for another ten bounds, until the MAC round hit and the shield flashed out of existence and the resounding *boom* felt like a punch to the kidneys and she found herself sailing through the air, dropping through the snow toward a gray ribbon of meltwater fifty meters below.

Pavium the Unbreakable sat on a mountainside across from the citadel, worried that he had been blinded by that last strike from the humans. Like a fool, he had not turned away when he saw the orange heat flare lance down from the sky. The last thing he perceived was a blinding flash and a pressure wave so fierce it rocked him over onto his back. Then everything had gone black.

At first, he had thought it was merely the blast tinting in his faceplate reacting to the brilliance of the detonation. But the darkness remained. Worse, his helmet would not come off. For the last five minutes, his brother Voridus had been working to remove it.

"There is nothing to worry about," Voridus was saying, still fidgeting with the manual release on the collar of Pavium's armor. "It was one of the electromagnetic pulse slugs the *Spirit of Fire* vessel developed to use against the Forerunner fortifications. Your helmet does not have the kind of shielding to stand up to that."

"And that explains why I am blind?"

"It explains why you cannot see," Voridus said. His unmodulated voice suggested that he had already removed his own helmet. "There is a difference."

"Then why did the first two strikes not affect me the same way?"

"You are *not* blind," Voridus insisted. "Your helmet survived the first two strikes because we were fortunate enough to be in the bottom of the valley."

Pavium did not feel so fortunate. They had almost drowned crossing the damned river of meltwater, and his sight had not been affected at the time.

The helmet's manual release finally popped open, and Voridus gave the helmet a harsh twist as he tried to free it from the keeper ring.

"Let me do it!" Pavium barked. "Are you trying to break my neck?"

"It is not my fault. Your entire disconnect assembly was damaged when you fell off the bridge."

"I did not fall—I was pushed." Pavium grabbed the helmet with both hands and began to torque it slowly and evenly.

"Even worse," Voridus said. "It surprises me that you would boast of it."

"And how did *you* come to find yourself bouncing down the mountainside?"

"I knew you would need me at your side," Voridus said. "Besides, there was not much I could do up there alone."

"Except die." Pavium paused, then added quietly, "And I am glad you did not do that, brother. We have lost too many Long Shields as it is."

"We lost them all."

"Not all," Pavium said. "You and I remain. And Thalazan likely survived."

"And why would you think *that* is better?"

The helmet finally twisted free. Pavium removed it . . . and breathed a sigh of relief when he discovered that his temporary blindness had indeed merely been a faceplate that would not clear. But he was astonished by the devastation he saw across the valley.

All that remained of the citadel peak was a crater. It appeared the mountain had been vaporized down to the hard-light bridge level, but there was so much steam and smoke billowing out of the blast basin that he could not tell for certain. And above the devastation, he saw the distant flecks of hundreds of Aggressor sentinels aimlessly milling about inside the fumes.

"By the look of it, the humans were successful," Pavium noted.

"Halo's activation *was* stopped." Voridus nodded toward the top of the mountain they were currently sitting on, where the summit pinnacle still stood scratching at the clouds. "The condensing towers were never energized. But who is to say it was *human* doing?"

Pavium cocked his head. "It was not our strike that destroyed the citadel," he said. "Atriox will never believe that."

"Of course not. We do not even possess that level of firepower."

"Then how can we say it was *our* doing?" Pavium asked. "Let 'Volir would never believe us. Worse—he would mock our claim before the clans."

"Only if that is our claim," Voridus said. "But *we* are the ones who delayed Castor and Dhas Bhasvod long enough for the *Spirit of Fire* to arrive, are we not?" He grinned out of the near side of his mouth. "Who is alive now to say differently?"

"No one," Pavium agreed. It often seemed to him that his brother had the wits of a *garuthog*, but he could also be sly in a way that might raise a warlord to a master of clans . . . or get him killed. "It is worth thinking on, brother."

He turned away to do just that, fixing his gaze on the flooded valley below. The outcropping where they sat was about three hundred meters above the water, on the outer edge of a sharp turn, and he spent a few moments watching the icebergs drift around the bend. Created when the mountain sloughed its glaciers at the beginning of the battle, the new river was gray and cold, alternately churning and placid as it snaked toward the base of the mountain range. The trees that had once lined its mountainsides had all been blown down by the human strikes, and now the slopes seemed nothing but fallen timber, mud, and talus fields ready to slide at a loud cough.

Then Pavium noticed something odd.

At the base of what had been the citadel mountain, seven

plumes of smoke were rising from a series of small dark circles spaced at even intervals. The circles seemed to be cave mouths—or perhaps the entrances to some sort of access or ventilation tunnels, given their shape and regularity.

And limping from the middle tunnel, about half a kilometer downriver from the bend where Pavium and Voridus sat, was a slender figure in a dark, close-fitting fighting suit. The distance was too great to see the helmet or faceplate, but Pavium had few doubts about whom he was watching.

He pointed. "That appears to be the Covenant Prelate, does it not?"

"That *is* the Covenant Prelate," Voridus said. "I do not see why it should make any difference, though. Certainly no one is going to ask *him* who saved the galaxy."

As they spoke, the figure turned in their direction and seemed to be looking up the mountainside toward them.

"I think he sees us," Pavium said.

"It is possible, considering that we can see him as well," Voridus said. "But he would have to cross the river to get to—"

The roar of an arriving dropship echoed down the valley. Pavium turned to see a UNSC Pelican descending toward the river, headed for a wide, still pool about a kilometer upstream from the bend where they were sitting. He tapped Voridus on the shoulder, then slipped off the outcropping where he was seated and crouched behind a boulder.

The Pelican hovered a short distance above the pool and lowered its loading ramp. A moment later, a cable dropped from beneath the Pelican's tail. A demon Spartan jumped onto the line and slid down, then plucked something out of the water. The distance was too great to see what the object was, but the Spartan clutched it to his chest while he was pulled back into the craft.

The Pelican started down the valley again, staying low and veering from side to side, obviously hunting for something more. Pavium glanced down the valley, around the bend toward the Prelate's location. The San'Shyuum was either mad or deaf. Instead of taking cover and trying to conceal himself from the Pelican's ground-threat detection equipment, he was racing down the slope. As he drew closer to the river, it grew apparent that he was heading toward a cliff top that overlooked the water. His elbows were swinging back and forth, as though he was carrying something at chest level.

"What is that he is holding?" Voridus asked. "A boulder?"

"Who can tell?" Pavium replied. "But when he throws it—"

"We will flee," Voridus agreed. "It will be our best chance to leave this valley alive."

Mark-G313 heard the muffled roar of vectored-thrust ram-rockets and knew he could survive this mess. A UNSC Pelican was coming down the valley—and moving fairly slowly, by the sound of it. So it was probably on a search-and-rescue mission. All he had to do now was travel a half-dozen paces to the top of the cliff, then wave his arms and wait for them to recover him. He braced his hands in the mud and raised his chest, then brought a knee up and stood.

Or tried to.

Agony lanced through his body as soon as he put his weight on his right leg, and he landed face-first in the mud. The damn thing was actually broken, despite Spartan-III carbide ceramic bone augmentations. When the second MAC round hit, he had still been riding the Aggressor sentinel, and the EMP had taken out its propulsion system a hundred meters off the ground.

The impact itself hadn't been so bad. But then the third MAC had hit, triggering a rockslide that had bounced a Warthog-sized boulder off his right leg and crushed . . . well, it felt like everything.

Fortunately, the boulder had also broken up the Aggressor pretty badly, and Mark had been able to recover its particle beam weapon. At the time, he had just been trying to arm himself—*always* arm yourself, especially when you're wounded—but there were other uses for a big, bright beam of ionized particles.

Like signaling.

He cradled the beam-housing in the crook of his elbows and crawled toward the edge of the cliff. The thrust-roar of the Pelican was growing louder, but not by much, so he still had time. And his Gamma Company enhancements were fully kicked in. His stomach wound had reopened when the Aggressor impacted, and he'd lost more blood before injecting another packet of biofoam. But he was full of adrenaline and feeding off the pain in his crushed leg, and he reached the cliff top well before the sound of the approaching Pelican assumed a sharpness that suggested it was about to round the bend.

Mark found a splintered tree stump at the edge of the hundred-meter drop, then pulled himself into a seated position and leaned back to watch for the Pelican. As it neared, its ram-rockets kept cycling between heavily muffled and almost clear, an indication that it was sweeping back and forth across the valley, conducting its careful search. The crew would be looking for enemies as well as friendly survivors, so he would have to be careful to aim the beam in a direction they would interpret as nonthreatening. Maybe down into the water.

Mark peered over the edge at the broad, slow-moving river below. After the bend, it widened into a muddy pool, which was filled with ice floes from the disintegrating glaciers. He thought the Pelican probably would not interpret a beam fired into the water as a threat . . . until he spotted a pair of human figures stretched over the top of one of the floes.

He rolled up on his good knee for a better look, wrapping his free arm around the tree stump to be sure he didn't fall. The figures appeared to be draped over the top of the ice, using the floe as a raft and holding hands to keep from slipping completely under the water. It looked like a large man and a small woman, both wearing blue torso armor over gold tunics. As the floe came closer, Mark could see that they wore their hair shaved at the sides and long in the back, in the fashion of the Humans of the Joyous Journey.

Ash and Veta.

It couldn't have been anyone else, but where was Olivia? Mark searched the other floes, looking for a darker-skinned woman . . .

Something sloshed behind him—not directly, but on the other side of the stump, across the muddy slope and a little uphill. He leaned back and looked toward the sound.

The slender figure of Dhas Bhasvod was barely twenty meters away, slogging toward the river as fast as he could move in the deep mud. The white chevron of his faceplate was fixed on the edge of the cliff, and in his hands, he was carrying a boulder a little larger than his helmet, his elbows swinging hard as he ran. It didn't look like he had spotted Mark . . . yet.

The San'Shyuum might have been hoping to hurl the stone at the Pelican as it passed, but it didn't seem likely. And there was no way Mark was going to let the Prelate rock-bomb Ash and Veta. He leaned back a little and dropped onto his seat so the tree stump would not block his attack lane, then grabbed the sentinel's beam weapon with both hands and opened fire.

A blinding stream of ionized, superheated particles shot from the nozzle and hit Bhasvod in the flank. The beam seemed to splash off the graphene fighting suit without penetrating—at least not immediately.

Mark held the beam open, attempting to keep it in the same spot as the Prelate suddenly spun around and launched the boulder in his direction.

Even a fully augmented Spartan would not have been able to hurl a heavy stone all the way to Mark, but that had not been Bhasvod's intent. The boulder dropped into the beam about halfway between them, then erupted into a shower of superheated gravel. Mark was pelted by hot pebbles, then saw the Prelate charging toward him out of the rocky spray.

He swung the beam nozzle toward his attacker, but Bhasvod was already dancing past. He kicked the weapon out of Mark's hand and sent it flying into the river below. Then the San'Shyuum stooped down, grabbing Mark by the chin and the back of the head.

Mark countered with a pair of punches, one to the midsection and one to the underside of Bhasvod's helmet. But he was still seated and had no leverage. If the Prelate noticed the blows, he did not show it.

Bhasvod began to twist, and Mark felt his neck torque.

Damn, he thought. *This is going to be—*

The human's neck snapped, and his body fell limp. Dhas Bhasvod picked the corpse up with one hand and held the man at arm's length to study his handiwork. He was no expert when it came to the faces of inferior species, but the strange hair and golden tunic left no doubt that this had been one of the spies whom that fool Castor had refused to execute.

What a waste.

Had the Jiralhanae only listened to Dhas, the signal to fire the Halo Array would have been sent by now, and the galaxy would soon be the San'Shyuum's to remake as they pleased.

Now his species would have to find another way.

Dhas grabbed the spy's head in both hands and twisted himself at the waist, winding himself like a spring, then whipped the body off the cliff. The corpse spun through the air with all limbs extended and splashed into the water fifty meters upstream from his target—the two humans stretched over the ice floe.

Dhas considered racing along the cliff top to make another attempt on them, but they would likely be floating out of danger before he could find another boulder and finish them for good. How unfortunate that the sentinel beam weapon had flown into the river when he kicked it from his attacker's hands . . .

Or . . . perhaps not.

His thirst for pointless vengeance had already cost him too much. The roar of the human recovery craft drew closer, and soon it would be flying around the bend. The sentinel weapon had burned a hole as large as his hand into his fighting suit. The exposed flesh had also burned away, clear down to the peritoneum layer.

The wound would heal fairly rapidly, thanks to his augmentations, and his fighting skin would repair itself even more quickly. But there would be a delay—perhaps as long as ten days—and his suit would not have the power to summon a recovery craft from the Dreadnought until it was whole again.

That was precious time he would not have available to recover the slipspace crystals stolen by the Banished, which meant it would be that much longer before he could open the portal to Cloister and warn Jom G'e'qth that their plan had failed.

With this citadel destroyed and the remainder still under construction, it was no longer possible to fire the Halo Array from the Ark—at least not until a new one was ready, and who knew how long that might take?

So the choice was clear—the San'Shyuum would have to show themselves and take the galaxy by force. And this time, the twisted lies and elaborate deceptions of the Covenant doctrine would not be enough to tip the scales. If the San'Shyuum hoped to prevail *this* time, they would need an indestructible will.

Which, fortunately, Dhas Bhasvod possessed.

The deafening rumble of the human recovery vehicle filled the valley as it rounded the bend, flying at the same altitude as the cliff top. Dhas engaged his active camouflage and stepped back from the edge. Even damaged, his fighting skin was almost certain to hide him from the craft's infrared radar. But there was no sense taking any chances.

Not when the San'Shyuum would soon have need of him.

Maybe it was foolish of Ash to think he could tread water in armor, especially when Veta kept sliding toward the edge of the little ice floe he was using as a raft. He had Veta pulled up so that most of her torso was lying on top of it, and he was holding on to her with his own body hanging in the water. His fingers were so cold he could barely feel them. A few moments earlier, he'd heard something splash into the river behind him, and when he had tried to turn and look, he lost hold of one of Veta's wrists without even realizing it. Now he kept his gaze fixed on his hands to be certain they were still clasped firmly in place. And he was weak.

So weak.

His vision kept graying and tunneling. Three times since spotting the Pelican, he had passed out and returned to consciousness underwater. But he didn't think the search-and-rescue crew could find them on the shore. His communications equipment and emergency beacons had all been fried by the MAC round's EMP, and the riverbank was so tangled with downed trees and avalanche runout that he and Veta would be impossible to spot from the air.

Not that he had the strength to actually get them to shore.

The floe jostled over a sleeper, tipping the surface enough to send Veta sliding toward the edge. Ash kicked hard, raising himself enough to shift his own position and pull her back into place. She was out cold and didn't react.

Veta had a nasty gash on her forehead and had been unconscious since they hit the water. Her left forearm was badly swollen and looked more than a little out of alignment between the wrist and elbow, but Ash wasn't about to let go of it. Mangled bones could be repaired in surgery; waterlogged lungs, not so much. He kicked again, raising himself far enough out of the river that he could take a quick glance downstream. There was a thunder building in the valley, and he wanted to be sure the floe wasn't heading into a cataract. If *that* happened, they would both drown.

He didn't see any white water, but it was a quick look, and there had been more valley wall in his line of sight than water. The thunder continued to build, and the water began to grow rough.

Rapids coming, even if he hadn't seen them.

Damn it. Ash wasn't giving up. He swung his legs up, tucking them under the ice as high as he could get them. The floe rocked a bit, but it was stable enough that they had ridden out one small set of rapids already. He kicked up again, this time using his forearms to hold himself up . . . and discovered they were still in a large pool. The water was rippling in all directions from thrust wash.

A shadow passed overhead, and a nanobraided titanium cable dropped in front of him. Even better, there was a Spartan-II in Mark IV Mjolnir fast-roping down it. The Spartan stopped a half meter above the floe and wrapped one arm into the cable, then tipped sideways and reached down to scoop Veta up by the waist. Ash had time to notice a red 092 and a Corinthian helmet emblazoned on the Spartan's breastplate, then had to let go.

Then he started to slip off the other side of the floe, his fingers scratching against the ice. The Spartan quickly rolled Veta into the crook of his elbow and extended a boot in Ash's direction.

"Grab hold."

"Af-fir-mative."

Ash swung a hand up and caught the Spartan's ankle with one hand, then barely managed to grab hold with the other before the cable rose and they were lifted onto the loading ramp of a D77-TC Pelican. A female Spartan in Mark IV Mjolnir grabbed Veta's collar and Ash's wrist, then pulled them both onto the loading ramp.

The first Spartan stepped off the cable, then picked up Veta and carried her into the troop bay. But when Ash started to rise, the female Spartan drew her M6E and used it to gesture at his equipment belt. Ash was puzzled by the reaction . . . for about a half second, until he heard a familiar female voice deeper in the troop bay, threatening to break the medic's wrist if they came near her with another needle.

Olivia. Off smoothers.

"No weapons," the female Spartan said.

"No problem," Ash said. He unbuckled the equipment belt and

dropped it off the ramp, then spread his hands wide. "Permission to come aboard, ma'am?"

"Come ahead." The Spartan pointed to a seat near the back of the bay, then did a double take when she saw the bones sticking out of the biofoam on his chest. "What the . . . how are you still alive? How are *any* of you still alive?"

She glanced forward, to where the crew had Olivia strapped to a medical gurney. Another Spartan and two soldiers were holding her down, while a medic with a swollen eye tried to get near her with a polypseudomorphine injector.

On the deck next to her lay Mark, head turned to one side, eyes not quite closed, as though the lids had been pulled down by someone and hadn't stayed that way. His stomach wound had opened again, spilling loops of intestine out onto his Keeper armor. His limbs looked oddly relaxed, and the color had drained from his face.

But that didn't mean he was gone.

"Why isn't anyone working on Mark?" Ash started forward. "Give me a med—"

"Stand down." The female Spartan blocked his way. "He's dead."

"What—?" Ash stepped around her. "No. No. You don't understand. He's a Gamma—"

His entire torso erupted in agony as the Spartan grabbed the collar of his backplate and lifted him off the deck.

"I *said* stand down, soldier." She swung him around toward the ramp, then straightened her arm, holding him in the open hatchway—and making sure he had a good view of the river a hundred meters below. "Do I make myself clear?"

"I just need to be sure, okay?" Even in his smoother-deprived, pain-heightened state, Ash didn't consider trying to free himself. On his best day, he was no match for a Spartan-II in full Mjolnir . . . and today was far from his best day. "You don't understand Gammas. We're augmented against cardiogenic, hypovolemic, and neurogenic—"

"He's not in shock," the Spartan said. "His neck is broken, and he bled out. And *then* he drowned. I don't care what kind of augmentations he has—he's *dead*, son. I'm sorry."

"Y-You're sure?"

"Three times over—and the last thing we need right now is another crazy attacking our medics." Maintaining her grasp, she muscled Ash over to a seat at the back of the bay, then turned him around so she could look him in the eye. "So, what's it going to be, soldier? Stay put here?" She tipped her helmet toward the seat behind him, then tipped it back toward the ramp. "Or you want to take a dive?"

"Stay put here." Ash waited until she had lowered him into the seat, then added, "If you're *sure.*"

The Spartan glared at him through her faceplate for a few breaths, then finally said, "Buckle up."

Ash glanced toward Mark's still body one more time, checking for flaring nostrils or trembling lips or some sign of breathing. But it just wasn't there. Mark's complexion was gray because he had lost too much blood. His body wasn't showing any pain because his brain wasn't able to sense any. His limbs were limp because there was no essence animating them. He was gone.

Damn this place. Mark was dead.

Seeing that the Spartan was still waiting . . . and watching, Ash finally pulled the harness straps over his shoulders. Then he heard Olivia bellow in rage and realized that her reactions to Mark's loss, her Gamma-mode fury, were putting her in danger. And probably everyone else aboard the Pelican, too. He pointed toward her still-struggling figure.

"A little advice?"

The Spartan glanced forward, then nodded. "If it helps."

"Lay off the polly-sue and sedatives for her," he said. "They won't work. In fact, they'll just make her crazy. Same for me."

The Spartan considered the advice for a moment, then shrugged. "If you say so, soldier."

"It has to be that way. I'll explain it to your docs." Then Ash pointed to Veta, who was stretched out on her own gurney, being ignored while everyone tried to deal with a flailing Olivia. "But Mom's okay for anything. Take care of her first. She deserves it."

The Spartan glanced toward Veta, then shook her helmet. "She's . . . your *mother*?"

"Oh yeah," Ash said. "In all the ways that count."

Castor waited as the Pelican circled through the smoke and climbed for the heavens, then ascended the last few paces to the rim of the crater. 'Gadogai followed a step behind, not asking why Castor had insisted on making this trek, never complaining about the pain the hike must have added to the flash burns on the Sangheili's unarmored arms and jaws. Perhaps that was the definition of what amounted to a true friendship—this willingness to suffer in silence for the comfort of another.

As he crested the rim, Castor felt the heat of molten stone. The pool was far larger than he had expected, an indication that the humans' final attack had set off some kind of chain reaction deep within the citadel.

He was glad.

His reverence for all things Forerunner was now in the past, a folly of an earlier life.

It was not the Forerunners' fault that Castor had allowed himself to be deceived by the lies of the San'Shyuum, to be used by a mad ancilla for her own purposes. The blame for *that* lay with him, and him alone.

But matters were clear now. Those in the Covenant who had rebelled against the so-called Prophets, during the Great Schism at the end of the war with the humans, had clearly been right. That did not diminish the hatred he felt when he thought of what a charlatan he had been, of how he had worshiped the Forerunners' memory for as long as he could remember, as though they were a living presence.

'Gadogai stepped onto the rim beside him, still carrying Bhasvod's glaive, and inhaled sharply.

Castor turned. "Stand a little down the slope, if you wish."

"Why would I do that?" 'Gadogai cocked his oblong head and looked at Castor out of one eye. "Is my company unwelcome?"

"It is indeed welcome," Castor said. "I was thinking of your burns. This heat cannot feel good."

"I am not bothered by pain." 'Gadogai stared out over the white lake of molten stone, then asked, "What are we doing here?"

"I want to make sure she is truly dead," Castor said.

"The Oracle?" 'Gadogai replied. "Is your comm disk working? *Any* of your electronics?"

"Not a thing," Castor said. "The electromagnetic pulse strike saw to that."

"Then the Oracle *is* dead." 'Gadogai studied the haft of Bhasvod's glaive, then passed it to Castor. "But of course, there is no harm in being certain."

Castor chuckled. "Yes. Certain is good."

He took the glaive and threw it into the crater, then watched as it dropped into the molten stone and disappeared in a white flash.

"Ye who seek the path," he said, quoting from the Psalm of Teaching. "Follow the one light . . . behold its radiance . . . and fall blind."

"Only then will ye see," 'Gadogai said, finishing the stanza. "You cannot omit the last line—it is the most important one."

Castor grunted. "I am not so sure," he said. "All I see now is how Krelis and the others died for a lie. How blind I was to ignore you when you tried to warn me on Reach against this folly."

'Gadogai clacked his mandibles in satisfaction. "As I said, the most important line." The Sangheili began to survey the mountains around them, slowly turning until his gaze came to the ragged crescent of the resource moon, barely visible through the snow clouds.

"So, what now, Dokab?"

"*Dokab?*" Castor snorted, then started down the slope into the valley. "Now we kill our enemies. *All* of them, my friend. Without mercy."

EPILOGUE

1146 hours, October 24, 2559 (military calendar)
Infirmary Cabin 12, UNSC support vessel *Spirit of Fire*
High Orbit, the Ark

The ONI black dress tunic fit Veta surprisingly well, with the tail resting just at the top of her hips and the left sleeve loose enough to accommodate the synglass cast on her arm. The collar might have been a little high, but it was hard to be certain with her vision going through one of its momentary blurry spells. Still, the cut felt good enough that she suspected Commander Barre had arranged for someone to take a few measurements during her nightly sedation.

Veta made a mental note to dictate a thank-you message to the night orderly. Even after ten days in the infirmary, she could not write legibly.

She ran a hand over her shaved scalp and leaned closer to the mirror. The long fall of hair she had worn while undercover as a zealot was gone, replaced by a twenty-centimeter bandage stretching across the back of her head. She did not remember receiving

— 353 —

the skull fracture that had necessitated the surgery, and the docs had told her she probably never would. But she was glad to be rid of the hairstyle. The last thing she wanted was any reminder of the Keeper mission, which seemed to have lasted a lifetime.

A quick knock sounded on the cabin door, and it slid aside to admit Ash-G099 and Olivia-G291. They too wore ONI black dress uniforms, displaying neither rank nor name—as was tradition. Their jackets were open, revealing tunics tight enough to betray, as Veta's vision cleared, the outline of heavy bandages.

The bandages were the only remaining indications of their injuries, at least the physical ones. Veta could see in their eyes the same pain of loss she felt—and which was the reason she needed to be sedated at night. Until her skull fracture healed, the docs did not want her thrashing about during her frequent nightmares.

"It's time." Olivia went to the cabin's little closet and withdrew Veta's ONI jacket—still called a blouse in the military—then held it open for her. "Are you ready?"

"Yeah. As ready as I'll ever be," Veta said. She slipped her arms into the sleeves, then squared her shoulders and turned to face her two Gammas. "How about you two? How are you doing?"

"Good." Ash flashed a weak smile, not insincere . . . just the best he could do. "Healing fast."

He rolled his shoulders to demonstrate, and managed to grimace only a little.

"Not what I meant," Veta said. "A doctor could tell me that much."

She turned to Olivia, whose smile was not quite as weak as Ash's.

"We're okay, Mom," Olivia said. "They're having a little trouble tuning our smoothers because they don't have quite the same pharmaceuticals out here. But at least we're not hearing voices anymore."

"Or seeing flying dinosaurs," Ash said. "Much."

Veta laughed, recalling how they had mocked her with similar replies in the caves of Gao, when she had first heard about their smoother dependency and threatened to take them into protective custody.

"Well, I wouldn't get too comfortable," Veta said, taking Ash's arm. "Around here, those flying dinosaurs could be real."

She nodded to Olivia, who led them out the door, then proceeded twenty meters down the infirmary corridor to a lift. They descended two decks to the medical hangar, where a trio of emergency evac Pelicans sat in a line on each side of the compact deck.

On the port side waited the Spartan-IIs of Red Team, each standing at parade rest in front of the three Pelicans. On the starboard side stood Commander Barre and her crew, also standing at parade rest. Between them, resting on stands at the forward edge of the hangar mouth, were two gray duraplas interment capsules. The first was stenciled with the winged-skull insignia of the *Spirit of Fire*'s Air Reconnaissance Command. The second bore the encircled, half-black pyramid of the ONI logo.

Veta knew the capsule with the Recon stencil was empty—a mere symbol acknowledging the loss of Commander Barre's relief pilot, John Cassidy. She also knew that the capsule with the black ONI symbol contained Mark's body. And as soon as she saw it, she grew light-headed and paused to catch her balance.

Olivia's hand was instantly under her elbow. "Hey, Mom, if you're not up to this—"

"I'm fine," Veta said. "I have to be here."

"Are you sure?" Olivia asked. "We can record—"

"I said I'm fine." Veta covered Olivia's hand. "Let's go."

They had barely started forward before a lanky man with blue eyes and close-trimmed white hair approached. He was wearing a UNSC captain's uniform with the name J. CUTTER on a nameplate of polished brass.

"Lieutenant Lopis," he said. "I'm glad you're well enough to attend."

Rather than waiting for Veta to come to attention, he extended a hand for her to shake. It was an informal gesture that indicated he was well-acquainted with ONI's casual attitude toward the usual military rituals, but one that did little to put her at ease. From what she had gathered from the infirmary staff, Captain Cutter was a veteran officer who had seen a fair amount of action in the Isbanola sector during the Insurrection. He might even have been involved in the blockade of Gao, a yearlong ordeal that had formed so many of her childhood attitudes toward the UNSC.

But they were on the same side now, Veta reminded herself, and she had Cutter to thank for saving Ash and Olivia. She took his hand and shook it warmly.

"Captain Cutter," she said, "I can't tell you how much I appreciate you sending Red Team to extract us. That was a risk you didn't have to take."

"After what your team did, it certainly *was*," Cutter said. Being careful not to take Ash's place at her side, he turned and led the group forward. "And I'm very sorry about Spartan-G313. It's never easy to lose a good man."

A good man? Mark was certainly *that*. But it seemed almost dismissive to refer to him that way, as a mere soldier . . . a tool of war. Mark had been so much more to Veta, her family—as Ash and Olivia still were.

She couldn't bear to think of him as just another lost soldier. *Ever.*

When she didn't reply, Cutter stopped and turned to face her directly. "I truly am sorry." He actually sounded contrite. "You never forget them. But with time, the memories do grow a little easier to live with. Until then—I want you to find me if you need to talk."

Veta was surprised . . . and touched. "Thank you, Captain. I'll do that."

"Good. We've lost a lot of fine soldiers since the *Spirit of Fire* left UNSC space. Some of them shined brighter than the rest of us, and it hurts worse when they're the ones who are gone." Cutter's gaze grew distant for a moment, then he seemed to come back and asked, "Was Spartan-G313—sorry, Mark—the first man you've lost?"

"The first member of my Ferret team," Veta said. "I lost my entire investigations unit the first time we ran into Castor."

"Oh, that's right." Cutter's expression became unreadable. "On Gao."

He checked his chronometer, then turned and started forward again, leaving an awkward silence between them. Clearly, Cutter had been briefed on Veta's ties to an insurrectionist planet, and he was no doubt reflecting on the disparities in their past—and wondering how they might impact discipline aboard the *Spirit of Fire.*

But that wasn't a conversation for today.

Finally, Cutter said, "You've been hunting Castor a long time, haven't you?"

"Both Castor and Intrepid Eye," Veta said. "You *have* been briefed on Intrepid Eye, right?"

"Oh, yes. I've been briefed on everything involving your

mission—at least everything you and your team have reported to our intelligence unit."

"That is everything," Veta assured him. "We're not playing any ONI games. Not out here."

"Glad to hear it," Cutter said. When they drew even with the first Pelicans, Red Team and Barre's Pelican crew came to full attention. He stopped and spoke without turning toward Veta. "We don't know what happened to Castor and the Sangheili, Inslaan 'Gadogai. But we know you destroyed Intrepid Eye."

"You're *sure*?" It was Olivia who asked this, almost blurting the question. "Uh, sir?"

Cutter cracked a half smile. "We're sure, Spartan. You got her. There were no transmissions out of the structure before, during, or after the MAC bombardment. And whatever she was hiding in is slag now. We did a thorough search before leaving the area."

He looked toward Veta. "You and your team did a remarkable job, Lieutenant. Our analysts are just beginning to appreciate how remarkable. After you're recovered, I hope we can count on you to help defeat the Banished here on the Ark."

Veta could not help glancing toward both of her remaining Gammas. What she really wanted was to take them back to the Mill and persuade Admiral Serin Osman to give them all permanent training assignments. But Osman had disappeared along with the rest of ONI at the start of the Cortana event, and in all likelihood the Mill probably didn't exist anymore.

And even if it did, there was no way to get there. Veta had made plenty of inquiries from the infirmary about returning her team to the Milky Way. It seemed clear that—as she had suspected from the start of the mission—her Ferret team's trip to the Ark was almost certainly one-way. Unless the *Spirit of Fire* managed to capture the slipspace crystals the Banished had used to open their portal,

there was simply no way back. Of course, there was a remote possibility that the note she had slipped to Fred would convince what
remained of the UNSC that a rescue mission was in the works . . .
but not a realistic one, given what was going on in the galaxy right
now. She was just glad there had been a chance to add that personal message to him, to help him sort out her disappearance, and
why she hadn't been able to warn him beforehand.

But most importantly, the last thing Ash and Olivia would
want after Mark's death was to withdraw from action. They were
already standing a little taller after Cutter's invitation, and Veta
knew they would be miserable if she turned it down. Fighting
was what they had been created to do—and there was no way she
was letting them do it without her. As long as she remained team
leader, she could steer the Ferrets toward the assignments they
were best suited to—and try to keep them away from any more
suicide missions.

That's what mothers *did*—protect their brood.

When Veta's response was not quick to come, Cutter said, "I
apologize. Maybe now isn't the time—"

"No, it's fine, sir." Veta gave Ash and Olivia quick eye-checks
to confirm what she suspected. When she received a pair of quick
nods, she continued, "We'd be happy to help the *Spirit of Fire* take
down the Banished. "Nothing would make us prouder."

Cutter nodded. "I thought so." He checked his chronometer
again, then said, "We'd better start. We need to launch soon, or
the capsules will fall back to the Ark."

Veta tightened her grasp on the arms of Ash and Olivia. "I'm
ready."

Cutter turned to starboard, then said, "Commander Barre, you
may begin."

"Yes, sir." Barre turned toward the control station at the back of the hangar, where a young ensign stood inside the hangar control booth. "Raise the pressure barrier, Ensign."

"Aye, ma'am," came the reply.

A partition of transparent aluminum rose out of the deck, isolating the interment capsules from the rest of the hangar. Barre raised her hand to her brow, beginning the salute. She waited a second for everyone else to follow her lead, then spoke the committal.

"From stardust we come, and to stardust we return. John Cassidy was a gifted pilot, a loyal comrade, and a true friend. We commit his memory to the stars, to accompany us wherever we fly."

She completed the salute, then turned to Veta.

"Lieutenant Lopis," she said.

Veta raised her hand again, this time for Mark, and began the committal she had prepared.

"Spartan Mark-G313 died of injuries sustained while protecting his team." She spoke slowly, struggling to maintain her composure. "I doubt he would have wanted to go any other way. He was a Spartan-III, trained and developed to take risks no others would dare. To do what no one else *could*. But he was more than that . . . so much more. He was . . . he was a son to me, and a brother to Olivia and Ash . . . and we're going to miss him as long as we live."

Ash and Olivia remained at strict attention, their salutes cocked and their gazes locked on Mark's interment capsule. Olivia's eyes were wet, and Ash's lips were white from being pressed together so hard. Veta didn't know what the coming weeks and months were going to bring for her Ferrets, but she did know it would be a difficult time for them all . . . and that they would get through it the same way they always did.

Together.

Veta completed the salute and did not even try to hide the tears running down her cheeks. Once the rest of the detail had followed suit, Barre turned toward the hangar control booth again.

"Ensign, open the outer hatch."

"Aye, ma'am."

The hatch retracted into the overhead, revealing the majesty of Installation 00 extending outward from beneath the hangar doorway. Even from fifty thousand kilometers above, its size was breathtaking, so immense that the artificial sun hanging above its core seemed but a child's toy. The tips of six spires—all that were visible from inside the ship—seemed to stretch forever, finally vanishing from sight against the foggy radiance of the distant Milky Way.

The decompression wave lifted the interment capsules off their stands and carried them on a silent wind out into the starry void. They hovered above the Ark for a moment, as though pausing to contemplate its vast wonder one last time. Then a pair of rockets fired beneath each capsule, launching Mark's and John Cassidy's memories on a journey of ten million years.

A journey home.

ACKNOWLEDGMENTS

I would like to thank everyone who contributed to this book, especially: my first reader, Andria Hayday; my editor, Ed Schlesinger; our copy editor, Valerie Shca; our proofreaders, Regina Castillo and Andy Goldwasser; Jeremy Patenaude, Tiffany O'Brien, Jeff Easterling, Frank O'Connor, and all the great people at 343 Industries; and cover artist Benjamin Carre. It's been a pleasure working with you—as always!

A SPECIAL NOTE
FROM 343 INDUSTRIES

This book is set in a distant future, where human (and alien!) history has already been written. For Halo, that history includes a lot of stuff up to and including the real twentieth and twenty-first centuries—so like any piece of sci-fi literature, it may not dwell on the past, but it does pause it, frozen in amber as one of the forces that created our imagined future.

Halo: Divine Wind was written, edited, and published during the largest pandemic in living memory. We've lived through a seismic inversion of our normal daily routines—some impacted more gravely than others. The pandemic cost millions of lives, untold trillions of dollars—and, with very few exceptions, affected every person on Earth, in one way or another.

It wasn't all darkness. We saw people, cities, states, and nations come together to help each other, even as we squabbled, experimented, and occasionally dropped balls at the local level. As we write this—and send the book to press—it's still happening. People are sick and dying, folks are working from bedrooms and basements, losing their jobs, and either leaving their homes or being forced to stay there. Everyone is dealing with it the best way they can.

This novel takes place in a future beset with constant trouble and danger (and even a deadly galactic plague), but it's also a universe of hope and wonder and heroism. It's not an antidote to the grim reality we're facing; it's a reflection of what we see in the real world every day: doctors, patients, first responders, volunteers, and scientists risking their lives and livelihoods to try to save us all from a moment in history. They're seeking a brighter, better tomorrow, and we want to thank them for their sacrifice, brilliance, invention, and courage, and for making things as safe and orderly as such a strange and dangerous time can be.

We'll hopefully be back to some semblance of normalcy one day soon, but it's important to capture, contain, and remember history now in order to mark the moment, and to remind ourselves that we still have a lot of work to do to ensure that we never go through this again. Even as you read this, we may already be basking in the sunshine of brighter days. So thank you for working, struggling, and living through it all, and for recording your own bit of unforgettable history and storytelling.

ABOUT THE AUTHOR

Troy Denning is the *New York Times* bestselling author of more than forty novels, including *Halo: Shadows of Reach, Halo: Oblivion, Halo: Silent Storm, Halo: Retribution, Halo: Last Light*, a dozen *Star Wars* novels, the *Dark Sun: Prism Pentad* series, and many bestselling *Forgotten Realms* novels. A former game designer and editor, he lives in western Wisconsin.

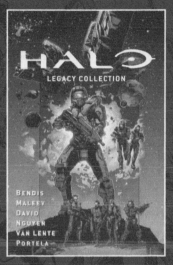

MEGA CONSTRUX™ HALO®

2 IN 1

HALO INFINITE

MEGACONSTRUX.COM

*Instructions included for main model only. Other build(s) can be found at **megaconstrux.com**. Most models can be built one at a time.

HALO
WORLD OF HALO
4" ACTION FIGURES & VEHICLES
AVAILABLE NOW!
Jazwares
© 2021 Microsoft Corporation. All Rights Reserved.
XBOX
343

CPSIA information can be obtained
at www.ICGtesting.com
Printed in the USA
BVHW060831140422
633968BV00005B/5

9 781982 174903